I0762267

About the Author

Michelle Miller lives in North Carolina with her husband, son, and far too many pets. When she is not writing fiction, she is solving scientific problems at her 'day job' or reading her way through an impossible TBR.

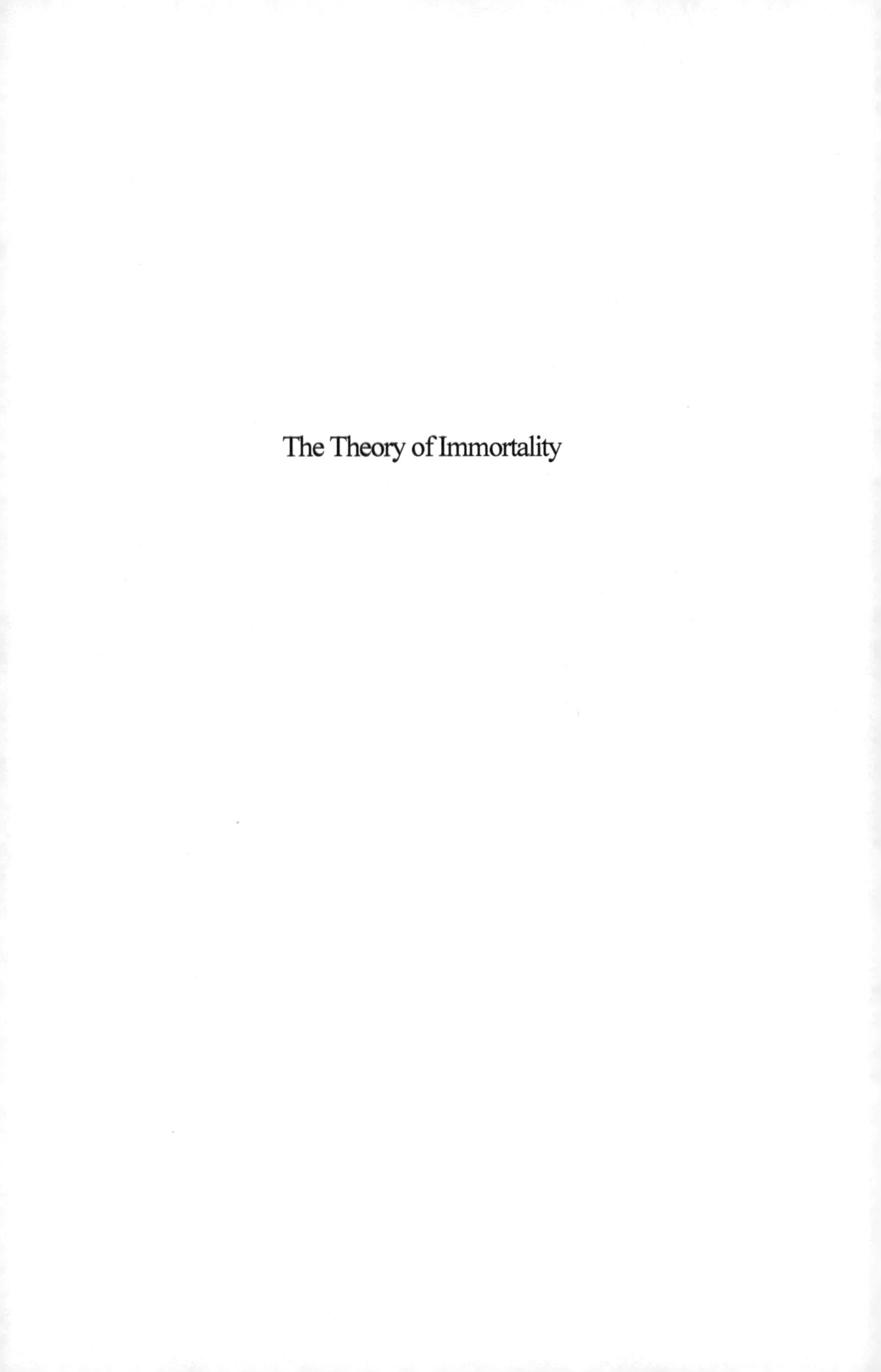

The Theory of Immortality

Michelle Miller

The Theory of Immortality

Vanguard Press

VANGUARD HARDBACK

A CIP catalogue record for this title is available from the British Library.

ISBN 978-1-83671-212-1

Vanguard Press is an imprint of
Pegasus Elliot Mackenzie Publishers Ltd.
www.pegasuspublishers.com

First Published in 2025

Vanguard Press
Sheraton House Castle Park
Cambridge England

Dedication

To my husband, who endorses all spice contained in this book.
Thank you for being my biggest fan, even though you don't read fiction.
You will always be my number one beta reader.

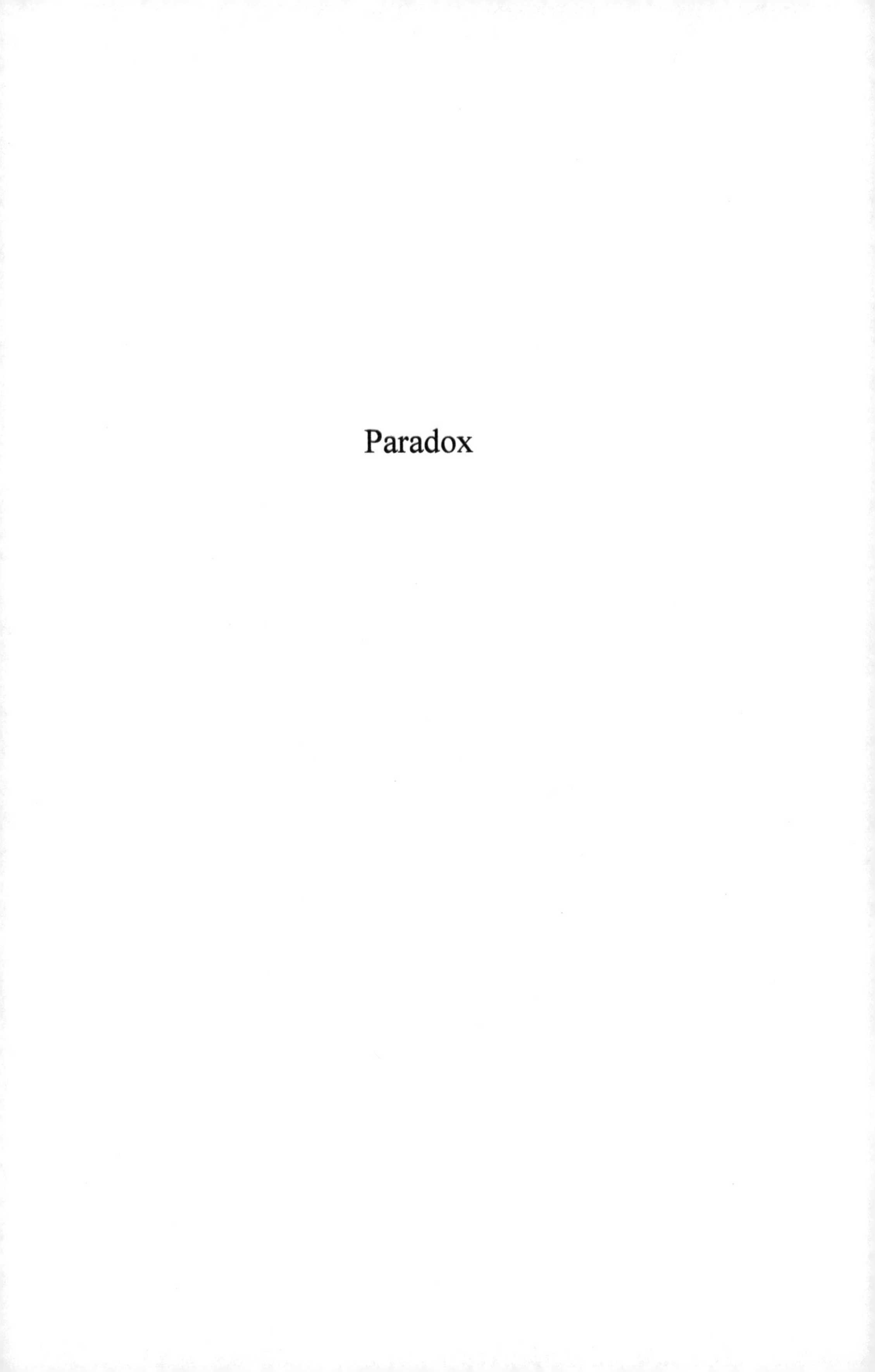

Paradox

Chapter 1

Dr. Mikaela Brookes did not leave unsolved riddles in her wake. She hated when something didn't add up. No. Hate wasn't a strong enough word for how it made her skin crawl and her neurons writhe in a short-circuiting fit of activity. She *loathed* it with a deep-rooted, unrelenting compulsion to make even the tiniest detail fit seamlessly into an orderly, comprehensible flow of information. Loose ends and half-formed hypotheses wiggled into her brainstem and ate away at her thoughts like parasitic little monsters until she found the reason, the *proof*, that they belong to something bigger.

Kaela chewed on the inside of her lower lip and scrolled through the Excel document on her tablet, her thumb flicking against the glass, a repetitive, agitated motion in time with the nervous tapping of her foot. Her gray eyes were unfocused, no longer registering the numbers sliding across the screen. This data set looked like the others that came before, inconclusive and distressing.

"Damn it."

The tablet hit the surface of her desk with a concussive crack, and she flinched. Replacement computers did not grow on academic trees. Taut muscles pinched her shoulders and bent her neck into an anxious hunch. She stood to stretch, breathing deeply to slow the angry beat of blood against her eardrums, and moved into a shaft of sunlight streaming from the solitary window. She squinted against the glare.

Below her third-floor perch was a tiny, paved square hemmed in by three tall buildings. Once, a miniscule green patch filled the area between. It had boasted a few accidental trees, and she often sat beneath the threadbare canopy at lunchtime, running her fingers through the clover that incessantly sprouted amidst the tough Bermuda grass and craving the slightest connection to something wild that existed beyond this synthetically planned public space.

Clearly, the improvement to air quality and mental health was outweighed by the practical need for parking permit revenue, and the clover was bulldozed in favor of asphalt last year. One anemic sapling was left, braced with tethers and wrapped in a protective cage. Four square feet of dirt was all the wilderness the university could spare.

Although the view did not inspire, Kaela was proud to have her very own portal to the outside world. When she started at the university, she was tucked away in a tragically tiny closet on the bottom floor of the oldest building on campus. While the mole crickets provided some company, those first few years were a lonely, mildew-riddled time of her life that she did not remember fondly. The older professors called it 'paying your dues.'

She suffocated in the absence of sunlight.

"Why can't he repeat those results?" she murmured to herself as she absently ran a finger down the window glass, her skin eliciting a high stuttering squeak of protest.

The sound barely registered over the churning of her brain while she mentally masticated the numbers from the data set, spitting out ideas and then discarding them one after another. A campus worker pushed a plastic trash bin across the parking lot, oblivious to the observer above. Kaela's eyes tracked the worker's movements by some primal instinct, a lizard watching the frantic scurry of a beetle. Her brain was busy connecting, disconnecting, considering, and rejecting, searching for a link or pattern.

She was missing something. There was a key to the problem that she had yet to identify.

"Damn it," she repeated and allowed a frustrated breath to squeeze through her tightly clenched teeth.

Once, Kaela would have called her mother for advice. Her mother wasn't a scientist. She wasn't even educated in the traditional sense of the word, yet she had been insightful on a different level. Her mother listened to the problem and then asked Kaela to explain the more technical aspects again in a way she would understand. They would go on like this for a time, Kaela searching for new vocabulary with which to communicate the scientific details and her mother pressing her about each part of the process, one after another. More often than not, Kaela's brain latched onto something mid-explanation that she hadn't noticed before, an imperfection in the weave, and the answer was close by. A mental blockade runner. That was what Kaela's mother had been for her. She never confronted science head-on, but she took her daughter by the hand and slipped around each of the bulky, difficult bits until they created a path for the answer to emerge. But her mother was dead, and now Kaela had to find her own way forward.

A knock on the office door startled her from her rumination.

"Come in," she called out, barely turning to look over her shoulder.

"Hi, Dr. Brookes!"

Jacob, an undergraduate research intern, one of three and just as helpless as the others.

"Come in," Kaela repeated when he hovered at the threshold, a nervous smile plastered across his face as he blinked at her with the eager anticipation of a puppy waiting for a treat.

"I wanted to talk to you about my course load and career plans after graduation, if you have a minute."

This time, Kaela swallowed the exhalation of air as she moved back to her desk. Her duty was to advise and guide the young people under her mentorship, even when she wanted to tell them to just 'figure it out like the rest of us.' Once he settled in a chair, the student began a long, agonizing recount of each grade he received and every volunteer hour he spent with Habitat for Humanity throughout the month. Kaela found her attention drifting but managed to catch the important parts. She recommended a few courses for him out of the selection he provided and sent him on his way with the advice to start attending a handful of interest groups in the area to network.

Kaela returned to her pensive asphalt gazing. Her fingers idly tickled against the large, leafy plant growing in a pot on her windowsill while she contemplated the circular continuity of life. She was certainly just as naive and eager when she was a young student, but the memories had been scrubbed away, replaced with false ones where she demonstrated greater maturity. It was the nature of the old to scorn the dewy-eyed optimism of youth.

The dark surface of the tablet on the corner of the desk was distractingly ominous, tugging at her peripheral vision no matter where she fixed her eyes. She needed to get out of this room. The stale recycled air of the building was pressing down on her, making her fidgety and claustrophobic. Kaela walked into the hall, pausing only to turn off the lights and lock the door before heading to the stairs.

In the darkened room, the plant on the window ledge extended one long growth, a creeping tendril that traversed the sill and slowly unfurled a new leaf.

The sun hit Kaela's head and shoulders when she stepped through the doors on the ground floor, dispelling the chill of fall in the air as it settled in a warm blanket across her body. She found an empty bench near the walkway and slumped onto the cold planks, closing her eyes and feeling the heat of the sunlight as a pulsing stream of life around her.

Her mind drifted to the ground beneath her feet, imagining the bright threads of energy connecting the grass and weeds that basked in the precious light while the days grew shorter and the hours of darkness longer. She let her hand dangle over the armrest, and the dry ornamental grass scratched a chaotic, light rhythm against her palm. She thought about the transfer of energy from one organism to another, the earthly divine interconnection of the ecosystem. Nutrients moved like thin threads of ichor, weaving their way among and between all beings.

A man crossing the courtyard shouted to the passing students, and Kaela startled back to awareness. Her fingers were tangled in the tall spikes of vegetation, and she carefully extricated herself while she listened to the voice drawing closer. The grass beside the bench boasted a spray of tiny flowers she hadn't noticed before. She pried her eyes away from this new discovery and peered past the bodies that brushed impatiently against one another on the sidewalk.

The man was now standing on the other side of the wide path, a sign held above his head. He was likely just another religious zealot evangelizing to the young crowds and not a threat to anyone's safety. She squinted her eyes to read the words scribbled over the cardboard in stark black characters.

The true measure of success is how many times you can bounce back from failure.

The chakras displayed beneath the letters belied his ties to a group commonly haunting the campus courtyards. He was a harmless pilgrim, but Kaela avoided eye contact and considered slipping back into her building. There was nothing worse for a scientist than being engaged in a theological discussion with someone who used feelings and beliefs in place of logic.

Their signs were always covered with new age truisms designed to inspire peace, love, and a greater sense of humanity.

Our greatest fear is to be better than those before us but not as good as those after us. Only through inner contemplation and acceptance of darker thoughts can we move toward a lightness of self. We are greater than the sum of our baser instincts.

Wouldn't it be delightful to think that way? Wouldn't it be easy and peaceful to truly believe that humans could rise from the reality that they are nothing more than cerebrally overdeveloped mammals?

Kaela lived in a world that thrived on logic and facts. Hers was the brain that would have been incompatible with the utopian Matrix. No paradise for Dr. Brookes.

Many years ago, she read poetry and spent time pontificating under the stars with friends. She remembered laughing around a fire pit and drinking red wine straight from the bottle. But those were the carefree days of youth when the world was a sparkling sea of foam-crested opportunities, ever changing, filled with unknown possibilities.

When she chose this career, she clipped off those spindly, fanciful parts of herself, pruning away the impractical to reinforce the cold core of deduction and drive. Her contributions to the world around her were better served if she focused on more tangible solutions to the problems plaguing human existence.

"Kaela!"

She looked up at the sound of her name and found another professor in her department approaching from the opposite side of the brickyard.

"Anjana!" Kaela raised her hand and stood in greeting. "Getting back from a lecture?"

"*Ugh,* yes." The short, slender woman scrunched her dark brows together and gestured to the laboratory building. "I need a cup of coffee before I start grading midterm papers. Care to join me?"

Kaela nodded and offered one final glance at the evangelical new age prophet before trailing Anjana back to the building. Perhaps caffeine would be the magical panacea for her troubles today. Anjana gave a gasp and came to an abrupt halt, causing Kaela to crash into her.

"Oh, no." Kaela followed Anjana's downturned stare to a tiny heap of feathers on the walkway. "I keep telling that admin to take down her stupid window feeder. This is the third one that has bashed itself into the glass in the last two weeks. Poor little thing."

Kaela shaded her eyes and squinted at the plastic feeder suctioned against one of the second-floor windows. When she leaned down to scoop the soft, still body into her palms, she felt the brief sting of disappointment. Humans still managed to leave potholes along the paths they paved with good intentions. The finch's beak gaped open, and its eyes were tightly closed in death. She was surprised to find the body warmed quickly in her hands as she offered a silent wish that it could have lived the rest of its short life in the skies.

"Don't pick it up! What if it has some type of disease?"

"I'm not going to contract a fatal case of avian influenza from a little songbird, Anjana." Kaela ran a thumb along its silky feathers. Did she imagine the movement of its tiny chest?

Before the other woman could respond, the bird shuddered against Kaela's palm.

"Oh, my god, it moved!" Anjana leaned closer. "It was dead!"

"Evidently not," Kaela retorted, delight crossing her face as the finch hopped up and blinked at her. "I guess it was just stunned."

"Could have fooled me."

The bird bolted into the air, a quick flutter of movement that startled them both, and disappeared into the distance.

"You better wash your hands twice. And use sanitizer. Here, I'll get the door. Don't touch anything."

Kaela rolled her eyes at Anjana's continued grousing and followed. At the door, she paused, her head spinning.

"Are you okay?" Her coworker peered into her face.

"I'm fine, I'm fine. Just a little lightheaded." Kaela waved off her coworker's concern and entered the building. Behind her, Anjana grumbled something about deadly bird flu pandemics and Kaela being patient zero.

On their way to the break room for the slightly burnt and barely palatable coffee, Anjana rambled about her children and their latest round of daycare-related illnesses, the bird completely forgotten. Kaela tried to remember how many children her colleague had and what their ages were. Keeping the details of a coworker's life in her mind was like squeezing a fistful of mud. There were a dozen vague impressions of conversations such as these, but the details squelched out between her mental fingers when she tried to hold on to them.

"Is your husband keeping the kids today, then?" Kaela scrambled for an innocuous question, hoping to disguise the fact that she remembered nothing about the other woman's personal life.

"Stephen?" Anjana crossed her arms, critically assessing Kaela's progress as she finished washing her hands in the break room sink and moved on to the coffee station. "No, he had classes to teach as well, so I dropped them off with my mother. If she insists on inserting herself into my life through the guise of caring about her grandchildren, she can at least care *for* them, too."

Stephen. There was a residue of memory, an educated guess really, that he was also on faculty at the university. Kaela took a sip of her scalding hot coffee and tried to devise some casual way of confirming this information. Anjana took several long gulps from her own mug, then filled it back to the brim.

"Well, I need to get these papers finished. Then I have to get home to make dinner before my mother decides to berate me for failing to perform my wifely duties. My marriage was a bigger cause for celebration than my doctorate or my medical degree in her eyes. I will see you later!"

Like the gale of a hurricane, Anjana exited, and the space in the room doubled. Kaela waited for her colleague to gain a sufficient head start, then wandered down the long hallway outside the laboratory spaces. As she walked, her mind slid back through the decades, thinking about her own mother and the disagreements which once enraged her but now filled her with a keen sort of longing.

A technician waved before they stepped into the open door to Kaela's lab, and she raised her hand in return. Mid-afternoon was the final push when the scientists struggled to finish their experiments, hoping to avoid the often-inevitable late night. Science kept its own hours, and they rarely coincided with a standard workday.

Kaela stopped in the doorway, setting her coffee on a cart in the hall before peering between the tall shelving that divided each section of benches. Through the various rows of glassware and stacks of plastic pipette boxes, she could see a few of her graduate students. One bent his head to his task in singular focus. Another bobbed to the music from her earbuds, the rhythm awkwardly out of synch with the one blasting from a Bluetooth speaker near the centrifuges. The third stood listlessly near the incubator stacks, staring out the window. Kaela considered her lab coat hanging just inside the doorway, wondering if her presence would improve or reduce the current level of motivation in the lab.

Before she decided, a fuzzy emptiness pulled forward across her brain, surprising her with sudden disorientation, as if she stood up too quickly from a reclined position. She placed her hands on the cool metal frame to either side of her body and took a slow breath. Thoughts of high blood pressure and low blood sugar were crossing her mind when a gravelly, soft voice spoke from just behind her.

"Checking in on your workforce?"

Kaela turned, ignoring the molten twist in her lower belly when her gaze met a set of shockingly vibrant green eyes.

"Who the hell are you?" She blurted the words, then cringed as soon as they left her mouth. "Sorry, that was rude."

The man before her was tall, well over six feet, which dwarfed most of the academics she was accustomed to seeing in this building. He was also thick with muscle, clearly active and fit despite the gray streaks in his hair. He had a hard line to his jaw, a strong, straight nose, and heavy eyebrows that framed jewel-tone eyes. A scar wandered across the light stubble of his left cheek, stopping just short of the full lips that were pressed into a disarming half smile.

"I am the one who should be apologizing," he replied, a faint lilt in the delivery of his words. "I didn't mean to startle you. We haven't been introduced yet. I am Landry Griffiths, a new professor of quantum physics. I just started a few weeks ago."

He extended his hand, and, like a complete asshole, she stared at it without moving.

"This isn't Stinson Hall. You're a few buildings away from the Department of Physics. Are you lost?"

"I am running a joint project with Dr. Fox." He didn't bat an eye at her thinly veiled hostility and gave no visible signs of discomfort as he returned his outstretched hand to his side. "I wanted to see how the experiments are faring. I know everyone is hurrying to finish up before the weekend, and I tried to put it off until Monday, but you must understand."

"Mikaela Brookes," she finally said, nodding at the 'Brookes Lab' sign by the doorway. "Neuroscience."

The abandoned, formal namesake rolled off her tongue with ease. She always introduced herself as Kaela, but the words escaped on their own, and she didn't know how to reel them back. She fixed her expression in what she hoped was a look of apology after her previous outburst. She didn't respond well to unexpected situations, particularly when her thoughts were actively locked on a problem or theory in another part of her brain. Although, to be perfectly honest, that was always her state of mind.

"Nice to make your acquaintance, Mikaela." When he spoke her name, the vowels light but dynamic like a song, she found herself reconsidering her dislike of the appellation. "I've read several of your papers. Your theories on the evolutionary changes in the rates of neuronal aging are unique. I am a physics man at heart, but I dabble in biological sciences from time to time, hence the joint project." He leaned one shoulder against the wall as he talked, both hands in the front pockets of his jeans, a picture of relaxation. "I saw an abstract out of your lab at a recent conference. Is it true that you are starting to introduce temporal aspects into your calculations to artificially influence cellular senescence?"

"If you want to steal my secrets, you shouldn't have told me you were a full-time physicist with an interest in biology," Kaela retorted playfully, regaining some of her social graces. "As a neurologist who dabbles in physics, I advise you to make better life choices that I have and turn back to your pure science while you can."

He grinned, a flash of startlingly white teeth.

"But to answer your question," Kaela continued, "Yes, I am attempting to design an artificial aging or de-aging chamber. Altering stress levels is one thing, but being able to manipulate temporal conditions is where the real magic happens."

"How very Wellsian of you; a little cellular time machine." He leaned forward ever so slightly. "Are you already partnering with a physics lab for resources?"

"Not yet." She sighed, slowly digesting his words and expression, gauging how much to trust him before she could verify his backstory. "The theoretical part of the project is in my wheelhouse, but now I am having problems reproducing some of the preliminary experiments. Until I get that data, I can't determine the resources I need and who I want to partner with."

"I assume the anticipation of some ongoing experiment is causing you to haunt this doorway, then." He looked past her into the lab space. "I would love to hear more about it when we both have the time."

Kaela's eyes followed his glance as he checked the watch on his wrist. She instinctively distrusted an attractive man in an academic position. He stepped a little closer, and much to her annoyance, her stomach fluttered in response. His cologne or aftershave reached her, a musky combination of cedar and pine. The warm scent felt inappropriately intimate, but that didn't prevent her from taking a slow inhale through her nose.

"Well, I don't want to keep you from your scientific time traveling," he joked, lowering his voice as if they were sharing a secret. "But perhaps lunch or dinner next week if you are free? I don't know my way around the area as well as I should, but you can send me an email if you'd like to take me up on the offer. I can even sign a confidentiality agreement so I don't abscond with any of your intellectual property if that would help."

She snorted as if she hadn't been concerned about that very thing. He offered a slow wink.

"It was very nice to meet you, Mikaela."

"You too, Landry." She placed her hand in his for a brief farewell, and he walked off with one final, dazzling smile.

Kaela shook her head. She scolded herself for her juvenile hormones even as she breathed in a last lungful of the provocatively rich smell trailing him down the hall. She scooped up her discarded coffee and turned away from the lab to continue her restless wandering. Her self-admonishment continued as she meandered to her office. She was on the latter side of her thirties, not some lusty twenty-year-old.

When she was younger, she was prone to distractions. She wanted to fall madly, deeply in love in the way movies portrayed, all fire and passion. From the wistful distance of youth, she looked to her future and saw the romanticized version of growing older. Then she lived another twenty years and realized that falling in love was a lot like ice skating. The idea of ice skating was a daydream, effortless and graceful. In reality, it was fraught with difficulty, disappointingly cold, and left one filled with regret at having attempted it. Kaela hardly remembered the starry-eyed girl she once was.

Maybe the disaster of her marriage took the thirst for adventure out of her. She spent ten years of her life becoming smaller and less extraordinary before she finally woke up one day and knew what needed to happen. Once the divorce dust settled, she poured herself into recapturing brilliance in her science and achieved it. Her work became everything.

Yet, she was now facing a substantial hurdle. She made broad-reaching conclusions and promises, which were rewarded with an excessive amount of funding, but eventually the piper had to be paid. She needed to deliver real results, but the experiments kept failing. She knew she could figure it out. There was an answer just waiting for the right question.

Kaela frowned at her empty coffee mug and decided she needed a different type of drink altogether while she contemplated the prospective end of her once promising career.

England – 1066

There was no room for thought or hesitation. A wordless battle yell poured from Landry's mouth as he hewed down soldier after soldier, a berserker on rampage. He found himself slipping into a trance, a pulsing pressure issuing from him in waves. The same feeling always came over him in battle. He would scarcely remember the fight later. It would become a blur of violence by the time combat ended.

Just beyond the edge of the battle was a hill that provided a high vantage point from which to observe the sprawling clash. There, the commander of the army and his wife, Lady Nisha, sat astride their mounts. The lady turned to her husband, a wild sort of certainty flashing across her face where her smooth, dark skin was coated in a fine mist of blood.

"Cassius, this one is very gifted," Nisha spoke, her voice a high, feminine shout that struggled to rise about the clamor of the battle. "Do you think he knows that he is doing it?"

The commander continued to watch.

No one except his wife would have suspected that this mercenary, a boy barely into manhood who left his home in the rural French countryside to fight in a war between kings, was the most dangerous adversary on the battlefield. The boy's companions were ordinary men, if extraordinary fighters, that taught him the basics of warfare without recognizing the underlying occultism that made him unique. Despite the overwhelming activity spread before them as the two forces sought to decimate one another, both the commander and his wife kept their eyes fixed on Landry.

Landry stood in the densest area of conflict. As the leaders looked on, he lowered his shield to block the swing of an axe aimed at his exposed side. He caught the attack, but the axe lodged into the wooden surface, slowing his movement. He turned his head in time to spot an arrow arching toward his back. For most observers, the arrow appeared to just miss its mark as it plunged into the dirt at his feet. To the two astute witnesses on the hill, the arrow altered from its deadly, accurate path just as Landry's eyes fell on it. He turned back to his attacker and used his shield to knock the opponent off balance, ripping the axe from their hands in the process. Before the man could recover, Landry delivered a killing blow with his sword.

Every time his sword swung, another opponent would fall. Some of the blows were direct hits, others glancing, but all of them resulted in death. With the demise of each opponent, a pulse of energy was emitted from the body of the dead, a watery stream like rapidly moving mist that slammed into Landry. Then another flick of his hand and an arrow would fall, or an attacker would lose footing, and the energy would fade. The cycle repeated.

"I think he knows he has an unusual ability to survive battles, but no, I don't think he understands what he is doing." Cassius observed the fighting for a time before continuing. "He is part of a band of men that regard one another as family. He will never leave them."

"That is easily fixed. I will make certain all his close companions die except one." Nisha's voice was flat, devoid of any emotion as she announced Landry's fate. "The last of them will be wounded near death. Who is the new healer we added to our ranks? The one I found in Fulford that causes the men to turn their heads when she passes?"

"I believe she is called Marguerite."

"Yes, that one. I understand her usefulness. I will have her treat the remaining man and seduce our recruit. He will need comforting after the loss of his family, after all."

Cassius gave his wife a sad, obedient nod and turned his horse away from the fighting. Landry continued carving a hole in the enemy forces, oblivious to the audience above and to the new future that had been decided for him as he fed rivers of blood to the parched earth below his feet.

Chapter 2

Saturday night, after a day spent once again wallowing in the unsatisfactory abyss of data brought forth in her recent experiments, Kaela parked outside the main entrance to her gym. The parking lot was empty, devoid of the weekday warriors who toiled away in the nearby business park and gathered here each evening to sweat out their stress while they waited for the weekend to arrive with its promises of household chores, shuttling children to their obligatory activities, and drinking too many beers at the neighbors' kid-friendly cookout. The absence of the expected bustle of bodies, half-dressed and gleaming with sweat, was dramatically noticeable in the empty locker room where Kaela tugged on her yoga pants while listening to the odd clicking from a water fountain.

Upstairs at the cardio equipment, the high ceilings swallowed the sound of the half-dozen occupied ellipticals within the sea of unused machines. What was meant to make the area less claustrophobic during busy days now served to amplify the feeling of emptiness as the noises faded into the air above. Kaela slipped in earbuds and claimed a treadmill at the end of the row. She warmed up and logged three miles, running at a reasonable pace while her mind wandered. Her feet automatically kept the cadence of the music she was streaming. Running was her mental cleanse.

Let there be no misunderstanding, running was hard. Excruciatingly so. It made everything on her body hurt by the time she finished a session, but when she was not running, there was the urge to do it again. Forcing herself to run with some consistency over the last few years resulted in a twisted dependency on endorphins. Kaela told herself there are worse character flaws than a masochistic running complex as she breathed against a sharp stitch between her ribs.

She thought about the end of her work week, the annoyance of the memory driving her to a faster pace despite the desperate pain in her side. She finished Friday with a restless agitation. Her mind, consumed with the unresolved scientific quandaries in her lab, couldn't shut down or disconnect. Her drive home shifted into a drive to a trendy ramen restaurant with a top-notch bartender. On many such Friday nights, she found herself traveling this path, seeking a quick solution for an overactive mind. It was out of the way enough that she wouldn't run into any students. Drinking in a dingy bar with newly minted adults that called her 'Dr.' and worried about her contributions to their GPA was past the very strict line in the protocol she followed to protect herself from scandal.

It was still early, so she had selected a seat at the bar, buffered by vacant stools to either side. She avoided looking at the couples leaning together across dimly lit tables and caught the eye of the bartender instead. He nodded, calling down the counter that he would be right with her. She returned the gesture, content to wait. He was faintly familiar with a warm, polite demeanor and what she considered a professional lack of extended chit chat as he engaged the other patrons.

Kaela's eyes wandered across the parade of liquor bottles sparkling in front of a full, wall-sized mirror. The directional lighting cast a bright glow on the wooden shelves, accentuating aged distress marks beneath the heavy layers of varnish. The building housed an apothecary many years past, and the furnishings retained some of the old charm. Like a wall-mounted crank phone or an antique hutch, they had a distinct quality to them, the detailed imperfection of handmade craftsmanship that was one part archaic and another part comforting.

A faint memory flickered to life, and she was standing in her grandfather's wood shop, staring at the meticulously painted face of a wooden whirligig owl. The offset angles of the two-sided wings fascinated her. She was only five or six. It was the last time her family visited before he passed away; heart failure after a lifetime of smoking. His face was a vague reconstruction, a reflection in moving water, but the smell of sawdust and the vivid pigments in the yellow painted eyes were still sharp. It's funny what details the mind will cling to over the years.

She tapped her fingernail on the edge of the bar as she waited, the light rhythm against the lacquered wood lost in the buzz of ambient noise. A tiny topiary in a concrete planter graced the counter in front of her. Similar plants hung from the ceiling, strategically suspended beneath skylights to give the impression of a forested canopy during the day. A swath of vertical plants spanned the wall behind her. She felt peaceful when surrounded by green things. She fiddled with one of the hanging branches of the countertop plant, gently turning a leaf back and forth while her mind slipped between memories.

"Good evening, and sorry for the wait. Can I get a menu for you, or is it just drinks tonight?" The bartender jarred her from her daze.

"I will take…" Kaela looked at the menu in front of her as if she hadn't already decided what she wanted before she walked in the door. "A pour of tonight's whisky, a glass of water, and an order of spring rolls."

The bartender mirrored her polite expression and collected the menu. When he drifted away to submit the order, a familiar voice breathed into her ear.

"Hello there. You haven't dropped by in a while. Why didn't you shoot me a text?"

Kaela shifted to accept a soft brush of lips on her cheek before the owner of that deep, clear voice took the vacant seat to her right.

"Hello to you, too." She gave the newcomer a cursory, bright-eyed once-over before turning to the drink set silently before her by the bartender.

While her new companion placed his own order, she took the opportunity to shamelessly ogle him. For several years, Kaela frequented this bar, initially staying for a drink or two and then leaving, a quick break on the occasional Friday between the bookend routines of work and home. She always arrived alone and left alone, dipping her toes in the post-divorce socialization pool. Since she barely conversed with anyone and didn't stay past nine, it was less of a toe dipping and more of a poolside sunbathing. On one of those evenings, she met Todd.

Sometimes the only solution for overcoming a difficult, rocky transition in life was to gather up your will, gird your metaphorical loins, and do something that seemed utterly absurd, such as going home with a random guy from the bar. At the time, Kaela felt daring and brazen in the most empowering of ways. In hindsight, she was appalled at the lack of concern she demonstrated for her own safety. Fortunately, Todd was not a psychopath, and the interaction was repeated on many occasions throughout the next year without any murders or abductions.

The whisky burned sweetly in the back of Kaela's throat as she ran her eyes over the light ridges of muscle displayed beneath a slightly-too-tight shirt when her companion leaned forward to better hear the bartender. This man spent hours at the gym maintaining his physique, and she didn't feel an ounce of shame in appreciating it. His hard work should not go unnoticed.

When Todd shifted back into his seat, Kaela slowly slid her eyes to his face. His pupils grew, and he leaned a bit closer, increasing the intimacy of the stare.

"See something that you like, Kaela?"

"You know I do." She chuckled easily.

In predictable exchanges, Kaela was more than capable of maintaining a coquettish rapport. She tried not to think about her abrasive lack of manners during the exchange with Landry. In her defense, it was ridiculous that she should be prepared to flirt at her place of work. Todd held her gaze, then relaxed with an exaggerated slump.

"Damn, I've missed seeing you. For the record, you're a goddamn tease."

Todd, the orator.

They slipped into a conversation that quickly pivoted to Todd's work at an investment firm. Kaela never really understood what he did or why he made such an ungodly salary. He and the majority of the patrons at this establishment were cut from the same insecure, self-obsessed cloth. She didn't dislike them for that. On the contrary, they took what could be considered weaknesses—people pleasing, attention-craving, deep-rooted narcissism—and turned these traits into lucrative careers in marketing and finance. Any bar in the business district of the city was sure to be swarming with them. After her divorce, Kaela chose to surround herself with this crowd instead of academics. There was a certain raw tenacity to their personalities that she appreciated, and she was practically guaranteed to avoid deep, soul-searing connections. It was a win-win.

Kaela dazed out, intrigued by a little offshoot on the plant that she hadn't noticed before. It was covered in delicate white flowers. Her interest in the new blooms was lost when she finished the last sip of her drink, and Todd circled back to a previous topic involving frozen stocks and an IPO. At that moment, she made eye contact with another person in the mirror over the bar.

Her breath caught in her throat when green eyes locked onto hers. The reflection of the shared look between them was disorienting, like spotting something bright at the end of a dark tunnel. She blinked and abruptly turned around. The eyes she thought were green were actually dark blue, and an ordinary-looking man in his mid to late twenties wore an expression of surprise in response to her sudden inspection. She immediately rotated back to the counter, taking a hasty drink from her water glass to cover the embarrassment of her mistake.

"Are you okay, Kaela?" Todd touched her arm.

Businesspeople always overused your name and threw away physical touches the way a chess player wielded pawns.

"*Hmm?* Yes. Sorry. I thought I saw someone that I knew, but it was a false alarm."

"I do that all the time." Todd abandoned his long narrative involving the stock situation to begin a new story about a time when he was on a video call with a group of representatives from a new client and could have sworn one of those people was the long-lost identical twin of his youngest brother.

He continued to ramble for some time, but Kaela noticed the way his eyes shifted suspiciously across the reflections in the mirror for the first few minutes, surveying the restaurant with an out-of-character intensity that was unsettling for someone whose entire personality could be summarized as 'casually flippant.'

Now, running on the treadmill with the cramp in her side conquered by sheer tenacity, Kaela found a new level of clarity. In the bar, she was too focused on ordering another drink and putting a chemically induced distance between her mind and the events of the day to let the red flag fly, but there it was. Why had he been concerned about her distraction? The rest of the evening progressed as anticipated until the final goodbye in the parking lot, but this one moment stood out in time, an anomaly that needed more investigation.

While she gained this new perspective on her evening companion, Kaela discovered a deep exhaustion flooding her body. It was the feeling of reaching her limit of endurance. She dropped the speed on the treadmill and began to cool down. Her knees emitted a warm pulsing ache, the aftermath of too many decades of use. She felt someone standing close by, a tingling of her peripheral nerves just before a fist bumped against her elbow. She removed an earbud and stopped the treadmill as she turned.

"Hey!" The perky, blond, perfectly toned athletic model in front of her flashed a big smile. "You must have had a terrible day if you're here doing cardio at eight o'clock at night."

"Hailey! I did need to let out some steam," Kaela replied, returning the smile.

"Well, remind me to make you do more farmer carries tomorrow. It's embarrassing that you aren't worried about being tired for our training session in the morning." The other woman punched Kaela lightly on the bicep and then nodded her head in the direction of the weight room. "Got time to spot a sister and tell me all your woes? I just finished my last PT session and haven't gotten my own workout yet."

"Of course." Kaela grabbed her water and followed Hailey, pausing to stretch a particularly tight spot out of her calf along the way.

Hailey was a personal trainer Kaela hired well over a year prior. They met at least twice a week for an hour, during which time Hailey provided dozens of exercises to prove that Kaela was a long way from being in top physical condition. In addition to being in Kaela's peer group, which was often enough common ground for friendship at their age, Hailey was incredibly likable. She was tough, sarcastic, and the human equivalent of an ant. She stood barely past Kaela's shoulder but lifted more weight than most of the gym bros. Kaela considered how unlikely their friendship was as she watched the trainer place an ungodly amount of weight on either end of an Olympic bar.

"What is eating you so much that you had to literally run away from it on the treadmill tonight?"

"I think the word you are looking for is 'figuratively', Hailey."

"Don't change the subject." Hailey shrugged off the correction and fixed Kaela with a no-bullshit stare. "Seriously, what happened?"

"I don't know," Kaela glanced away, but proceeded to explain as she moved behind the bench to spot Hailey's first set. "I have a lot going on at work that is making me anxious. I keep struggling with the same problem. It's frustrating, to say the least. I also met someone, and I have a strangely difficult time not thinking about him. I don't know what it is that makes him stick, but I'll be doing something, and *whoops,* there he is, taking up brain space."

"No more Captain Shallow then?" Hailey had several pet names for Todd that she rotated through depending on the topic at hand.

Kaela considered the final part of her Friday night adventure. She and Todd were several drinks in, cozied up at the bar with the foot of her crossed leg firmly pressed against his calf, the heat of him soaking into the tops of her toes. His hand rested on the exposed knee below her skirt, and as he chatted about his work, his hand inched higher, his thumb occasionally wandering across her skin with a calculated absence of thought.

“You didn’t respond last time I texted you, but I’m sure you were busy.” Todd finished his second drink and leaned back to look Kaela over. “I don’t suppose you want to get out of here already, do you?”

She gave a thoughtful tilt to her head.

“I don’t know,” she replied in a tone crafted to be equal parts hesitation and invitation. “I’ve been pretty clear about exactly what I’m willing to commit to these days, and you were the one who might have balked at those terms. Nothing has changed on my end, so you tell me if we should leave or not.”

He answered with a devilish grin.

As a divorcee with no intention of getting roped into another relationship, Kaela found a new appreciation for superficial engagements. She and Todd spoke on the topic only once. He suggested more of a commitment between them, and she was painfully blunt about her stance on the subject. That was their last conversation before tonight.

A few minutes later, the bar tabs were closed, and bathrooms were visited. Todd escorted Kaela to the parking lot. His oversized truck was parked behind the building where the lighting was less effective and the pedestrian cross-traffic nonexistent. Kaela’s car was a few spaces away, but she stopped at the back of his vehicle, pulling the latch to release the tailgate. Todd’s eyes tracked her movements with cautious interest. She laughed at his uncertainty and pulled herself onto the now open truck bed. A fuzzy euphoric buzz drifted through her, spurring this mischievous attitude.

“I just need a few minutes before I drive to settle.” Kaela paused, appreciating the way Todd’s attention slid to her knees where they draped over the end of the tailgate and then moved up to her thighs, which were slightly parted despite the impropriety of the position. “See something you like?”

“You know I do.” He returned, having a difficult time looking anywhere other than at the object of his desire.

“Not many people around.” She laughed again, impish in her amusement. “It’s a slow night. Want to pretend we’re horny college kids and make out in a bar parking lot?”

Todd’s answering chuckle held more of an edge as he stepped close, stopping with his hips between her knees, the tailgate impeding his forward progress.

“As I said earlier, goddamn tease.” He leaned in but didn’t touch her.

Kaela brought her face closer, letting her lips hover centimeters from his, feeling the warm air from his mouth caressing her skin.

“You can always back off,” she whispered.

He closed the distance, pressing his mouth to hers and parting her lips. His tongue delved in. She scraped her teeth across the surface of it, taunting him with an edge of pain. Instead of pulling back, he thrust it harder, deeper. One of his hands snaked along the inside of her thigh while the other tangled into the hair at the base of her neck. He wasted no time getting straight to the point.

Kaela’s hand ran up the front of him, but she froze when her thoughts betrayed her with a flash of emerald eyes and the imagined feeling of a smooth scar crossing a stubbled cheek. An attractive, fit man was frantic to get under her skirt in a situation with a healthy dose of voyeurism, but her mind chose to wander off to another man entirely. She opened her eyes and tried to focus on the familiar feel of Todd against her skin, scratching her nails across the curve of his thick shoulder like she had dozens of times before.

She wanted to untether herself from the heavy weight of her work. It was constantly grabbing, pulling her under the crushing expectations of success. She wanted to remember how it felt before she became mired with too much responsibility. Todd’s thumb found its way past the last of her clothing, and he made a guttural noise into her ear. Kaela closed her eyes again, panting softly against his cheek.

That smell, cedar and pine. There was a sweet undertone to the masculine combination, a hint of warm vanilla that made it softer, fuller somehow. The memory of the scent filled her nose. The phantom sensation pushed through the carnal feelings and made her skin crawl in a completely new way. She braced her hands against Todd’s chest and applied gentle but firm pressure.

“Todd.”

“*Mmm?*” Todd moved his head to nibble along the side of her neck, chuckling at the small gasp she gave.

Kaela glanced over his shoulder, half expecting to see someone watching, but the parking lot remained empty.

“You want to take this back to my place now?” His smug expression faded as he finally leaned back and saw her face. “Hey, are you okay? What’s the matter?”

"Yes. I mean, no." Kaela laughed and awkwardly tugged her skirt lower over her thighs. "I mean, thanks but no thanks? I know I'm dripping with mixed signals right now, but I just realized that I forgot something and need to run back to the lab. I don't want to cut our evening short. It's just really important."

"Okay." Todd let the heaviness of her sudden change in behavior hang in the air for a moment. "You're welcome? Takes the wind out of my sails from a superior performance I had in mind, but I can take a rain check on what I was planning next. Do you want to just meet me at my place after you handle your work situation?"

Part of her did want to take him up on this offer. A larger part of her lost all interest thanks to the inopportune wandering of her thoughts. It seemed the idea of making out in a parking lot was much more exciting than doing it and realizing halfway through that you were thinking about another man. The serious mantle of adulthood settled back across her shoulders.

"As much as I would like that, I think I'll need to head home by the time I finish there."

She hoped he believed the lie. He really was a nice guy. She just couldn't get her head straight at that moment. He accepted her chaste kiss and waited for her to retreat to her car before turning away.

Kaela should end their relationship so he could find someone with more to offer, but she also really wanted to go home and get a good night's sleep. She put off any further responsible decision-making to another day. In the morning, she picked up her phone more than one time to text him the modern equivalent of a Dear John letter. In the end, she chose to be a coward and bury herself in her work instead.

"No, I think I've finally decided to cut that fish loose." Kaela marveled at the way Hailey effortlessly benched something that she would have dropped on her ribcage in an instant. "The other someone I met is a new coworker. It's probably just a weird stress response. I was in the middle of a lot of disappointment this week, and he showed up at the lab like some angel with good tidings. I'm sure he's just another vapid, hot guy."

"Hot guy, *huh*?" Hailey grunted between reps. "I mean, there's nothing wrong with meeting a hot guy and thinking about him. You need someone to bang it out with if Terrible Todd is really marked off the list."

"Oh, my god!" Kaela exclaimed as she helped Hailey replace the bar.

"I don't have a list. And I was just considering talking to him about some of the research I'm doing over dinner. He's a physicist that recently joined the faculty. I don't think that really counts as a date and certainly doesn't imply we would 'bang it out'."

"A hot guy who might be as smart as you." Hailey said with a tone of amused disbelief. "I don't know what could possibly cause this attraction. Maybe he's someone actually worth spending time with and not just a literal space filler."

"Figurative," Kaela corrected.

"I said what I said," Hailey rebutted.

"Again, oh, my god!"

Hailey released a loud guffaw before resuming her exercises.

"I don't want to meet someone." Kaela's words were soft and hesitant as she continued. "After Jason, I swore off those kinds of relationships. I can't give pieces of myself to someone that takes and takes until there's nothing left of me to give."

She fell silent as Hailey finished her next set and then racked the weight.

"Kaela." Hailey sat up on the bench, turning to face the other woman with an expression that indicated she was about to depart some level of profound wisdom. "Just because you spent years pouring yourself into a marriage with a person who didn't deserve you doesn't mean that there isn't someone else who will deserve you. Having feelings beyond lust isn't a weakness or a waste of time. You're allowed to feel things. Honestly, I was starting to think you'd become a sociopath. Sex is great. Having a connection with someone is probably better. Why worry about it? Just spend some time with this guy and figure it out as you go."

"Says the woman who has no deep connections in her life."

"Well, I have you."

"Absolutely does not count."

"I am open to feeling things, unlike you," Hailey retorted, lying back down to start another set. "I just end up spending too much time with people who are even more egotistical than I am."

"You worry about me being a sociopath, but you also avoid dating anyone with depth. Hey kettle, pot calling."

"I do not avoid it. I just don't prioritize it. My only requirements are physical at the moment. Now shut up and make sure I don't hurt myself like a good spotter."

Kaela laughed and did as instructed, a feeling of lightness spreading through her as the delayed runner's high mingled with the happiness of a amiable conversation with a friend. Hailey was one of the only friendships she had left. The longer she lived, the more it seemed that friends were a luxury of youth and not something that stood the test of time.

After she showered and left the building, Kaela sat in her car under the glow of the parking lot lights and typed an email on her phone to one Dr. Landry Griffiths.

England – 1066

Landry followed the woman along the winding path created by a border of fires and small sub-camps. He did not register the faces or the murmured voices of those men. He only knew that he placed one foot in front of the other in a slow but steady approach to the great hill.

"This first tent belongs to Lady Nisha and the commander, Lord Cassius le Roux." The healer turned to him as she spoke. "They are expecting you. I will take my leave here."

"What is your name, if you don't mind?"

"Marguerite. I will care for your friend. I hope you will return soon to check on him. Bon nuit."

With that final sentiment, she retreated down the darkening path, leaving Landry alone at the entrance to the tent. He stood looking back across the encampment. He had seen men die his entire life, and yet today, he felt a shifting in his core that rearranged the fibers of his soul. He knew that he would no longer fight as a mercenary; that part of him had died beside his companions.

He pushed through the tent flaps. Yellow light washed the inside of the shelter, shifting with each tiny flicker that disturbed the flames from the lamps. Landry found himself facing a large, heavy-set man with graying hair at his temples and a thin black mustache highlighting his otherwise clean-shaven face. The man's olive visage was impassive, and his gray eyes hard as he scanned Landry.

"Milord, Commander." Landry offered a bow of greeting.

"You are called Landry, are you not?" The commander's voice rumbled deep within his bearlike ribcage, and Landry nodded. "Tell me. Why do you not wear the Christian cross around your neck like the others, no trinket to invoke or honor your gods? Are you a man under no gods?"

Landry looked into the eyes of the man questioning him and answered frankly, without forethought or concern to the consequences. "I see no gods when I am on the battlefield. We live and we die. We do not do so for the promise of an everlasting, peaceful kingdom of heaven or Valhalla. We do so because there is no other way to live. Those trinkets around men's necks are like the fingertips of the drowning, groping upwards for some stray moment of hope that never comes. Men who cannot accept our darker natures wear silver crosses and pretend that there is a god who condones their every action."

He waited in silence, wondering what emotions were moving behind the dark countenance of the commander as he considered Landry's atheistic sentiments. At last, the commander's face broke, fracturing into a wide-mouthed grin that displayed his long, white teeth.

"My boy. You have barely seen twenty harvests, and yet you speak more clearly than men thrice your age. I am sorry that you have come to see the world so. We ask our young to shoulder such moral burdens. Perhaps it is unavoidable."

At this, fresh gravity took over the commander. Landry belatedly realized he had been instructed to sit at one of the stools around the strategy table, and he moved quickly to cover the delay.

"I wish to be truthful with you," the burly man began. "I have known of your group for some time prior to this campaign. I commanded several of them on a short assignment before you joined their ranks. I thought very highly of their skills. I always travel with healers of my own, and I assigned one of them to your group. She tells me that there is one who may yet live, but the others will not last through another dawn. You have my sympathies."

Landry nodded but did not trust himself to reply.

"I previously spoke to your leader. Ebrulf, I believe his name was." The commander leaned forward with his hands braced on his knees and observed Landry's reaction as he addressed him. "He knew you to be a good man who treated everyone equitably but who would suffocate under the yoke of a purposeless existence. He spoke of finding direction for you. He said that without a leader, you would fall into your cups and your women until you ceased to exist."

"I do not disagree, Milord, that I should like to have a purpose other than the continual infighting of our peoples."

"He was concerned for your future because I am recruiting you into my personal vanguard, and he only ever wished for you to be content."

Landry physically started at this unexpected revelation.

"Why would you do that, Milord?" he managed.

"There was once a young boy very much like you. He had strange gifts and thoughts about how the world around him should work. He fought valiantly to help grow a kingdom for the wrong kind of leader. There were wars and battles meant to absorb the world, and what started as a shining empire of dreams became a slow, all-consuming disease. That young boy grew to understand there is an intrinsic need for shepherding among the masses.

"People who have darkness in them must be watched and controlled to protect those with innocence in their souls. There are some with great abilities that can step forward to serve that purpose. You are one of those people. Without being able to stop the turning of the world or to alter the way of men's hearts, we are little more than prisoners to our discontent. What if there were a way that you could become an instrument of good in this world for many lifetimes yet to come?"

"I would ask, what must I give to be part of such a future?"

Cassius drew his stool closer to Landry's.

Chapter 3

Despite her best efforts to avoid thinking about her spontaneous weekend email, Kaela spent Monday morning refreshing her inbox once every three minutes. Her very professionally worded correspondence to Dr. Griffiths had offered her congratulations on his new faculty position at the university and suggested a working dinner to discuss their research projects in more detail. By half past eight, her anxious clicking finally resulted in one new, unread message. They arranged to meet at a fusion restaurant near campus the following evening.

Kaela's low heels clicked against the pavement as she navigated the sidewalk on her way to dinner. She tried to convince herself that the extra thirty minutes spent selecting the perfect outfit that morning had nothing to do with Landry. The dinner was simply a professional meeting of the minds to talk about science.

She maneuvered around a sidewalk vault, eyeing the ten-foot drop through the metal grating with suspicion. After watching a morning show segment about the rising number of injuries sustained due to faulty covers, she refused to walk across them. She checked the time and admired the flash of her freshly painted nails in the process.

A faded sadness washed through her, tinting the edges of her thoughts in overtones of gray. Painted nails and perfectly styled hair were the top priorities drilled into her by Grandmother Anicette. Only the first lesson really stuck. The usual series of memories clicked by at the thought; the astringent smell of a hallway, the suffocatingly tight space of a patient room, the constant clicking, and mechanical beeping of machines crammed into every inch of space around the hospital bed, and the long colorful spaghetti of wires connecting a frail body to monitors. New nurses appeared each day like random cards from a shuffled deck, but the stream of chatter drifting past the cracked door was constant. Kaela saw her hands on her grandmother's toes, applying a bright pink lacquer to each small, yellow nail as she talked with her, speaking in halting French during times when the confusion set in. There were long hours spent filling the air with cheerful nonsense to keep them both distracted and long nights spent alone, researching treatments.

Her mind broke through the crust of recent memories into the deeper ones. There were also happy days when her grandmother remembered every face around her and every detail of her life. There were trips to the salon where their fingers were meticulously shaped and polished, and they laughed through familiar family anecdotes. There were hundreds of snippets from farther into the past that should hold sway, but the sadder times protruded the most, hard, knobby memories that were more difficult to process. They were the memories of events that took place after the minor signs of dementia darkened into evidence of Alzheimer's.

Kaela filled her lungs with air to physically displace the sadness inside her, diluting it out into her body. The swallowed tears dissolved, unshed. The memories were unexpected. Ordinarily, she kept them locked up within a tidy box in her head, only releasing them when she was alone and needed a good cry. The pain of loss had become just another part of her. Carrying the burden of sadness was like sliding into a hot bath; she eased into it, bit by bit, letting her body gradually settle into the feelings until she hardly noticed the water was near boiling. She shook off the melancholy, forcing herself to focus on the placement of each step, one after the other.

Landry was standing close to the restaurant entrance, scrolling through his phone. His blue blazer stretched over a plain white shirt, and he was wearing another pair of perfectly fitted jeans. He ran a hand through his hair, tousling the black and silver locks before looking in her direction. His green eyes brightened when he saw her approaching. Filtered golden light from the setting sun fell across the sidewalk, accentuating the bronze tone of his skin.

"Mikaela!" His dimple flashed, and he beamed at her boyishly. "I am glad that you took me up on my offer for a dinner date. This place has excellent reviews."

Kaela's throat dried out when the word 'date' left his mouth, and she swallowed as he leaned in, brushing warm lips against her cheek. An involuntary shiver spread across her body. His hands dropped, and he took a small step back.

"I'm sorry, that was very European of me. I hope I didn't make you uncomfortable."

"No! Not at all." Kaela replied too quickly, willing her stomach to stop swimming. "Are you? European, I mean?"

"Well, I'm not sure. I have been in the continental U.S. for quite a long time. I suppose you could say I used to be European but now I am a bit of a lost soul."

Kaela pondered the response as he pocketed his phone. He held open the restaurant door, then followed close behind, his hand hovering near but not touching as she moved past.

Among the litany of chauvinistic triggers Kaela could claim, the hand applied to the lower back with the intent to steer a woman took a high spot. Yet the absence of his touch now made her skin crawl. Her rational mind condoned professionalism, but a different part of her mind wanted him to initiate something else entirely. His cedar and pine smell plagued her again as the doors closed, wafting his scent forward. Her muscles clenched, and she bit back a groan of frustration. She reminded herself that humans were creatures of chemically driven instincts and as professional as she might want to act, her body was still a sucker for a good smelling man. Biology was a bitch.

The hostess seated them right away, and once established at the table, they didn't have time for chit-chat before the server appeared.

"Dr. B!"

There was a long pause while Kaela racked her brain. They were in her Tuesday class this semester, second row. They were taking the class with their girlfriend and performing much better than said girlfriend on every test. For some reason, she couldn't remember their name, and she tried to navigate around it.

"Hello, good to see you outside of the classroom."

"You, too! Madison and I have been wondering if you'll teach a higher-level course next year. We high-key love your class so much and would definitely sign up for another."

"*Um,* that is something that is decided above my pay grade. It will depend on enrollment numbers and the projected demand for the higher-tier course." Kaela tried to look apologetic as she gave the less than helpful response.

"Makes sense," they replied with an unaffected shrug. "Did either of you have any questions about the menu?

The remainder of the exchange hinged on drink selections and dinner specials before they moved on to the next table. When Landry and Kaela were finally alone, they looked at each other in silence. She was terrible at small talk and was still searching for an easy topic of conversation when he broke the silence.

"I don't want you to feel like I am intruding on anything here. Please feel free to tell me to go to hell if I cross any lines," Landry paused, looking into her face as if deciphering a cryptic message. "I am very interested in your research. I want you to know that if there is any way my lab can support you in a partnership, I am absolutely interested in hashing out the details. Outside of that, though, I really want to know how you arrived here and what your motivation is for this project."

"Why do I feel as if this is an interview?" Kaela peered at him with suspicion. "Am I going to read about this online tomorrow?"

"Perhaps, in my scientific celebrity tabloid." He chuckled freely and shook his head. "At the risk of being a fanboy, I want to understand how the idea of temporal senescence came about. You spent the bulk of your early career dealing with neural changes associated with aging. Your research focused on repairing faulty pathways. What made you jump from interventional therapeutic strategies to playing God, if you will? When did you decide that age, and therefore neural state, was negotiable if you had the correct set of temporal parameters? And why would you derail your entire career to pursue that? Is it a Ponce de León endeavor for you?"

"I am not trying to find the Fountain of Youth. I am researching a better way to treat aging diseases." The beeping of someone's phone alarm at another table had the cadence of a heart monitor. She glanced in that direction but shoved the memories of the hospital away again, refocusing on Landry's face. "Think about cells that are terminally differentiated. You can't replace old neurons with new neurons like you would with skin cells. Sure, some of them regenerate at a very slow rate, but you know what I mean. If you could make them replicate, then you could replace damaged cells, but even then, you would acquire the same random mutations and changes that are associated with age.

"So instead of replacing them with aging cells, why not take the damaged cells and revert them back to their healthy, youthful state, repairing the damage on a cell-by-cell basis? You could treat a neurodegenerative disease like Alzheimer's or even certain types of dementia with one therapeutic to stop disease from advancing, then you could use my research to convince the damaged neurons to regenerate or revert. You would not only treat a disease, but you would also help someone go back to who they were before the disease ever started!"

Kaela's cheeks were pink, and her eyes feverishly bright as the words poured from her mouth. She couldn't staunch the flow of emotion, and she didn't want to. She had willingly gagged herself to accommodate the insecurities of others for a large part of her adult life and refused to do so now. Her forcefulness only seemed to amplify the spark in Landry's eyes as he leaned in on his elbows.

"Yes," he wrapped a great deal of meaning into that one word. "That is the fire I imagined you would have."

They peered at each other silently, assessing.

"But what if you could use this to impart immortality?" he finally asked.

"And why would anyone want that?" Kaela retorted, pinching her eyebrows together and wrinkling her nose at the thought.

They shared another tense moment, Landry's expression unreadable and Kaela's slightly confused. The server appeared with drinks and an appetizer. Landry and Kaela politely thanked them.

"No one wants to age and die," Landry finally said once the server left, as if the answer were obvious.

The blackberry and pepper tang of the wine rolled around her tongue as Kaela took a large sip. "Maybe they should, though. How does one person deserve hundreds of years of existence? Instead of one person living three hundred years, you have three generations living a hundred each. What's the difference?"

"Maybe that one person has a greater role to play in the course of human history, but a hundred years isn't long enough. Maybe immortality would let them fulfill that purpose."

Kaela leaned forward, matching Landry's position, her skin still colored with emotion.

"Here is the secret. No one wants to admit that there is no purpose. No divine intent. No one wants to admit that we just are and one day we just are not. A blip in the time of the universe. Here one second, forgotten the next."

"Spoken like a true scientist," he responded. "But divine intent aside, what if I told you that one person could make a change that impacted the future direction of humankind? One person could work in small steps over hundreds or even thousands of years to sway or steer decisions on a small scale that impact the overall picture. Think of what that person could achieve by preventing a mass genocide or redirecting a war to a peace accord."

"I would say you were full of shit." She leaned back into her seat. "Pardon my language. Do you know why people love to read fictional stories? The characters have a purpose. They have a focused need to achieve something. We read it, and we feel like we, too, would have that ability to overcome and conquer something evil. Through them, we then have the suggestion, the briefest feeling, of a greater direction for our lives. But that's not the truth. It's fantasy. In reality, people have a biological drive to take care of themselves and a few others in their pack. We aren't built to care for the entire species *en masse*."

"You don't accept that any one person could be altruistic? Maybe that, in itself, is what makes a person worthy of this immortality. Maybe there are very few people who check that box, and you haven't met them. You are jaded by your own experience with our 'species *en masse*'." He continued to fix her with his stare as if willing her to accept something. "Maybe you should consider the outliers."

"Maybe you are an eternal optimist, and we won't ever agree on this."

"No amount of new age positive affirmations every morning will make you an optimist with me?" His eyes were twinkling, and Kaela tried not to notice the way they were shot through with gold flecks or the way her body responded to him.

"Ugh, my least favorite philosophical movement." She grimaced playfully. "I much prefer existentialism."

"Dr. Brookes, are you telling me you don't believe in being present and connected to your own inner light?" Now he was definitely teasing as he settled back, chiding her with an audible *tsking* noise. "You would rather think that we are all going to die, therefore, we should live each day like it's our last?"

"We create this system for fooling ourselves and our thoughts in order to feel better about our lives. Focus on the now. Be present. Let that shit go. Say it however you want, but the bottom line is, we just cling to anything that takes away the sadness that we are fleeting, and we will go back to being star-stuff when we die, atoms in the great cosmic void. Is it that difficult to simply embrace our impermanence and realize that's okay, too? It's a beautiful, short life that shouldn't be wasted on trying to make it something it's not. We are given a hundred years to live, but shouldn't we *all* be given that amount of time free from disease and neurodegeneration to make of it what we will?"

"Well." Landry's expression shifted into a lop-sided smirk, and he paused for a long moment. "You are certainly filled with visions of sunshine today: an eternal realist."

"I think we dove right into the deep end of the philosophy pool before we even finished appetizers." She laughed.

"Yes, I typically save that kind of doomsday prophesying for dessert."

His wink drew out one of her slow grins. Kaela realized how much she needed to converse with someone like this. At work, conversations were focused on staffing or office politics with her coworkers. At home, intellectual discussions were never an option when she was married, and now that she lived alone, she would be talking to the toaster. She certainly wasn't engaging Todd in deep cerebral discourse. They were always busy with more physical things.

A flash of embarrassment colored Kaela's cheeks when she thought of Todd. Fortunately, Landry appeared preoccupied with the plate being set in front of him and didn't notice. The server reached across the table with Kaela's entree and accidentally clipped the edge of her wine glass.

Kaela reacted in slow motion, her hand rising from her lap as if to grab the drink, but Landry's hand was faster. As his fingers closed around the goblet, she imagined a thump in her chest like the concussion from a subwoofer. He straightened the glass and slid it further away from the plate. She could have sworn it reached a nearly horizontal position before he righted it, but not a single drop of wine left the stemware. Kaela touched the base of the glass, a light contact to ground her senses, as the server exclaimed over Landry's quick reflexes.

"So." The server left, and Landry restarted their conversation before she could think about the surreal mechanics of the wine glass incident any further. "How did you end up at the university?"

The usual autobiography began to tumble from Kaela's mouth. At a certain point in her career, listing her credentials and detailing key aspects of her resume became second nature, a knee-jerk response to a stimulus. Landry listened attentively, but the furrow of his brow progressively deepened as she made her way through her work history. When Kaela finished painting her academic career in broad strokes, he interrupted.

"You did more in the last four years than you did in the ten years prior. Why the change of pace?"

"I was married. For a while." An involuntary cringe threatened to seize her features at the confession. There was a stigma with broaching this subject on a first date, but Kaela reminded herself that she was not on a date. She was having dinner with a male colleague. Somehow, this only worsened the feeling.

"And that held you back?" Landry didn't bat an eye when he asked the question.

"Yes, it did."

He simply nodded as if the information helped him put together a puzzle that was missing pieces. There was no pity in his expression, nor did he seem put off by the topic, merely inquisitive.

"Well, you clearly made up for lost time and came out ahead. How is your food?"

Kaela found herself relaxing more with each exchange. Landry smoothly navigated every potential pothole in the conversation. The next thirty minutes passed quickly with comments about the food and stories about trips taken where food was a key part of the experience.

They discussed Landry's career. His name was not one that Kaela remembered from publications, but their field of research was a big, diverse world, and they were specialized enough that this wasn't surprising.

The conversation finally arrived back to the topic of Kaela's research, and she openly revealed the latest experiment that was troubling her in the lab. She detailed the way her staff handled cells in culture to try to demonstrate neuron regeneration without division. Then explained an experiment she personally performed several weeks ago.

"It was beautiful. It gave the exact results I dream of – an early-stage profile consistent with de-aging of the cells. I had my postdoc repeat the experiment, and it failed. Then I repeated it, and it worked. Then he did it side by side with me and with my lab technician. I am the only person who can get positive results."

Landry raised his hand and slowly scratched the hint of stubble along one side of his jaw. "Did you prepare the initial cell culture separately?"

"The first time, yes; the second time, we used the same source vial of cells and then split them up between us to set up the experiment."

"Are you using all the same reagents and equipment? And are you feeding your cells on the exact same schedule?"

"Yes, and yes."

“Do you sing to yourself while you prepare your cells?”

Her laughter at what she thought to be a joke quickly died when she realized he was waiting for an answer to the question.

“You can’t be serious.” She snorted.

“I think that you are a brilliant scientist who has gone through every single aspect of the process to try to troubleshoot this. The number one difference between these scenarios is the person who initiates the experiment. It was an honest question but think about it at a higher level. Is there any little thing that you do differently when you set up the experiments compared to your lab staff or postdoc?”

“No.” She monitored every movement her staff made when they were performing the lab work, but now she second-guessed her assumptions. “I mean, I don’t think so. I just get into a certain headspace, and I’m completely focused on the cells. I think about the pathways that need to be activated, the cellular mechanisms that must be triggered within them, the DNA repair, and the final, pristine product I hope to achieve. It helps me focus on why we’re doing this. I don’t sing to them. But I do yearn for them if that’s possible.”

Kaela came to a clumsy halt and stared off into the now busy restaurant interior, mindlessly watching a waiter deliver heavy plates of food to a nearby table, listening to the dull chatter and the clink of silverware. It was such a silly concept that something about her presence would make a difference, but she was at the end of her rope, and she entertained the idea for a few long moments. She didn’t want to tell him the full truth, that those times when she was working in the lab, her mind was occupied with the past. Thoughts of the steady deterioration of Grandmother Anicette’s mind were too personal to expose here in this public place in front of someone who was still a stranger.

When Kaela finally stopped fidgeting with her napkin and raised her eyes to the man across the table, she found Landry observing her with a soft but serious expression. The concern and intensity of that look was in sharp contrast with the casual demeanor he maintained throughout the evening. He blinked, and the moment was broken.

“Can I get either of you dessert or anything else?”

Kaela tried not to start at the sudden appearance of the server and politely declined their offer. Landry did the same and took the check.

“It’s on me, really. I have thoroughly enjoyed this, and you can consider it a bribe to let my lab be your number one choice for a partner moving forward, no pressure." His exuberant flirtation was back, and Kaela decided to let him win this round. "If you don't mind, I'll stop off at the restroom, and then I would be delighted to have you escort me safely back to campus. I was told that I can't be too careful at night in a college town."

The server returned to drop off the copy of the receipt and followed Kaela's gaze to Landry's retreating figure with a chuckle.

"That man is hot."

"I didn't think he was your type," Kaela teased.

"I'm not blind," they retorted and turned to leave, calling back over their shoulder. "That one is a snack and a half, if you're into that kind of thing."

Kaela was still laughing when Landry met her at the restaurant door.

"Shall we?"

This time, when they exited, his hand skimmed lightly across her back.

Kaela pointed out a few restaurants and shops on the way to the faculty parking lot, rambling about interesting things to do in the area as a cover for the heartbeat pounding in her throat when Landry's shoulder or hand brushed against her body. They were walking closer than necessary on the sidewalk, but every time they started to drift away from one another, they were pulled right back together by some invisible, attractive force between them, two masses locked in rotation.

They paused at an intersection, shoulders barely touching as they waited for the signal to cross. A low yipping tugged at Kaela's mind. She turned her head in concern. She heard it again, faint and low but muffled. She couldn't find a clear direction, but some instinct drew her to the dark alley behind them.

"What is it?" Landry glanced backwards.

"I'm not sure."

Kaela walked to the alley opening without waiting for his response. The passage was just a narrow space between the backs of the buildings with dim lighting and rows of trash cans. A stack of empty tomato boxes teetered beside the door to a restaurant, propped up by an equally unsteady pile of empty milk crates. Kaela's eyes snagged on a single box, wrapped in layers of duct tape and barely visible in the shadowed gloom cast by a waste bin. She glanced at Landry, reading the wariness in his features as he peered down the alley.

Kaela noticed the way he stood to the side, close enough to grab her, but his attention shifted constantly through their surroundings.

"Did you see something?"

"No, but…" Kaela trailed off, unable to explain the feeling, and walked closer to the box. "I'm not sure what it was, but I think it came from this."

Landry placed a hand on her arm when she moved to touch the dirty cardboard surface. A door swung open a few feet away, and a teenager with headphones stepped out carrying a plastic trash bag, which she promptly dropped, releasing a tiny high-pitched scream of surprise.

"You scared the bejesus out of me!" The girl glanced at the box near Kaela's feet, then backed up. "What are you doing?"

Before Kaela could respond, she heard the tiny noise again.

"There's something in here!" She ripped into the box with her bare hands, circumnavigating the tape and tearing a hole in the side where her fingers easily clawed through the waterlogged material.

"A puppy!" the teenager squealed in Kaela's ear, leaning over her shoulder in excitement. "Is it okay?"

Kaela held the cold, skeletal body on her lap, rubbing her hands gently over the thin skin. She could feel a tug in the pit of her stomach, a pulling sensation that must have been sadness. To her relief, the puppy took a few shallow breaths and lifted its head. The girl yelled at someone through the open door, and then a towel was being thrust into her hands by a lanky man in a dirty, white apron.

"Here, wrap it in this. Poor thing is skin and bones. What kind of asshole leaves a dog in a box?"

In a whirl of activity, the puppy was whisked into the warm building, and the kitchen staff of the small German restaurant crowded around the little furry creature, offering it saucers of water and little chunks of cooked meat. Kaela watched in a listless daze. Her arms were heavy as they hung by her sides, and a dull ache pounded behind one temple.

"Your nose."

Landry was holding a Kleenex out to her, and she registered a damp feeling under one of her nostrils. She used the tissue, and when it came away from her face, there was a bright spot of blood. He observed her just as he did during dinner, his face a mix of concern and curiosity, as if contemplating the answer to a particularly challenging question.

"Do you feel all right?" he finally asked.

"Yeah." Kaela balled the tissue in her fist, eyes still fixed on the puppy as it wiggled its entire body back and forth in a happy, serpentine dance. "I think so. I just get tired of people being garbage."

"Hey." He pulled her to his side, his hand rubbing the top of her arm in a comforting gesture. "One person was garbage. One person left that dog out there to die. Six people in this room are making up for that. Seven, including you."

"Definitely an eternal optimist." She bumped into him with her shoulder to emphasize the statement.

The puppy was now standing up on its back legs, licking at the mouth of the restaurant manager, who had a delighted expression on his face.

"What made you go back to the alley?"

Kaela was waiting for the question but still didn't have a satisfactory response prepared. She remembered the clammy, lifeless sensation of the dog's skin pressed beneath her fingers. She pictured the seams of its closed eyes and the sluggish way it started moving as the slow transfer of her body heat appeared to revive it. Her answer felt ashen in her mouth, disintegrating with her own disbelief even as she spoke the words.

"I heard it barking."

France – 1522

A stooped, shawl-covered figure moved through the grove of tightly spaced trees. Daylight was beginning to seep into the foggy valley, but wispy patches of darkness still clung around each tree and hollow. The woman wove through the shadows, seemingly unaware of Landry's presence as he viewed her progress from the top of an embankment. She took a few slow steps, then bent close to the ground, eyes carefully inspecting an object. She straightened and moved on, repeating the cycle while occasionally placing items from the ground into the basket that dangled from her arm.

The cloud of Landry's breath drifted in the air before him, though it was not particularly cold. The sun shifted above the mountain ridges in the distance, and a thousand drops of dew on the leaves and grass caught the bright rays of light. For a brief span of time, the valley sparkled with points of bright silver nestled among the clusters of night stubbornly hiding in the thicker vegetation. He let the morning air fill his lungs, soaking in the marvelous sight of the countryside awakening and wondering if he could etch this scene into his memory for eternity.

More and more, he recognized that memories like these faded into vague impressions with the passage of time. The image and feel of the country spread out before him would eventually disappear from his mind as it became one moment in a long line of lost experiences. He had more than enough time to forget this day.

"I suppose you are here to ask me to reconsider my decision on behalf of your master?"

Landry looked at her with a half-smile on his face. In contrast to the hunch of her body while foraging, she now stood straight and proud beside him. She was only a dozen years older than his outward appearance of twenty-one, but he felt each of those years was a millennium. She was still beautiful, but now she wore the tempered beauty of a mature woman, the angles of her features lessened as the tension in her skin eased, and her body shifted to a softer composition. Her chocolate eyes were still warm and open, but at each corner, faint creases trailed to her temples that hadn't existed when Landry last saw her.

"No, I am not here to harass you on Cassius' behalf, Marguerite," he responded gently. "I know you well enough to leave you alone when you make up your mind, although I can't say that I like the choice you made."

"I know that you do not understand, mon ami," she replied, perusing his features in a deeply understanding way. "You and I are different, Landry. We always were. You will live for thousands of years and never lose your humanity. I cannot and I will not."

He did not reply, and Marguerite turned to face the horizon with him, their sides barely touching. The sun continued on its path, and they listened to the birds calling out for one another. She was first to break the spell when she heaved a long-suffering sigh.

"Why are you here?"

"I came to see how you are. Truly!" Landry laughed at her suspicious tone. "I was in Paris and knew you were living here. I anticipated that you would be out gathering."

"You are never in Paris," she retorted.

"No, I have not been in Paris since before the Pestilence."

"And why have you now returned? Are we Parisians and French not the lowest on your list of acquaintances?"

"Marguerite," he scolded. "You know that we left France before the Plague could take us all. It was a cesspool of death."

"Yet your French remains perfect," she teased drily. "What a lovely surprise."

Landry, who had been conversing with her in French the entire time, gave an unamused look.

"Did you think I would forget the tongue of my birth?"

"It has been four hundred years. We forget much."

When Marguerite looked at him again, he felt that she could see everything he was feeling that morning. She could always read his mind like it was a sheet of parchment stretched before her. He shrugged and looked away.

"You have changed," she murmured. "You never concerned yourself with the same spiritual maladies that some of us were consumed by. Did the black death teach you fear, or is this just a maturation of the soul that I am finally witnessing?"

"I am sure it is but a temporary difficulty." He offered a half-heartedly devilish grin. "I woke up this morning without my usual sense of purpose.

I shall find it again once I go into town and locate a tavern."

"And a brothel, no doubt," she teased. "Landry." She placed her hand on his arm to impress the seriousness of what she was about to say. "It is okay to be lonely. I am married now with children of my own. I shall raise a family, and then one day I will die as an old woman with a broken body if I am fortunate enough to live that long. I do not expect this type of life to fill the void you find inside you. You have an infinite amount of time on your hands. Take part of it and dedicate yourself to knowing what you require to feel complete. You are a man that will always need a mission and a purpose, just like Cassius. Determine if those callings for you align with those for him. If they do not, find your own. Do not be shackled by your fear or sadness. You must build your own happiness."

Landry placed his hand over hers and kissed her on the cheek.

"Thank you, mon coeur. I do not know who I shall go to for such words when you are gone. You will take a piece of me with you. Know that."

She returned his sad look, and they wandered together down the long path. When they drew close to the homestead, a boy, a near exact image of his mother, caught sight of their approach and set into a hard sprint in their direction, face lit with happiness. Just outside of the open doorway was an older girl. Landry considered her bronze skin and upturned, watery eyes the color of an afternoon thunderstorm. Where her younger brother favored Marguerite, she must have taken after her father in features. Her long, lean form was that of a child on the cusp of maturity. He would have placed her between ten and twelve but knew her to be younger since Marguerite had no children when she left their group only nine years past. Marguerite grabbed his arm and drew him near before the children were close enough to hear her words.

"Promise me," she whispered fiercely in his ear. "Promise me you will watch after my children and my children's children. Promise me that long after I am gone from this short mortal life I've chosen, you will keep them safe."

"I promise, mon coeur," Landry whispered in return. "As long as I live, I will watch over them."

Chapter 4

Three days without any contact from Landry. Kaela shouldn't be counting. She should be more concerned with the advancement of her research and less concerned with the progression of her love life. Yet her feet had a mind of their own as they took her away from the well-worn path she traveled at the end of each day. Instead, she found herself walking a circuitous route through the bell tower yard, which meant she passed directly in front of the physics building.

The staff at the German restaurant had assured her the puppy would be well taken care of, and after Landry exchanged contact information with the owner, she agreed to leave it with them. While Landry walked alongside her to the university parking lot, their conversation was sedate. She shared stories of her childhood dog, a retriever with a heart of gold and a head full of lead named Alchemy. Her father insisted on punny names for every pet in their household.

At her car, Kaela turned back to face Landry, acutely aware of their proximity. His eyes rested on her lips for the briefest of moments, and by some hidden strength of character, or perhaps some streak of cowardice, she didn't lean in to close the slight, but significant, physical distance between their bodies.

"Thank you for dinner and an exceptional conversation tonight." His voice was still soft and deep, but it contained a slight strain. "Perhaps I could convince you to do this again soon?"

"I would like that." She pulled out her phone and looked at him expectantly. "Give me your number and I'll text you. Then you'll have mine."

He complied, and his phone chimed as Kaela sent a simple: *Hey*. She tucked her phone away and searched for her car keys. Once she extracted them from her hip pocket, she returned to the uncomfortable stalemate.

The shorter days of fall meant they were observing one another under the intensity of the fluorescent bulbs illuminating the dark lot. Most, but not all, of the vehicles had left. The majority of those remaining likely belonged to young, untenured professors attempting to fit far too much work into a single day. Kaela realized she was staring at Landry's mouth, but when she shifted her focus to his eyes, the tension only increased. Landry leaned forward just enough to pull one of her hands to his face and softly kissed the inside of her wrist.

Kaela was certain that her body was spontaneously dissolving into a puddle. She managed to suppress the sound that threatened to escape her parted lips. She placed her palm along one of his cheeks and brushed her lips across the opposite side of his face. As her mouth made contact, she registered the smooth section of skin dividing the scratchy stubble. She had inadvertently kissed his scar. She felt him shudder beneath her hand, but his eyes were clear and his expression calm when he dropped her wrist and stepped away.

"Just message me if you want to plan something."

She moved purposefully, concentrating on getting into the driver's seat of her car without giving any indication of her frenzied emotional state. She checked the back seat for a hidden serial killer and locked the door behind her before starting the engine. Landry walked down the line of parking spaces before he turned out of sight.

Hey back.

Kaela looked at the text from Landry. Three days since their date, and she still hadn't replied. It would only take a few seconds to initiate a conversation. Her thumb hovered over the empty response field. Instead, she locked her phone and slid it into the pocket of her jeans. She had performed this same dance dozens of times, but despite the wonderful dinner they shared, she couldn't bring herself to type a message.

Work was a series of nightmare scenarios that day: a departmental meeting that turned into a public admonishment when she disagreed with the department head, office hours full of sob stories and requests for extra credit, and finally, a lab technician who accidentally dropped an experiment on the floor. Kaela was currently standing in her driveway just outside the closed car door. She tilted her head back and breathed the chilly evening air deep into her lungs, the clicking of the vehicle's engine the only thing loud enough to register in her head as the stars slid in and out of view behind a thin layer of clouds. She stared up to the seven sisters, the Pleiades, which graced the evening sky again after their summer hiatus.

Such a terrible, bullshit example of what women endured over hundreds of thousands of years of homo sapiens existence. Sisters were stalked by a testosterone-ridden sex fiend of a giant, and instead of that imbecile getting his just desserts, the women were turned into stars. Thank you, Zeus, for setting the bar of oppression low. Maybe he should have focused on something godlier, like swan-flavored bestiality.

Kaela was riding a wave of heightened anger and indignation. Departmental meetings at her university began once a quorum of attendees was reached. In theory, that was an appropriate strategy since it was impossible to account for everyone's schedules, and absences were to be expected. However, holding the meeting at half past four on a Friday afternoon meant that the two other female professors, both with children under the age of ten, were unable to attend. Arguing with a room full of old white males and having no allies to lean on was something Kaela was used to, but it wasn't something she enjoyed. She found it difficult to remain calm or professional when her words fell on deaf ears and her ideas only received careful consideration after they were restated by a man.

She released her lingering frustration, shaking out her arms and giving a throaty exhale. She abandoned the skies and turned to enter the house, nearly dropping her keys in surprise when something furry darted out of the shrubs by the stoop. Her pulse thundered in her neck, but she belatedly realized the shape was just a cat, an orange tabby with long fluffy hair and a white chin. It wove in and out of her legs.

"What are you up to, fuzzball?" Kaela reached down, and the cat bumped a soft cheek against her extended fingertips. "Do you have a home, or is accosting strangers your path to a meal ticket?"

It moved to the door; eyes squinted.

"You look like a stray," Kaela squinted back, and there was a momentary stand-off before she leaned over to put her keys in the lock. "If you have fleas or if you pee on anything, I'm kicking you right back out, no explanation needed."

It jetted into the interior of the home the moment the opening was wide enough for its slim body. Kaela followed behind, hanging her keys on a hook and kicking off her shoes. She navigated to the kitchen by the soft light of the foyer and placed her laptop on the counter. When she retrieved a box of cereal from the pantry, she was able to locate a can of tuna in the dark recesses of the shelving. The can opener was a siren's song to the feline, and it rubbed along her calves with renewed fervor, low wailing cries issuing from its mouth. Kaela flopped the can onto the floor and carried her bowl of cereal to the living room. She sank into the couch cushions, socked feet resting on the coffee table.

She had moved into this house during the separation that preceded her divorce. It was an older build with 'good bones.' Her father used to talk about houses as if they were living creatures with memories and personalities. Her ex, Jason, was horrified by her love affair with historic properties. She never shared much of the details surrounding her childhood with him, and he couldn't understand the way renovations connected her to a father that died too early. Whenever something would slip out that revealed her blue-collar upbringing, Jason's lips would flatten, and his nostrils would flare with mild contempt. He never came right out and said that he found her bloodline distasteful, but he didn't need to.

She once noticed tiny bubbles along the drywall in his office when visiting his firm. She remarked that the workers should add a drop of dish soap to the joint compound, like her father always did before applying the mud. Jason had looked frantic, his expression pained as he peered back into the hallway and closed the door.

"Don't talk about that where people can hear you."

It would be a great embarrassment for the other partners to know that Jason Arnolt married a poor girl.

The windows in Kaela's living room were large and beautiful, overlooking a little green field during the day. Tonight, it was too dark to see anything except the interior of the house, reflected in the glass like a mirror. Kaela stared at her shadow double. The deep brown of her hair and faded gray of her eyes dissolved into the darkened windowpane, giving the *other* Kaela an unnerving appearance like a ghostly specter in a horror film. The house was eerily quiet except for the constant scrape of the tuna can against the tiled floor in the kitchen.

Kaela settled a little deeper into the overstuffed couch, turning away from the window to spoon wheat flakes into her mouth. The cat finished banging the can against the kitchen cabinets and jumped up next to her, shuddering with purrs.

"Hi." Kaela ran a hand down its spine, and it arched up to meet her touch. "I had a terrible day. How about you?"

The cat closed its eyes, purring louder. She gently picked it up and gave a perfunctory evaluation to its nether region. Its little body stiffened in protest, but its claws remained sheathed.

“Lady parts. Not that it matters, but I wanted to know what you’re working with. At least you won’t be offended if I tell you about the misogynistic jerks I work with, right?”

She laughed at the cat’s insulted expression. It settled further down the couch and began to bathe itself. She moved her phone from her pocket to the coffee table and picked up a half-read novel, happy to sit alone in the silence of her home.

Kaela was always alone these days. She rarely felt attachment to others around her beyond inconsequential affection. In truth, she found that people were too self-focused to participate in relationships that fulfilled the emotional needs of both individuals. Friends didn’t truly care about her; they were just filling space in their lives with a convenient body. Jason hadn’t been much better.

She met her ex-husband in college. He was there because his trust fund and connections meant he could attend any university he wanted. She was there because she worked two jobs through high school, made all A’s, and volunteered for every nonprofit in her hometown.

He dazzled her. His life was a fantasy, and she was happy to hide who she was so she could have that life too. He never cared about her academic successes. If anything, her intelligence was on the same list of unmentionable attributes as her home improvement skills. The women in Jason’s family kept their mouths shut, their bodies cosmetically enhanced, and their legs open. When they tired of that last part, they gratefully overlooked the collection of mistresses who followed.

Jason was different at first, but when the apple falls from the tree, it doesn’t grow into an oak. She brushed off the problems for years, but the more effort she put into becoming the perfect wife, the less effort he put into treating her as a partner. Leaving him was never her choice, it was a decision he made for both of them the day he stopped seeing her as a person worth respecting.

Kaela replaced the bookmark after rereading a paragraph multiple times and tossed the paperback onto the table. She was doing more introspection than usual these days. That particular wound was closed on the surface—not healed but contained. She would like to seal it up tightly again.

“What is wrong with me?” She exchanged a glance with the cat. “Don’t look at me like that. I know it’s normal to be attracted but I’m four years out from a failed marriage, and he's technically a coworker. I can't just bang it out and move on, despite what Hailey thinks."

The feline's stare was unyielding.

"I mean, not really a coworker if we aren't in the same department, but still."

The piercing yellow eyes didn't shift.

"Fine, I will text him."

The cat returned to meticulously grooming her inner thigh hair.

Hey! Haven't heard from you this week (or seen you). How are you?

She grimaced after hitting send, immediately regretting the overuse of the word 'you,' and set the phone face down on the table. She shouldn't feel guilty for acting on a physical attraction. Most humans placed entirely too much stock in abstract concepts, thinking that holding themselves to the unattainable goal of remaining chaste would somehow make connections deeper than physical need. Aside from disease and surprise pregnancies, Kaela couldn't figure out what was wrong with sex. The simplest solution was to scratch the itch, which would level her out and get her back to a better mental state. Easy-peasy. Deeper, emotional connections could be completely independent of physical engagements.

She scrutinized the dregs of her cereal as if divining her gastronomic future and tried to decide what else to eat. The phone buzzed, and there was a delayed chime on her smart watch. She tapped into a stubborn vein of willpower and refused to check either. Instead, she retrieved a selection of food from the kitchen and forced herself to eat one unhurried bite after another, staring blankly at the unlit fireplace until she was finished. Only then did she pick up her phone and check Landry's response. Small, arbitrary victories felt important.

Sorry, been a busy week. I would love to take you out for another dinner if you aren't otherwise occupied. Just leaving campus now.

His message was direct and straightforward. The coy, teasing persona from the other evening was absent. Kaela frowned and looked over to her new companion. The cat studiously ignored her. It grasped the tip of its tail in both paws, chewing on a stubborn spot.

I just finished dinner but could go for a drink or dessert.

Pick you up or meet you out?

My place? You bring the dessert. I have drinks.

Kaela belatedly gasped at her own audacity and waited for his reply, trying not to read too much into every second of delay.

Seems like the perfect way to end a long work week. I need to stop by my apartment, and then I'll pick something up. Sure, you're comfortable giving me your address?

"Kaela, you idiot," she muttered to herself. "Ted Bundy was charming."

An in-depth sleuthing session on the web after their first date (not that she was calling it a date) allowed Kaela to verify that everything he told her was truthful. Even so, putting a safety check in place with someone was the intelligent thing to do when inviting a man that she barely knew to her home. She didn't have any friends who weren't somehow connected to her ex, and those people were obviously off the list. Who did that leave?

She sent a quick text to Hailey with her address and a short message to tell her the general situation. Kaela promised to check in later that night and again in the morning to let her know she was safe. Hailey sent an eggplant and confirmed she was on the job. Only then did Kaela text Landry the address.

I've taken some safety precautions in case you're a serial killer.

Of course, can't be too careful. See you around eight.

Kaela's stomach churned, and her body tingled as if it was disconnected from her head. She jumped off the couch and started the long sequence of events that were required to prepare for an unexpected date. The cat observed the commotion with a look that fell somewhere between concerned and unimpressed.

After nearly an hour of cleaning, showering, dressing, and generally fussing over the appearance of herself and her home, Kaela stood in the living room wearing a nice but casual outfit that attempted to give an 'everyday look' vibe. She checked her watch – ten minutes to spare. She had never invited a man to the house. With this realization, the nervous twinge in her stomach evolved into a heavy stone.

She noticed a cup sitting on the table by the window. She took it to the kitchen and plucked a mint leaf from the plant next to the sink. Chewing on the leaf, she moved back to the living room and straightened a blanket on the chair.

She moved the blanket to the couch.

She put the blanket back on the chair.

Candles? No, that was too much. The air already held a sweet, sugary scent thanks to the lilies blooming in the living room window. She picked up her book and perched on the edge of a chair, trying to read but really just waiting, caught in a suspension of time resulting from the combination of her impatience and agitation. She gave herself a mental scolding for the embarrassing level of anxious energy coursing through her body.

Before she could truly embrace the self-loathing, there was a knock at the front door. Kaela sprung to her feet but paused to let the dizziness of a head rush pass. She forced herself to walk slowly as she moved down the hall to answer. Landry waited on the stoop, one hand in a front pocket, the other holding a paper box. His bright smile and vibrant eyes sucked the breath right out of her. She told herself it was a normal, physical response, the words echoing in her head like a desperate mantra.

"Mikaela." Her name was a gentle caress, the vowels tilting and floating over the 'L' like a song. She was struck by the familiarity of it. "Looks like I'm in the right place. This is a nice, older neighborhood." He leaned forward and kissed her softly on the cheek. "You must have purchased at the right time. It's hard to find one on the market these days."

"Yes, I've been here for about four years." She fought the warmth rising up her neck and stepped back, yielding space as an invitation.

Before Landry completed his step across the threshold, a furry body hurdled past him and out into the night. He hesitated in surprise.

"Was that your cat?"

"*Um*, no?" Kaela peered into the dark, tracking the feline's trajectory. "I think it was a stray. I let it in and fed it, but I guess it got what it came for. You know how it is with cats, the universe gifts them to the right person at the right time. We aren't allowed to ask questions."

She shrugged with amusement as Landry entered the foyer, closing the door behind him. He removed his shoes and fastidiously placed them next to hers on the rubber shoe tray. He was dressed in jeans again, but tonight he donned a fitted black half-zip fleece. He offered her the paper box.

"Paulie's Pastries on 29th," he stated. "This box should contain a few life-altering cannoli if the reviews are correct. I also got a macaroon and biscotti in case cannoli are not to your taste."

Kaela's mouth started watering.

"Are there people who don't like cannoli?" She accepted the proffered treats and gestured for him to follow to the kitchen. "What can I get you to drink? I have wine, a few different types of beer, and some harder brown stuff in the living room cabinet. Or water, of course."

He leaned back against the counter, letting his eyes wander around the kitchen and then over her. Her pulse jumped, but she pretended not to notice.

"Honestly, a beer would be great after today."

She retrieved two beers, leaving the cannoli on the counter for the time being and leading Landry to the living room. They moved with the comfortable rhythm of two people who enjoyed being together. Kaela briefly marveled at the lack of tension before her motions became more stilted, as if noticing the ease of the other's company made her suddenly distrust it.

She settled on the far end of the couch and Landry took a seat on the opposite side, facing the wall of windows. Kaela tucked a foot under her body and propped an elbow on the back of the sectional, forcing her movements into a natural cadence.

"Long day?" she asked.

"Very long day."

Her eyes were transfixed by the bobbing of his throat as he took a drink. For a moment, his shoulders curved forward in a slight hunch, and his face looked drawn. She felt her body shifting closer to him, compelled by a reflexive need to provide physical comfort in response to his obvious malaise. The surge of emotion caught her by surprise. While she scrambled to yank back on the impulse, he emerged from his melancholy. His back straightened, and a warm expression flooded slowly across his face like the breaking of dawn. When he turned to her, he had transformed into the jovial flirt she was expecting.

"I am sorry this date is last minute." Kaela's chest tightened as he used that word again. "I'm glad you didn't have other plans."

"I mean, with my crazy social agenda these days." She winked at him and took a swig of her beer, focusing on keeping her fingers from picking at the bottle label. "Is everything okay? Just work politics or something else?"

He fixed her with the stare that was becoming familiar, the one that suggested he was considering something about her that he wouldn't put into words.

"Only work." He set his drink on the table, taking care to use a coaster, and adjusted his position to mirror hers with one arm resting along the sofa, his fingers brushing her elbow. "How about you? Did your week improve after we last spoke?"

“Mostly.” She discarded the still-fresh memory of bigotry at her work meeting and tried to remember if anything went well over the last few days. “The experiment still hasn’t been reproduced, but I did have excellent feedback from a grant review.”

Lightning was shooting up her elbow from the lazy tracing of his fingers along the outside bend of her arm. Landry appeared to be unaware of the extreme agitation his actions were causing, as if they were unaffected, spontaneous gestures more so than an engineered tactic of seduction. Whatever the motivation, she found it difficult to focus around the contact.

“That is excellent news. Since you have an impressive funding history, I am not surprised. I’m sure the resolution for your experimental troubles will also come along soon.”

She blinked in surprise at the supportive tone.

“Tell me about those plants,” he abruptly redirected, looking over her shoulder.

“The plants?” Kaela set down her drink and turned, physically orienting herself to the subject. The absence of his fingers against her skin was as distracting as their presence had been. “I like to garden. In the fall and winter, all I have are my indoor plants, and I decided to go overboard. Are you a houseplant aficionado? I’m not judging, just surprised, is all.”

“Not typically.” He left the couch to inspect the plants in question. “I wouldn’t expect to see such happy plants in November.”

“Like I said, kind of my thing.” She followed him, letting her finger affectionately tickle the frond of a fern. The proximity of his body to hers made her skin tingle with a heightened awareness. “It’s not that complicated, really. I just make sure they are on a good watering cycle and get plenty of sunlight. The windows do the hard work. And some of them only like to be watered every other time. But otherwise, it’s easy.”

He chuckled as he walked the length of the flora collection, stopping in front of a pineapple plant. Kaela breathed a little easier with their increased separation.

“That one is my pride and joy. It takes about four months for the pineapple to mature, but once I clip it, another one starts right back up! It’s amazing. I haven’t bought pineapple from a grocery store in years.”

He turned and stared at her for a long moment.

“You are joking?” he asked.

“*Um*, no?” She tipped her head in confusion.

Landry frowned.

“Kaela, pineapple plants take years, plural, to mature, and they only produce a single fruit. Then they must reseed from the mother plant, and a new plant grows which also produces only a single fruit.”

“Shut up,” the valley-girl response popped out of her mouth. “Maybe this is a different variety. And why do you know so much about pineapple plants?”

“I spent some time in Honduras,” he responded cryptically. “And there aren’t any other varieties. Are you sure it’s the same plant that produces the pineapple each time? Or do you have a new plant sprout up from under the roots of the original?”

“It’s the same plant.” Kaela slowly pulled her phone out of her pocket and brought up the web browser. “Not that I don’t believe you, but…”

“Trust but verify.” Landry shrugged noncommittally and then watched her reaction as the results appeared on her phone screen.

She clicked and scrolled through one hit after another, certain that she would find a source to corroborate her story. Her eyebrows inched closer together until her frown lines were in danger of splitting her forehead in two. The pineapple plant was the first thing she purchased when she moved into this barren home. She was shopping at the grocery store, and right there in the produce section was a display of them. She thought, *what the hell, why not grow a pineapple or two,* and brought it home.

“What about this lily?” Landry gestured to indicate the light pink Easter Lily, the syrupy odor of its flowers close to nauseating at this proximity. “How often does it bloom?”

“All the time,” Kaela responded tentatively, watching his expression for a reaction. “It puts up new blooms every few weeks. It’s pretty much constantly flowering.”

Again, the long, mystified stare as he processed her statement.

“Easter Lilies are genetically programmed to bloom once a year for a few weeks. It’s why they’re called *Easter* Lilies. Have you honestly never realized that you have—unusual plants?”

“No.” She huffed with annoyance. “I’m not a botanist. I have perfect light in this window and get a little heavy-handed with the fertilizer. I’m sure I’m not the first person with these one-off oddball plant situations.”

“Maybe not.” He shrugged away the suspicion in her tone, looking at the pineapple plant pensively. “Well, if you’re against discussing this alternate universe you’ve created with your plants, I guess I’ll let it go. I will simply chalk it up to you being an exceptional gardener and agree to ask you all plant care questions from now on. Although, I don't have a single house plant. I can't commit to the upkeep."

"I had a roommate like you." Kaela's face lit up with the memory, and she cataloged the plant concerns for more research later. "She was my randomly assigned partner in the dorms as an undergrad. She hated all the plants I grew in our room. I had a little coral plant in a container, have you ever seen those? She accused me of growing pot in our dorm room. She was absolutely convinced that I had cannabis in our window. I'm surprised she never turned me in.

"One day, the fire marshal came around to do an inspection while I was in class. She had broken her ankle a few weeks before and was on crutches. When he knocked on the door, she absolutely lost it, falling all over herself to get that plant hidden in the closet under some dirty clothes. I only know about it because I told a mutual friend that I found one of my plants in the closet, and he let me in on how it got there. God, what a great memory! I wonder what happened to her."

"She probably sells legal weed at her head shop in Colorado." Landry joked, and Kaela giggled at the thought.

"What about you? You must have one or two good undergraduate college stories."

Landry took another drink of his beer and crossed to the coffee table to set it back down. When he returned, he stood close to her again, and she felt his nearness like the soft flickers of a fire.

"I was too busy worrying about exams and getting into the best graduate programs to make any memories worth recounting."

"Right." She chuckled nervously. "Like you need an impressive resume to get into Oxford. I'm sure you could just bat those pretty eyes and get the grades you wanted."

"Pretty eyes?" He raised an eyebrow and moved a fraction closer. "You think I have pretty eyes?"

"I mean, they're okay." Kaela suppressed the urge to fidget when those breathtaking eyes slid down to her mouth. "I've seen worse."

He took another step forward, and she had to tip her head back to keep looking at him. She was hyperaware of the disparity in their sizes with him only inches away, but it wasn't fright that sent her pulse scurrying. He lifted one hand, tracing it lightly along the edge of her jawline. Kaela's skin exploded with a rush of heat, and she shuddered. His breath was warm against her face, and he gave a low, satisfied chuckle at the obvious effect of his touch.

"Well, I'm glad they don't completely disappoint you." His hand drifted down, and he lightly gripped the base of her neck.

Kaela's body was simultaneously taut and loose when he drew her forward, bringing his mouth down to brush against hers. Her body melted into him, the hard press of his legs and chest making her ache. His lips parted, and he tangled their tongues in a single, slow movement that made her knees tremble. Her hands gripped his waist, pulling him, encouraging him. He traced his fingers under the edge of her sweater, running them against the bare skin of her lower back. He spread his hand, pressing her tightly against his body.

She was instantly frustrated with the multiple layers of clothing between them. She tugged at the fabric of an undershirt where it was tucked into his jeans, needing to feel his skin beneath her hands. He backed up to the couch, pulling her with him as he sat down until she was straddling his lap, their faces nearly even in this position. Kaela leaned back, creating enough of a gap between them to pull her sweater over her head. Her entire body thrummed and vibrated, feverish with anticipation. He ran hooded eyes over the thin, lacy material of her bra.

"Mikaela," he rasped, his hands gripping her hips, pulling her harder into him despite the hesitation. "You barely know me."

"So?" She kissed him again, more urgently this time, biting down the side of his neck and feeling his body tighten beneath her as a groan escaped his lips. "I don't need to know you for this part."

He stood in a single fluid movement, turning to lay her flat on the cushions. Now it was her turn to moan as he dragged his tongue up the centerline of her stomach. The sensation washed over her, the pure satisfaction of it pushing out the too solid concerns of her professional life, filling her with a singular, buzzing focus on the physical feeling of him.

There was a hard knock at the front door.

"Wait, wait," Kaela panted, pushing Landry back a few inches to listen. "Did you hear that?"

His hands paused at her waist, where his fingers had been burning lines into the sensitive skin above her hips.

The knock sounded again.

"*Ugh*, I could ignore it?" she offered helplessly as she reached for her sweater.

"No, it's okay, I can wait," Landry winked, his voice uneven.

Kaela slid off the couch, pulling her shirt over her head, and combing through her disheveled hair. She paced quickly to the door and peered into the peephole.

What fresh hell was this?

Todd stood on the stoop, hands shoved into his pockets like he was cold. As she spied on him, he glanced at the street and then straight back to the peephole. Kaela stepped away in surprise. Seeing no other choice, she cracked open the door and stuck her head through.

"Hey, what are you doing here? Is everything okay?"

Todd evaluated her flushed skin and seemed to come to a rapid conclusion, attempting a glance over her shoulder. The inside of the house was obscured by the door, and he returned his eyes to her face, his expression a strange mingling of amusement, anger, and reproach.

"You busy?" His question finished in a sneer, and his eyes took on an unhinged wildness.

"A little." Kaela pulled the door even tighter against her shoulder. "I have company over. What's going on?"

"I need to talk to you. About the other night." His speech pattern was off, and although it looked like Todd, she was struck by the thought that this person was a stranger.

"Well, now isn't the best time. Maybe we can meet up tomorrow or something?"

He glanced at her bare feet, then over to the pair of obviously male shoes sitting just inside the foyer. "Why don't you grab *your* shoes and come out here to chat. It'll just be a minute."

"I don't think so." Kaela started to step away and shut the door on the deranged person standing on her front steps.

He anticipated the response and kicked the door from her fingers before she could close it. His hand shot straight out to her throat. The attack came in slow motion, Kaela's mind attempting to reconcile the dangerous man before her and the irreverent pretty boy she associated with this face. It was like learning that a chinchilla was a deadly, venomous predator. Her mind couldn't accept the unexpected dichotomy. Pretty things shouldn't be dangerous.

For a moment, she thought she leaned far enough away to evade his attack, but then his fingers closed around her neck, and she was being dragged forward through the open threshold. Something large *whooshed* past her body, the displaced air blowing her hair and clothing against her skin while a concussive thump reverberated deep in her ribcage. It collided with Todd. He released her as the impact sent him backwards through the air, landing in a sprawl across the front lawn. There was no blood on him and nothing on the ground nearby that would indicate what hurled him into the grass. Kaela stood at the foot of the stairs in momentary shock, willing her brain to process the scene.

"She said get lost, *Theodore*." Landry's voice blasted through the air, forceful and aggressive, issuing the name like an insult.

Kaela turned her head, watching him advance from the living room, and was once again overcome by the feeling of seeing someone for the first time. Landry's movements were fluid and intentional, a hunter that hadn't spent a single day of his life unsure about his actions. To her other side, Todd was back up on his feet, malice stamped across his features.

"No one asked you, *Guardian*." Todd spat on the ground and raised a fist.

The ground shook, and Kaela fell to her knees like a rug had been pulled out from under her feet. A harsh rumbling echoed inside her head. Her hands were braced against the sidewalk, and she stared at them, watching the small pieces of dirt and rock bounce against the shaking surface. The vibrations faded, and she looked back at Landry. In place of her door was a giant sheet of rock. A boulder, five feet across, was crushing her front stoop.

She was in shock. She must be.

Her body refused to move, and all she could do was stare at the granite surface of the mysterious slab as if answers would flow from it. A hand closed on her upper arm.

"I told you to grab your shoes," Todd grumbled as he dragged her to his car and attempted to shove her into the back seat.

The trance broke in that instant, and a survival response finally surfaced. When her back hit the seat, her bare feet kicked out, catching Todd in the stomach. It was a mistake as she was aiming for his groin, but he moved.

"Fuck you," she shouted, scrambling to get out of the car.

“Kaela, Kaela, such a tease,” he tutted, grabbing her wrists and cinching a zip-tie around them.

He swept one of her legs when she started to run and tossed her to the ground with practiced ease. He zip-tied her legs so quickly she didn’t have time to process her next move. He picked her up to put her back in the car, and she squirmed. When he loosened his grip, she flung her only free body part into the fight, smashing her forehead into his face with a considerable amount of force. Unfortunately, he didn’t drop her despite the expletive that left his mouth. He deposited her in the back seat, and she felt a glimmer of satisfaction at the blood streaming from his nose and upper lip.

“How do you like *that* follow-through?” she hissed.

He stood stock-still, an angry half glare contorting his bloody face. Then he slammed the door.

England – 1536

"This is an interesting scene." Theodore drifted into the open space, acknowledging the three people he knew well and then eyeing the group of armed men that he did not recognize. A smooth dark stone danced between the fingers of his hand. "Whatever is the matter?"

"It would appear his majesty ordered these men to seize Charles," Landry stated, his voice flat. "I was just asking how that could be, as Lord Dale is a loyal servant to the crown."

"Ah, well. That is... milords..."

The man speaking was clearly ill at ease with contradicting men above his station. As he stammered, the other armed guards, swords in hand, moved to surround the group. Landry, Charles, and Sarah slowly drew their weapons. Theodore continued to toy with the stone, an impatient look on his face. The tension grew. It was Sarah who finally broke the silence, her hands tightly clutching the twin daggers that she'd slid free from hidden pockets within the folds of her voluminous skirts.

"You cannot take him. Do whatever it is that you think will work to force his capture."

One guard grabbed her by the arm. She managed to slice his bicep open and tried to slam the blade up under his chin. The much larger man caught her wrist and wrenched the knife from her before it made contact again, pressing it to her throat instead as he pinned her tight against him. Her face was contorted with rage, but the blade at her neck kept her still.

At the same time, the other three guards lunged to engage her male companions. Their initial attacks were rebuffed. Charles wielded his blade awkwardly. His life as a courtier never required actual swordplay, whereas his opponent was trained to kill. Landry moved with ease, his sword graceful and deadly in the hands of a master fighter. Even Theo used a short blade for the occasion.

"Put down your swords or I will slit the lady's throat," the man holding Sarah yelled, pressing his blade down with enough pressure to elicit small beads of ruby blood that trickled along Sarah's throat and gathered inside the crevices of her collarbone.

"You would harm a gentle lady of his majesty's court?" Charles questioned in disbelief.

"I am sure his majesty would not notice this one's absence."

Landry and Charles stared at the man in anger. Theodore made eye contact with Sarah, and an understanding passed between them. She grabbed the man's arm and pushed the blade from her neck with every ounce of strength she could muster. At the same time, Theo's hand shot forward, and something flew through the air, whistling as it smashed into the face of her captor. Sarah collapsed to the floor with her hand pressed firmly to her throat.

Landry's arms fell limply to his sides, and he issued a harsh, wordless yell. The three remaining guards sagged like marionettes whose strings were abruptly severed, and faint wisps of light poured from them. A concussive sound wave rolled over the group, and the phantom lights reversed, sending the guards' bodies backwards until they slammed into the thick stone walls with a series of sickening thuds. Landry sank to his knees, sucking down deep, wheezing breaths. Theodore stared at Landry with surprise and another, more cryptic emotion.

Charles rushed to Sarah's side. The blood which oozed between the fingers of her hand was cooling in a dark, gelatinous puddle in front of her. Her breath was shallow and quick. Charles tried to look at the wound, but she shoved him away.

"Wait," she croaked.

Theodore approached Landry, helping him up. Once upright, they exchanged a heavy look. Landry nodded, accepting whatever apology and agreement he read there, and then briefly glanced at the guard that fell to Theo's attack. The small rock was lodged deep in the front of the man's head, and his eyes bore the vacant stare of death. Landry could not muster regret or sadness for the man as he turned to Sarah. She was breathing more naturally now. Charles still clung to her free hand, desperate but too afraid of the wound to remove the hand that was staunching the flow of blood.

"Sarah?" Landry asked.

At his voice, she raised her eyes and let her hand fall away. Beneath the smears of blood was the pearly white skin of a new scar.

"That was a little too close," she replied, giving Theo a smile that didn't reach her eyes.

"Thank God," Charles blurted out. "I thought, well, I don't know what I thought. I am still not sure of your powers, and the wound looked deep."

"She is far more resilient than you give her credit for," Theo stated, drawing Charles' sharp stare.

"You are the one that put her in danger." Charles rounded on him, a new target for his frustration. "That was idiotic and unnecessary. I could have convinced that man to let her go if not for you!"

"Charles," Landry stated calmly. "We did not have time for you to practice your charms, as convincing as they may be. The task needed decisive action. These are the choices you will face from now on. It is best that you grow accustomed to them. Sarah was never in real danger, were you, my girl?"

Sarah snorted with derision and brushed off her clothing.

"You could have done a bit more than throw a stone at someone," Charles muttered at Theo instead.

"Would you have me bring the entire keep down on our heads?" Theodore asked, continuing to respond over his shoulder as he retrieved the rock from the dead man's forehead. "I do not think I should start moving rocks around inside a stone palace. Perhaps next time we will engage our opponents in a field, and I can really impress you, Little Lord."

"Don't call him that," Sarah cut in before Charles could rise to the bait. "Shall we pretend to be friends and get out of this hall before anyone notices the blood?"

Landry nodded and smoothly took command. Cassius's missive that morning demanded a full retreat from the country, and with the addition of Theodore, he now had his full contingent of immortals together. It was time to leave the court for good.

Chapter 5

"If you kick me in the head, I'll wreck the car, and we will both die." Todd looked in the rearview, wary of the manic glitter in Kaela's eyes.

"Fifty-fifty chance I crawl from the wreckage in one piece which seems better than whatever sick, sadist shit you have planned for me." She let her rage flow through her, knowing that if it faded, all that would remain would be shock and fear.

"I'm not a sadist and I'm not going to rape you, or whatever it is that you think I'm planning. Besides, we've already had sex."

"It is always rape if it's one-sided you dip-shit." Kaela continued to glare at his reflection, incensed beyond reason. "What is wrong with you?"

Todd studiously focused on the road. Kaela kept her eyes locked on him in the mirror as she subtly pulled against her restraints, testing their integrity. Looking for landmarks at night was disorienting, but she knew they were heading to the main highway, driving away from the city center.

"For what it's worth, I'm sorry I left that giant sinkhole in your yard."

Kaela blinked, trying to remember exactly what happened during the chaotic moments of her kidnapping—the explosion and shaking of the ground, the inexplicable appearance of a rock at her door. He hogtied her in her front yard like she was an unruly animal. There hadn't been much time for her to inspect the mysterious monolith. Once they were speeding down the block in his car, another explosion had occurred behind them.

"A sinkhole," she repeated, still processing the words. "That boulder thing caused it. What was that?"

Todd laughed darkly and dug a napkin out of the console. He glanced back at her in the mirror as he dabbed away the blood around his nose.

"Well, if you're a neurologist, I guess you could call me a geologist."

"Is that supposed to be funny?" Kaela's deadpan expression only incited his mirth. "How did you make that rock appear? Did it drop from something above my yard?"

"Jesus!" He wiped tears from his eyes but continued to chuckle at her expense. "You really don't know, do you? I pulled that shit up from the ground, therefore the sinkhole where it used to be."

Her stare was an unflinching thing of art.

"You are actually insane."

He just laughed harder.

Kaela tried to commit the name of an unfamiliar gas station to memory as the car rounded a corner.

"Is Landry okay?" She finally let the question slip out.

"Landry? Yeah, I'm sure he's fine. Unfortunately. He hasn't survived a thousand years to go out that easily. Looked like the two of you were getting cozy. Did you decide I wasn't keeping the kitty satisfied lately?"

There was a lot to unpack in that particular series of sentences, so Kaela chose to remain silent, counting blocks. Clearly, this Todd was a sarcastic jerk. She assumed the man she dated for the better part of a year was physically sitting in the driver's seat, but the person she 'knew' was a complete sham. She was disgusted at herself for believing the deception. She tried to remember any warning signs that she overlooked, but not once had she gotten a strange or uncomfortable feeling about him. Until the other night, of course.

Maybe he was too vanilla. Maybe she should have been suspicious that an attractive, well-employed, forty-year-old man with no obvious emotional baggage was single. Scenarios raced through her mind, mostly originating from her minor obsession with true crime podcasts. He was probably a jealous lover about to murder her in the woods. She didn't see a gun or knife, but the way he summoned the restraints out of thin air meant he could have other items hidden on him.

She needed to get him talking, to try to get more information. Then she could sneak out a text from her cell phone. Her cell phone was sitting on the coffee table. Expletives ran through her head when she remembered that she was too busy putting on her shirt to grab it before answering the door.

The giant rock took over her thoughts again. There was no explanation her brain would accept. Was it dropped from the sky? Pulled up from the ground? Pushed up from the ground? Was the entire event an optical illusion or exceptional special effects, and there really was no rock?

"If you aren't a murderer who abducts women that break up with him, why am I tied up in your car?" Kaela decided to take the 'get them to talk to you' route for the time being.

"I've always wanted to tie you up." Todd grinned. "And for the record, I don't feel scorned. You never actually broke things off and we never agreed to be exclusive."

"Read the room, dickhead." Despite her best efforts, Kaela couldn't hold back her anger. "Not fucking appropriate if you want to reassure me you are not, in fact, a rapist."

"It was just a joke, Kaela." He let out an exaggerated sigh. "It's seriously not as bad as you're making it out to be. You should have grabbed your shoes. Your new man caused things to escalate. I was going to ask you to take a drive with me because I need you to meet someone. I didn't realize *he* was with you. I had to get you out of there in a hurry while he was detained."

She held up her bound hands.

"Seriously? And you couldn't think about using more of your big boy words instead of abducting me? Besides, I've never invited you over or given you my address, which makes it kind of hard to play the 'I'm not a creep' card at this point."

Empty silence stretched between them, and they merged onto the highway. Kaela counted the mile markers, reaching five before Todd took the car down an exit ramp. She frantically attempted to map each turn and street name in her mind as they moved deeper into the suburbs. The houses grew larger and more pretentious until they reached a long sweep of hedges where only the occasional silhouette of a multi-pitched roof was visible from the road. Todd pulled in front of a solid, iron gate and punched an entry code into the keypad, gaining entrance to a driveway that ended at a plain but monstrously large house in the Mediterranean revival style.

"Are there palm trees around the pool in the back?"

Todd furrowed his brow at Kaela's sarcasm and parked. He walked around to extract her from the back seat, standing clear of any potential kicks. Kaela started to exit but froze when the open pocketknife in his hand caught her attention.

"If you promise not to run and not to kick me, I will cut your legs loose. We are just here for you to talk to someone, that's it. I promise."

"Fine." She snarled, fixing him with a cold stare. "I won't kick you unless you get handsy."

"Fair enough," he responded and sliced through the plastic straps. "I don't like that I had to grab you. There is a lot that you don't know yet. I hope I'll get a chance to explain."

He abruptly stopped talking and glanced over his shoulder as if checking to see if anyone heard his words. Kaela rolled her ankles; thankful the ties had been over the legs of her jeans. Todd stepped back, and she set her bare feet on the cold pavement. The house was surprisingly well lit with a carefully maintained yard and high walls around the perimeter. There were no movements or noises to indicate the presence of other people.

"I assume you have a name other than Todd that I can call you."

"Actually, I go by Todd most of the time. It's too hard to remember fake names, and I don't want to have a wallet full of IDs. My full name is Theodore, but some people call me Teddy if you prefer. Or Theo."

"I'll go with Theo." She scowled at the amused tilt of his head, simultaneously grimacing at the thought of calling him Teddy. "Do you live here?"

"No," his reply was sharp enough to catch her off-guard. "I only stop by for business reasons. Speaking of, let's go."

He gestured to the front stairs, but Kaela hesitated. Clearly, someone in this house made him uncomfortable. She considered stalling and asking more about the 'business' reference but cautiously made her way up the stairs instead. The door boasted an ornate metal knocker shaped like a snarling gargoyle. She stared at it, her zip-tied hands resting in front of her body. Laughter bubbled up her throat, filling the hollow space left behind by the ebbing adrenaline with a situationally inappropriate humor.

"What in the Bram Stoker is that thing?"

Todd gave her a concerned look and reached around, swinging open the unlocked door. Her mirth quickly dissolved as he pushed her forward with a firm hand on her back. Kaela elbowed him away and stepped through on her own volition.

The interior of the home was stylishly decorated and brightly lit. Kaela's skin soaked in the welcoming billow of air as she entered, the warmth of it giving her body a false sense of comfort. She conducted a perfunctory survey of the foyer, her stare lingering on the large staircase and the unlit entrances leading deeper into the home. A painting hung between two of the darkened doorways. It was ghostly, a dark pigmented dreamscape of a mother kissing the forehead of a tightly embraced child. The lines were blurred, insubstantial, like images ripped from a recently experienced but rapidly fading dream.

Todd closed the door, and the click of the latch echoed unnervingly. He gestured for her to follow as he moved through an arched entryway to the left, his shoes creating a staccato chorus of squeaks on the polished mahogany floorboards. Kaela tore her eyes from the painting and walked behind him, her bare feet whispering along the short, open hallway and into a large room.

"I see you convinced her to come with you."

The cold, feminine voice belonged to a woman standing near a ridiculously oversized desk. Her eyes were so dark they seamlessly swallowed the obsidian of her pupils. Her bored, impassive expression when speaking was unsettling. Her delicate bone structure made her appear small and non-threatening, but the strange aura she gave off made Kaela suspect that her physical appearance was a deception, like the doe-eyed face of a leopard seal or the cuddly-soft fur of a honey badger. To her left was an equally striking female with a perfect, dark complexion and features that suggested middle eastern descent. She looked familiar, Kaela thought they must have been acquaintances, but when they made eye contact, a sharp pain at her temples distracted her from these thoughts. Her mouth tasted coppery.

"Thank you, Ramla. You can go now." This abrupt dismissal came from the first female.

The tall, exotic beauty sauntered out of the room; kohl-lined eyes filled with haughty contempt as they traveled across Kaela's body in passing. Kaela was instantly transported to middle school, when the unsolicited hatred of other females first became a regularly occurring staple in her social life. On closer inspection, she didn't recognize her after all. The first woman scanned Kaela with a less judgmental interest, stopping briefly at her bound hands before turning to Theo, lip curled in disgust.

"Take those off her. I told you to convince her to meet with me, not sling her over your shoulder like a giant gorilla. I hope she did that to your nose." She turned back to Kaela while Theo complied, ignoring his not-so-subtle grumbling. "I did not intend for you to be treated barbarously. I just wanted us to get to know one another. My name is Nisha."

Kaela glared at Theo as he cut the ties, not bothering to respond. She rubbed the pain away from the pink welts on her wrist.

"I understand if this starts us off on the wrong foot. Perhaps we could sit for a moment, and I will explain why I wanted to meet you. Theodore can stand over there and keep his mouth shut." Nisha didn't so much as glance his way as she said this. "He has done enough damage for now."

Kaela followed her hostess to a set of symmetrically opposed couches spaced apart by a metal coffee table. A large window overlooked the side yard, and moonlight spilled across the sill. In college, Kaela rented a single apartment that would fit inside this one room. Nisha sat and gestured for Kaela to do the same. Her eyes communicated that the silent instruction was not a request, and Kaela meekly perched on the edge of a cushion across from her.

"Can I get you something to drink?" Nisha gestured to a bar against the wall.

"No, thank you," Kaela finally replied.

"She speaks!" Nisha's eyes crinkled in amusement, and she placed her hands in her lap, looking as innocuous as a coiled snake. "If you do not mind, I can tell you more about myself to begin."

"That would be nice," Kaela offered blandly. "I assume you already know plenty about me."

"*Ah.*" She pursed her lips as if chagrined. "I do apologize for how that must feel. If it helps, I did not dig into anything deeply personal, mostly just your professional work history. I know that you are an accomplished scientist for several reasons, but chiefly owing to your specific personality traits. You are intelligent, highly analytical, and excel at combining complex modalities into cohesive singular theories. You question everything and adapt your theories as you receive new information, a skill set that will hopefully allow you to be open-minded during this conversation."

Nisha paused and crossed her long, thin legs at the ankles. Her gray pantsuit was perfectly pressed with a distinctly bespoke quality of fit. She wore simple gold jewelry, and her short black hair was tucked behind her ears. Her spine was perfectly straight, and she radiated an off-putting level of controlled power. She reminded Kaela of a corporate executive, or a cat eyeing a mouse. She hoped it was more of the former than the latter.

"I was born during the Qin dynasty. Since you are an educated person but not a historian, the details of that statement might be missing. I am over two thousand years old. I have a unique ability that no other person possesses. Theodore is also able to do things that defy your current grasp on the laws of reality. Mine is a bit different. Let me give you an example, and then you can ask me questions. There are three birds sitting on the front wall to the right of the gate. If you look through the window, you should be able to see them just around the corner."

Kaela waited for someone to break character and laugh. She looked at Theo. He continued to stand with his arms folded, blandly returning her gaze. She looked around the room for signs of a hidden camera or a group of people waiting to jump out and shout, '*Ah hah!*' The room was silent other than the faint sounds of the outside world continuing its normal course: a distant car horn, a bird song, a dog barking. Nisha was watching with a threatening stillness.

"Two thousand," Kaela finally repeated.

Nisha nodded, her canines showing as her lips slowly retracted in a semblance of a smile.

"That's biologically impossible. I should know."

Nisha gestured to the window again as if her age was the least important aspect of what she previously stated. Kaela rose, keeping both of them within her field of vision as she stepped sideways to the indicated spot. In the front of the house, three mourning doves were tucked together along the wall that shielded the home from the street. The lights from the house bathed them in a bright sheen and they fluffed their feathers against the cool evening breeze. There was no angle that would allow either Nisha or Theo to see them from their current locations.

"Interesting parlor trick." Kaela didn't see any cameras or mirrors, but even if Nisha couldn't see the birds from where she was sitting, she could have known they were there prior to Kaela entering the room. "What is the purpose?"

"There is a spider behind the curtain to your left, halfway between you and the ceiling." Nisha cocked her head slightly to the side as if listening. "And another bird just landed in the trees near the driveway. It's close to the squirrel that's been getting settled in a nest up there for the last half hour."

Kaela checked each of the statements, straining her eyes to detect the bird in the shadowy limbs of the tree. The squirrel was impossible to see, leaving that claim unverified. She turned back from the window, uncertain about the direction of this little game. Kaela glanced at Theo again. He had the gall to look exceedingly bored.

"I have a unique connection to living things. I can feel where every creature is within a certain physical and mental radius. I can also detect when people have particular abilities."

Kaela shouldn't have reacted to the clearly disturbed individual in front of her. She should have nodded and played along until she could escape. She should have done a lot of very reasonable, safe things every day of her life, but she somehow always chose differently.

"And that is how you've lived through two millennia?" Kaela disregarded the hand wave indicating she should resume her seat.

"No." Nisha laughed, but it did nothing to ease the tension. "Well, yes and no. This ability is why I was gifted with a long life, but it does not stop me from aging. Someone much like you did that."

"And how old are you?" Kaela cut her eyes over to Theo.

"He is much younger. Theodore was a stone mason in the late Middle Ages. Aren't you around eight hundred?"

"Close enough," he answered with no hint of emotion.

"And you move rocks?" The question snaked out before Kaela could smooth the sarcasm from it.

"Something like that." His characteristic smirk returned.

"Theodore, get the tray from my desk."

Kaela fully expected torture implements on the deep silver tray that he retrieved, but when he was close enough for her to make out the shapes, she saw that it held several types of stone instead. He placed it on the coffee table and sat on the vacant sofa. Kaela struggled against a wave of curiosity but ultimately moved closer, peering over Theo's shoulder as he selected a fist-sized stone. He held it up as if peering through it in the light from the ceiling fixture. He offered it to her. She stared at his hand, still not understanding the ruse.

His smirk grew.

Kaela's expression soured but she took the stone, feeling ridiculous. She found nothing remarkable about the surface. It was not as heavy as it should be, but she suspected it was a geode.

"Break it," Nisha demanded.

"In my bare hands?"

She nodded. Kaela half-heartedly squeezed it between her palms, then handed it back to Theo with a shrug.

"Quartz." He placed it flat in one palm and tapped the top firmly with the index finger of his opposing hand. It split into two perfect hemispheres with a loud crack. He handed one to Kaela, and she marveled at the miniature cave of crystal sparkling inside.

"Another nice parlor trick," she grumbled.

"I told you this demonstration wouldn't be worth the effort." Theo muttered and reached forward for a large block of concrete. "Here, give this a good inspection."

The block was much heavier than he made it look, and Kaela nearly dropped it on her toes. It was unremarkable. She tapped the sides, shook it like a Christmas present, and squeezed it. She passed it back to Theo, and he put it on the table. His fingers danced across the surface as if caressing something living and precious. With each pass, a little of the concrete crumbled away, littering the table with chips. An ornate *fleur de lis* took shape. He blew the last of the dust away to reveal a beautifully carved relief. Kaela walked around the couch, feeling the surface of the stone in amazement.

"Tell me how you did that." She took him by the wrists, inspecting his palms and searching under the edges of his sleeves for anything that would explain what she witnessed.

There was a reason Kaela avoided magic shows and mentalist demonstrations. There were people who spent their entire existence finding elaborate and convoluted ways to trick others for profit. Poorly performed shows were a waste of time, and well-performed shows left her annoyed that she couldn't see past what was obviously a deception.

"I told you; I have a thing for stones."

"Acid etching? It's clearly not aerated concrete." She rubbed her fingertips into the carved surface and then smelled them for residue. "Some type of electrical pulse or vibration?"

"Are you going to lick it too?"

Theo wiggled his eyebrows and then handed her the final stone. It was solid granite, almost too heavy for her to inspect. When she returned it, he gestured for her to step back. He placed the rock on the tray and gave her a sly look. He raised his hand and dramatically formed a fist. At the exact moment his fingers closed, a small explosion reverberated through the room and the rock shattered into a thousand tiny pieces. Kaela barely stifled a gasp of surprise.

"You really did make a boulder shoot out of the ground." She gaped at the pile of rubble littering the table.

"Thank you, Theodore." Nisha stood and retrieved an orchid from her desk, setting it on the table next to the stone debris. "Now it is your turn, Dr. Brookes."

"What?" Kaela looked from the flowerless plant on the table to Nisha's composed expression. "I don't explode plants."

"You misunderstand," Nisha replied patiently. "Theodore's talents are of a brute, physical nature, though I admit he creates lovely artwork when he is so inclined. Your talents are very different. I want you to make the plant bloom."

Kaela processed this statement slowly, digesting each word. The only conclusion was that Nisha read Kaela's publications and decided that the speculation about applying her research to aging cells was concrete evidence of something outrageous. Every scientific paper overstated the findings in a grandiose conclusion. It was expected that you would do this to validate the importance of your research by suggesting long-reaching implications and thereby secure more funding for future work. Kaela's conclusions inevitably leaned into the ability to manipulate the effects of time on living flesh, suggesting that science could speed up or even reverse the aging process. She considered Nisha's earlier claim of being thousands of years old.

These people thought Kaela could grant immortality.

That was the only explanation for this circus. Nisha wanted to see a demonstration of time manipulation by having Kaela age the plant forward to full bloom.

"I don't think you understand how my research works," Kaela replied carefully, fighting the rising wave of panic squeezing against her lungs. "It's all completely hypothetical. I can't alter time. I can't take a living thing forward, or backward, in development."

"I think you can." The corners of Nisha's lips dropped, and she leaned forward just enough for Kaela to notice the shift in weight. "I think you just haven't found your motivation."

Now the panic was pounding in her ears, a full-body flight-mode onset. This woman was clearly not mentally stable. Why did science always bring out the crazies? Some people couldn't accept the cold, data-driven facts, and they had to take information out of context, twisting it into something fantastic, something beyond reality.

"Is this the part where you torture my loved ones in front of me and scream at me to try harder?"

Though she had never been in this situation before, never been so scared that something terrible was going to happen, sarcasm was Kaela's normal stress response. The snarky words tumbled out on their own accord. To her surprise, Nisha let loose a short, rusty cackle. Theo abruptly straightened, looking at the other woman with surprise.

"I don't think fear is a great motivator, Kaela. In your case, I think your overwhelming drive to put the solution together will be enough. You need time for this unsolved mystery to wear away at you until you rise to the challenge. Your skepticism is remarkable, and I admire it. If you were the type of person who believed everything they were told or trusted the unreliable information provided to you by just your eyes, we would not be having this conversation. No, I think you just need time to digest everything that we discussed. The unresolved questions are enough incentive for a mind such as yours."

"You're going to just let me go now?"

"You were never my prisoner!" Nisha's eyes widened in surprise. "Despite Theodore's lack of delicacy in bringing you here, you were free to walk away at any time. I am not in the habit of abducting people. Particularly not people who I respect as much as you, my dear doctor. I must apologize, once again, for the situation in which you arrived."

"And you aren't going to do anything to ensure my silence after telling me about, all of this?"

"Who would believe you?" Nisha stood and handed Kaela the unbloomed orchid with an air of finality. "I think we gave you the information you need to get started. Perhaps we can talk again soon when you have more questions. I want us to have a mutually beneficial relationship, but I understand you will need a bit more time before you are ready. For now, your Knight in Shining Armor is about to arrive, and it's time for you to go out front. Theodore, please make sure that you don't incense him any further. I do hate when the two of you destroy things that belong to me."

Unbelievably, Nisha turned and walked out of the room without saying another word. Theo stood and stretched as if he had been watching a game on TV, not engaging in this dog and pony show.

"Well, come on. You can keep the rock, too."

Kaela looked down at half of the geode still clutched in her hand. She didn't remember picking it up. In her other hand was the orchid, a queen at coronation with her ball and scepter. Perhaps that's what they wanted, a queen for their madness. A shock-induced laugh tried to exit her body, but what emerged was a choking kind of cough. Theo waited patiently near the door and turned to lead her to the driveway. Kaela inspected the back of his shoulders, thinking through their interactions again.

"Have I been your mark this whole time?" He didn't break stride when she abruptly called out the question. "Have I just been someone your boss wanted you to keep an eye on? I assume we didn't meet by chance at that bar."

"Yes."

No sugar coating, no apology, just a simple admission.

She remembered her guilt for stringing him along. She thought he was a kind, if self-absorbed, person, and she was doing him a disservice by staying involved when she didn't take his company seriously. They never went into any depth during their conversations. They mostly talked about his work, upcoming sporting events, or new workout routines for the gym. Kaela suddenly realized they had spent an entire year sharing superficial, garbage conversations. She never wanted to connect in a non-physical way, and she had assumed he wasn't very intelligent. She wanted to believe he lacked complexity, so she didn't question anything. She was willingly naive the entire time.

"Well, I guess I don't have to feel bad for thinking you were just a good lay and not wanting a real relationship."

Theo barked out a laugh as they exited the house.

"Kaela, I don't think you ever have to apologize to a man for that."

"Theodore, I think that despite living eight hundred years, you are unwisely underestimating the emotional capacity of your gender."

"I did enjoy the time we spent together, Kaela." The quiet seriousness of his words caught her off guard. "I wasn't ordered to sleep with you. That was your decision to make, and I, for one, don't regret that."

She stared at him, off balance.

"Of course, everything I told you was a lie, and I did write an entire dossier on your personality from our time together." Asshole Theo made a triumphant return as he winked and faced a set of headlights approaching through the still open gate. "Time to talk your boyfriend down from the ledge. I'll try to stay calm this time. I just really can't stand that guy. He always brings out the worst in me. Maybe I can tell you about it sometime."

"I don't think I want to hear anything else from you." Kaela snarled.

An SUV pulled up too quickly to be a casual visitor and a very angry

Landry launched himself from the driver's side door. There was an aching pull in Kaela's belly when she watched him stalk directly at Theo, a palpable throb of energy shimmering in the air around him. He was a seething hulk going into battle, and some animalistic part of Kaela took notice. Her ears started to ring, and the hairs along her arms lifted.

"She is perfectly safe and unmolested!" Theo held his palms out in a sign of surrender. "Nisha just wanted to talk to her, and I was about to return her now. Nisha also asked if you would please refrain from attacking me and potentially destroying this property out of respect for your ongoing friendship."

"Talk?" Landry sneered at Theo but hesitated and looked up at the house when Nisha was mentioned. "Next time you want to 'talk' to someone, try not breaking down their front door and snatching them out of their home. 'Out of respect' for *your* boss, I won't teach you a lesson in manners right here and now. Don't ever come near her again unless she specifically gives you permission, or I might forget to play nice."

"She being me?" Kaela scowled, drawing Landry's appraisal. "*She* is going to walk down the street and call an Uber. *SHE* is tired of dealing with whatever deceptive insanity is taking place with all of you. As flattered as I am with this protective display of yours, I don't think we have quite reached the point in our relationship where that is even appropriate."

"Mikaela, I am sorry." Landry flinched, and his face softened into a mask of remorse, the raging energy around him fading back to a low hum. "Are you okay? I brought your shoes, and I can take you home now if you'd like."

She noticed a pair of her running shoes clutched in one of his hands. They were sitting by the door when Theo snatched her. What person had the foresight to remember shoes in that situation? She glanced past Landry and through the open door of the SUV. Another man she trusted. She invited him into her home. He clearly knew Theo, and he clearly knew Nisha since he found his way here in short order. The conversation about immortality and his comments about the plants in her house sat differently as she pulled the pieces of these connections together.

"I'll take the shoes."

He placed them next to her feet. She handed him the orchid and the rock so she could pull them on. She looked at the gate, too exhausted to follow through with calling a ride.

“You can take me home.”

Theo remained silent as Landry opened the passenger door and Kaela climbed into the vehicle. As they pulled away, a flicker of emotion that might be fear or concern crossed Theo’s face. Kaela closed her eyes and leaned her head against the seat, too tired to worry about trading one lunatic for another and just trusting that Landry really was taking her home.

“Mikaela,” The sing-song word was soft and careful on Landry’s lips.

“Don’t,” she interrupted him without opening her eyes. “Please just take me home. I don’t want to hear it.”

“Okay.” He fell silent and stayed that way.

Kaela listened to the blinker as they made a turn. The tires ticked out the constant rhythm of the interstate, which was only broken by the occasional rush of a passing car. She couldn’t focus on a singular aspect of the night. Her mind was caught in a dizzy spiral filled with overlapping snippets of conversation and snapshots of events. Her mind spun and spun as she lost herself to the road noise.

When she finally opened her eyes, she looked at Landry’s face, illuminated by the dash and the headlights of oncoming traffic. He was ruggedly handsome with his scarred cheek and dark features. She let her eyes move across his disheveled hair, past his lowered brows, and along the straight line of his nose, skimming down his profile past his shoulder until finally running across his arm. His hand was tightly clutching the steering wheel.

She always hated Jason’s hands. His fingers tapered past the first knuckle, giving them a strange, small appearance. Having never performed any type of manual labor, they were altogether too soft. When they were dating, it seemed such a trivial observation. Later, after they were married, she found herself staring at his hands with a feeling of disgust at random times. Landry’s hand was thick and callused. She could discern the small wrinkles and scars that accumulated when people used their hands to build and shape things.

What a ridiculous thing to think about after the events of the evening. She glanced at his face and found him looking back at her. A light blush crept across her cheeks, but he was already looking at the road again.

“They told me that between the two of them, they were thousands of years old.” The words escaped her mouth without thought.

Landry sighed and shifted uncomfortably, maintaining his silence.

“That would be completely insane.” He still didn’t speak, and she continued her halting soliloquy. “Those tricks that they showed me could be explained a hundred different ways, but the age? Absolute insanity.”

Kaela fell back into silence, watching the cars on the opposite side of the interstate fly past.

“You know them, both of them. Did you know Todd was following me? Were you part of this twisted little plan of theirs?”

“Mikaela, I— ”

“Nope, I’ve changed my mind.” Kaela held up a hand, cutting off the deep rolling timbre of his voice. “I don’t actually want to know.”

They sat in silence for several miles before Landry grunted in frustration. “You weren’t part of a plan,” he blurted out. “I don’t work with Nisha or Todd. I’ve known them for a very long time. I had no intention of doing anything other than starting a scientific partnership. I didn’t realize I would be attracted to you. It is my own fault for letting myself go down that path when I should have remained professional.”

“How long have you known them?”

He took a deep inhale and let it out slowly through his nose.

“A long time.”

“Not going to cut it.” She turned in her seat to face him. “How long?”

The lights from oncoming traffic washed his face in a temporary, pale light.

“Centuries,” he finally said in a near whisper, as if willing her not to hear the words.

Kaela closed her eyes again, ignoring the pounding surge of blood behind her jaw. She couldn’t do this. She needed to be at home, alone, in her pajamas, pretending this entire evening didn’t happen.

“Shit, Mikaela,” he trailed off. “This isn’t how I was going to talk to you about everything.”

“No, I suppose not,” she managed to reply. “At least I hope kidnapping wasn’t on your agenda for the evening. Just get me home. No more talking.”

Kaela angled her body away from him and pointedly stared out the passenger window at the half-moon gliding above the tree line. This time, the silence remained unbroken for the rest of the car ride. When they pulled up to her house, the cat was sitting on the stoop with no stone monolith in sight. A strange sprinkling of dirt and sand covered the walkway. Landry offered a lame statement about having taken care of the ‘boulder issue.’

Kaela remembered the second, unexplained explosion as she was driven into the night.

"And the cat?" Kaela stood with her arms crossed, an exaggerated distance between them.

"What about the cat?" His confusion seemed genuine.

"Odd coincidence for it to show up tonight of all nights. I can't believe I'm going to ask this, but is there another one of these people that thinks they control animals?"

He blinked at the suggestion, face thoughtful.

"As far as I know, the cat is just a cat."

A tremor started in one of her thighs, and nausea curled inside her abdomen. Todd was flippant about snatching her from her home, as if it was an everyday occurrence to violate someone's sense of safety. There were trees and shrubs near the house, but surely someone should have seen what was happening. Kaela looked around and noticed just how dark and remote her front yard was. She could barely make out the porch of her neighbor's home, and judging by the dark windows, no one was awake. She was rubbing phantom zip ties on her wrists, and Landry noticed the movements with a worried expression.

"No one else will come here for you tonight, but I can stay if it will make you feel safer."

Kaela laughed, angrily. "Having you here would not make me feel safe."

He looked wounded for the briefest moment.

"I realize that you have no trust in me. I lied to you. Never directly, but through omission, which isn't any better. There are many things that I want to tell you, to explain to you. What happened to you tonight may just be the beginning. There are a lot of people like Nisha who are watching you. I won't push you to talk to me if you aren't ready, but I will try to keep tabs on those people while giving you space. When you want to know more, I am an open book."

"It's all just a misunderstanding, right?" Kaela heard the faint desperation threading through her own words. "There is a group of people that think I can do something impossible, and they just need to realize that I am an ordinary person who has nothing to offer. Then they will leave me alone."

"But you aren't ordinary, Mikaela."

She met his eyes. Nothing made sense. Why would Landry want to protect her while the others… She didn't know what the others wanted. What could she possibly do that compared to crushing a stone with nothing but a thought?

Kaela started to walk to the door. When Landry took a single step forward, the cat launched itself off the stairs, a streaking bullet of fur and claws, aiming for his stomach with a gravity-defying leap. Landry back peddled, the cat landing short of its target. He stared at her in surprise when she hissed and growled, her tiny body doubled in size as she pranced sideways, every hair standing on end.

"The cat is just a cat," Kaela said sarcastically, retrieving the deranged feline.

Its little body was stiff but yielding as Kaela scooped her up. Its eyes remain fixed on Landry, dilated pupils overtaking the yellow of the irises.

"Please leave me alone." Kaela looked back at him, her hand on the door handle. "If I decide to talk, I will let you know. Until then, I don't want to see you."

He nodded, but she was already turning away, slipping over the threshold. She stood with her back against the cool, solid surface of the now locked door as the stillness of the house pressed in on her. She took deep, gulping breaths, ignoring the tightening of her throat and burning at the backs of her eyes. She willed herself not to cry.

She would not dissolve into an emotional mess.

A hard vibration against her ribs soothed the panic. She took the cat into the kitchen and retrieved a new can of tuna from the pantry. Kaela looked around, noting the pastry box still sitting on the counter. She took a large knife out of a drawer and carried it with her as she threw away all evidence of the date. She circled the house twice, checking doors and window locks, pulling blinds closed. Finally, she sat on a chair with her back to the wall.

"*There are a lot of people who are watching you.*"

She shuddered and gripped the knife tightly.

England – 1818

Landry held up the glass, and Theodore was instantly captivated by the dancing points of light sparkling in the amber like tiny stars in a honey sky. Landry turned the liquid back and forth in one hand while his other traced lazy paths through the fur of the dog next to him.

"You really do not remember anything that happened earlier today?" Theo resumed his critical appraisal of Landry.

"Tell me again." Landry closed his eyes with a resigned grimace and balanced the glass on one knee.

"When we arrived, there were three men instead of one." The general attendance at the gentlemen's club was low this early in the night, but Theodore kept his words hushed and leaned forward to deliver them. "You were set up. They were armed to the teeth and clearly prepared to kill us. Before either of us could do anything with more finesse, you ripped, something, from the first one, and he collapsed as if dead. The second rushed you, and you did it again. Then the third turned to run, and you made them all explode. I don't know how else to explain it. One second, there were three bodies, and then there was nothing but mist and bone."

A server began to move in their direction, but Theodore waved him away.

"I remember our arrival," Landry began, his eyes shifting behind his lids as he revisited the moments in his mind. "The carriage was parked at the last reasonably safe cross section, and we traveled a dozen blocks on foot. Nothing along the way was particularly concerning other than the whore standing by the dark red door that was entirely too attentive to be what she seemed." If he'd opened his eyes, Landry would have seen Theo nodding in agreement at this part of his narrative. "We slipped around the back of the building, expecting no one to notice. My informant had assured me the man I was seeking took his midday meal alone in the back of the store each day, but when we entered the room, there were three men, and one tried to kill me. Anything beyond that is gone, a hole where a memory should be. Unless you said otherwise, I would think that I lost consciousness in the attack."

"It is obvious they expected us. Who knew you would be there that could have betrayed you?"

"I am not surprised that they were waiting. There are too many crossed threads for this to be a clean extraction of information, and I should have been more careful. The bakery itself is a sham. The bread is stale and terrible, and the real business is the opium they trade for sale in the dens down at the Limehouse slums."

"Cassius sent you, knowing you might be caught," Theodore made the suggestion too casually, as if commenting on the weather.

"He knows I am capable of dealing with those types of situations when they arise, regardless of any prior warnings."

A low growl issued from the dog at Landry's feet, and the sudden appearance of a uniformed man caused Theo to twitch with surprise. The soldier stood near Theodore's elbow but offered a curt bow only to Landry and held out a letter.

"Settle, Jacques." Landry gave a dismissive gesture to the dog and then accepted the envelope from the messenger, scrutinizing the seal before stowing it in a pocket, unopened.

"Is that related to our little adventure today?" Theodore followed the soldier's retreat as he spoke.

"It is not." The glass of amber liquid caught the light again, sending a scattered burst of brilliant sparks along the carpet as Landry took a long swig. "I suspect it is an update on a particular family in whom I maintain an interest. They moved from France to Prussia in the last generation, and after the fall of the empire, I had them tracked down."

"Are these the children of the children, some number of times over, of your former lover?"

Instead of responding to Theodore's question, Landry held up his now-empty glass as a signal to the servers. The two men sat in silence as one of them approached, filled the glass, and left. Only then did Landry choose to answer.

"Marguerite was many things. I made a promise to her."

"She has been gone for three hundred years. Surely you fulfilled your promise by now."

"I will continue to fulfill it for as long as I live." When Theodore started to speak, Landry held up a hand to stop him. "These are matters that do not bear further discussion."

They sat in silence for a long time after this statement. Landry swirled his glass but did not drink, staring out of the closest window, lost in memories older than the building in which they sat. Theodore drank from his own glass and eyed his companion, wondering about the depth of connection that Landry shared with Marguerite and refusing to let himself think about the wife and children he himself lost for fear of where those emotions would lead.

"How did you stop me?" Theo looked up at the question and found both Landry and the hound watching him, the sudden shift in the feeling of the exchange suggesting that the time for reminiscing was at an end. "When I was killing those men, not aware of what I was doing, I didn't kill you. What did you do to keep yourself safe?"

Theodore stared deeply into his glass and then swallowed the last of the liquid within. When he finished, he placed it on the side table and stood, a little unsteady at first but gaining confidence once his feet were settled. He analyzed Landry's face, searching for something even he didn't understand.

"I didn't do anything. You killed those men, and then you fell to the ground. I don't know if you were a danger to me, but I suppose we are both fortunate that I didn't have to find out. We have been through the details enough times now, and there is nothing left to learn. I'll retire for the night. I have a long journey tomorrow."

Landry nodded in acquiescence. Whether or not he suspected that Theodore was hiding something, he was willing to end the conversation where it sat. Theo returned the gesture, wishing Landry a pleasant evening and taking his leave through the main door. As he stepped into the carriage waiting for him, he thought back to the small stone that conceivably saved his life earlier that day.

Cassius gifted the stone to Theodore hundreds of years ago, telling him to keep it secret and to only use it in the direst of circumstances. At the time, Theo hadn't understood the implications of what Cass told him, but after today, there were several very important questions he needed to ask their Chief Commander.

Chapter 6

"...and finally, I would like to thank the organizations listed here, who currently provide the funding for my lab to complete this research. With that, I am happy to answer any questions."

The room filled with the sounds of clapping hands and rustling bodies as Kaela closed out her presentation. She set the pointer down on the podium and focused on carefully taking a sip of water, her movements awkward under the knowledge that she was being watched by the crowd below.

Having just provided a twenty-minute session detailing the latest data from her laboratory, Kaela would now be subjected to the equivalent of an open mic night in the scientific world. For five minutes, any of the hundreds of people in the audience could use the microphones standing at the midpoint of each aisle and ask whatever question came to mind about the research presented. On rare occasions, these types of questions provoked some bit of reflection and could help in future experimental design, but most were just rubbish statements from researchers who wanted to feel important by simply having their voice heard. Occasionally, Kaela even attracted a Class A mansplainer who was compelled to begin with detailing the importance of his own research in the field, skip the actual question entirely, and conclude by pointing out some flaw that he perceived in the core logic of her life's work.

This time, there were three questions without anything of substance, and Kaela finally finished answering a fourth when a familiar, heady feeling swept through her.

"Dr. Griffiths, Professor of Quantum Physics. Thank you for the presentation, Dr. Brookes. It was quite exceptional, and you've made it clear that your lab is lightyears ahead of others in the field."

The room seemed to shift ten degrees, and Kaela skin warmed as Landry's silky baritone came through the speaker system. She held back a smile at the thinly veiled snub he included for the group of men sitting near the podium who continually grumbled throughout the Q&A. They were from other academic institutions, and their postdoctoral students were presenting data in the same session. They were the 'Boys Club' of aging-related research and historically capitalized on any opportunity to discredit Kaela's contributions to the field.

"I think the preliminary data that you show with these signaling pathways and cellular degradation products are quite promising, but I wondered if you could speak to your next steps. You haven't shown data where you applied the proposed atomic bioreactor, and that part of your work remains theoretical at this time. Is that correct, and do you have plans to move in this direction?"

"Thank you, Dr. Griffiths. You are correct that nothing shown today incorporates the bioreactor. However, that is certainly the logical next step. We were awarded a grant specifically to build this device and repeat some of these basic experiments. If everything goes to plan, I hope to present a more comprehensive overview at the AAB meeting this spring. But as we know, science never goes according to plan, so perhaps you should expect to see it at the annual meeting later next year instead."

The expected wave of chuckles drifted through the room, and the session chair stepped forward to announce that although they were out of time, all speakers would be available in the panel discussion at the end of the track.

Kaela returned to her chair at the long table of speakers on stage, her eyes following Landry's retreat from the microphone. He sat and placed his arms on the backs of the empty seats to either side, his suit jacket falling open and the polo underneath pulling tightly across his torso. He tipped his head to listen to a comment spoken into his ear by someone sitting in the seats behind him. He nodded and turned back up to the stage, where he caught Kaela's gaze before she could look away. He gave her a secretive wink.

The slow burn sliding up Kaela's neck threatened to become an incriminating blush, and although she shifted her attention to the current presentation, she couldn't help the answering quirk that played at the corners of her mouth.

It had been weeks since the incident. She didn't sleep well that first night. As she sat in the living room, listening to each creak of the house and clutching her kitchen cutlery, she considered her options. She started to call the police, but she managed to type a '9' and then a hesitant '1' before changing her mind. What would she say?

“A man named Todd kidnapped me, and then someone else brought me back to my house. The first guy used some kind of magic to keep this second guy from helping me. No, they didn’t hurt me. No, there isn’t any evidence of foul play other than a big hole in my side yard. No, I didn’t call right away because I was contemplating the existence of magic.”

She eventually texted Hailey that the date was over, and she was safe at home. The dishonesty of the message made her tongue stick in the back of her mouth, but ‘survived a kidnapping, all good now’ would have required a great deal of explanation and she didn’t have the emotional capacity for that.

Three in the morning came around, and Kaela was searching the annals of the internet in the hope of finding some small piece of information that would let her process the evening events. Page after page of superstitious trash dedicated to telekinetics, unexplained psychic connections, and witchcraft left her exhausted and angry, but no closer to sleep than before.

The geode and the orchid were sitting on her stoop the next morning when she let the cat out. She stared at them, bleary-eyed from lack of sleep and wavering between throwing the items directly into the trash can or keeping them as proof that the entire experience wasn’t a delusion. Movement at the top of her yard caused her to look up as one of her neighbors approached from the street.

“Katherine!”

She waved in greeting, watching the man navigate her lumpy, half-dead lawn with a spryness that still surprised her. He was a kind soul who lived by himself a few houses away. The day she moved in, she dropped a large, framed picture on the sidewalk, the glass shattering across the cement. She remembered standing there in shock, paralyzed by the addition of that one small mishap to the towering stack of awful things that were happening in her life. Before the frustrated blurring of tears in her vision could morph into a full emotional disintegration, George had appeared.

He marched down the sidewalk, dragging a shop vac and an extension cord behind him, his thick chest puffed out and his gray eyes flashing with purpose like a firefighter on his way to rescue a cat from a tree. After he found the nearest outlet and cleaned up the mess, he helped her move the remaining items from her car. As they talked, she discovered he had a quick wit and a deep love for philosophy. If her father were alive, they would have been the same age, but George prided himself on maintaining his physical strength and was a rather imposing figure despite his advanced years.

Unfortunately, his hearing wasn't very sharp, or perhaps the differences between her American pronunciations and his British ones caused some confusion. Either way, when she introduced herself, he mistakenly thought her name was Katherine. After letting several uses of the appellation slip past without correction, Kaela realized it was too late to redress, and she had continued responding to her new name over the next few years.

"Katherine, I brought you a new book. This one is Hume," George's deep voice rolled through the yard, and he waggled the bound volume in her direction as he neared the porch. "Your statement about the nature of men being neither good nor evil inspired me. I know this one will provide some provocative discourse in our future."

"'Heaven and Hell suppose two distinct types of men, the good and the bad. But the best of us floats between the two'. Or something close to that?"

Kaela laughed when his eyebrows lifted in surprise.

"You already know his work!" George nodded appreciatively as he reached the stairs.

"Only what helped me avoid going to church with my grandmother on Sundays." Kaela shrugged. "I have a really good memory, and some of it still rattles around in there."

"*Ah.*" He tapped the book on his leg and considered the response. "It can be hard for bright, skeptical minds to stay within the bounds their parents and grandparents set. I can appreciate having a difficult family member that doesn't always agree."

"Well, it wasn't really a hardship," she admitted. "As long as I had sound reasoning for not going, she respected my decision. Therefore, the foray into philosophy. She would not accept my wanting to stay home strictly on the basis of it meaning I could sleep in on the weekend. I believe she used the word 'sloth' during that discussion."

"Glad to see she took the deadly sins to heart," he responded jovially. "I admit, I find it difficult to imagine someone with such firm convictions being quick to accept yours if you disagreed about the most basic tenets of her religion."

"She was a unique individual." The memory of a warm hug and the scent of honeysuckle drew a nostalgic smile from Kaela. "She always reminded me that if you waste all of your energy judging people, you have none left to really love them."

George evaluated her with a strangely emotional and considering look on his face.

"She does seem to have been a remarkable woman."

"She certainly was." Kaela's expression turned wistful as she continued. "Before she started to go downhill, she was complex in personality but led a very simple life. Alzheimer's."

The beeping of the monitors and the astringent smell of a hallway filled her ears and nose.

"'In recognizing the humanity in each other, we pay ourselves the highest tribute.'"

Kaela pulled herself from the memories and looked at him quizzically.

"Hume again?"

"No, Marshall, United States Supreme Court." He gave her an easy grin and then gestured down to the items sitting at her feet. "Gifts from a suitor?"

"No." She responded a little too quickly but tried to cover it over with her own disarming smile and reached out for the book. "Thank you for the reading material. Perhaps we can continue our discussion when I've managed to get through some of it."

"I would like that, very much, Katherine."

After she retreated into her house, the orchid, the geode, and the book became a trio of dust collectors on her counter, and she tried to forget everything that happened during her abduction.

But yet, she stared at the orchid in her kitchen until her eyes burned every morning, willing it to *change*.

She stood in her side yard for a few minutes each day when she returned home, inspecting the sinkhole.

Her best solution was to forget the entire thing and do her best to safeguard against any future attacks, but she couldn't overlook the evidence of the event all around her. After the initial shock and confusion wore off, her thoughts turned to Landry. She went back over their interactions before the night of the abduction. He was never insincere. He was always direct in asking about her research and waited for her to initiate at every turn. Kaela didn't have to be angry at him for not immediately disclosing his full story. Would she handle it differently if their situations were reversed?

The big questions remained, of course. Was Landry telling the truth about his age, or was he delusional? Did he accept a job at the University just to pursue her, or was it a coincidence that brought him into her life? What was the bigger picture for this little conspiracy Kaela was glimpsing, and were there more people involved? Nisha called him a Knight in Shining Armor. Did that mean he was protecting Kaela from them all along? And last, but probably least, what was going on with her houseplants?

When she should be grading papers, Kaela found herself looking out of the office window and wondering if Landry was walking around campus just beyond the next building. While preparing her lecture notes, she typed his name into her browser search bar. For all the internet digging, she never found anything unusual about his past. She discovered pictures from his graduate lab at Oxford, a headshot of him on a postdoctoral listing at the University of Glasgow, and an early career photograph of him at MIT. The pictures started with a man that looked to be in his early twenties and aged appropriately through the timeline. They were completely inconsistent with the concept of him being centuries old.

As the weeks passed, Kaela realized she was disappointed. If Landry was intent on being truthful and if he was on her side of whatever situation she now found herself in, how could he just give up? He should at least send an email or a text to explain his actions.

There was no contact with either Todd or Nisha. She considered Todd and Nisha as a unit and compared them with Landry. Why were they the same age? If someone wanted to live for eternity, would they choose to be forty? Kaela spent the better part of a week on the pros and cons of that particular question. Then, one morning, two days before her flight to California for the conference, she received the long-anticipated email.

Dear Dr. Brookes,

I will continue to respect your expressed desire for me to leave you alone. However, I feel I should warn you that I will be attending the annual meeting of the Society for Biomolecular Physics in a few days. If we are to cross paths at the conference, I wouldn't want you to think that I was stalking you. Please reconsider the radio silence. I truly desire to speak with you again and to clarify upon a few questionable interactions. Please say hello to the Hellcat for me.

Sincerely Yours,

Landry

Kaela tried not to respond to his email. She deleted it. She moved it back to her inbox. She started to reply but let the email save to the draft folder without sending it. She deleted that one as well. She stood in front of a mirror and lectured herself on women who had fallen victim to men with nefarious intentions throughout history. In the end, she sent a response.

Dear Dr. Griffiths

Could we please move past the part where we pretend that we don't know each other's first names? I am glad you will be attending the conference. If we do run into one another, I will try not to call the police or lodge an official complaint about you as a stalker. I am open to more discussion over lunch or dinner. The Hellcat is currently undecided.

Yours Truly,

Mikaela

In the days leading up to the conference, there were no further exchanges and Kaela suddenly found herself trying desperately not to meet Landry's stare while the last presentation in the symposium concluded. She wanted to ask him roughly five hundred questions pertaining to the meeting with Nisha but also felt an equivalent urge to pretend they could start over with the cannoli date and omit most of the events that occurred after he arrived that night.

Landry's green eyes slid from the person standing at the microphone, and the scientific discussion faded to white noise. They shared a long, fixed stare. He raised one eyebrow, and she did a poor job of suppressing the responding smirk that threatened to break across her face. The session officially ended, and the moment dissolved as the crowd began to disperse, and people moved between them. By the time Kaela left the room, Landry was nowhere to be found.

The next evening, a confident woman wearing red lipstick and an unapologetically tight black dress gave a self-satisfied look to Kaela in the mirror. When she was younger and new to her career, Kaela dressed down, adopting frumpy, conservative clothing to make her look older. Years spent listening to comments about women's appearances convinced her that to be taken seriously in her career, she needed to be as asexual as possible. Pretty women didn't go into academic careers. Intelligent women couldn't also be attractive. Young women didn't lead.

Embracing the idea that she could command respect regardless of her hairstyle or the location of her hemline was a difficult process which still required constant reinforcement. She now bypassed the thick-heeled, sensible shoes for impractical pumps whenever the mood struck. She applied bold red lipstick and flaunted manicured nails without apology. She was comfortable and happy in her body and would rather own that sexuality than give in to the idea that her very liberation invited denigration from her peers.

Kaela's fingers aimlessly fidgeted with her earrings, and she double-checked her watch. When there was finally a knock at her door, her clutch and shawl were already in her hands.

"Dr. Brookes!" Kaela's postdoc, Caleb, greeted her with a pleasant expression on his face. "Ready?"

Caleb was the quiet, studious leader of her lab. She always took him to conferences, and he was a brilliant contributor to the scientific portions, but he never participated in social events. Before the trip, Kaela gave him explicit instructions to attend the President's Gala. The anxiety that rippled from him in response was palpable, but while she wanted to be sensitive to his excruciating introversion, he needed to make stronger connections at other institutions to advance his career. She insisted, suggesting that he bring his much more sociable partner on the trip as a plus one. When his partner developed a cold the day of the gala, Kaela was determined enough to stand-in as Caleb's personal moral support. The deep-rooted dread with which he approached chit-chat was familiar to her, so she promised to ease him through the initial conversations and only set him free when he was comfortable.

"You look very professional." Caleb managed to appear both modest and pleased with himself at Kaela's praise. "I approve of this entire ensemble."

He had opted for a light blue suit jacket over a classic white button up, which perfectly framed the ebony of his face. A pocket square with precisely folded edges peeked out of the jacket, a genuine Type-A calling card. He was twenty-eight years old, just beginning on his career path and filled with vibrant, youthful energy. Kaela remembered the start of her career. She was too methodical and anxious then about the arbitrary rules of how to present herself to be quite as eager as Caleb. The nerves, though, were the same.

Kaela let her mind wander as they took the elevator to the ballroom. She felt and saw Landry that afternoon around the conference center when they passed near one another in the poster presentation area, spied each other across the vendor booths as they investigated new tech, or locked eyes across the audience while attending the same sessions. They formed their very own two-body problem, tied together in a disruptive orbit but never meeting. Romance at a science conference. Kaela snorted at the dichotomy, drawing a quick glance from her postdoc.

"Any particular projects or programs that seem compelling enough to steal you away from the Brookes Lab?" she asked, prompting him work through a rapid listing of the intriguing science he experienced over the last few days.

His stumbling, excited recitation continued all the way into the gala.

They arrived late enough to miss the commencement speech, sparing them from that boredom. Kaela immediately spotted a contingent of people from other institutions that were a good match for Caleb's interests and set about getting him established in the conversation. As soon as they delved into deeper scientific debates, she offered a silent question to Caleb, and he happily nodded to grant her release from her duties. She slipped away to one of the bars stationed throughout the room, considering whether she wanted to mingle or haunt the edge of the party like a pariah.

A familiar sensation crept up her spine.

Landry was standing near the front entrance to the ballroom. He approached slowly, his eyes trailing over her.

"Landry." Kaela smiled as she stepped in, just a bit closer than a professional acquaintance should, and accepted the customary light kiss across her cheek.

"Mikaela." His lips lingered for a moment, and she could almost feel her name rolling along his tongue. "You look radiant. I hope my text last night didn't wake you."

She reveled in the heady feeling as he spoke the words softly into her ear. Her phone had chimed the night before with a simple message.

Goodnight, I look forward to seeing you at the gala tomorrow.

She was in her bed at the hotel, working on a grant application and feeling hopelessly preoccupied when it popped up. It was masterfully timed, and she hadn't stopped thinking about it since.

"Not at all." Kaela accepted her drink from the bartender and turned to Landry. "I was just stepping into the shower when you sent it."

His eyes sparkled mischievously as he ordered and collected his own refreshment. His hand barely brushed her shoulder when he moved past, the contact a feathery kiss that left a trail of goosebumps along her flesh. There was a measured distance between them as they wandered to a conveniently placed cocktail table. Kaela could feel the pull and circle of their bodies, tugging a little closer now.

"I see you lost your date."

"Caleb. Yes, he is off in search of new opportunities, I'm afraid. He does look quite handsome tonight, though, don't you think? Rather like a young Idris Elba. Now there is a man who can pull off black tie. But you don't seem jealous enough. Should I have arrived with the real Idris instead?"

"I don't get jealous of eager young men." His eyes never strayed, and the room drifted further away as he leaned in to whisper these next words. "I have a great deal more experience than any of them. I'm not concerned with a little competition." Kaela was worried she would never find the words to respond but he broke the moment, leaning back and continuing in a normal voice. "Besides, I doubt you would cross that line with one of your staff."

"Well, I won't tell him you said that," she finally managed to tease back. "I'd hate to make him feel undesirable."

"And how did you enjoy the talks today?" He changed the topic after a long pause during which his eyes drifted across her, a visual caress against her skin.

"I managed to recover from your attempts to distract me, if that's the question. The morning presentation on neural linking by the associate professor from UCLA was very interesting. I have her on my list of people to meet this week."

"I am glad to hear that my presence alone can be distracting to you." He winked.

"And are we going to continue pretending you weren't connected to a recent abduction of mine?" She blurted the words, the importance of the question contradicted by the flirtatious tone with which she delivered it.

"I am following your lead," he replied easily. "I thought you would eventually like to discuss everything that happened, but if you are planning to compartmentalize and have a casual conversation for now, I can do that as well. I just need to know what you want."

In that moment, the overdue discussion felt abstract and unnecessary, as if the passing of time and a change of scenery made it a thing of the distant past, an anomalous blip in the storyline. Kaela tried to summon her list of questions, her concerns, and her demands for explanations.

"I want both." She sighed and closed her eyes in an exaggerated blink.

"Mikaela, you get to decide."

Landry reached over and caught her fingers in his, stilling their fidgeting such that her partially crumpled cocktail napkin fell back to the table. Kaela pulled her hand away quickly, almost thoughtlessly, as if his touch singed her skin. She startled herself with the reaction and looked up at him, taking in his slight frown.

"It's not about you and me." She glanced around the room and then shifted to create a larger space between them as she attempted to explain. "It's about all of the women at this conference and how those old chauvinists treat us. I can't let my guard down and act like a normal person when I'm here."

Landry followed the nod of her head, his eyes scanning across the male-dominated crowd. His face smoothed over in understanding.

"Well, maybe we could have a discussion about partnering together instead." He leaned back, a picture of professional engagement. "I am still convinced that my lab has the exact resources you need for your next steps, and we are very well funded. You wouldn't have to shoulder the financial burden yourself. What do you think?"

Kaela scrutinized his posture and unreadable expression. She considered what he was proposing as she let her eyes drift back across the room.

"Is this about everything that happened with Nisha, or is this about scientific research? I'm having a difficult time separating these things."

"It's about both. I don't think you can separate them. If there was no Nisha, I would still be attempting to form a working relationship because you are the key to creating a scientific solution the likes of which haven't been seen before," he replied earnestly.

A silver-headed man across the room caught Kaela's eye. Her face instantly changed beneath a wave of frustration and anger, echoes of a past conflict she couldn't quite forget about every time she saw him at this meeting.

"Time after time, when I have accomplished something, there is always a man to take credit for it." Her voice was even, but her temper bubbled higher with each word given air. "I spent the majority of my career being just another feather in some man's career achievement cap. It's exhausting to work two or three times harder than my male colleagues to achieve the same recognition. It's even more exhausting to explain that this is happening and to be asked to provide evidence that men are considered more promotable because everyone is in denial. I'm a fighter. I go after the things that I want, and I don't back down easily, but at a certain point, I don't want to spend every moment of my life clawing and scratching to get what I already deserve."

If Landry was surprised by this rant, he certainly didn't show it. He watched without expression as she drew slightly closer to him. The sense of indignance was a raging beast, rattling inside her, and she fought to push it down, to remember the original purpose of their discussion. He remained silent, waiting for her to continue.

"As a graduate student, I was asked if I was an undergrad. As an early-stage professor, I was asked about my PI, as if I were still a grad student. It was not because I looked young. It was because I am a woman in a male-dominated line of work, which makes me an easy target for marginalization. I have had my own thesis explained to me by somebody who wasn't even in my field. I have been told that I will never make it in an academic career, and have I considered going into the industry where a good manager could give me direction? All of these things have been said to me by older men. Yet despite this experience, which is fairly common for females in this profession, I am told that I should be more assertive and confident in order to advance my career."

Kaela paused, her eyes sharp and focused as she searched his face for a hint of emotion, gauging his reaction to her rant. Landry returned the look, his eyes drifting to the delicate flare of her nostrils and the visible beating of her pulse in the skin along her neck. He gave a single curt nod, his sincerity clear when he finally spoke.

"You don't need my validation, but for what it's worth, I agree. It is beyond absurd for a brilliant, motivated, and accomplished person such as yourself to be forced to prove something that doesn't need proof. If I gave you the impression that I intend to contribute to that, I am deeply sorry."

The animal in her chest stopped screaming and coiled, wary.

"Do you understand why I can't partner with you?" Kaela looked down at his hand, resting a foot from hers on the table. "I never wanted to partner with you. If we are being completely honest, I was hoping we would never have this conversation, and we could just go on a few dates while you tried to get in my pants. I plan to find a female-run physics lab."

"My motivations for partnering with you are largely selfish, but I don't want to work with you to steal your scientific merit. I don't want to take your grant money. I don't want credit for your research. What I want is for you to be successful at finding a cure for aging."

She offered an apologetic shrug.

"Even if you aren't going to claim my work, someone else will do it for you. They will list you first, send questions and applause your way, then eventually leave me off the credits entirely. Ask Rosalind Franklin or Esther Lederberg how that goes."

Another quiet moment passed before Landry replied.

"I want to support you and walk away from my request, but I don't think you really understood what you were shown a few weeks ago. This isn't about awards and careers. It's about something bigger, and I think you don't want to accept that shift in your life. Don't let what has happened to you in the past blind you to an opportunity now. Small changes over time, Mikaela."

"I can't make you immortal." She hissed the statement, afraid someone might overhear what they were now discussing. "The very concept of immortality is absurd."

"You can stop me from aging." He returned, just as quietly. "And you won't be the first person to do it."

Nisha's forgotten words ran through Kaela's head, *someone very much like you.* She was distracted and overwhelmed at the time and didn't register the meaning.

"If there is someone who can already do this for you, why chase me around?"

"He is dead. At least we all think so. No one has seen him in almost twenty years."

The pattern finally emerged in the puzzle. Immortality was something Kaela could only justify in the furthest, most obscure applications of science. If someone did discover an effective way to manipulate aging at a cellular level, her brain could then accept the idea of a two-thousand-year-old woman. What she couldn't grasp was the concept of someone doing this without modern technology.

"Let's pretend for a moment that I believe everything I have been told thus far. I saw pictures of you online from the last twenty years, and you've aged. All your education matches up. It didn't make sense. But from what you just said, twenty years ago you started to age again, which means the pictures I saw are real and don't discredit your immortality theory."

Landry continued to watch her with a calm assessment that was practically habitual for him. Kaela gave a surreptitious glance around the room, checking for any unwanted interest, but no one was close enough to hear their hushed conversation over the noise of the party.

"Yes. Twenty years ago, I got to remember what a 'normal' life is like."

"If Nisha was given longevity by the same person, that means he understood how to do this when Roman aqueducts were the height of technology. Did he publish his work anywhere? Can I see anything that will tell me how he did it?"

"No. He wasn't exactly doing science in the way that you think about it. You're an oddity. Most of us have a specific connection or intellectual proclivity toward our—abilities, but we don't understand it in intimate detail. It's more about being governed by feelings and impulses."

"Like Todd, I mean Theo, being a mason?" She tried to remember everything that was said at Nisha's house. "He really does 'like rocks'. He wasn't being a condescending jerk when he said that?"

"He is always a condescending jerk," Landry responded with annoyance, and a spark of something that could have been jealousy crossed his face. "I'm sorry you were conned by him. You and I are similar. The scientific details don't give us our ability, but the understanding of it lets us focus and control the use to prevent chaotic ripples."

"How can you know that when I have never used this 'ability' as you call it?"

Landry hesitated, crafting his next statement carefully. "You do use your ability. Frequently, if I were to guess. The experiments in your laboratory are just the beginning. That puppy you rescued behind the restaurant wasn't a series of accidental events. I haven't quite figured out how, but you were using your ability to fix whatever was wrong with it, and you pulled some of that energy from your own body."

"That's ridiculous." Kaela's voice held a certain weakness, and the denial fell flat, dead before it even gained a spark of life.

"There must be dozens of times when similar, unexplainable events took place. They aren't flukes that you happened to witness, Mikaela. They were supernatural events driven into existence by you."

A large moth with tattered wings flopped along the edge of a wooden deck outside Kaela's home. She was a child, perhaps ten years old. She scooped the dying creature into her palms and looked up to the black, wire-enshrouded bug zapper hanging from the post with disgust. The anger rumbled through her, traveling down her arms and into her hands, a tingling wave of electricity. When she looked back down, her hands cupped only air, and a single red drop of blood fell from her nose onto an outstretched palm. The unblemished, luminescent wings of the moth fluttered past her face as the insect rose into the night sky.

One memory in a bank of an unknown number.

As a child and even as an adult, Kaela dismissed those incidents as the product of an overactive imagination. Surely, ten-year-old Kaela invented the damage to the moth's wings in a fanciful remembrance of the occasion, which then became an integral part of the memory, an overlay of fiction across the foundation of reality.

But what if Landry was telling the truth? What if, after all this time, Kaela could finally accept all those memories that were carefully sorted out and set aside in her mind?

"And what is your superpower?" Kaela decided at that exact moment to take the plunge and suspend her skeptical disbelief, or at least to try.

"Are you willing to accept that I have one?" Landry's excitement at this turn in the conversation was clear.

"I mean, I'm familiar with the X-Men. I can follow along."

"It isn't like that," he grimaced. "There is no mutation that anyone can identify. I think most people never manifest, even if they have an ability, because it is difficult to master something this abstract. Mine can be subtle or explosive, and there are always repercussions. Take a drive with me to the desert after the conference ends on Friday. If you're ready, I will provide a full disclosure and demonstration."

"Why the desert?" she prodded.

"A long time ago, we would find places that were isolated where we could safely practice our abilities. It was particularly important when training those with recently discovered skills. That is the nearest location where I know that I can show you what I do and not risk exposure. Then you'll see with your own eyes and be able to pass your own judgment."

"And between now and then?"

A woman passing by accidentally clipped Kaela's elbow just as she brought her drink off the table. A small splash of wine escaped the glass and beaded on the glass tabletop. Kaela reassured the apologetic woman and when she turned back, searched for a napkin.

"Here, let me." A mischievous expression split Landry's face, and he moved his hand forward, several inches above the table. Beneath it, the napkin slid across the surface, gliding as if on a breeze and stopping when it reached the spill. "A little preview. Until then, you can let me try to get into your pants. Your phrasing. And there is also a conference we are supposed to be attending in a professional capacity, so…"

"Right, our day jobs." Heat bloomed in her cheeks, but she focused on the way Landry flexed and then relaxed his hand. "Did it hurt you to do that?"

"No, but the energy has to originate somewhere."

Kaela considered this response, watching the way he shook out his hand like someone who opened too many pickle jars for their grandmother.

"That's why I feel weak and sometimes have nosebleeds."

Though she said this as a statement more than a question, Landry bobbed his head in affirmation.

"I can show you how to channel it differently, so you don't pull from within but rather channel it from around you or from a stored source."

"After we finish our current occupational commitments, of course. We wouldn't want to lose our jobs for the sake of magic. Unless being a professor at a school for gifted youngsters is your full-time occupation and the university is just a front?"

"Do I now have to tolerate superhero references?" Landry lifted his eyebrows in mock surprise.

"I have a derisive sense of humor. It's important we establish that expectation now." Kaela's laughter bubbled up easily and she cocked her head to the side as she searched his face. "Why do I still feel comfortable around you? I still shouldn't trust a word you say, but here we are."

A man was waving to them from near the entrance and Kaela turned away as he approached the table. Landry managed to hold in whatever response was about to leave his mouth, and his pained expression smoothed over.

The next two hours were filled with Kaela and Landry moving between conversations. Sometimes they were together, talking to the same people. Other times, they drifted into parallel discussions. It was the organic flow of a social event, but always there was the undertone of their unfinished words, pulling Kaela's eyes back over to Landry when he glanced her way.

"Is that the new physics professor?"

Kaela was standing with Anjana, who also attended the conference as a representative from their university. They were discussing a presentation by one of Anjana's graduate students when the other professor noticed Kaela's preoccupation.

"Wow. Please tell me that the two of you are seeing each other."

"What?" Kaela looked back at her with a carefully controlled expression of innocence.

"Please, Kaela." She paused and took another slug of her wine. "I may be married with three kids, but I remember those little coy glances. He has been eying you up half the night, and you don't seem to mind."

"We work at the same university," Kaela offered as an excuse.

"Sometimes I really do think you live under a rock, my friend. Half the college has slept together at one time or another. Daniel Fredrick, in micro, is sleeping with someone in the statistics department, and he's married. No one actually cares about these things. Stop acting like you'd be doing something improper. Worst case scenario, someone gossips about it in the staff lounge, but they'd only be doing it because they're jealous. My god, that man is good-looking."

"Anjana!" Kaela scolded her friend. "You are embarrassing."

Anjana abruptly changed the subject.

"How about that presentation of the link between polymerase functionality and lifespan? That was a new one. I think the evidence was compelling but certainly incomplete."

"I did find it interesting, but the connection was a little stretched for me as well," Kaela replied, wondering about the sudden turn back to science. "I would like to see more direct linkage. It was heavy on supposition."

"I constantly wonder how much conjecture is just for funding and how much people really believe about their own work." Landry's bass rumbled into the conversation as he stepped close to Kaela's side, extending his hand. "Hello, Landry Griffiths."

“Anjana Mathison.” The other professor returned the greeting and offered Kaela a suspiciously broad smile to the side. “I work with Kaela. How are you enjoying your time in the physics department so far? I hope Kaela has been able to show you around the university and make you feel welcome.”

Kaela tried not to widen her eyes at the shameless wink her friend delivered along with this last sentence. Landry reported that he felt quite welcome and enjoyed his time both at the university and with Dr. Brookes. Kaela focused on her determination not to fidget as Anjana made a show of checking her watch.

“Well, it was very nice to meet you. It looks like the scientists have had enough drinks to start dancing, and that is my cue to go back to my room to FaceTime my husband. Some of these idiots act like this is their niece’s wedding instead of a professional conference. I hope he survived getting the kids to bed without me tonight!” She placed her empty glass on a nearby table and called back over her departing shoulder. “Kaela, really, no one cares.”

Landry lifted a quizzical eyebrow, but Kaela faked nonchalance and waved away Anjana’s comment.

“So, Dr. Brookes, would you like to dance?”

“I will not be joining those drunken fools in the Cha-Cha Slide.” She surveyed the group that had kicked off their shoes and taken over the parquet square at the front of the ballroom. “If you would be so kind as to accompany me, I believe I am ready for a change of scenery.”

Landry didn’t blink as he offered his elbow. Kaela took it just as smoothly, emboldened by Anjana’s statements. If anyone cared enough to notice them leaving together, let them see.

Greece – 1827

"My team has done its part. When Charles died, I told you that this blind offensive of hers was misplaced grief, and she should not be allowed to take on a mission with such a low probability of success. Did I not tell you that this would end poorly? Do you see her, Cassius? Do you truly see what she endured as their captive?"

"You knew there would be a cost, as there always is during war. I gave her autonomy, and she chose this task. That is the part of being a leader you have never been able to stomach. You cannot control every decision or keep everyone safe. She did her job, now do yours. Lead your team until we complete our mission here."

Anne heard the overlap of the angry voices, the words sinking into her brain even before she was aware of her surroundings. The mental fog gradually lessened, and the memories of her captivity clawed to the forefront of her brain, one painful gouge at a time.

After Charles' death, she charged into the fight and took the first, most reckless assignment available. She was a mole, embedded within the enemy ranks until someone sold her out. She was thrown into a cell, and she thought she would die there, but Landry stormed the jail to retrieve her. It was only a few weeks, but she suffered many things at the hands of her captors during that time.

Cassius and Landry were still arguing, but there was another, heavier blanket of sound that filled her ears, smothering everything else with its constant droning. She opened her eyes enough to peer into the brightness, placing the noise and the feeling of dampness that permeated the air around her. The high walls of a tight, tree-covered ravine rose before her. Halfway up the embankment, a thin sheet of water broke free of the rocks and shrubs, tumbling down into a deep, cloudy pool of amber and green below. She followed the frenetic sparks of light across the top of the waterfall and the rippling dance of the ferns below as the mist sprayed across the foliage.

Charles was gone.

That one, clear fact surface, displacing any other thought. Her entire reason for taking on the Ottomans head-first and the source of her deep, unshakable sadness, remained unchanged.

She flexed her fingers first to check for injury but found one hand trapped. Not trapped, though, held. Her eyes fluttered over and met Cleda's. Anne's breath constricted, an unreleased sob aching within her lungs at the emotion in those eyes of endless ebony swirling within a warm pool of caramel. Never once in all her captivity had she let herself despair. She stayed focused on getting through her task, not letting herself consider what she might lose in the end. Now, as Cleda ran a hand over her cheek, leaving a blazing trail of warmth behind, she felt every ounce of terror and regret surface from under that stone barrier she erected within herself to survive.

"Anne!" Cleda breathed, her words full of joy, anger, and worry, all woven together as she leaned down to touch their foreheads in a gentle embrace. "I have healed what I can. You should be able to sit up and move without any pain."

"Thank you." Anne knew the words were woefully inadequate, but all other statements of longing or love were tied up inside of her.

"Anne." Landry stepped to her side, the outrage and violence gone from him as he gave her a careful inspection.

"My savior." Her words were sarcastic, but they held no bite as she nodded to him. "I am sure I would have found a way out of there eventually, but your early intervention was welcome as always."

Landry smiled, happy to see that she was capable of joking. She stood, slowly moving each part of her body and pressing against her muscles in various places to assess her overall condition. Cassius waited several feet away, silently observing the exchange.

"Commander." Anne nodded and executed a slow bow when she made eye contact with him.

"Anne," Cassius returned with a nod. "Glad to have you back."

"Thank you, milord," she replied, accepting Cleda's support under her arm, if only to enjoy the nearness of her body. "I have gained additional insight into the enemy's plans and tactics in the last few weeks. Men have loose lips when they assume you will never leave their company."

"Then I expect a full debrief once you are reasonably recovered. I am to rendezvous with the head of our combined fleets at sea tomorrow before the final attack. I expect you to join me."

"She can provide you with the information now." Landry interjected.

Anne gave Landry a warning glance. "I will join you as ordered, Commander."

"Then I will accompany her to the launching point and travel with you to the fleet," Landry stated. "The rest of the team will join the ranks on foot near the lower end of the bay."

"I expect you at dawn, Lieutenant Commander." Cassius' eyes were filled with an icy reprimand as he looked at Landry. "You are to be focused and ready to fulfill your duties without question. Am I understood?"

"Yes, milord." Landry's jaw clenched.

"Good."

Cassius shifted his focus and waved his hand at the trees behind Anne. A half dozen men appeared, a private retinue. The men waited for him to stride past, nodded respectfully to Landry, and then closed ranks, silently marching back into the woods. Landry faced Anne, his mouth opening to issue some angry sentiment.

"Don't," Anne cut him off before the air even left his lungs. "You are my commander, and I respect your decisions, but do not make me play the part of a victim. I am a soldier. I have survived my captivity, and now I must see this through to the end. Would you feel the same if it had been Bron held in that cell?"

"That is not a fair question," Landry stated gently. "You know, as well as I, that men are more creative in the ways they torment female prisoners."

"No, they aren't. It is the same story every time. I can handle it."

Landry peered into her face as if a deeper story would be written there.

"I thought I would lose you." The sadness in Cleda's soft voice made Anne wince with regret. "I do not want to feel that way again. If you must go on that ship, then go. But don't you dare stay for longer than you need to. Do not make me search the depths of the ocean for you when the fight is over."

"I will come back to you in a few days." Anne clutched Cleda's hand but could not bring herself to make eye contact. "When this has ended, we can go away for a while. Perhaps back to England to enjoy the spring in the countryside."

Landry gave a resigned shake of his head, and Anne drew up her chin.

"Let me finish this. For him. For Charles."

"It was always your choice, Anne," he said sadly. "Winning this fight will not bring him back, but I do hope it will bring you some peace."

Death of a loved one floods the veins and takes up residence in some deep part of you like cancer. It inhabits you. The feeling never really goes away, but eventually you begin to function around it, incorporating it as just another part of the weave that forms your heart and your actions.

Landry had experienced it all before and knew that the shift from a new pain to an old pain was coming for Hailey. She was still desperate to understand the additional weight on her soul, too busy finding a crutch to support it that she didn't realize she was slowly growing accustomed to the burden. Soon enough, she would carry it without even knowing the effort.

Chapter 7

Kaela pulled the oversized sweatshirt to her nose and took a slow inhale, letting the smell of woody citrus settle through her as the floors ticked by on the digital counter and the elevator slowly made its way down from the highest level of the building.

Here, it's for my own protection. I can't have you wearing nothing but that dress much longer, or I'll lose my self-control. Also, it's cold.

She shivered despite being perfectly warm under the bulky, thick material.

When she left the gala with Landry, Kaela had every intention of going to the hotel bar, but the lobby was packed with other conference attendees, and she found a very different plan tumbling out of her mouth.

"Are you staying in this hotel, too?" she asked, coming to a halt at the edge of a very loud, and very drunk, crowd of scientists.

"I am."

"Should we go to your room for a drink then? The bar is probably filled with people we both know, and I think we should have a longer conversation without worrying about being overheard."

"It would be my pleasure." Landry led her into an open elevator and pressed the button for the topmost floor, a sly expression tightening the corners of his mouth. "Yours too, if you would like."

"Will I ever live down the comment about getting in my pants?" She laughed, hoping it sounded relaxed despite the rapid fluttering of her stomach. She pulled a strand of hair off her suddenly sweaty neck.

Once the elevator doors closed behind them, Kaela leaned against the handrail, her arms out to either side as she looked at her companion. He returned the stare, his green eyes traveling over the excited pink of her skin. Her breath snagged in her throat. Being alone in the small space was suffocating, the air thick with anticipation. Landry quietly stepped closer, his proximity pushing against her with an invisible pressure. In a fit of boldness, she reached out and grabbed his shirt with one hand to tug him forward.

His kiss was soft and unhurried. She remembered the feeling of him against her, but this time it was different, less frantic but somehow more intense. Her hands drifted, fingers beginning to trace the planes of his stomach underneath his jacket, but he pulled away. He took her hand and turned to the door. Kaela smoothed the front of her dress in a quick, slightly shaky gesture before letting her shoulder rest next to his. The elevator continued to the top of the building.

"I wanted to do that all day." His voice was full of gravel and restraint as he led her through the doors.

Kaela noticed the wide spacing of the hotel rooms on this floor and wondered if she should have requested an upgrade at check-in. Landry stopped to open one, and they stepped into a small entryway filled with soft light. At Landry's gesture, Kaela moved deeper into the suite, shamelessly nosey as she let her eyes rove the contents. The entry opened onto a large living room hosting a pair of bright blue couches. Beyond the furniture were two walls on the corner of the hotel building, both filled with floor-length windows overlooking the bay. Lights from the city skyline trailed off into a twinkling sea of black. To the right was an eat-in dining area, also containing a window-filled wall, and a large kitchen.

Kaela's heels echoed across the hardwood flooring. She set her clutch on the table near a single-stemmed orchid in partial bloom. She glanced at the dancing spots of light in the water far below before giving Landry a weighted look.

"I'm glad I didn't suggest my room. Physics must treat you well because this is definitely not within my departmental budget."

"I don't always stick with the university resources." He chuckled, moving to stand near her in the dim light. "Call it a perk of being financially tied to this hotel. Do you still want a drink? There is a fully stocked bar in the kitchen."

Kaela found herself staring at the orchid, her mind drawn to the events with Nisha.

"Show me again." She gestured to the pot. "Make it slide over to me."

Landry flicked his eyes to the flowers.

"I don't typically provide frivolous displays of my powers. There are too many repercussions and potential side effects from indiscriminate manipulation. Not to mention that the energy to move that object would make me feel a bit taxed if I drew it from myself."

“So, you can’t move it then?” Kaela managed to deliver the question as both goading and disbelieving.

Landry drummed his fingers in a quick, agitated movement, then shook his head at her, a slight sideways motion, before heaving a sigh. Dry scraping drew Kaela’s eyes back to the table as the orchid came to rest against her outstretched hand.

“I thought it was a trick earlier, with the napkin.” Kaela swallowed; tongue thick as it pressed into the dry roof of her mouth. “This is magic.”

The sentence tumbled out, something halfway between a statement and a question. The fact that she was witness to an extraordinary phenomenon which was too spontaneous to be explained away as a trick or manipulation should be a shock to her system, a paradigm-shifting revelation. Instead, she felt distant, an actor in a play, feigning surprise during a rehearsed scene. This was the part where she should gasp and let her eyes fill with wonder and excitement.

“Where did the energy come from this time?” Her brain clung to the calming familiarity of theoretical calculation, seeking the solace of something easy to process.

Landry vaguely waved his hand in the air. “I tried to spread out the pull of it. I think the plant in the kitchen may now be dead, but that’s the nature of things when I don’t have time to plan more precisely.”

She blinked away the words, too focused on the implications of this newly formed understanding to hold onto the significance. Magic was real. Which meant that everything she was told about herself might also be real. A gurgling sort of nausea formed in her stomach at the thought. She slid the pot back a few inches and then held her hands out, willing her body to release whatever strange powers it was keeping locked up inside.

“Teach me what to do.”

“My first suggestion would be to relax.” His breath was hot against her cheek as he moved behind her, sliding his hands lightly down her arms and adding a gentle pressure until her palms settled onto the surface of the table. “You aren’t conducting an invisible orchestra, you are rearranging a few very complex temporal conditions, changing an invisible dimension for just one object. You are feeling the natural order of forces and plucking a single string to shift the balance in the direction of what you desire.”

“Oh, is that all? That sounds exactly like some biblical description of a deity conducting a great cosmic orchestra. Or maybe just a mouse pretending to be a sorcerer.”

"*Touché.*" The rumble of his laugh against her back was distracting, and his nose trailed against the exposed skin of her neck. He drew a slow inhalation. "Try to connect to everything around you. Feel the movements of life, the flow of energy. You want to steal just a tiny bit from each living thing. It shouldn't be enough to notice. Or you can pull from yourself. If you pull too much, well, you've felt some of that before. Haven't you?"

Her thoughts were erratic, and a deep throbbing started to spread through her core. She tried to think about his words despite the distracting effect of his touch.

"The fainting and the nosebleeds. I had them sometimes as a child, too, but those memories are out of focus, like something I dreamed and then remembered later. I thought they weren't real." Thinking about anything beyond the feeling of him against her was impossible, so she turned, her hands slipping under his jacket again. This time, she slid her fingers into the top of his belt and pulled his waist gently but firmly against the front of her body. "I hope this isn't your usual method of teaching, or I'll need to be concerned that you seduce every new student of yours."

"Was that a seduction?" He grinned wickedly and ran his fingers up the small of her back. "I didn't realize."

She gave up on a witty retort or a response at all as his fingers found the top of her dress zipper, slowly pulling it until it stopped at her waist. His hands were warm and rough as they moved across her skin. She needed this physical sensation, the normalcy of it driving away the lingering traces of panic that formed when the ordered physical foundations of her world were thrown into chaos with a simple conjuring.

Landry caught her mouth with his, and she pushed his suit jacket off his shoulders, letting it fall to the floor even as her fingers moved deftly through the barrier of bowtie and buttons left behind. The hands at her hips lifted and pushed until she was perched on the edge of the table with him standing between her knees. His hands slid along her thighs, revealing more of her skin beneath the thin material of her dress. Then he pulled back his head, breathing thick but controlled, like he was pacing himself mid-marathon.

"Why did you stop?" Kaela ran her nails down the exposed skin of his stomach, satisfied by the tiny shudder this elicited.

"I'm giving you a chance to change your mind."

She listened to the underlying desperation in the careful metering of his words. His obvious desire spawned in her a deep-rooted satisfaction, and some feral thing in her body purred. Landry's eyes sparked when she released a breathless laugh and pushed the dress off her shoulders, letting it pool around her waist.

"I think we're beyond that, don't you?" The calm, sultry quality of her voice surprised and pleased her. "I believe I invited myself to your room, after all. Were you wanting to settle on safe words before we continue, or?"

He followed her index fingers as she traced the exposed skin from the top of his hips, down the sloped lines until they disappeared under his waistband. Then he gently redirected her from his zipper and lowered himself to his knees instead. Her hands fisted in his hair and she gasped. She leaned back, lost in the sensation.

She felt immense, spread out across an entire plane of existence, her corporeal body forgotten. The waves of pleasure became everything, her body arching off the table as he worked her higher in slow but sure spirals, first with his mouth and then with the added fullness of his fingers.

In that instant, she wasn't Dr. Brookes, the career-driven professional. Her reservations and logical decisions fell away, leaving an entity of feeling and desire. Cries issued from her mouth with no regard to who heard them. Her body writhed against him, needing and taking. When she finally screamed out her release, he gave a low, satisfied sound in response.

Kaela slowly pushed up from her elbows, looking down at him with an indolent, satisfied expression. She drew his lips to her when he stood, marveling at the taste of herself.

"Your turn."

"I can wait." He carefully pulled up the dress, wrapping his arms behind her to zip it in place while scraping his teeth along the edge of her ear, inciting a full body shudder from her.

"What?" She leaned back and stared at him in disbelief. "What man has ever said 'I can wait' to a mostly naked woman?"

"Kaela," he lectured in mock seriousness. "You will learn that I am a very patient man who plays the long game with things that he cares about. Wait until after the trip to the desert tomorrow. Then you can decide what you do or do not want from this relationship."

She continued to stare at him dumbly, and he slid her off the table, helping her straighten the dress back over her thighs. She let her eyes sink to the bulge in his pants, stepping close and lifting a hand to firmly cup that generously portioned part of him. His breath hitched and then hissed back out into her ear.

"I'm going to need that drink now or else I might put you back up on the table." Her body tightened and liquefied at the same moment as he turned and walked away, her playful laughter escorting him from the room.

Now that Kaela was alone, a wave of exhaustion hit her, dragging her arm as she wiped imagined smudges of mascara from under each eye. She tried to shake the feeling as she waited, and the orchid drew her back to the table. It was doubled in height with a veritable bush of leaves spilling over the edge of the pot. There were two new stems, both completely covered in vivid purple blooms.

"What the hell?" she muttered to herself.

Landry returned, holding a sweatshirt. "Here, it's for my own protection. I can't have you wearing nothing but that dress much longer, or I'll lose my self-control. Also, it's cold and... What is it?" He registered her expression and then followed her gesture to the plant. "*Ah,* it looks like you're starting to get more in touch with your abilities. That's quite impressive."

He inspected the plant like he was being shown a new experiment in a greenhouse, no sign of surprise on his face, only curiosity. Kaela looked at her hands in disbelief. They appeared as they always had. She looked at the plant again. Landry glanced up, delight playing across his face along with something like pride. He read the shock in hers. Her hands were still held gracelessly in front of her, but he folded them into his own, pressing them against him.

"I remember how dumbfounded I was the first time I realized I had done something that couldn't be explained away with common reasoning." His voice was gentle, and he placed a finger at her chin, slowly turning her face until she was staring up into his eyes. "What you can do is special and beautiful. Let that be the first thing in your mind right now. Put that screaming, logical part of your brain on pause for a moment and let yourself feel the wonder of what you created over there."

"That shouldn't be possible." Kaela stumbled over the words.

"And yet it is." He released her and stepped back.

"I didn't even touch it or look at it." She moved slowly, wanting to feel the new blooms but somehow afraid to do so, as if by confirming they were real she would be stepping through the looking glass. "Where did the energy come from? Me? How could the cells have replicated that quickly? In a handful of minutes, an entire month of growth took place."

"I think you already invented a dozen different hypotheses on how that could be possible." Landry set the sweatshirt on the table. "Here, put this on and let's start the discussion we keep putting off."

"I think I need that drink after all."

"And maybe a snack?" he suggested.

Kaela considered this suggestion, realizing that in addition to being tired, she was ravenously hungry. "Yes. I could use something to eat. How did you know?"

"Energy transfers. You're running at a deficit now."

"My nose isn't bleeding." She checked her nostrils, and her fingers came away clean again in confirmation.

"You either didn't use as much energy, or you successfully borrowed from another source nearby. Maybe both." Landry shrugged as if this were a simple concept and then headed for the kitchen.

While she waited, Kaela tugged the sweatshirt over her head and finally allowed herself to run a finger across one of the flowers. It felt just like a flower should, no tingling or sparking issued from the contact, no portal opened to another dimension. She was sitting stiffly on a couch, staring at the plant as if it was a viper that would slide off the table, when Landry returned with two glasses of amber liquid and a protein bar.

"You are full of questions." He observed, sitting near her. "Just start asking them as they come to you, and I'll answer what I can."

"Everything you and the others said is true."

"That's a statement, not a question, but yes, all true." He nodded.

"My house plants. I've been affecting them, haven't I?"

"Yes."

"How long have you known what I am?"

"For years before we officially met."

"Years." The gravity of that statement sank in, and Kaela waited to see if this new detail shifted her feelings for him. "Were you stalking me that whole time?"

"No. Not in the way you think. Nisha knew what you were long before I did. I'm still not sure how she discovered you, but I think it was accidental. She approached me and we had a long conversation over how to handle your existence, but we didn't agree on a few key points. I haven't really interacted with her since. I went to one of your presentations afterwards and watched you from a distance. I realized you didn't know what you could do or how to channel it. I decided to help you however I could, but I needed to find a way to do that without scaring you off. I applied for a faculty position knowing you would need more resources for your project. I thought I could start by helping you with your research and gradually make you aware of the bigger picture. Nisha forced my hand when she had her errand boy snatch you."

"Why do you hate Todd? Sorry, Theodore?"

The look of disdain on Landry's face when she mentioned the other man was clear.

"We have history together. We haven't been civilized in almost two centuries. I also saw how he was handling you and didn't approve."

"Then why didn't you stop it?"

"I didn't think you were the type of person to appreciate a self-proclaimed savior swooping in to interrupt something that was, by all observable accounts, consensual on both sides." His face twitched as he spat out the words.

"Consensual and catfishing are hardly two terms I'd interchange. When were you born? Oh, and where?"

"France in the eleventh century."

"Holy shit, how can I possibly believe that?" Kaela washed down the last of the protein bar with the remaining liquor in her glass. "You are telling me you are a thousand years old. Why don't you have a French accent?"

"I came to England by way of the Norman Conquest." Kaela's face remained blank as he began to explain. "I forget how little American scientists know about history sometimes. William the Conqueror invaded England in the eleventh century. He brought his forces from Normandy and other areas of France."

"I'm not going to respond to the slander you just aimed at my profession." She narrowed her eyes but stuck to the storyline. "So, you became British?"

"I lived in Wales off and on. In total, I may have spent hundreds of years there. I have a place near a small coastal village. I consider it my home."

There was a long break in conversation as Kaela stared at the plant on the table, processing, considering, and squashing down her skepticism as it tried to insert itself back to the forefront of her brain.

"Do you remember all of those years?"

"Not all." His eyes became slightly vacant as he followed the passage of time so immense that Kaela could not begin to fathom it. "Big events, certainly. Some are vivid, like they happened only days ago. Most of it has softened, becoming a series of emotions and impressions that are dull and surreal. I don't think the human mind is meant to contain that much information at once."

Kaela thought back to some of her earliest memories and wondered if that was how he felt looking fifty years into his past or five hundred. She remembered a lot of the time she spent in high school, but not every day in full detail. She remembered even less about elementary school. How much time could you collectively lose from memories spanning a thousand years? His forgotten experiences might fill a hundred lifetimes, perhaps even two hundred. Twenty years to him would be a week to most people.

"Did you have a family?"

"Once." His eyes came back into focus. "I left home to go to war when I was sixteen, and I don't remember anything about them. I had siblings but can't remember how many. I then became perpetually twenty-one years old. How could I have a committed relationship if I was unchanging over the years? No children, no connection to the generational passing of time. I formed a new family with some of the people like me, but most of them have been lost to time as well."

"Me neither. The children part, but I guess you know that. I decided a long time ago to prevent it from ever happening. I never told my husband about the surgery. He thought it was an appendectomy. He was too distracted with his own important life to pay much attention anyway."

The story was too personal, too freely given for this stage of their interaction. Kaela didn't mean to share it, but Landry's openness sank its teeth into her, slowly putting her caution to rest like belladonna leaching into her brainstem. The understanding expression on his face never faltered when she said it, making her fall a little deeper into the comfort of the conversation.

"And my parents passed away in the last decade. No siblings. I guess I understand the feeling of disconnect, if not the duration." Kaela cleared her throat and shifted.

"I'm sorry about your parents." His hand traced a long line down her leg where it rested near him. "How did it happen?"

"My mom died in a car accident, and my father had cancer."

Just saying the C word made Kaela's stomach flip. Whenever she talked about her father, she wanted to scream out the truth of his death. He knew Alzheimer's was coming. When he received the cancer diagnosis first, he treated it like an exit strategy. He gave up. He quit when he should have fought, and he left her by choice. She choked back the anger and the sadness. It was a little easier to snuff the feelings out each time.

"Why did you just recently decide to pursue a higher education, Dr. Griffiths?" She abruptly changed the subject as if she hadn't just traipsed through the debris of her shattered heart.

"This is my fourth doctorate, five if you count my medical degree from the 1800s," he boasted, smiling at the shock on her face. "A man gets bored from time to time and has to pursue new intellectual challenges."

She grunted, distracted by his fingers still resting on one of her knees as she considered the endless stream of questions she had yet to ask. She decided to focus on the ones with more immediate relevance.

"Who made you stop aging? And why did they pick you?"

"The second part is easy. They picked me because I can manipulate matter and energy. The person who did it was named Cassius."

"And this Cassius disappeared twenty years ago, and you started to age again. Does he have to be around you constantly for it to work, the immortality part?"

"No." Landry's body assumed a stillness, and he stared out the window to the dark bay below. "He and I went our separate ways in the mid-1900s, and it had no change on me. Which is why I think he is dead now. I think he died, and then we all started to grow old at once."

"And that is why I am getting dragged into this. You, Nisha, Theo, and anyone else who is now aging like an ordinary human are looking for a new source of eternal life and the word on the street is that I'm your Huckleberry. Where does Nisha fit into the picture? Was she friends with this Cassius person? She seemed like she was used to giving orders."

"She was his wife."

Kaela tried to imagine spending a thousand years with another person. Then, she simply tried to imagine living for a thousand years in the first place. Generations of people would come and go, their lives vibrant but fleeting like butterflies, and she would remain unchanged. How quickly would that existence become filled with loneliness?

"What was it like when you realized your body was aging again?"

Landry considered her question before answering.

"I didn't know the exact moment that it happened. There were surely signs that I missed. If you stare at the same face in the mirror for a millennium, you notice even the small changes, though. First, I found gray hair in my beard. Then more gray hairs appeared on top of my head. The parts of me that never hurt before were stiff and sore in the morning for no apparent reason. Joints started complaining a bit more after a particularly taxing exercise.

"The strangest part of the experience was that it all happened so quickly. I was used to a different tempo for the passage of time, and then I gained twenty solid, tangible years seemingly overnight. I will catch a glimpse of my reflection from time to time, and I have to pause to readjust to the person looking back at me because he doesn't quite match the image in my head."

"I will let you in on a little secret." Kaela slid closer to him, letting him tuck her against him in a comforting gesture. "That happens to all of us at this age."

She closed her eyes and rested her head against his body, listening to his slow, steady heartbeat. Their fingers were tangled together in his lap, and his thumb traced lazy circles on the back of her hand. She couldn't remember the act of clasping them together. She had more questions, but the long day of professional interactions combined with the evening festivities left her drained. Her eyelids were heavy as she breathed in his warm smell.

Not long after, Kaela managed to pull herself together in a moment of clarity and make her retreat with the promise to meet at the front desk the following afternoon after the concluding session of the conference. In the elevator, reminiscing over the spicier details of their exchange drove Kaela to bite the collar of the sweatshirt in agitation. This time, the elevator came to a halt on the floor of her own room. She took a step through the metal doors as they slid open but stopped short to avoid colliding with another person.

"Wow, you didn't have to get all dressed up for me. I'm sure that looks much better without the sweatshirt swallowing you."

Kaela's sudden fear of running into a colleague when she was dressed for a walk of shame evaporated, and her mouth dropped open in shock.

Theo slowly perused her body, lingering on her exposed legs.

"You have got to be kidding." Her blood pulsed rapidly, and her adrenaline spiked, but her sarcastic mouth didn't miss a beat. "Did you just happen to come to California and end up in my hotel, or are you going to admit to stalking me this time? If I scream, everyone on this floor will hear."

"Well then, please don't scream." He was the picture of relaxation with one hand in his front jeans pocket and the other at the elevator threshold, preventing it from closing. "I am stalking you, as it turns out. I need you to come with me again, and I will be sure to use my big boy words this time. Will that work for you?"

"It's late," Kaela replied, uselessly pushing the button to close the doors. "And this is clearly the wrong floor. If you'll excuse me."

"I'm afraid it can't wait." Theo took a slow step forward, placing himself just inside the opening. "Please. We just need to drive past the mountains for a meeting. I know it's late, but you can nap in the car."

Kaela stiffened. She wanted to hide her fear from him but couldn't keep herself from physically recoiling. She knew the situation was going to end poorly very soon.

"It's been a long night. Why don't we talk about it in the morning at a reasonable time, like after the sun has come up?" Her body was begging her to step back, to create more space, but she refused to move another inch.

"Kaela, I'm serious." A pleading look crept into Theo's eyes that didn't translate to his body language or his snarky tone of voice.

"So am I."

Kaela's eyes darted to the hallway on either side of him, suddenly realizing he wasn't alone, and that the haughty display was not for her benefit. "I am not going with you right now. You'll have to wait. Last time I checked, there aren't a lot of big rocks for you to throw around in this hotel. Now, back off or I will scream until I'm hoarse."

"For fuck's sake!" A voice came from the right side of the doorway, and a man Kaela didn't know stepped up to the open doors. "Grab the god-damned girl and let's go."

She opened her mouth to scream, but the air in her lungs refused to obey. In fact, she quickly realized she couldn't breathe at all.

"Dude, stop before you kill her." Theo snarled at the short, balding man and moved a step closer to Kaela.

Shrinking away in panic, ribs jerking frantically with the effort to move air, Kaela slipped on the smooth metal of the elevator floor. The last thing she registered was a blinding pain on the side of her head.

England – 1922

Sarah, Anne, Elizabeth; whatever she wished to be called in this lifetime, she was still the same devoutly moody individual she had always been. She looked just past Landry through the large picture window, her features shifting as she digested some particularly troublesome thought. Landry was used to her moods after all these years, and he allowed the silence to continue as long as she felt necessary.

He took the opportunity to consider her appearance more completely. She was always happy to scandalize a household by her choice of behaviors, and when Landry arrived at the estate unannounced, he found her dressed in a chore shirt and breeches, pummeling a richly embroidered cushion clutched in the hands of a very bewildered young footman.

When he first entered the room, a wolfhound was lounging in the corner, one eye on the sparring and another on the outraged butler hovering just beyond the doorway. The dog's lazy, unimpressed attitude immediately dissolved on Landry's arrival, and it leapt from the ground with as much speed as its heavy, lanky body could manage, executing a long, tail-wagging bow before rushing to his side.

"Hello, Jacques." The dog's tail beat an enthusiastic rhythm against the nearby bookcase at the mention of his name. "Have you been keeping her in line for me?"

After a few minutes, the frantic licks against Landry's fingers subsided, and the hound leaned its head firmly into Landry's hip, tongue lolling while it enjoyed the feel of the fingers combing through its long, wiry hair.

"Well, Elizabeth?" Landry called out loudly, walking across the carpeted floor to a table near the window and pouring a drink from the decanter there. "That is what you are going by these days, I am told. No warm words for your long-lost partner in crime? Only Jacques appears to miss me."

"I assume that you are here because Cassius sent you, not out of some mais ou sont les neiges d'antan that made you crave my company." Elizabeth waved her hand to dismiss the mortified servant and then glanced at Landry's drink as she spoke. "Pour me one of those?"

"As long as it will not serve to make you more quarrelsome than you already are," Landry returned, but the words were spoken lightly, and he brought her a partially filled glass. "I am glad to see you have not gone completely feral, living outside of high society over the last few years. Your French, at least, has improved, n'est pas? Where is Cleda?"

"She is upstairs, cleaning up after a full day of terrorizing the help in the gardens."

"I only wish it were a simple desire for your collective company that brought me here." He settled into a plush chair, and Jacques moved closer, draping his warm body across Landry's feet. "Cass has us withdrawing our physical support of the current situation and will be refocusing on something new. He requests that you and Cleda play the usual parts."

"Il ne bat plus que d'une aile." Elizabeth snorted with derision. "He should never have involved us in the first place, and now he is backpedaling."

"Il faut reculer pour mieux sauter," Landry rejoined. "Do not hide behind your witty French retorts, mon ami. You may disagree with most of the decisions he has made, but Cassius is still our leader. He has already given us hundreds of years to share, and he would let you walk away if you chose to. No one is infallible."

"What are a few hundred years between friends if you are unable to enjoy them?" Elizabeth swirled the glass in her hand, her voice fading as she lost focus on the conversation again.

"Come now, there were many years where we could laugh with one another."

"We had Charles to help us with the laughing then," she whispered sadly.

The great clock in the corner of the room ticked away an uncounted number of seconds as Landry waited, giving her time to traverse the individual memories of a shared past. When she finally turned back to him, there was a growing hardness in her expression.

"You will keep her safe during this task." It was a statement, an order, an undeniable contract of duty that was already sealed the moment the words left her mouth.

"I will not be there. You must keep her safe this time. If this is too large of a request, I support both of you in refusing. You know I will always be on your side." He hated to pull them into danger, but none of them knew any other way of life, and ultimately, the decision was not his to make.

"We can discuss this further over dinner with Cleda." She downed the last of her drink in two large swallows and set the empty glass on a side table. "I suppose I can change, although I really do not see the point in maintaining the façade that we are part of high society."

"We can dine en famille tonight. I won't be changing into white tails, but you should at least put on something reasonable, to keep the staff from being completely scandalized. I am intrigued to hear how Cleda, the gentlest spirit I have ever known, has come to terrorize them."

"Ah, well. She does have very specific opinions about the flowers and insists on digging around out there herself. The gardener is positively convinced that she will dismiss him and take over his responsibilities. She was meant for this type of rustic life."

Landry straightened and gave her a stiff bow of his head as she made her exit. Just before she departed through the door, however, she paused.

"I am glad to see you again, you know. I am just not very good at showing it."

And with that, she was gone.

Landry stared at the now-empty doorway, wishing that he could have arrived simply to say hello instead of being the bearer of another lengthy assignment. Elizabeth was family, his sister. He wanted to protect her from what was waiting in their near future but knew he could not. She would go in with her guns blazing, literally or figuratively, with no regard for her own well-being and no concern for the emotional damage it would inflict. When everything was over, he would scoop her up and take her to another country house in another location and let her recover. He lost count of the times they had gone through this dance.

Chapter 8

A rhythmic thumping resonated through Kaela's body. She swam up from the dizzying black recess of her mind, gaining more awareness in her body with the passing of each minute. She tried to understand the humming vibrations transmitting through her muscles, fighting against the stubborn sludge of sleep.

Beneath her cheek was fabric. She was lying on her side, and the surface beneath her was moving, a disorienting but familiar sensation; the gentle swaying and shifting of a vehicle moving over a paved road. Her balance tilted as the car leaned into a bend.

Kaela's ears were ringing, but the pounding in her head started to lessen as her heart beat a slow rhythm. She counted with her pulse. *One Mississippi, two Mississippi, three Mississippi, four...*

When the pain was a dull ache instead of a raging throb, she opened her eyes. Tan upholstered seats with sagging pockets. Ambient light, bright enough to make her eyes water. Kaela tried to sit up but let her head fall back against the cushion as her equilibrium spiraled. Her chest tightened. She had stopped breathing. No matter how hard she tried to pull in air, her lungs hadn't been able to expand, and she'd slowly suffocated in that elevator until she passed out.

She drew a sharp breath at the realization, savoring the sensation of fresh air filling her body like a balloon. She sucked it in until the back of her throat hurt, and her ribs could have burst from her body. Her entire left side ached. She remembered a sudden impact just before losing consciousness.

"Looks like I didn't kill her after all." The amused observation drifted from the driver's seat.

"This isn't a joke," Theo's voice was stiff with anger. "You do realize that she is the only way out of this. Are you all right, Kaela?"

Kaela finally managed to get herself upright, but it was a slow process. She first struggled to push up from the seat, only to realize that she couldn't orient her hands appropriately. They were restrained by some unknown force. When she tried to place her feet on the floorboards, the motion pulled oddly at her ankles. She was trussed again. She blocked out the screaming pain in her right knee and forced herself to move, swinging both legs down and tucking her dress under her with shackled hands. She opened her mouth to provide a scathing response to Theo's concerned question but was immediately interrupted by the bald man in the driver's seat.

"I control that precious air in your lungs." He hissed at her in the rearview mirror. "If you like being able to breathe, do what I say. You even think about throwing yourself out of that car door, and I cut you off again. Got it?"

Kaela didn't bother to acknowledge the threat, snapping her mouth closed and looking through the windows instead. The sky had grown lighter in the time she was unconscious, and it was nearing full daylight. The same scenery greeted her every direction she turned, grayish sand ridges giving way to hills and then mountains in the distance, both covered in scattered brown-green desert scrub.

"Hey, are you okay?" Theo's genuine expression did nothing to lessen her all-consuming hatred for him as he reiterated his concern.

"My knee is banged up, my face hurts, and I have a pounding headache." She squinted but held his gaze, pouring every ounce of her anger into the stare. "Other than the fact that I'm tied up like a fucking calf back here, I'm fantastic."

"I told you she was fine. Jesus, that mouth of hers." Baldy glanced through the rearview once more, then kept his focus on the road.

"Listen you hairless asshole." The last of her shock burned away, leaving only raging insolence. "I am sick of you already. What's your problem? Start losing your hair in the last few decades, and decide that you need someone to give you more than a bottle of Rogaine? Twenty-year-old girls think you look old and now you can't get laid?"

"Wow. Harsh but not too far off. Don't get pissy, you asked for it." Theodore started laughing as Baldy's head turned crimson, then he looked back at Kaela. "I guess you're up to speed on the situation we're all in?"

"Yes, I get the big picture, but what I don't understand is this: if you need me to make you immortal again, why treat me like a disposable commodity? If I decide I don't like you, then why would I ever agree to grant you eternity?" As the words left her mouth, Theo exchanged a nervous glance with the driver. "Well, maybe chew on that for a while and then decide to treat me more respectfully."

The road was a single lane in each direction. On the passenger side was some type of gigantic lake. A sand and dirt shore vanished into a shockingly blue body of water. On the far side, bucolic mountains of faded azure rose from a hazy horizon. Seagulls circled above, and flocks of waterfowl were grouped in the shallows, tiny, winged flotillas undulating over the gentle movement of the water. By contrast, the driver's side window revealed only more rough, sandy terrain.

"Why are there pelicans in the desert?" Kaela tried but failed to keep her curiosity in check as they passed a decrepit wooden sign, sunk to an angle in the sand with faded white letters emblazoned upon it.

"That is salt water," Theo responded. "Some weird tourist thing in the mid-1900s, I think. I don't know or remember the details. It was a popular destination for a few years, but it ultimately failed. Now it is just a sad, run-down place where people occasionally stop to take a selfie."

"Can you untie me? I can't feel my toes. It's not like I'm going anywhere at this point. In case you were concerned, I won't be diving out of a moving vehicle."

"Sorry about that." Theodore's eyes ran across her, surprisingly devoid of any sexual undertones. "You had to know you couldn't get away when you were cornered in that elevator. Why bother resisting?"

"I suppose you would just meekly go along with it if someone tried to kidnap you." The banter with him was almost comforting, a familiar face and exchange that contradicted the seriousness of her situation.

"No, but I wouldn't try to escape when I was trapped like that." His expression grew hard as he looked at her, reminding Kaela that this was not the same person as the Todd she once dated. "I would go along with it until I had a real opportunity to get loose, and then I'd rip them to shreds."

A shiver moved up her spine, and she wholeheartedly believed that he would physically tear another human being apart given the chance. The darker side of her rose to the surface in response, convincing her that she could sink her thumbs into Baldy's eye sockets and make her escape once the car stopped. Theo's eyes flashed in approval at what he saw on her face, and he turned forward to address his companion. Had she imagined his planted suggestion? She couldn't understand why he would want her ready to fight when he was the one who initiated this situation in the first place.

"I don't see the harm in cutting her loose now, do you?" Theo was addressing his companion again. A brief discussion ensued, but they eventually agreed to free her hands. Theo leaned between the seats, cutting through the ties at her wrists with a familiar pocketknife.

"Any chance you have refreshments to offer for this little joy ride?" A half-eaten bag of beef jerky landed on Kaela's lap. "Breakfast of champions. Why do you have me out here in the middle of nowhere? Not that I don't enjoy a good sightseeing trip."

"Come on, Doctor." Baldy found his voice again. "Surely you can figure out what we want."

"I hate to break it to you," Kaela mumbled around a wad of jerky. "But I am really not in touch with my all-powerful side. *Teddy* here should have told you as much."

There was another silent exchange in the front of the car before Theo replied.

"Someone disagrees with my assessment."

"That's ominous." She popped more of the salty dried beef into her mouth and masticated in silence for a few minutes. "How are you going to try to force it out of me this time? Back to the torture idea since shock and awe didn't pan out before?"

Now the silence wasn't just ominous, it was downright threatening.

Baldy turned the car off the road and started across the open sand along a barely discernible path that was marked by short posts jutting haphazardly from the ground. Kaela considered her options for escape while she was jolted around in her seat. Running straight into the desert was a terrible idea, but also the only one she had at the moment. She wondered if there was a physical limitation to the reach of Baldy's ability. It was possible she could run quickly enough to be out of range before she passed out again.

How could someone control air? She was just coming to terms with what Landry demonstrated, but this new ability was returning her to the land of make-believe and delusions. Although controlling air wasn't that far removed from controlling stone, perhaps just more abstract.

She regretfully thought about her phone. She must have dropped her clutch in the elevator. Hopefully, someone would find it and realize she was missing.

"Rules." Kaela wanted to slap Bald Man's superior little snarl off his face as he lectured her. "When I park, you will exit the vehicle without a fight. You will stay between me and him the whole time. I will put an air curtain around us to limit sound, but if you make a single noise or try to run, I'll pull the air from your lungs again. Got it?"

Kaela gave a begrudging scowl but was distracted by interpreting the meaning of 'air curtain.' Was it a thickening of the particles in the air to prevent the passage of sound waves? Sound could travel through solid surfaces, even steel. Therefore, it wouldn't just have to be solid, it would need to acoustically decouple their noises from the area outside of this supposed curtain. It could be a moving barrier meant to deflect the sounds upwards.

Her breath hitched, the tiniest constriction, but enough that she knew her lungs were being manipulated. Her eyes shot to the front of the car again.

"I said, did you get that?"

"Yes." Kaela seethed at the invasion of her body but knew this was not the appropriate time to fight back.

Theo gave her an unmistakably sympathetic look but didn't add to the discussion. Instead, he casually typed into his phone, keeping the screen tilted just far enough to prevent his co-conspirator from being able to read it. The secrecy was suspicious, but Baldy was too interested in Kaela's reaction to the instructions to notice. He parked in a flat section of sand.

Kaela's surge of excitement at seeing other cars faded back to an anxious pit in her stomach when she saw they were all unoccupied. Theodore stepped out of the vehicle, slinging a backpack across his shoulders before moving to extract her from the back seat. When he opened the door, he held out a pair of old athletic shoes, and she realized her high heels were missing. He cut through the zip ties at her ankles after giving her an assessing glance, likely considering whether she would attempt to kick his teeth loose. At least he'd learned something from the last time. She tugged the shoes onto her feet, trying not to acknowledge the unsettling fact that they were the correct size, and stepped into the uncomfortably bright light of a cloudless desert sky.

The naïve concept of desert landscapes in Kaela's mind was derived from too many childhood cartoons and picture books. What surrounded them did not match her expectations. To begin with, the ground wasn't unending, pristine sand. The rolling hills were thick with dry, brown underbrush that looked like dead sticks, not living plants. The occasional tree clawed up through the low shrubs, and a random smattering of reddish rocks interrupted the open spaces. Sand free of plant growth extended away from the parking area, winding into the brush. Kaela could only see about fifty feet down this path before it curved away. Although it wasn't terribly hot, it was utterly dry, and she felt her throat losing moisture with each arid lungful. Hopefully, Todd was carrying a significant amount of water in his backpack. She didn't look forward to dying of dehydration right after surviving suffocation.

"Let's go." Theo indicated the path with a nod. "It's not that far to hike. We will keep a decent pace. Just let me know if you need a break or water."

"Stop playing nice with her, she'll be fine."

"Are you sure you put enough sunblock on your head?" Kaela glared at the back of the shiny scalp, hoping Baldy's skin was about to fry to a crisp, but she didn't receive the satisfaction of a response. "Are you going to tell me where we're going?"

Theo glanced at her but gestured to the path again without answering. Kaela kept pace just ahead of him and behind Baldy.

The scenery was interesting but unchanging. An occasional bird or lizard broke the monotony, but Kaela quickly found her mind wandering. If there were any practical applications for her abilities that everyone kept telling her about, now would be a great time to figure out how to wield them to her benefit. Thus far, she made a few plants grow, but if she could control life, wouldn't that also imply power over death?

She had seen enough movies and read more than enough books to know how this type of magic was portrayed across various genres. The abstract concept of a soul was too firmly based in religion for her to consider pulling a person's essence from their body a possibility. She also couldn't fathom making someone crumble into dust for a variety of reasons, basic laws of physics being the greatest of these.

But what if she could make them age more quickly? This concept she could wrap her head around. She considered a biological solution that involved an increase in metabolism and cellular processes. She then considered the alternative, which was meddling with temporal parameters rather than biology itself. A new series of hypotheses rattled around in her brain, distracting her so thoroughly that she trudged across the desert for nearly an hour, oblivious to the bits of sand that worked into her shoes and exfoliated the inner edges of her toes.

"We are here."

Theo's voice drew her up short. He was standing at the top of a hill next to Baldy, facing away from her. She was in the back, following them with the docile obedience of a sheep while her brain worked through the various scenarios. When she reached the top of the slope, she finally cringed at the grainy abrasion of her feet and the throbbing protest issuing from her right knee. Theo handed her a bottle of water, and she drank it in long, greedy gulps.

The path continued down the other side of the hill into a large, thick grove of palm trees backed by a mountainous ridge of rocky soil which extended into the desert in both directions. The tops of the trees were covered in dense green fronds that faded to brown near the ground. There were hundreds of them, and their tight spacing made it impossible to see past the edge of the thicket.

"Is that an actual oasis?" she gaped.

Neither man responded as they started forward again. Kaela risked a backward glance, considering. Rather than being brought to her knees by a sudden lack of air, she decided to follow them, biding her time. The temperature continued to rise as the morning passed, and sweat was dripping along her spine in thin but insistent rivulets. She was just beginning to struggle out of Landry's sweatshirt when they stepped into the first section of trees, and the temperature dropped dramatically.

Inside the oasis, the air was heavier, deadened by the closeness of the palms. The ground under Kaela's feet was covered in long strands of grass, trodden flat into a trail. The towering vegetation completely blocked the sun, creating a cave-like ambiance. She followed the two men onto a raised wooden walkway, and her ears were accosted by the singing of dozens of birds. The grass thickened, and the humidity climbed. To the left, the trees receded, revealing a small, still pond fringed by green plants. The flat surface of the water reflected the palm trees reaching tall into the sky, creating a disorienting world below to match the one above. Ahead of her, the dry brown sections of the fronds were cut away to provide clearance for those walking across the boards, giving the appearance of tiki huts lining the path.

"What is that?" Kaela came to an immediate stop as their destination through the fronds became visible.

"It's a tunnel." Theo assessed the degree of panic on her face then offered more detail. "A light bender monitors this location; a person that controls light the way I control rocks. She makes the entrance look intimidating to deter the occasional trespasser."

“A light bender,” Kaela repeated carefully, staring into the never-ending black depths of the tunnel opening before them. “Is that a term I should understand? And should that make me okay with strolling into the mouth of hell?”

“Dramatic.” Theo turned and walked straight into the gaping hole in the rock face.

“Well, get on with it, Doctor.” Baldy roughly nudged her forward.

She held her breath as she followed. The darkness was so complete she expected a physical resistance to the air, as if she were wading through tar. Instead, it was like walking into an open room with her eyes closed. The air moved against her skin, and the rustle of the body moving in front of her registered in her ears. She breathed in the earthy but nondescript scent through her nose. The ground felt soft, sandy, but easy to tread across.

Her eyes were open wide, searching back and forth in the darkness and straining to detect even the slightest hint of a shape, but no light penetrated the black. She pushed against the impulse to sweep her arms around in front of her body, but her skin still crawled, goosebumps rising as her hair stood on end. Her muscles involuntarily tensed at the slightest shift in air pressure, anticipating a sudden collision. Then, she was standing on the other side.

“About time you got here,” a masculine voice called out in accusation.

Kaela blinked against the bright light. They were back in the desert, but this time they had company. To her left was a pair of twenty-somethings wearing blank expressions. The male was sitting on the ground, denim-clad legs crossed at the ankles above a pair of sneakers. His eyes drifted to her briefly before returning to the phone in his hand. His shirt was emblazoned with the name of a punk band from the late 1980s. Ordinarily, Kaela would consider this humorous, the strange youthful fascination with past pop culture, but in this instance, she didn’t know if this youthful-looking man was twenty or if he was born prior to the previous century. The shirt could be nostalgic.

The female standing next to him was leaning casually against the surface of a large boulder. The similarities between them were clear from their striking, dark features to the shoulder-length onyx hair. Her attire was gothic, whereas his was grunge. A cluster of bodies to her right consisted of three men around Kaela’s age dressed like they were prepared for an afternoon trip to the Hamptons with their uniform of polos and linen shorts. Near them was a familiar petite female sitting on the ground.

Kaela stared at Hailey in shock, the handcuffs on her friend's wrists indicating that she wasn't a willing participant in this sand party. Baldy yanked Kaela forward before she could react beyond a widening of her eyes, and the taller of the three men next to her continued to talk, asking why they took such a long time and if there was any trouble. The words barely registered as she scrambled to understand what was happening. Her eyebrows pinched together, and she mouthed the word 'okay' to Hailey, searching the other woman for signs of injury. She received a curt nod in response.

When Kaela looked back to the man speaking, she realized he was inspecting her. He was tall, his hair the gold-lined brown of someone that spent a lot of time in the sun. His icy blue eyes cut into her, making her skin crawl unpleasantly. She stubbornly refused to break eye contact.

"Can I help you?" Kaela managed to ask the question in an aggressive and slightly bored tone.

Theodore smothered a laugh.

"Jackson, meet Dr. Kaela Brookes. She is a kind, caring person once you get past the smartass façade."

Jackson flicked his eyes to Theo, no hint of amusement at the jest, and then returned to his cold perusal.

"Why do you let yourself age like this when youth is at your fingertips?"

His voice was distant, the question delivered rhetorically. Something in his voice was off, an emptiness in place of emotion. His eyes carefully followed the traces of gray in her hair and hovered around the hint of crows' feet forming at the corners of her eyelids. He shook his head slowly, disapproving.

"Wow, you just cut right to the insults with no introductions." Kaela glared back at him, angry at his blatant and dismissive critique of her appearance.

"She really can't use her powers yet?" Jackson ignored the outburst and turned back to Theo and Baldy. "We don't have time for this. Has she shown any signs of being able to wield her abilities?"

"No, she has not," Kaela cut off Baldy just as he opened his trap to speak. "I am right here, you know. No need to marginalize me by pretending I can't speak for myself."

Jackson turned slowly back in her direction as one of the other men spoke up.

“Don’t tell me you’re one of those whiny women who think that any time someone treats you as unimportant, it’s because we’re sexist. Women vote, get over it already.”

“Inequitable treatment of females isn’t an opinion, it’s a basic truth,” she stated with a calmness she didn’t feel. “And I don’t think he was being sexist. I think he was being a superior asshole.”

“You’re basically a prisoner right now, Sweet Pea. Why don’t you shut your pretty mouth?”

“*Ugh,* I’m going to be as wrinkled and ineffectual as all of you by the time she makes me immortal,” another voice cuts in, belonging to the Goth Girl. “Can we skip all the bullshit posturing and torture her friend already, Jackson? Obviously, your group of fuck boys over there isn’t going to convince her of anything. And she isn’t that pretty.”

Kaela turned and looked at her with surprise. The girl was still slouching on the rock as if this was the least interesting event she had ever participated in. She returned to her phone, muttering loudly enough for everyone to hear.

“I mean, you are kind of old.”

A harsh laugh barked out of Kaela’s mouth, but on the inside, her heart was thundering. Would they really torture Hailey as a pressure point?

“I’m seriously not capable of whatever it is you think you can frighten out of me. I was told what you think I can do, I tried to do it, and I haven’t shown any signs of being able to.” It wasn’t the truth but there was no way any of them knew about the plant in the hotel with Landry, so she plowed ahead. “The research in my lab is the most promising lead you have right now. Let Hailey go and let me get back to my work. I am this close to stopping aging. I just need a few more years and the right tools, and then you can have what you are after. I won’t keep it from you. Having her here isn’t going to change anything.”

There is a long silence during which Kaela risked a glance at Hailey. The trainer stared back, a pleading expression on her face. Theo shifted uncomfortably. The Goth twins were still happy to remain in the background, playing on their phones. Baldy was standing with the polo crew, all three of them looking to Jackson for his decision.

“Grab the other one and bring her,” Jackson finally responded; his tone bland as he gestured to the desert behind him. “It’s getting hot out here, and we should do this in the shade. Let’s see how quickly we can inspire Dr. Brookes to use her powers.”

"I have no idea what's going on, please let me go. I won't say anything to anyone." Hailey was pleading with the larger of the polo men as he dragged her up by the links of the handcuffs. "Ask Kaela. We are just acquaintances from the gym. I don't even know her middle name or her birthday or anything! She can't possibly care about me that much."

"She's right, I barely know her," Kaela offered to Jackson, wanting to reason with him without appearing desperate. "She's only my personal trainer. She knows my squat and bench numbers, but that's it. She has nothing to do with any of this."

Even as the words left her lips, Kaela knew Hailey wouldn't be allowed to walk away. They had conceivably dragged her here across the country, not a small distance. Now that she was thinking about it, how did they get her this far? It was practically human trafficking.

"You have no friends or family that you contact with any regularity. You have your coworkers, your ex-husband, a few estranged friends that probably took his side in the split, distant relatives who send you Christmas cards, but no birthday wishes, and an occasional fuck buddy, Theo being the longest running one of those. This woman is the closest thing you have to a friend, and we are about to find out if you are capable of the human emotions that lead to lasting relationships or if you're a sociopath like the rest of us."

For once, Kaela couldn't think of a good retort, and she stared at him, feeling shame creep into the back of her thoughts as she realized everything he said was accurate. She didn't connect with people. Her friendships never lasted, mostly because she quickly stopped caring enough to invest her energy in the other person. She now led a life unencumbered by toxic relationships, but in a few pointed sentences, Jackson reduced her life to a sad, relationship-less void.

Kaela tried to shake off the feeling. She knew what he was doing. She stayed married to an emotionally minimizing man for years, and the churning in her gut was familiar. But understanding his intentions did not immediately erase the effect of his words.

"You do realize that we know everything about your life." Jackson walked away as she continued to stand in silence.

"Dick," she half-heartedly called after him as the twins and the douche squad followed with a frantic looking Hailey in tow.

"They aren't serious about torturing her, right?" Kaela screamed-whispered to Theo, the only person still standing near her. She felt her panic rising as she clutched his forearm. "Please tell me they aren't completely crazy, and you aren't really one of them. You couldn't have spent the last year pretending to be nice. No one is that good at keeping up a front. I know you're a decent person. You've got to help us."

"I'm sorry, Kaela." He glanced at the group that was moving deeper into the desert, his voice low. "I didn't really have a choice. You'll understand eventually. Look, I'll try my best to get you out of here in one piece, okay?"

"But why are you helping them?" She refused to move, scraping through her brain to find some way to influence him. "I know you aren't dumb, even though you spent the last year pretending to be. I'm sorry I didn't see through that. I am sure it was degrading to pretend to be that person."

"A bit." His eyes narrowed with amusement at her admission. "You wanted me to be an uncomplicated, easy lay and I went along with it. I can't say it was all difficult, though. You and I had some fun too."

"Right up until the time you wrecked the front of my house in a jealous rage." She seethed, still wishing she could punch him in the nose and make a run for it but knowing she couldn't abandon Hailey. "You still haven't told me why you're with them."

"I don't *want* to do any of this." Theo dropped the roguish pretense and lowered his voice to a murmur, leaning close to her ear so Kaela could hear him clearly. "I'm here for you. Trust me. I hope I can explain it all to you soon." He brushed her cheek with his fingertips and then turned, pushing her roughly along in front of him even as he continued talking in a soothing tone. "Just go along with whatever they ask. Use those powers that are buried deep down. You say you can't, but I can tell you're hiding something. Then I'll get you out of here. Now, come on."

This time, there were no rambling slopes of brush, and Kaela could see straight across to the waiting group of people. They were gathered a dozen yards away, conversing and occasionally gesturing down to Hailey, who was cross-legged in the sand. The heat was getting more intense, but her skin was dry, the sweat instantly evaporating. She and Theodore were still walking in full sunlight, but a long section of shade covered the others. A quick glance confirmed that the rays of sunlight should have been unimpeded over their heads.

"Seriously, what is a light bender?" She breathed to herself, eliciting a glance from Theo.

"This is one of the locations for training newly discovered talent. It's remote, meaning tourists won't stumble into something they shouldn't, and the new talent won't accidentally blow up something important. Although we haven't seen many people with those big, showy abilities in decades, long before Cassius disappeared. The sunburns were a nightmare. A light bender made this sunshade. Think of it like a big invisible beach umbrella."

"I can't even begin to mathematically summarize the physics of that," Kaela responded, temporarily distracted from the situation by her scientific interest.

"That's just the beginning, Kaela. You need to stop thinking linearly. There is a whole level of existence you've negated with your black and white logic."

"Was that a scientific reference?" Kaela stumbled in surprise.

"I'm just saying, Dr. Brookes, that it is a three-dimensional world you live in, but you need to reshape your thoughts. It's all fun and games until someone shows up with a Mobius strip."

She gaped at the shallow, unintelligent man she dated for over a year.

"Who even are you?"

"Someone you may hate again in just a few short minutes." His eyes were heavy with this statement, and then he turned back to the group, raising his voice. "Someone else needs to have prisoner duty next time."

Theo shoved Kaela at the last moment, and she fell forward onto her knees. The protective statements and concerned actions were deeply confusing when followed by this behavior. Hailey offered a single, desperate look before she was dragged to the side by one of the men. Her face was pinched as if she might burst into tears at any moment. The confident, action-taking persona Kaela was accustomed to was replaced by someone reflecting the same panic Kaela was feeling herself. Hailey's fear scratched at the edge of Kaela's calm outer shell like wind eroding sand. Baldy was at Jackson's elbow, presumably awaiting further instructions from the ringleader.

"She needs to demonstrate her abilities on someone," Jackson stated.

"I think Brady should volunteer." Theo flicked his eyes to the man at Jackson's elbow, and Kaela finally knew Baldy's name. "He is very anxious to get a taste of his youth again. He didn't age as well as the rest of us."

Brady cast an annoyed glance Theo's direction but nodded to Jackson.

"Time to show us what you can do, Dr. Brookes." Jackson twisted the honorific into an insult. "Turn back the clock on our friend here."

Kaela looked from Jackson to Brady and then back to Jackson.

"I thought you wanted me to stop aging, not reverse it."

"Cassius could do both," Jackson responded as Brady moved to Kaela's side. "I don't see why we should expect any less from you. Now take a decade off him."

"I told you; I have no idea how to do that."

Jackson held Kaela's gaze for a long moment before he turned and nodded to the two men standing with Hailey. One of them pulled her to her feet and punched her in the face. Hailey gave a loud cry of pain and crumpled to the sand.

"What the hell!" Kaela screamed and her body involuntarily moved in the direction of her friend, only to be stopped short when Theo's muscular arm wrapped across her waist. "Why would you do that to her, you piece of shit?"

"Make him younger." Jackson's calm, cold voice seeped into her brain.

"I don't fucking know how!" Kaela frantically shoved Theo, trying to break loose. "Beating her to a pulp isn't going to change that."

Jackson nodded to his thugs again. This time, one of them pulled Hailey upright, and the other took her forearm between both of his hands. She was crying and pleading with them. Kaela was yelling nonsensical threats and thrashing against Theo's renewed restraint. There was a horrific crack, and despite the lack of any obvious effort, the man snapped straight through bone. The shriek that tore from Hailey's throat made Kaela's mouth sour, and she sank against Theo, dry heaving as Hailey bent over the broken arm, falling back onto the sand with a low wail of pain.

Tears streamed down Kaela's face, and a pulse of anger washed over her, smothering the nausea. She turned her eyes back to Jackson, hate radiating from her in waves. He returned her look with one of amusement.

"Stop it." She hissed.

"Again," he replied.

Before Kaela could do more than turn, they broke Hailey's other arm.

"STOP!" Kaela was screaming at the top of her lungs now. Theo released her when she whirled and grabbed Brady's hands. "I'll try! I'll try! Please just stop hurting her! Please!"

A blanket of silence fell over the group. Brady's eyes locked on her face, pure excitement showing despite the horror of what was just done to Hailey. Jackson's expression was triumphant. Hailey's low keening continued, matching the silent cry of helplessness that was echoing inside Kaela's own head.

This was actually happening.

A wave of heady disorientation passed over Kaela, and she looked back at the tunnel, confused by the familiar feeling.

No one was coming.

She strained her eyes, but this time, no knight in shining armor appeared from the black opening. She was alone with no way out.

Kaela willed herself to do something, anything, to convince them that she was capable of this magic. If she couldn't, they would kill Hailey. She had to try. She let a stillness settle inside her, searching for Landry's instructions last night as she took long, slow breaths.

I need to stay calm. I need to think.

"I would advise against stalling, for your friend's sake."

She wanted to murder Jackson. She was nearly blind with hatred and could visualize stabbing a knife through one of his eyes. She would be doing the world a favor.

Kaela set her loathing to the side and focused on Brady. She placed one hand on each of his forearms, gripping him tightly. She closed her eyes and tried to remember the feeling of connectedness. There was a mental space, a level of dissociation, and yet a hyper-focused intent she needed. She took more deep breaths to slow her adrenaline-fueled heartbeat.

Try to connect to everything around you. Feel the movements of life, the flow of energy. You are feeling the natural order of forces and plucking a single string to shift the balance in the direction of what you desire.

Kaela could feel the air, motionless around her. The living creatures hidden within the plant-shaded crevices of the sands, the trees stretching out of the earth, all the life in this barren place, paused for just a moment as she reached out with her mind. She imagined she could hear the tiny whirring machinations of the cells in Brady's body spinning along their metabolic courses. The air filled with buzzing, humming, the sound of a beehive when all the bees were hard at work.

The body was a glorious cohesive unit filled with a million microscopic epicenters of activity, all interconnected throughout by tiny threads. Each little part was autonomous and yet belonged to the whole, sending messages and resources between one another in a hundred different ways: biochemical, physical, electrical, mechanical. The air that filled the lungs, the food slowly making its way through the digestive tract, the blood racing through the tiniest of capillary paths, the glycogen feeding the muscles, the neurotransmitters jumping across neural junctions. Kaela could instantly feel the vitality of it all.

While she reveled in this beautiful connection with a living being, a miraculously unified system that was as complicated as it was simple, she felt the anger and the darkness of her current situation creeping in. Everything was delicately balanced to sustain them, and yet here they were, giving this brutal human display instead of reveling in the magic of existence itself. Her friend was reduced to a crumpled heap just on the hunch that Kaela could prolong the lives of these few selfish individuals.

She thought about all the processes that were occurring in Brady's body right then. She let herself sink into the complex map of pathways and grabbed onto her disdain tightly as she went deeper. What if instead of restoring all those aged, dead ends, she made more of them? What if those cells that were slowly churning out the basic units of energy needed for this life were placed in fast forward, just for a brief span of time? What would he look like if he continued to approach death despite his best efforts to delay it?

Kaela was humming a wordless tune, reveling in these thoughts, when a pair of hands grabbed her and roughly pulled her away from her task. There were shouts and cries of disbelief. When she opened her eyes, she first saw the shocked expression of Theo, who was grasping her on the upper portion of her arms. Still in a stupor, Kaela turned her head toward Brady.

What should have been a forty-year-old bald man was replaced with the wrinkled, aged visage of someone well past sixty. They wanted Kaela to rewind time and bring him back to his youth, and instead, she managed to do the opposite.

She laughed.

Waves of mirth took over, and she howled as the tears rolled down her cheeks, a crazed cackling that poured out of her mouth. She felt disconnected from her body, and all around was chaos.

Jackson backed away as if she and Brady were lepers. Brady grabbed at his face, looking at himself with his phone camera. Theodore shifted her behind his body, shielding her from something. The twins were straight-backed and determined as they joined hands. The two thugs near Hailey moved away from the tunnel, their eyes fixed on something as they retreated in the direction of Jackson. They looked as if they were afraid of turning their backs on some new threat that had emerged. Kaela finally regained enough composure to peer around Theo to see what held their attention.

Landry had appeared, seemingly out of thin air, and he was angry.

Germany – 1945

It was the beginning of an end. Ten of them defied direct orders, so Landry supposed it was a mutiny at last. He reminded himself that Cassius was the reason for this, even as he met the angry accusation in his commander's eyes.

Alban was present in his usual capacity on the night Cassius refused to grant permission for Landry to extract Elizabeth and Cleda, a silent shadow in the background, personal guard, and firestarter for their commander. No amount of yelling or desperate pleading from Landry could change Cass's decision, and when Landry left, his next move was already decided.

He called together his team the following night and found that Alban counted among those gathered in the room, along with three more of Cass's personal guards. Landry chose transparency and revealed the full situation. He explained who was being held and how. He provided full details of the orders from Cassius to stand down. Just discussing his plans for an unsanctioned attack on the hidden bunker was committing treason. He offered the team a choice: return to Cassius's side to do nothing or stay and fight.

The entire group chose to stay.

In addition to Alban's team of four, every member of Landry's trusted cadre would participate. First was Agatha, his shadow collector; then Bron, who could harness wind; followed by Ahtah, a spirit walker from America, and Kofi, a heart keeper who was close to Charles before his death. The day after the plans were set in place, Theodore appeared. Landry suppressed his anger, choking back the deep-rooted memories of hate, and allowed Theo to state his case. He was invited to join the team after he made one simple statement.

"Please, let me do this for her."

It was the first and only time Landry could tolerate Theodore's presence after the loss of Charles, but they both knew the mission was more likely to succeed with the two of them working together. Once Cleda and Elizabeth were safe, they would become strangers once more.

The women were held in a clandestine research facility. They were embedded as spies in the upper echelons of the regime, but just before the fall, they were betrayed, and the truth of their abilities became the subject of much interest to their captors.

The team managed to infiltrate the secret bunker, eliminating any opposition along the way. Several dozen prisoners were being held at that location. When Landry and his group arrived, less than a third of those were still alive. Landry pushed away the memory of finding Cleda's lifeless body, of dragging Elizabeth away from the divider between their cells, of being too late to prevent the torture clearly inflicted on them both.

Landry peered at Cassius in silence, arms crossed. Cassius returned the stare, giving no indication to his state of mind.

"At last it comes to this," Cassius said flatly. "You have finally grown tired of being second in command."

"That is not what this is about," Landry returned with equal calm.

"Is it not? You knew that there would be orders you did not agree with. You were to trust me to lead you through the ages when you chose this path. Yet here we are. You have reached a point where you believe your own judgment has surpassed mine. You took your team into a battle today against my orders. Beyond that, you recruited members of my personal guard. I suppose you will next inform me that they are to be part of your retinue in the future?"

Landry assessed Cassius carefully, noticing the hint of wildness in his eyes even though he kept his voice even.

"Elizabeth is not a sacrifice I could make, and you should not have been able to make it either. She has been my own second in command for centuries. She was not a pawn on your chessboard to do with as you like. You used her in this war, knowing that I would follow."

"Everyone is a pawn on the great game board of the gods," Cassius replied quickly, his voice deepening now with anger. "But you are right. I saw your conviction fading, and I knew that you would stay involved if only to keep her safe."

"And are you a god now, Cassius?" Landry's voice grew quieter in turn, an ebbing of emotion to balance the flow of it from his companion.

"The animals that inhabit this world need someone to care for them." The anger was gone, and in its place was something more dangerous. "That was always the understanding. There were no gods to make them act as

they should. There were no repercussions to living in violence and hate. In the absence of gods, we become our own."

"Even the lives of animals should count as more." In the darkness, Landry could not tell if his words were being recognized or if they were lost within the deafness of Cass's righteous anger. "You no longer value the same people for which you claim to fight. I cannot keep going into these wars just to throw away lives on a whim. That was not the reason I chose this existence. We were to change the inequities and the violence. We were to make them work toward a better existence and a greater purpose."

"And doesn't murdering fifty men in cold blood make your statements feel hollow?"

After removing Elizabeth from the bunker, Landry returned with a few of the others and killed every last person he could find that might have been part of Cleda's death. He refused to feel any remorse for his actions.

"Those were not men. They were monsters. Their lives were forfeit the moment they crossed that line and tortured those people to death. You did not see what I saw today, Cassius, or you would not accuse me so."

"Would you expect Jacques not to bark?" Cassius practically snapped the words at him. "People are animals just like all the other creatures in this world, stuck within the confines of their own biology and behaviors. It was ingrained in them from birth. We may serve as the judge and jury for the future, but we are not executioners."

"Yet you have sent me to act as the hangman time and time again. You told me that if there are people that cannot find a way to evolve, their lives are forfeited. Sometimes the darkness must be removed, not just steered in a different direction. You know as well as I that those men could never come back from the things that they have done."

"Even so, their souls were not yours to take." Cassius snarled.

"And why is that, Cass? Simply because you did not order it?"

"No," the other man bit out. "They were not yours to take because there were other options. Death of that entire building of men was not a last resort that you delivered with sadness in your heart. It was with joy that you snuffed out their lives. It was the darkening of your soul that I cannot abide."

"And what of your soul, Cassius?" Landry's voice continued to soften, struggling to find the words as he faced this stranger in the place of his former commander. "What being can weigh and measure your intentions

to ensure your grand designs are unblemished by hubris? You cannot be your own god unless you have a system by which to frame your morality. These statements you make, they are not rooted in fixing the problems, they are the words of someone afraid of giving up power."

The words hung in the air between them, and Landry finally felt it, the breaking of their friendship. It started as a crack formed when Cassius began to retreat into himself, withdrawing from his personal connection to the people around him. In the end, however, it was the deepening connections Landry made with the few members of his own circle that tore it into a rift. The choices they each made for those around them led to this fracturing. They were shattered by their own loyalties; Landry's to those by his side, Cassius to some unattainable ideal that would drive him mad. What could have been a shared vulnerability became a dividing line in the sand.

Cassius would give everything to save his ideals.

Landry would give nothing that threatened his family.

"You do not begin to understand how I have tried to save all of you." Cassius looked away, caught in the depths of his emotions. "For thousands of years, I have tried to protect you, but even I am not free to follow my own will."

For a moment, Landry was confused by these statements, a feeling of uncertainty preventing his immediate response.

"This is the end for us then." Cassius continued. Sadness and anger were intertwined in these words, spoken barely louder than a whisper but given to the air around them, an open secret for anyone to hear.

"Goodbye, Cassius."

"Goodbye, Landry."

Chapter 9

The desiccated remnants of a hundred dead cacti littered the sand. Kaela asked Landry about it in the aftermath of the conflict. When she pushed the additional energy into Brady to burn through his cellular processes and jump him forward in age, there was a consequence, the eternal give and take, where energy was neither created nor destroyed. She managed to pull the necessary energy from the life sources around her instead of her own body, but plants and at least a few small reptiles paid the price. She learned Landry's first lesson a little too well. It was reckless, using a power she didn't understand. Although the results were surprisingly effective.

Kaela's deranged laughter was still dying on her lips when Landry had appeared behind Hailey's prostrate form. He locked eyes with her, and she swayed, untethered in her relief. There was fury on his face as his stare raked across her body. He paused on the bruised cheek, his expression taking on a feral edge.

Power pulsed from him in palpable waves. Even dozens of feet away, the sensation was akin to standing directly in front of a roaring fire, but Kaela realized that whatever was making her hair stand on end and her neck stiff with tension wasn't a tangible threat, it was the feeling that something was about to happen, as if he were wrapped in layers of potential energy.

The group appeared to be sizing up Landry and considering their options. He paused to check Hailey and then stepped past her, standing just beyond her slumped body, shielding her from what was about to occur. The pulsing around him grew more intense.

An answering hum kicked up to Kaela's right, and she scanned the desert in that direction to find the twins. The female's eyes were closed in concentration, and the male's eyes were fixed on his hand that was extended in front of his body. There was a loud *whoosh*, and a pulsing fireball, two feet across, appeared in his upturned palm. With a dramatic flinging motion, the boy launched the fireball at Landry, and it sizzled through the air, a hissing comet with flames trailing in its wake. The scream of warning died on Kaela's lips when Landry calmly raised his own hand, as if engaging in a game of catch. The fireball reached his fingertips and dissolved into the pulsing aura, first the main body and then the tail. One moment it was there, blindingly bright, and the next it was gone.

Landry swung his arm away in a horizontal arch, flicking the air with the back of his hand. The pulsing paused, air collapsing inwards like the desert was a living thing inhaling a steadying breath. Streaks shot from Landry, visible ripples of energy that shimmered with refracted light. The waves hit each member of the semicircle except for Todd and Kaela, throwing their bodies twenty feet in the air on impact. The concussive crack accompanying this flow of power swept past Kaela. She recoiled, expecting the noise to coincide with a physical force, but she was in a bubble, untouched. Kaela stared in disbelief at the people now strewn across the sand.

Landry's attention fixed on Theodore. To his credit, Theo appeared unperturbed by the turn of events and simply returned the stare, pulling Kaela tighter against his side. Landry scrutinized Theo's hand where it gripped her shoulders, his eyes holding the promise of violence.

In the background, Jackson slowly rose from the sand, angry but hesitant. His wingmen worked their way to his side on slow, gingerly placed feet. Once they were reunited, the whole group edged closer to the unmoving shape of the twins. Landry's gaze shifted back to them, a warning in his eyes.

"So, you found us, Guardian," Jackson's voice called out over the distance, full of spite. "I didn't realize you were claiming her as one of your own. How did you find us, I wonder? I assume I have a spy on my team. It isn't difficult to figure out who that might be."

Jackson's eyes flicked to Theo, and Kaela stiffened. She realized that the concern had been genuine after all. Landry's scowl only deepened.

"Did you come to rescue the good doctor and recruit her into your little elite group? I assume you are building your own army now that your precious Cassius is gone. Too bad she doesn't realize you and the rest of your *special* team will abandon her like you have everyone else that wasn't good enough. You only collect people with bright, shiny morals. Did you see how she tried to kill Brady?"

Jackson clicked his tongue disapprovingly and glanced at Kaela, the pity on his face glaringly disingenuous.

"Don't place your insecurities on her, Jackson," Landry responded calmly. "Your less-than-impressive skill set was just the beginning of our concerns with you. Sometimes a bad apple is just a bad apple, and sometimes self-defense is just self-defense. Kaela did what she had to because you forced the actions from her, but nothing would have made you a better person."

"Always so fucking superior, aren't you?" Jackson sneered.

The twins were on their feet. Theo took the opportunity to whisper in Kaela's ear, and without further warning, a wall of sand shot up around Landry in a thick, swirling cocoon. Theo dropped a kiss on the back of one of Kaela's hands and, before she could react, ran to the tunnel entrance behind the rest of the retreating group.

After Theodore disappeared into the dark opening, the swirling column of sand and the unmoving heap of flesh that was Hailey were Kaela's only remaining companions. Stones continued to rise from the ground, whizzing through the air and pummeling into the cyclone around Landry. Kaela finally snapped free from her shock and rushed to Hailey's side. Each time a stone collided with the barrier above them, it shattered into dust and the particles swept into the whirlwind or rained down into the surrounding desert. Kaela did her best to use her body as a shield while she checked Hailey's vitals; alive, but unconscious.

The pulsing energy began again, beating through the sandstorm in a rapidly increasing tempo. Just as it merged into a continuous screaming pressure, the debris exploded. Kaela hunched over Hailey's face, protecting them both from the fallout. When she looked up, she saw only Landry, covered in a fine film of sand. The three of them were alone on a partially demolished stretch of desert.

Time was an ethereal thing to Kaela. She spoke only a little after the sand settled, asking a few disjointed questions. Then she stood in silence and stared at the dead flora surrounding her. It could have been days since the final encounter, but it was probably closer to an hour. She glanced back over her shoulder.

Hailey's eyes were still closed. Landry had settled her in the shaded part of the sand, her broken arms gingerly positioned at her sides. Kaela insisted on calling an ambulance in the first few moments when the shock was still settling over her. Somehow, Landry's insistence on 'giving Hailey time to wake up' made enough sense that she acquiesced, falling silent not long after. In fact, Kaela couldn't find the words for any of the questions that came to her mind. Instead, she stood in that spot, rooted deep into the sand and staring out at the aftermath of the battle.

She was clutching a water bottle. It likely originated from the open backpack on the ground next to Hailey. Her mind was blank, the bottle simply appearing in her hand. The sweatshirt was tied around her waist. She had no memory of removing it. A slight breeze rippled the thin material of her disheveled evening wear. She needed a change of clothes. And food. All she could do was look at the dead cacti.

Kaela stared and stared at the detritus, knowing she would need to move her body again but unable to do more than lift her hand to sip the tepid, flat water.

"How did you know where to find me?" She felt Landry approaching.

"People have been following you." He stopped just outside of her personal space. "They were interested in your movements, and I suspected they were either part of Jackson's contingent or associated with one of two rogue groups. I thought they would try to snatch you at some point, and I had a hunch they would bring you here. Maria is the light bender who watches over this area. She sent me a message after they grabbed you from the hotel, and then I tracked Hailey's phone to be sure."

"You tracked her phone." Kaela digested this new information. "Why would you have access to something like that?"

"I have access to a lot of resources, Mikaela. I spent centuries building networks. Why wouldn't I be able to track phones?"

"You came here. The light bender, Maria, hid you, and then you walked right up to the group." She replayed the event in her head. "I assume she left as soon as her job was complete to avoid the fighting. Why did you wait until I changed Brady to make yourself known? I felt you, but I couldn't see you."

"You looked right at me," he replied. "How did you know I was there?"

"I always know when you're close by." Kaela struggled with finding words to explain something she didn't begin to understand. "When you get near me, I have this strange dizziness. Is that normal for people like you? Like us?"

"Not that I know of," he replied, head tilted and expression cryptic.

They stared at one another.

"So, why did you wait?"

"I wanted to see if you could do it," Landry finally admitted.

"Did you let them break Hailey into pieces just to see if I was capable of using my abilities?" A disgusted anger rose in her again. "You were here in time to stop them."

"No." He sighed. "I didn't let anyone do anything to Hailey she wasn't prepared for. You'll have to ask her about that when she is awake."

"I'm asking you now." Kaela squared off with him, nostrils flared, and feet planted. "Are you just as bad as the rest of them, torturing an innocent bystander just to 'see if I could do it'?"

"Hailey isn't a bystander. She's a bone setter." Landry stared Kaela down, unyielding despite her vehemence. "She is not responsive right now because she put herself into a healing coma. It's something she's done dozens of times before. When she wakes up, she will have no more broken bones or abrasions. She was here because she chose to be. She painted herself as a victim in order to be close to you."

"What?" Kaela blurted the unintelligent response. "Why would she do that?"

"For starters, she did it because she cares about you." Landry crossed his arms but deflected his stare out at the desert. "She knew this situation would create an opportunity for you to learn how to harness your powers, but she didn't want someone who couldn't heal to be the victim of torture. She thought this was the best way to stay close to you and to also protect you."

"Since I didn't know she would be okay, I don't think it protected me from anything," Kaela snapped back. "That is some seriously messed-up reasoning. They could have killed her."

"I've seen her go through much worse. It wasn't anything she couldn't handle. I would have stepped in sooner if it was."

"I hope you at least had a sign or something in case it was too much." Kaela grumbled, angling her body away from him. "I have very few people in my life to begin with, and now I am finding out that half of them were planted as part of this insane, ridiculous world of yours."

Landry waited patiently beside her.

"Where is this light bender?" Kaela finally broke the silence.

"She left as soon as I was released from her protection. I told her it wouldn't be safe to hang around."

"Were they all immortal once?"

"No." Landry shifted his weight as he structured his response. "Only

Todd and Brady were part of Cassius's group. The others were just children before Cass disappeared. He found them when they showed the signs, tested them to see how they behaved, and then judged them by his own secret standards. He ultimately found them wanting. You heard how bitter that made Jackson. He was a young boy when Cassius and Nisha tested him, but there was something dark and twisted in him that they weren't willing to risk.

"For the first ten or so years after Cassius disappeared, I worked with Nisha to search for Cass, to try and understand what happened. During that time, she told me about the recruits that weren't turned. I helped her hunt them down in case they were in some way connected to Cass's presumed death. That's how I met Jackson. He joined together with other outcasts in a fringe society, but we could find no evidence that these new talents had ever interacted with Cassius. The two younger ones, the boy and the girl, are new to me. Jackson must have found them somewhere and enlisted them. I'm surprised he could find a fire thrower. Most children with those types of destructive abilities accidentally kill themselves not long after they manifest."

"Shouldn't they know Hailey is one of you?"

"No." His expression held a mixture of complicated emotions. "She was kept a secret from most of the others. She was very good at infiltrating the opposition and more useful as a ghost. She fell out of favor with Cassius the same time I did, and she never looked back. She hasn't even seen Nisha in all this time. Theo knew her, but it appears he chose to remain silent for whatever reason."

"So, now there is this rogue group of people with special powers led by Jackson, another group that works for Nisha, and then the random stragglers like you and Hailey. Are there other groups? I'd like to know how many more times I'll be snatched in the night."

"The only others I know of are a group in Spain and a few smaller clusters scattered around the world. The Spanish group was independent for centuries before Cass left, but I haven't heard anything from them in recent years. And they would never associate with Jackson. There is a power vacuum with Cassius gone. I still don't understand the end game for all the players yet."

Kaela let this information process, filing the details away for when she might need them.

"Can each person only do one specific thing with their abilities?"

"Yes and no. Most people can only manifest one particular skill set. It's hard enough to focus your will on a solitary task, much less divide up your control in multiple directions. Theo only focuses on stone, Hailey heals her own body, Maria can manipulate light or at least the perception of it, and Jackson is able to move small objects, similar to telekinesis. More than one of us working together makes things appear more impressive. Moving air and using telekinesis can make quite the sandstorm. We think there is only one real source of power, but it manifests differently for each person based on how they are mentally structured to frame that focus. Sometimes families will show the same type of power across generations, but then you have situations like Maria's light-bending talents, which are very different from the rest of her family. They were all herbalists and healers."

"The One Power." Kaela chuckled, surprised at her ability to find humor after the events of the day, drawing a confused look from Landry. "You can't say these things and then not expect me to make fantasy or superhero references. Never mind. Why can you do multiple things?"

"At the core of it, my ability is just a manipulation of matter at an atomic level. So, it isn't really a multifaceted ability, just a widely applicable one." He shrugged as if admitting to a natural athletic ability or a hidden vocal talent. "I can create a surplus of energy doing something small and then carry that energy into initiating another reaction that returns even more energy at the end. Linking together sequential reactions provides enough energy for a big final output, like shattering a giant boulder or throwing someone across a desert. It's a butterfly effect. Or, if I have a big enough energy source to start with, I can simplify the process.

"That fireball earlier required all the metabolic energy those two youths could pull from their own bodies. She manipulated the air to create a flammable gas pocket, and he initiated the spark. I would guarantee they didn't know what they were doing, but they have a physical limit when they do that type of demonstration. When that fireball reached me, I diverted the energy into the movement of the molecules around me, and I threw out waves of compacted air. The energy source wasn't my own body. I can also create an aura around myself that holds potential energy like a battery. It allows me to collect that first needed bit of power to start a reaction ahead of time."

“I could feel it around you when you first appeared.” Kaela’s body shivered with the memory of that hidden power. “You were pulsing with it. I understand the basic concepts of what you are telling me, but there are dozens of holes in your explanations.”

“If it were a simple scientific process, anyone could do it.” Landry surveyed her skeptical expression. “These are the easiest explanations I have for what is happening. I know they don’t hold water at the formulaic level, but it helps add a framework to my ability and some rules for its use. That is probably what keeps me from blowing myself up or bleeding all the energy from my body.”

“When I did… whatever I did, with the orchid in your room yesterday, some of that energy came from within me?” Kaela thought back to how tired she felt afterwards. “Then today, I pulled what I needed from around me instead.”

“It would seem so. Usually, that requires time and discipline to understand the connectivity and make use of it. With practice, you could learn to pull just a bit from each living thing to keep from killing them.”

“And can I pull energy from another person?” she asked, slightly horrified by the answer that might be waiting.

“Yes.” Landry looked away; his voice heavy as he admitted this. “Not many people realize that’s possible. Most don’t even realize plants and animals are sources of energy. They continue to pull from within. We never taught anyone to do otherwise. It was a way of keeping them controlled.”

“Keeping them from becoming killers, you mean.”

Kaela’s words sliced through the air even though they came out as little more than a whisper. She could have killed someone today. She could have done it at any point in time without even understanding what she was doing. Landry’s grimace at her final statement remained. His mind was preoccupied with a series of memories and blank spaces that continued to haunt him.

“You worked for Cassius. Nisha was his longtime partner. When he disappeared, you and Nisha went your separate ways. Then, somehow, Theo is in the picture and he is helping Nisha. The people today were a fringe group, but Theo is helping them, too. If you don’t think Nisha is involved in what happened today, Theo must be bouncing around, hoping that someone will be successful at making him live forever.”

Kaela dismissed thoughts of Nisha and returned to the reality of her current situation. She was abducted from a reasonably public area. She was restrained and transported for hours in a car against her will. She was made to watch as her friend was tortured. She could have easily died by those same hands or in the ensuing firefight, and no one would have found her body as it crumbled to dust in this desert.

Kaela closed her eyes and took a deep breath. Bile rose in the back of her throat, but she swallowed it down. Tiny tremors passed through her muscles as the last of her adrenaline faded into an exhausted combination of shock and dehydration.

"May I touch you?" Landry was still at arm's length, but his eyes roved her face and shoulders as he asked this.

She nodded.

He stepped forward, his movements slow and cautious as if approaching a wild creature. His hands were gentle when he gripped her shoulders.

"You went through a lot today."

"I should thank you for coming to my rescue—again." Kaela tilted her chin up, submitting herself to the comfort of his touch. "I know that I am stubborn and proud, but I also know that if it weren't for you, the situation would have been even worse for me in the end."

"If they did anything to hurt you, I would have killed every last one of them." The muscles in Landry's face tightened in anger, and she knew beyond any doubt that he was telling the truth. "I haven't formed a connection with anyone new in many, many years. I'm out of practice. If you'll let me, I'll do a better job of keeping you safe from now on."

Some knot in Kaela loosened at these words, and she felt tears forming at the corners of her eyes. She blinked them away, regaining her composure before responding.

"I'm not used to people going out of their way to protect me." She offered him a crooked smile and rested her hands on the outside of his forearms. "But to be honest, I've never been in mortal danger before. I want to tell you I'm more than capable of taking care of myself, but that is painfully untrue at the moment."

"Yes, well. The most difficult part of taking care of you will be the part where you let me do it." He gave a gentle laugh and brought his head lower, delivering the next words in close proximity. "You don't like accepting help."

“It wouldn’t be any fun if you didn’t work for it.” Her lips trembled as she attempted a flippant smile.

“I’ll help you learn to protect yourself, too.”

Kaela gave a slight nod of her head in agreement. Landry’s breath was a steady, comforting rhythm when she sank against him. His arms were firm, reassuring in their strength. She pulled him into her, using the press of his body to smother the aftershock of the morning’s violence. Her head swam, and she became aware of every inch of contact between them.

“Good thing I’m not on my deathbed while the two of you are canoodling out here.”

Kaela shoved Landry away and lurched in the direction of the voice, an instinctive motion. Hailey was standing just a few yards away, her arms remarkably whole where they were crossed against her chest. Without a second thought, Kaela dove into her, wrapping her in a hug and drinking in her shocked laughter.

“I thought you weren’t a hugger,” Hailey mumbled into Kaela’s shoulder.

“I thought they were going to kill you.” Kaela’s joy abruptly soured as she remembered what Landry had revealed. She pulled back and ran her hands hesitantly over Hailey’s forearms. “Are you okay now? Did you heal? And why the hell didn’t you tell me who you are? Do you even understand how screwed up that was to watch them beat you and not realize you would be okay? And who says canoodling?”

“That is a lot to process all at once, my friend,” Hailey replied with an intense, reassuring look. “I’m fine. I didn’t tell you because you are a terrible actor and would have given me away. Also, it’s a weird conversation. ‘Hey, Kaela. Today, we’re working on your abysmal box jumping skills. Also, I used to be immortal.’”

Kaela lifted an eyebrow at the snarky tone.

“I assume that you have no food in your stomach, and we need to find some before we both have hanger-induced meltdowns,” Hailey continued. “I can tell you about everything over some breakfast tacos.”

“It’s nearly noon.” Landry approached her, his expression filled with relief. “But we can still have tacos.”

“Glad you finally decided to show up to the party this morning.” Hailey gave him a quick embrace. “Those guys were dicks. I thought there would be a little more foreplay before they got down to the bone-breaking. Well, you showed up before it got too hardcore. That’s what matters.”

"You seemed to be having a good time, and I didn't want to interrupt." Landry held her elbows, and they stood together for a long, comfortable moment.

"You know that was a cakewalk compared to other times," Hailey's voice dropped as she said this, but she was quick to return to the lighthearted banter. "Should we head back into town now?"

"I need clothes and a shower, but I'm fine starting with food," Kaela replied, too overcome with relief that her friend was uninjured to argue.

Getting out of the desert was a matter of hiking back through the oasis then taking a short path that led to a different parking area. Kaela trudged along, continually glancing at Hailey's arms as they swung by her sides, struggling against the feeling of wrongness that the scenario provoked. At what point would her brain adjust to this new reality and accept the things that were happening at face value?

Landry drove them to the 'town' which turned out to be a set of semi-dilapidated buildings clustered together near the entrance to a small grid of trailers. The restaurant may have once been an old gas station. The whitewashed walls of the rectangular building gleamed alongside freshly painted wood pillars; a roadside dive if there ever was one.

"I know it doesn't look like much." Landry turned his bright emerald eyes to Kaela as he unfolded his long body from the vehicle. "But they serve the most exquisite albondigas. If you aren't in the mood for something hot, I'd recommend the turkey sandwich."

"You must be joking," was all she could think of saying. "I worry that I should have gotten a preemptive Hep A booster."

"I've known the owners of this restaurant for a long time," Landry responded lightly, clearly unbothered by her skepticism. "The current owner is Maria, but I knew her mother, her grandmother, and her great-grandmother."

"Why do you know the family so well?" Kaela was annoyed by the inappropriate flare of jealousy in her stomach.

"When you live for many, many years, meeting the various types of people that make their way through life, finding a person or group of people who are genuine in their actions as well as their words is a meaningful event."

Kaela stared at Landry, wondering exactly what type of person he thought himself to be.

"I will literally starve to death while the two of you discuss this." Hailey grumbled. "Just come inside and we can eat while you try to connect on a deeply human level. I could consume thirty enchiladas and still not make up for my calorie deficit."

"You know I hate it when you say 'literally', Hailey." Landry abruptly turned and followed her through the doorway. "Because you never use it correctly."

Kaela's laughter faded as they stepped through the door into a peculiar blend of roadside diner and college dive bar. Old wooden booths lined the walls, and rickety metal folding tables draped in checkered plastic tablecloths filled the open floor. Posters advertising hunting competitions were taped to the plaster, displaying endorsements for various bird hunting competitions and something called 'Dove Season.' The dining room was empty other than an older couple at a table tucked into the farthest corner from the door.

A woman approached, the sharp observational intensity with which she tracked every movement in the room revealing her as the proprietor of the establishment.

"Maria." Landry rested his hands on the woman's shoulders, leaning down to place a light, respectful kiss on her cheek. "*¿Cómo has estado?*"

"*Bueno, ahí vamos.*" She patted Landry on the cheek, a tender maternal gesture which was in striking contrast to the disapproving look she turned on Hailey. "And I see you've managed to come out of captivity unscathed."

"*¿Qué tal?*" Hailey bumped Maria's bicep with a fist. "You know I'm good at handling a little rough play."

"It was a stupid risk to take, *Chavita*." The older woman gestured for them to follow, mumbling additional chastisements under her breath until they reached a booth. "I'm sorry for the other customers. They are almost finished. When they leave, I will lock up until you are done talking."

"*¡No hay bronca!*" Hailey offered a shaka with her right hand as she responded.

Maria just shook her head, the picture of exasperated patience.

"Please don't apologize, Maria. We should be thanking you for your hospitality."

Landry shot a warning look at Hailey, who miraculously remained quiet as Maria patted Landry's hand and walked away. Kaela glanced between her two companions, then slid onto a bench seat. Landry settled next to her in the booth. When Hailey slid onto the opposite bench, Kaela's eyes snagged on her arms.

"Are you in any pain? I still haven't forgiven you, if I'm being honest, but seeing you go through… well, seeing what they did to you takes most of the anger out of me."

"Please, always be honest." Hailey reached across the table to take Kaela's hand. "I will return the favor. I was involved in wars, Kaela. I have been a prisoner and suffered things that you would not begin to understand. I chose to be the victim for this encounter because I know that after everything I endured in my past lives for various causes, a little man with an ego issue breaking a few bones wasn't going to be a terrible hardship for me. I know my limits. This was nowhere close to exceeding them."

"You don't deserve that, any of it." Kaela's thoughts traveled into the dark recesses of her mind, where scenes of torture and war crimes collected over a lifetime of cinematic depictions were stored. "You might be a jerk for hiding the truth from me, but no one should endure those things for any reason."

"I chose to go through them because I thought the end results were worth the temporary pain." She squeezed Kaela's hand, then broke contact. "I was never forced to do something I didn't want to do. And if we are going to get into the heavy details of my past, I am going to order a big serving of tequila with my enchiladas."

"Fair enough." Kaela blinked back the wetness gathering at the corners of her eyes to peruse the strange assortment of American and Mexican food tangoing across the pages of the menu. "Food and tequila first. Unpacking our various emotional baggage second."

Hailey released a loud guffaw, and Landry gave a side-eyed wince.

"Food and tequila it is," he agreed, nodding to Maria and watching as she sent a young woman over to take their order. "And remind me to get something from Maria for those terrible bruises on your face and shoulder. I don't know what happened when they were grabbing you from that hotel, but you certainly put up a fight."

Kaela blushed and focused on her menu to avoid explaining that she didn't fight with anything other than the elevator during her abduction. After placing an obscenely large order of food, Hailey took up an easy sprawl and fixed her eyes on Landry. Landry leaned back with just enough tension in his body to give the impression that he could uncoil at any second. He alternated between monitoring the surroundings and returning Hailey's stare.

With their actions no longer driven by the urgency to secure food, Kaela became painfully aware of her disheveled dress and the shivering weakness of her joints, residual trauma from being tied up in the back of someone's car only hours before. Yet here she sat, waiting for a plate of tacos. A strangled laugh spilled out of her at the absurdity.

Hailey broke from her sharp focus on Landry long enough to give Kaela a small, understanding look. Landry placed an arm across her shoulders, the weight of him reassuring. Kaela's laugh trickled away, and she leaned her head back, staring up at the air ducts and electrical wiring in the open ceiling. She traced a conduit with her eyes.

Deep breath.

She felt the flow of oxygen into her lungs, reminding her that energy moved through her, power that could be harnessed.

Deep breath.

She was safe now. She would learn to protect herself.

"Why is it that everyone who hates you calls you 'Guardian'?" As her body settled, the questions fluttering in and out of Kaela's awareness began to assemble themselves into a more organized stream for investigation.

"They mean it as an insult." Landry shrugged as he stated this obvious fact. "It is a term over a hundred years old for a specific collection of people Cassius surrounded himself with. I led one of the teams that were part of this. We were intensely invested in the direction of society and saw ourselves as protectors or 'guardians' of humanity. Others gave up on making the world a better place and broke away from Cass."

"Guardians of… never mind." Kaela discarded the joke halfway through. "It's increasingly difficult to avoid superhero references when you say things like that. You were one hundred percent serious about the small changes across centuries. Where is the rest of your secret organization of immortals?"

"May I just say that you being in the know about our superpowers makes me incredibly happy." Hailey chuckled as she finished off her third glass of water and refilled it from the pitcher sitting on the table. "Landry and the others were always too serious for my taste. No one ever appreciated my humor. I think you and I will be wonderful allies in tormenting him from now on."

“I have a wealth of pop culture references on this topic.” Kaela grinned at the look of disapproval firmly stamped on Landry’s face in reaction to their irreverence. “Marvel, DC, you name it. I dated a comic nerd once, and I have a natural ability to retain information.”

“I would rather you call it magic or witchcraft.” Landry grumbled and Hailey giggled.

“If you’ll excuse me, I have over-hydrated.” Hailey was still chuckling as she slipped out of the booth.

“She hasn’t always been this flippant,” Landry volunteered after Hailey was out of earshot. “She went through a very dark period after the second world war. We both did. I am glad to see how much she enjoys your company. I hope you’ll forgive the deception we played on you. I didn’t see another way.”

“I’m getting over it,” Kaela replied with honesty, still leaning into his arm on the back of the bench but reaching over to also take his free hand. “I like that you’re protective. What I don’t like is you making imperious decisions about my well-being. You are not charged with taking care of me like a parent. What you can do is talk to me about what you think is happening or what the best course of action might be. I know I am the world’s biggest skeptic, but I can’t deny this anymore. Just don’t hide things from me, okay?”

“Okay.” He relaxed a little and gave her hand a reassuring squeeze. “There is a lot for you to catch up on, though. Please be patient if I accidentally omit things that I should explain from time to time.”

Hailey’s return coincided with the delivery of their food, three glasses, and one large bottle of tequila. Hailey shoveled down an entire enchilada in three bites, then started pouring drinks for everyone before Kaela managed more than a mouthful. The unblemished wholeness of her arm when she slid a glass of tequila across the table surface still caused a fuzzy disorientation in Kaela’s mind, a glitch in her ability to process reality from dream.

“Are you the only ‘bone setter’?” Silence met Kaela’s question for a long moment.

“No, there was another bone setter before,” Hailey finally offered, holding up her tequila glass in a resigned salute. “Guess it’s time to get started on the heavy talk then. Cheers!”

“You don’t have to.” The reassurance rolled softly out of Landry’s mouth, and Kaela marveled at the tender concern in his voice.

“It has been long enough.” Hailey was sad but firm. “I can handle the retelling.” She took a swig from her glass. “Her name was Cleda. She was born in the 1700s in Salem, Massachusetts. I’m sure you’ve heard of it. If she was born fifty years earlier, the witch trials would have caught someone with real abilities instead of just chasing superstition. I met her after Cass brought her into the fold. The two of us were inseparable until she died. She couldn’t heal herself, you see, only others. I can’t heal anyone else, just my own body. We were the worst pair to get caught in a bad situation together, but there you have it.”

Hailey swallowed the rest of her tequila, refilled the glass, and stared at Landry with her eyebrows raised in challenge. He said nothing but didn’t look away either. She switched to a sour expression and shrugged. She gazed blankly across the room as she continued speaking.

“We had the exact same ability, even though we directed it differently. That’s why we think you could do the same as Cassius. He was able to act on himself and on others. It stands to reason you could do any combination therein. We just don’t know what you’re capable of yet.”

“I’m sorry, Hailey.” Kaela struggled to think of the right words to express the tangle of emotions that had formed in her chest. “Loss never goes away. It fades a little with time, but then you just feel guilty when the memories hurt less.”

Hailey’s eyes flicked back to her, expression softening. They briefly clasped their hands across the table, and Kaela picked up her own glass of tequila, raising it without voicing the implied toast. All three of them drank in silent acknowledgement.

“I realize I’ve paid you to be a companion in the past,” Kaela said. “And that you were spying on me without my knowledge. But for what it’s worth, I’m glad that we are friends. I really do appreciate what you did for me this morning, even if I disagree with some of the details.”

“You paid me to guilt you into extra planks, and I wasn’t spying so much as monitoring. The friendship was just a really nice perk.”

They shared another look across the table.

“Do the two of you need to be alone?” Landry broke in. “There are some big emotions flying around this table for two of the most aloof, detached women I know.”

They shared a laugh, the tension and seriousness of the exchange relieved as Landry continued. “I don’t think that group will come for

Mikaela again anytime soon after what she demonstrated. They're too afraid of death or winding up like Brady to risk it. They'll regroup and strategize with whoever their ringleader is before making any more moves."

"And who is the ringleader?" Hailey asks around a mouthful of her meal. "That is the million-dollar question. Jackson doesn't have the connections to know about her. There is someone else."

"We'll figure it out," Landry responded.

Kaela shook her head as a feeling of disbelief flared again. "All this for immortality."

"Mikaela," Landry faced her. "There is nothing some people wouldn't do to achieve immortality. Don't trust anyone. Don't believe anything. You must always be on your guard if you want to navigate whatever happens now that we all know you exist and what you can do."

We. Now that we know you exist.

Kaela looked at Landry and then across the table to Hailey. They were both accustomed to the idea of living forever. They should be just as desperate as the others after twenty years of facing their own mortality.

"Mikaela?" Landry was looking at her as if waiting for an answer.

"I'm sorry, I was lost in thought. What did you say?"

"Are you okay with having someone clear out our hotel rooms and bring everything here instead of the other way around? We can stay with Maria's family and then take a flight from the Palm Springs airport tomorrow."

"Yes," she answered, trying her best not to appear distracted. "That's probably the better way to do it. I'll need a new phone, too."

"We can take care of that." He waved his hand dismissively as if this were a common request. "They can bring a new one to you after getting it set up."

"Well," Hailey grinned broadly at the two of them, "that calls for another round of drinks before we head off to the showers."

Kaela returned her smile, but the last words that Theo whispered in her ear before he escaped echoed through her mind.

Trust no one. I'll see you soon.

Germany – 1954

Something sharp was pressing into Landry's side. He shifted to alleviate the pressure against his ribs and realized that it was his own elbow causing his discomfort. He turned onto his back, exhaling in pain as a heavy pounding set in behind his eyes. His left arm was cold and numb. When he tried to place a hand on his forehead, he slapped himself across the nose with the unfeeling appendage. It must have been pinched beneath him. He opened his eyes and shook his head in an attempt to clear the heavy cobwebs from his thoughts.

He remembered meeting with Kofi, but nothing else.

Everything hurt. His arms and legs were lead anchors, pinning him to the cold, hard floor. He moved the fingers of his right hand, letting them caress the smooth surface of the floor under him. Marble or a similar polished stone met his touch. A shuffling revealed someone past his feet. Another noise, this one on the opposite side of his body. Two people at a minimum.

"Welcome back, my boy."

Cassius's deep voice washed over Landry. He couldn't quite believe the sound for what it was. Nine years. He had not heard one word, not received a single letter, from him in nearly a decade. Yet he knew that voice from the first syllable that left Cass's lips. Landry slowly drew himself up to sitting, waiting for the throbbing in his brain to subside before looking around. Cassius stood close to him, his face a grimace of concern.

From the looks of the oversized fireplace and grand piano, they were in the sitting room of a large house. Landry's eyes moved to the other occupant of the room, and he couldn't stop the reflexive straightening of his spine nor the deep scowl that contorted his features.

"I'm glad to see that my presence still brings you joy, Landry."

The words were spoken by a tall, slender female with rich caramel skin and wide-set eyes. Landry's expression took a feral edge, his lips retracting to a sneer. She merely tilted her head in amusement.

"Why do I wake up in the company of your pet mind bender with a surprising gap in my memories?" Landry leveled the accusation at Cassius even as he continued to stare at the subject of his malcontent.

"I did not have her enter your mind," Cassius stated, giving the woman a warning glance as she hissed at Landry. "She was here in case I needed her when you awoke. She will keep her fingers to herself, won't you, Ramla?"

"He never took issue with my wandering fingers before." Ramla blinked her long black lashes and bared her teeth in an aggressive grin.

"Your noncorporeal fingers, my dear." Cassius gave her another stern stare. "And please refrain from goading him."

She huffed and dropped loosely into an upholstered armchair sitting near the fire. She threw one leg across the other and appraised Landry with a mischievous smirk. Landry did his best to dismiss her and focused on getting himself off the floor. The ground shifted beneath his unsteady legs, but he stubbornly rooted through his feet and straightened. He suppressed a groan as his joints stretched back into their normal positions.

"I suppose placing me on a soft surface was too much to ask for?"

Cassius chuckled and held out a glass of water.

"You were unconscious for a few hours while we drove here. You were only on the floor for a few minutes. I am certain you have survived worse."

Landry took the offered drink, and they stared at one another in silent anticipation. "Why am I here, Cass? I thought our separation was quite clear all those years ago."

Cassius frowned, his eyes shifting between Landry and Ramla. Finally, he gave her a pointed look and a directional nod, a silent order. Ramla blew Landry a kiss and then left through a set of tall, curved doors. When they were alone, Cassius faced his former protégé. Landry ran his fingers over his face, inspecting a nasty scab beginning to form across one cheek.

"I have kept an eye on you ever since you left my side." Cassius waved away Landry's aggrieved grunt as he said this. "I know I can be overbearing at times, but it did come from a place of concern. Truth be told, I intended to confront you this past evening, but I did not time my arrival well. You had already left your room, and I had to search you out. When I found you, you were in such a state, and I chose to bring you here until you recovered."

"But what happened, and where did you take Kofi? Is he waiting in another room while we have our reunion?"

Cassius paused, considering Landry's tone of voice and posture. "No, Kofi is dead. It would seem he did not survive your misguided plan of revenge."

Silence filled the room as Landry digested these statements. He oscillated between anger, sadness, and confusion as he scraped his brain for memories of the night's events. Vague images floated around, ghostly specters that were too fragile and insubstantial to stay when he tried to hold them in his mind.

He and Kofi had set out to kill the last of the men tied to the military operation that tortured Elizabeth and killed Cleda. The last 'Doctor' responsible for that atrocity was supposed to be at home, surrounded by his family. When they went into the building, they found too many men confronting them. The intel was faulty. After that, he couldn't piece together the storyline. He thought that he had panicked and attempted to neutralize a full room of people at once, but then his memory faded to a black uncertainty.

"You know this beyond any doubt?" Landry finally asked.

"Yes, I saw it with my own eyes. He is dead."

Landry instantly lost the little energy he had recovered and found his way over to the recently vacated chair, slumping defeatedly into it.

"He was a good man."

"He was," Cassius sympathized, moving to the other chair.

"How did it happen?"

"I do not know." Cassius paused as if deciding how much to share but Landry was too deep in his own thoughts to notice this odd response. "It appeared that one of your enemies managed to kill him before you finished the man off in return."

"Did we get our target?" Landry fought against the darkness, his mental fingers running through the barrier like water, unable to gain any traction to force the remembrance. "Did Kofi die for nothing?"

"From what we could see, there were no survivors other than you. I sent several men to clean up the mess, and we removed you. I was not sure what to expect when you awoke, but I am glad we arrived before you could have been taken into custody or entangled with the local police. There was no saving him, Landry."

Landry nodded and regarded the hearth, remembering other nights over the centuries that he spent with Cassius in a similar tableau, mourning their losses. It was stunning how quickly he could fall back into a rhythm with this person he had known nearly all of his long life. He let Kofi's loss ache within him for a few long moments before he tucked the feeling away.

He would mourn the man when he was able, but for now, he needed to confront the matter at hand. He and Cass exchanged many words in anger the last time they spoke. He still didn't understand how any of this happened, and yet here he was, letting the deceptive calm of familiarity dull his reactions.

"Why do I not remember what happened if you didn't have her *work on me while I was incapacitated?"*

"Your brain does not want to remember. Or perhaps it can't. Sometimes the human mind only holds the information that it can understand and rejects the balance. You should not dwell on it too long."

"Swear to me that you have not been meddling in my brain, Cass."

"I swear it to you."

Landry leaned forward, his eyes riveted to the man he once considered a father.

"Did I kill Kofi?"

Cassius turned back to him sharply. "We both know you are responsible for his being there tonight."

"Do not lecture me. You know what had to be done."

"You have spent ten years killing in cold blood," Cass's voice lowered as they waded into the familiar territory of an old argument.

"No, I spent five years helping my sister piece herself back together, then another five helping her get revenge." Landry stood, no longer interested in rehashing old feelings. "It is justice."

"You act as if you are the head member of a vigilance committee."

"Isn't that exactly how you always operated, Cass? It is precisely why you surrounded yourself with yes-men and soldiers who do not have the faculties for reason. You cannot deny me this since I am not yours to command. I will take my leave. Thank you for the help, though it was a misplaced effort. Clearly, we still do not see eye to eye."

"You killed the last one, Landry. You took your revenge in full, and you have broken my heart with the selfishness of it. Let this be an end to the killing and let this be an end to us if it is what you desire. I will not chase you. You will behave by the same rules as those we endure in Seville, and I will suffer you to continue life as an outcast."

"You have not changed," Landry snarled the accusation.

"And you have. Perhaps you do not shoulder the same burdens that your conscience once found heavy, but do not forget the price of your

revenge. Kofi's death is yours to bear. Perhaps that mark on your face will remind you until you find a healer to erase it."

Landry turned and left. He did not acknowledge Ramla when she made a snide comment in the hallway. He ignored the guards near the entrance who nervously watched him. He walked out into the night, set on putting as much distance between himself and Cassius as he could before figuring out how to get back home to Elizabeth. All the while, Cass's words lingered with him, burning their truth into the darkness.

"His death is yours to bear."

Chapter 10

The pavement in front of the house dropped to a sandy walkway, and Kaela stumbled forward in a graceless lurch at the unexpected change in elevation. She tossed an embarrassed look back at Landry and Hailey, who were following close behind. Hailey's idea of one more round had turned into two more rounds. Kaela was just tipsy enough to feel no remorse for the early afternoon indulgence and just sober enough to realize she should start drinking water if she wanted to be a functional human being for the rest of the day. Hailey laughed at the misstep, a tittering, juvenile sound, and then proceeded to botch the transition as well. Landry held back a reprimand, choosing to move around them and open the front door instead.

"Thank you, sir," Kaela remarked, stepping into the uninteresting and sparsely decorated living room.

"*Ew*, this air is stale." Hailey followed and wrinkled her nose, looking around at the less-than-contemporary furniture with distaste. "Does anyone live here?"

"They keep it for visiting family." Landry ignored Hailey's disgust and checked the thermostat. "It doesn't get much use."

"Well, I'm sure we can find a candle or air freshener somewhere. If we have running water and soap for the shower, I'm happy." Kaela turned a bright look to Hailey, who squinted her eyes in mock annoyance at the chipper retort.

"Well, you two have fun in your five-star accommodation. I'm going to stay with Maria." Hailey turned to leave, giving Kaela a devilish grin and speaking a little too loudly. "I have a long shower and some additional sleep to take care of, and I don't expect to hear from either of you until many hours from now when you surface for dinner." Before Kaela could say anything in return, Hailey closed the door.

A knot formed in Kaela's stomach as she became acutely aware that she and Landry were unchaperoned. The previous night in his hotel room could have been a lifetime ago, but just the thought of it made her skin crawl.

“You can shower first.” Her voice was a bit higher than planned, and she fought against a blush in her cheeks at the realization.

“If you’d like.” He looked at her, his expression unreadable. “I think they provided some clothing in the bedroom. As much as I like seeing you in that dress and my sweatshirt, it might be time for a wardrobe change. Maria told me she left a jar of ointment in the bathroom. Her sister, Marlene, is an herbalist and said that it will take care of your bruises.”

“That was thoughtful.”

The silence between them had the tension of an overstretched rubber band. Kaela didn’t know where to look. Landry angled his head ever so slightly in amusement and then retreated to the bedroom without further discussion. When he was no longer standing in front of her, Kaela’s heart rate dropped into a normal range, but the memory of his skin beneath her hands kept her palms clammy. She shook herself and stalked to the kitchen, rummaging through the cabinet for a clean glass.

The tap water was flat. The odd metallic flavor twanged against the back of her tongue, but she gulped it down and looked out at the empty stretch of sand on display through the window over the sink. The stillness was unnerving. She pulled the blinds and turned her back to it, surveying the interior of the home instead. It was a tiny structure, barely larger than a double-wide trailer but probably stick-built.

Kaela could practically hear her dad complaining about the cramped wall spacing and the low ceilings. This would not have counted as ‘good bones’ for him. The constant click and flow of a respirator echoed in her head, but this was not the time for those memories. She refilled her glass and squished them down.

In the living room, she situated herself in an overstuffed armchair, attempting to relax while she waited for her turn in the bathroom. The side table hosted a stack of three books, and she slid her eyes across the spines. The first was the Bible. Underneath was a guide to desert wildlife. The final book was written entirely in Spanish, but careful extraction from the bottom of the stack revealed the bare torso of a man with smoldering brown eyes offering her a rose on the cover. She skimmed a few pages, disappointed that her Spanish wasn’t better.

The rattling of water in old pipes distracted her with a shockingly detailed mental image of Landry in the shower. Kaela closed her eyes and took a long, slow breath. She pulled her lower lip into her mouth, picking at the skin with her teeth. She wasn't accustomed to these feelings. There were plenty of attractive men in her life over the years with whom she went on dates and had physical relationships. Maybe plenty was an overstatement, but there had been Todd and a few other one-off dinners. The point was, they did not drive her to distraction. She never found herself silently salivating in a daydream over nice abs and devastatingly attractive eyes. What had gotten into her?

"I left you plenty of hot water." Landry stepped out of the now open bathroom door, ushering a wave of steam into the room with him.

Kaela twitched in surprise and opened her eyes. He stood in the hall, shirtless but with loose sweatpants slung low across his hips, rubbing the moisture from his hair with a towel. She couldn't stop herself from staring. He lowered the towel and gave her an impish, quizzical expression.

"You still want a shower, don't you?" Kaela stood up too quickly, attempting to regain her composure as she set the book on the table and walked stiffly to the bedroom. "Let me know if you need help."

Her spine stiffened further at the teasing, and she blindly grabbed the stack of clothes from the edge of the mattress, rushing into the small bathroom with a desperation to close the door between them. A floral shower curtain dangled precariously from a thin gold curtain rod above a cream-colored tub. The squares of porcelain crawling along the wall from behind the little pedestal sink into the tub area were dusky rose. They were marbled with darker veins that matched the mauve of the carpeting that covered everything from the toilet lid to sections of the flooring. She had stepped into a time capsule from the 1970s.

The pipes restarted their loud protest when Kaela turned the knob above the faucet. She began stripping out of her disgusting clothing, frowning at the sand stuck to her skin beneath the fabric. She took inventory of her physical condition as she stepped into the shower. Her shoulder and hip were turning a deep purple where she hit the wall and floor of the hotel elevator. Her fingers lightly traced the surface of the bruised skin, the panic of not breathing and the pain of the impact flitted across her mind as phantom sensations.

Kaela refused to let the thoughts take root, refused to feel like a victim. After she scrubbed every inch of her body and her skin was approaching the color of the wall tiles, she turned off the water. The pile of fabric she snatched off the bed contained a full set of clothes that were small and likely intended for her, along with a large men's T-shirt that was clearly meant for Landry. She once again ran hot and cold as her mind conjured the sight of him in nothing but sweatpants.

Two could play that game.

Before leaving the bathroom, Kaela risked a glimpse into the mirror. Her cheekbone was tender, but the discoloration was less dramatic than she originally imagined. There was a jar on the counter, and when she unscrewed the lid, an unusual combination of sweet and bitter fragrances wafted into her nostrils. She dabbed a small amount on the magenta half circle under her eye and gasped when the skin instantly returned to a normal beige tone. A quick slathering of the unguent across the side of her face removed all evidence of her injuries in seconds. Kaela shook her head in disbelief. How much money could someone make off such a treatment? She began to wonder what else these people kept secret from the rest of the world.

Landry was sprawled carelessly on the couch, reading the trashy romance novel as she returned to the living room.

"This book is very graphic. I can't believe Maria—" He stopped talking when he finally looked up.

The oversized shirt ended just below the apex of her thighs, and her long bare legs were on full display. Her hair was damp, leaving little drips across the shoulders of the white material. Landry's eyes slowly trailed down to her toes and back up to the jar of cream in her hand. He closed the book and placed it on the couch next to him without blinking. His nostrils flared as if scenting the air.

Kaela held out the ointment.

"You did offer your help, didn't you?" She raised an eyebrow in what she hoped was a sultry expression. He stood, moving closer with measured steps.

"I certainly did." He stopped a foot away.

"My side and shoulder are a bit difficult to reach." Kaela kept her face relaxed, but her heart thundered as he retrieved the small jar from her hand and traced the neckline of her shirt with one finger.

"A little hard to get to at the moment."

Kaela slid the shirt over her head and turned to the side, listening to the sharp intake of air from Landry as she stood in front of him, fully bare. He slowly, painstakingly, unscrewed the lid of the container and dipped his fingers inside.

“That’s quite an impressive salve,” she nervously filled the silence. “Do you have cures for every potential ailment?”

“Most, but not every.” His voice was tight, restrained, as his ointment-laden fingers traced her collarbone and glided across the top of her shoulder, eliciting an eruption of goosebumps. “What we don’t currently have could easily be made, though. Herbalists can treat anything from bacteria or viruses to simple physical trauma.”

“Is that how you remain alive, after all this time?” An involuntary hiss of pleasure fought to escape her lips as his fingers wandered below her arm to her exposed ribcage. His fingers lingered over the tattoo crossing her side. The slow tracing of his skin against her threatened to drive all reasonable thoughts from her head. “You can still become sick, but the herbalists treat whatever you may contract in order to keep you healthy?”

“Yes and no.” Kaela didn’t remember either of them moving, but somehow Landry was now close enough that his breath caressed her neck just below her ear. His touch still followed the inked feathers along her ribs, and the dull pounding in her core started to shift into a throbbing need. “We are incredibly resistant to infection, but if it occurs, our herbalists are more than capable of curing us. I am not without vulnerability, of course. If you wanted to cut open my throat right now, no healer would be able to save me in time. We could always die, even when we didn’t age.”

As he said this, Landry brought his mouth close enough to her ear that his teeth brushed against the outer shell. Kaela shuddered, keeping her head carefully turned away from him, forcing herself to focus on the empty, white wall across the room to gain some level of control over her body.

“Do any of your treatments only work on immortals?”

“No.” Landry pulled back, staring down at her face, though she still refused to meet his eyes.

“But you choose not to provide the world with these medicines? You could cure malaria, cure AIDS, but yet you keep these treatments for yourselves.”

His hands rested against her hip, where he had been applying more salve. He lifted his fingers to her jaw and gently turned her head, meeting her defiant stare without shame.

“If we gave the world a cure, they would pick it apart to determine why it worked. When they couldn’t find a reason, they would ban it from use. No government agency would approve a treatment without a specific mode of action and a decade of supporting scientific study. It would be relegated to back-alley exchanges and illegal medicinal shop sales. Who do you think would benefit from that? The world is not ready for medical miracles. Maybe it will never be. Don't you think if there was a chance, a legitimate way to save all those lives without endangering our own, I would take it?"

Emotions flitted across his face. Frustration and pain were visible one second but gone the next. Her thoughts softened as she followed the change.

"I'm sorry. I should have given you more credit than that."

He nodded, then replaced the lid on the jar of ointment as he moved away, setting it on the kitchen counter. When he turned back, he managed to keep his eyes on her face despite the fact that she was still unclothed.

"You left it to me to decide what I wanted from you after I got to know you better." Kaela shifted forward, closing half of the distance and waiting.

"Yes, I did." He remained motionless, eyes now locked on her lips.

"Are you going to make me say it?" Kaela tilted her head up and stepped even closer. Landry's face was now angled down, and their lips were less than an inch apart, sharing the same air. The heat of his body was a gentle caress on her naked flesh.

"Yes." His voice was even, but his breath was ragged.

"I would like this." Kaela let one of her hands trail down his body until it rested against the hard fabric at the top of his pants. "Inside me. As soon as possible."

"You've been drinking." His words had a painful edge.

"I am a big girl who knows her own limits. I am perfectly capable of making this decision."

"I don't want to take advantage of you. I meant it when I said I am more interested in the long game. This can wait."

"I don't want this to wait." Kaela pulled at his neck, bringing him down to tug on his lower lip with her teeth. "Like I said, I'm more than capable of deciding."

His kiss was bruising when he finally relaxed into her. He lifted her up until her legs were wrapped around his waist, and he was pushing her into the nearest wall. Her hands fisted in his hair, teeth scraping his neck as he bent his head back. When she let go, he brought their mouths together again, nibbling and sucking her lips between kisses. His hands at her hips lined her up against the strained material of his sweatpants, the feel of him flooding her body with need. He let out a pained moan, then set her back on her feet and pulled away. Before Kaela could protest, he dropped to his knees, trailing bites down her front. He placed her bent knee over his shoulder and ran a long, slow lick straight up between her legs. Kaela gasped and tangled her fingers into his hair, bracing herself against the wall as her entire body shuddered.

She struggled to stay standing as he took his time with her. Her cries grew louder before they reached a crescendo, and he slid away, kissing along her thigh and teasing her with a few feathery touches before stopping entirely. She sagged against the wall as the pleasure faded, but he scooped her up, shocking her with ease of the motion before he carried her into the bedroom. He lowered her onto the bed and then stood back, eyes questioning even as they roved across her body.

"I already said yes." Kaela reached up and tugged at the waist of his pants.

Landry groaned a frustrated complaint and closed his eyes, rubbing his brow, trying to gain some distance from the situation.

"I will yell at you if you ask me to just cuddle."

"Mikaela… there are things I still need to tell you…"

A thick, syrupy feeling of rejection began to pool in her stomach. Her head filled with a low buzz. There was no reason two consenting adults couldn't have a physical relationship. Why was he trying so hard to prevent this? The dizziness she often had when he was nearby became overpowering. She felt a gathering resentment at his hesitation, a frustrated need to *push* against his restraint and against the feel of his nearness that throbbed through her veins. The sensation was familiar, a pattern similar to that of her powers flowing through her in the desert when she'd finally acted against Brady. She let it ripple from her in a sudden release.

Landry's hand dropped, and his eyes snapped to hers as every item in the room slid several inches away from Kaela. A lamp fell to the floor when a side table crashed into the wall, and the furniture screeched against the hardwoods.

"What did you just do?"

Kaela looked around in shock, seeing the radial pattern in the movements and understanding that whatever happened had originated from her.

"Mikaela, what did you do?"

"I don't know!" Kaela shrank from the intensity in Landry's eyes as he crouched in front of her. "I was frustrated, and I was mad at you, and I just wanted to shove you like a stupid little child. I didn't mean to push *everything*. Did I really do this?"

"No." Her attention flew from the broken lamp to Landry's narrow-eyed assessment, confused by the hesitation in his voice. "That was like a string being pulled from a sweater. Except the sweater was my ability, and I wasn't pulling the string. You were."

"I don't understand." She stared blankly at him. "That has nothing to do with the powers you keep telling me I have."

"I know."

Kaela searched for the thrumming pulse of her ability but felt nothing except the dull emptiness that always accompanied the drop in her blood alcohol after sobering up. She tried feeling for anything living around her.

"Whatever it was, I can't feel it now. Has that happened to you before? Can you be sure it was really coming from you?"

"That has certainly never happened before, but I know my power. I can feel every part of it like an extension of myself. I controlled those objects, but the choice to do it was yours. I don't know how else to describe it. Did you know you were doing anything unusual?"

Kaela shook her head as he sat on the mattress, wrapping a blanket around her shoulders and earnestly observing her reaction.

"I felt you standing there, that same thing that happens whenever you enter a room. Then there was this weird urge to lash out. Is this another ability that people can have, controlling others' powers?"

"If it is, I've never heard of it," he answered quickly. "Do you think you would be able to do it again?"

"I wouldn't even know where to start." Her head shifted slightly from side to side in an understated motion of denial.

"Think of it like inertia." He paused, choosing his words before proceeding. "I always have the ability to manipulate matter or move objects, but I don't use it. To me, it's like a ball sitting at the top of a hill. For me to start that chain of events leading the ball down the hill, I have to push it past the friction keeping it in place. You were the push. I just kept the ball rolling."

"Stationary objects sliding across a flat surface aren't picking a downhill path. That's telekinesis, not manipulating potential energy."

"What physical aspect of the world keeps those objects seated on a surface?" he returned, his expression shifting to something lighter.

"Are we in a basic physics lecture now?" She lifted an eyebrow and cocked her head, slightly annoyed at his amused expression. "Newtonian gravity."

"And what about the breakdown of the gravitational force law near black holes?"

"You are talking about disproving the theory of universal gravity, but the space and time components on Earth, in this room, are not the same as those near a black hole."

"Unless there was another phenomenon like a black hole that we haven't realized yet." He was overtly teasing her now. "What about dark matter? What about novel subatomic particles?"

"Now you're just being ridiculous." She was beginning to enjoy the conversation. "You know as well as I do that there is no room for new particles in quantum field theory. We are talking about objects in this plane of existence for which we've described all the observable energy. If you start talking about bending spoons, I am going to have to leave."

"I'm just saying that if a law breaks down over a few extreme circumstances, who is to say it doesn't break down in other places as well, but we don't have the ability to describe that yet because we aren't aware of it in the first place? Just because our established laws and forces don't leave room for gravity to be negated doesn't mean that it can't be."

"Magic is just an event that we have yet to describe with math and science," Kaela recited under her breath. "Don't you ever get tired of the fact that science can provide proof that something is true but can never UN-prove anything?"

"No."

She considered his answer for a moment.

"Yeah, me neither."

"What do we do now?" Although the blanket covered most of her body, Kaela was hyperaware of her nakedness beneath it.

"I don't know, but please keep this between the two of us for the time being until I figure it out. I'm worried about what others would do if they knew."

"Okay." She pulled the fabric more firmly against her.

Landry leaned forward, elbows on knees, while he rubbed his brow again. She wondered if her use of his powers drained his energy. He would be running low after the events in the desert, and the unexpected exertion wouldn't be easy. The fact that the objects only moved a few inches instead of slamming and shattering into the walls might indicate how low his energy stores really were.

"I'm going to clean up, and then we can get some sleep." Kaela avoided his eyes as she stepped away.

In the bathroom, she leaned against the inside of the closed door, willing her head to clear. Why was she not thinking of an exit strategy? Despite the physical attraction, she should be considering a quick climb through the nearest window. Instead, she could only worry about Landry and lament the interruption of what should have been a very satisfying exchange. The thought of his careful caresses and his talented hands in the hallway sent a shiver down her spine. She splashed cool water over her face and administered a stern mental scolding in the mirror.

Listen, you. This is a phase. You are lusty and working on a weird version of White Knight Syndrome. Enjoy it, don't guilt yourself, and move on when it is time.

She donned the plain cotton undergarments and soft sweats that were intended for her and returned to the bedroom. Landry was lying against the pillows with a sheet pulled halfway up his body, one arm thrown behind his head. She hesitated for a fraction of a second but slipped in beside him at his gesture of invitation. Her toes brushed against his calf when she curled into his side.

"How do you have such cold feet?" He gasped, tightening his arm around her.

"How do you have such warm legs?" She snuggled her cold nose into him for good measure. "At least I know you aren't a vampire."

The only response was another of his long-suffering sighs.

"Seriously, though, are people like you the reason for those legends?" The thought suddenly occurred to her, and a dozen related ideas popped into her head along with it.

"I don't think so, but it's possible." His face scrunched up pensively. "Supposedly, Porphyria was partially to blame. There are also the tales of *strigoi* from what is now Croatia. I think I met Stoker once in England. He was good friends with Oscar Wilde, you know. They were both obsessed with the idea of immortality but had no idea that it had been achieved by some of their own acquaintances."

"Do you mean to tell me that you were an *acquaintance* of Oscar Wilde?" There wasn't room in her brain for the onslaught of questions.

"Me? No. I met him a few times, but it was Hailey that knew him well. She was close to Constance, his wife. Constance was a radical feminist. She and Hailey bonded over suffrage and rational dress. I think Hailey was going by the name Anne at that time, or was it Elizabeth? Honestly, I don't remember much from those decades. I was involved elsewhere."

Her head was still against his shoulder, but her toes were no longer wiggling.

"Mikaela?" he prodded, tucking his chin as he peered into her face.

"I'm processing."

"I know it's a lot." He took a slow breath. "There are plenty of famous people I have never met, and a multitude of critical shifts in the course of history that I was not part of. Just think, a hundred years from now I could brag that I have met THE Dr. Mikaela Brookes who discovered the cure for Alzheimer's disease."

"Ha, only if I can figure out this so-called 'gift'... no pressure." As she said this, Landry idly stroked his hand up her arm, and she traced a slow circle on his chest with her finger. "Does the thought of my failure and your being forced to live a normal human lifespan from here on out frighten you?"

"I don't know if I have accepted that idea enough to feel afraid." His hand came to a stop, gently cupping the back of her elbow. "I struggled with mortality after Cassius died. There were days where death felt like a heavy weight, pressing the breath out of me every time my thoughts turned that direction. There were days when it felt abstract and less important. When you have eternity, there is no real pressure to regret decisions or to improve as a person. You can be an absolute monster for a century if you want. There are still endless centuries to make up for it. Now though—"

"Now you suffer the same spiritual maladies as the rest of us mortals," she joked, feeling him go deathly still beside her.

"What did you say?"

"No man ever threw away life while it was worth keeping." She shifted to look up at his face in the dim light. "It is okay to feel sad about the passing of time. Shit, I feel depressed any time I think about it, too. That is just part of the human journey."

"You are an enigma, Mikaela Brookes." He searched her face, hand tracking across it from temple to hairline before he twirled a dark lock of hair between his fingers. "Sometimes you say and do things that remind me of a friend I lost centuries ago. I didn't peg you for being a philosophy enthusiast."

She just shrugged.

"You never told me where you got this." Kaela carefully touched a finger to the mark on his cheek, enjoying the way his eyelids lowered at the contact. "I find it hard to believe an herbalist like Marlene couldn't have dealt with this scar."

"That is a reminder of who I don't want to become," he responded cryptically, seemingly uninterested in providing more detail. "My actions resulted in the loss of a very close friend and companion. I choose to keep it so that I never forget the cost of negligence."

"And this?" Her fingers moved down to his ribs, where a tattoo depicting a six-headed wyvern crawled across his skin. The bluish tint and blurred edges indicated that it was a very old piece of work, perhaps even inked before he became immortal.

"A reminder of who I was when I started in life."

"And is that who you want to be now?" She followed the outline of the tail as it dipped close to his hip.

"No," his voice was heavy and tired. "I just don't want to forget that part of me either. What about yours?" He touched the tattoo along her side, and she shuddered again. "What does it mean to you?"

"I think it's pretty self-explanatory."

He followed the curves of the phoenix before he nodded in agreement and took her hand, brushing it against his mouth in a quick kiss. She nestled her head into his shoulder and snaked a leg across him.

"Thank you, Mikaela."

"For the 'almost' great sex?" She scoffed.

"Thank you for giving me a chance. The fact that I didn't tell you the truth about myself before was a betrayal of your trust. I would have understood if you never wanted me near you again."

"I'm glad I did." She closed her eyes. "Just don't lie to me. I do have limits to my ability to forgive."

"I promise," he murmured into her hair. "No more lies from now on."

She closed her eyes and thought about how strange and interconnected life could be, of the repeated patterns of existence that popped up when you were least aware. There was no time in a person's life when they stopped forming relationships; there was only a continuum of opportunities to connect and decisions to take a chance or to remain alone.

His heartbeat slowed under her cheek, and his breath began to move in deep, repetitive movements like the constant flow of waves. She drifted into a memory of the beach when she was younger. She would drive there by herself on the weekends when she was an undergraduate student. She sat for hours, staring out into the ocean. The ebb and flow of the water was like a sonic meditation, guiding her brain through endless channels of connections, chasing the solution for some complex question. Sleep came quickly as she was pulled into the hypnotic rise and fall of Landry's chest.

France – 2008

Despite the fair weather, a chilly breeze was blowing in from the north, and Landry drew his coat a little tighter as he wandered between the moss-laden headstones. A feral cemetery cat cast a startled, yellow-eyed stare in his direction, then disappeared through a cracked mausoleum door. The uneven cobblestone path became less substantial as he walked, until it disintegrated into a dirt track. The shiny headstones and sepulchral monuments at the entrance dwindled and faded into dull lichen-covered markers along the way. By the time he reached his destination, they were irregularly edged stones boasting hand-chiseled letters that were too misshapen and worn beneath centuries of harsh seasonal abrasion to be legible. Landry stood before a small headstone nestled among the roots of a thick-trunked oak, leaning down to offer a small bouquet of muguet, tiny sprigs of white dripped in memory.

"Bonjour, mon coeur."

A raven in the oak gave a harsh cry and was joined by a chorus of crows in the higher branches. For a moment, Landry considered the bird. Ravens were rare in France, eschewing Paris altogether, but each time he returned to this grave in the countryside, one stood vigil in this tree. The bird's thick, proud beak parted to deliver another call, this time a warbling series of croaks that rose and fell in tone and volume. The feathers along its throat fanned and vibrated.

"You must be Muninn, come to return my fading thoughts." It tracked the movement of Landry's mouth with a single, bright eye. "His eyes have all the seeming of a demon's that is dreaming."

The raven fluffed its silky feathers in response to Landry's whimsical nonsense and took flight, leaving the strange man to his odd human behaviors. Landry observed its effortless glide.

"Well, Marguerite, I find myself filled with melancholy again. What did you always call it? A spiritual malady. Some days, I think it is just a product of living much longer than any human should. You told me so many times and in so many ways, but I didn't have the ears for it. I am living in

an endless loop. There are scientists who study this phenomenon now. They call it Periodic Time Cosmology; a scientific theory that cosmic history repeats itself exactly. If you distill it down to a smaller scale, you may conclude that because humans never learn from their past, they keep making the same, selfishly motivated, ethically blind decisions over and over again, ad infinitum. But you always knew the nature of men. You knew that the passage of a thousand years should never be observed from a single vantage point. That way madness lies."

Landry stared blankly into the distance and remembered the recent encounter that brought him on this mission of absolution. Cassius was gone. Years passed during which Landry searched the world for any hint or sign of his former commander. He finally accepted his mortality and was attempting a new type of life when Nisha contacted him in her usual, deliberately provocative fashion.

"Why are you here, Ramla?" Landry stood in the doorway to his home, eyes squinted in suspicion and a ripple of disgust passing through him.

"Don't be like that." She pouted her plump lips and stepped closer, one long, lean leg sliding between his as she formed her body against him. "What if I said I missed your touch and wanted to remind you of all the good times we've had together?"

"Funny, I don't remember any good times. I thought it was just a little desperate fucking that stopped when you couldn't keep your slimy tendrils out of my mind."

A low growl came from behind Landry just then, and Ramla stepped away, her sudden movement proving that her fearful distaste for dogs remained unchanged. Landry affectionately patted the gray muzzled head that peered around him.

"It's okay, Jacques. She isn't staying. You can go lie down."

The dog gave a dramatic snort and returned to his bed, his steps slow and arthritic as his claws tapped out an irregular rhythm against the flooring.

"At least he is going to die soon."

"Still the same heartless bitch, Ramla." Landry stepped onto the porch and closed the front door behind him. "Glad nothing has changed. You have thirty seconds to tell me why you're here before I forcefully remove you from this property."

"Nisha sent me." Ramla picked at her nails, appearing bored with the interaction.

"With what message?"

"She wants you to know that she found a replacement for Cassius."

Landry digested the statement, letting the revelation sink in.

"How?" he managed to croak out.

"Me." The boastful, self-satisfied look on Ramla's face made the hairs on Landry's arm stand on end. "Cassius had a very special relationship with one particular family for all these centuries. You wouldn't know since you abandoned him. He was obsessed with them in a way I've only ever seen him act with you, but he watched them from a distance."

"What do you mean by special relationship?" Landry's mind was reeling from this information, searching his memories for any associations that would tie into this strange story.

"He stalked them, never made any kind of contact until they were much older, sometimes in the last decades of their lives. He would bring me along and make me wait while he had a private conversation with them. Afterwards, Nisha would tell me to erase their memories. A couple of them were more difficult than others, and I had to erase them multiple times. Tell me, doesn't that seem suspiciously like they wanted to control something that was a threat?"

"Do you mean to tell me that there's one left and Nisha thinks they can manipulate age the way Cass could."

"It makes sense, doesn't it? He was never one to shy away from eliminating threats to his own power." Ramla peered into Landry's face as he came to a similar conclusion. "She was the last person that he visited before he disappeared."

"If you suspected all of this, why are you just now telling Nisha?"

Ramla narrowed her eyes and placed a finger on her forehead.

"It took these awful new wrinkles and the noticeable effect of gravity on my perfect breasts to overcome my absolute hatred for that manipulative cunt." The provocative purse of Ramla's mouth smoothed over when she realized Landry wasn't noticing. "Besides, it was a while before I pieced it together and figured out the identity of the person he saw that day. Do you want to see her?"

Ramla had taken him to a nearby university and sat with him on a bench outside of a familiar building. His stomach churned with dread when lectures ended, and students began to stream out into the sunlight.

"That one." Ramla nodded at a young woman who passed close to the

bench, the arm of her arrogantly handsome boyfriend draped across her shoulders, and a look of adoration on her face as she turned her gray eyes to him.

Even weeks later, Landry's stomach turned over at the memory of that moment. He looked up into the tree and observed the crows hopping between branches high overhead.

"For twenty-five generations, I kept my promise to you. I checked on them as they aged and kept them safe from harm, but they never knew I was there. Only Katherine's family line has continued through the years, and after all this time, there is one left. She even looks like Katherine. It amazes me, the way certain genes can survive five hundred years of transfer." Landry trailed off, his eyes shifting and refocusing on a far-off point. "I don't know how they found her, mon coeur, but I will continue to do anything I can to keep her safe from them. Her name is Mikaela, and she is the last of your children."

Chapter 11

Kaela was curled on her side with an empty bed stretching in either direction. The faint scent of pine and cedar from the sheets brought the memory of strong arms wrapped around her and a warm body pressed to her back. Landry should be close by.

There had been a dream of the ocean. A never-ending net of fishing line was tangled before her, but she picked each strand free, carefully pulling apart one knot at a time to loosen the threads. The feel of the sand between her toes competed with the cold press of the sheet against her outstretched hand. Kaela slowly pushed herself into a seated position and rubbed the grit from her eyes.

"Hamiltonian equations," she muttered while her brain pulled itself out of the residual grogginess of sleep.

There were voices coming from the front of the house. The door to the room was closed, but the deep, easy timbre of Landry's voice and the higher, bubbly tone of Hailey's drifted through the gap at the threshold along with a wide beam of light. Kaela groaned against the stiff ache of her muscles as she leveraged herself to her feet.

An unfamiliar male joined in the discussion outside. There was a brief exchange between this new person and Landry, followed by the sound of the front door opening. Kaela stopped; hand frozen in the process of turning the knob when a voice she recognized only too well called out a greeting. She yanked open the door and stalked down the hallway as Landry's angry snarl reached her ears.

"Nothing you say will excuse what you've done to her. You have one minute to leave on your own, or I will make you."

"Are you joking right now?" Theo shouted back. "I kept her safe. Something you don't seem capable of doing these days."

Kaela stepped clear of the hallway, making eye contact with Theo, who stood in the frame of the open front door, the dim light of dusk silhouetting him in a warm backlit glow. Hailey was standing in the middle of the room, one hand pressed to Landry in restraint. The owner of the unfamiliar voice stood to the side, a look of panic on his narrow face, his eyes flicking back and forth between the two men.

"Last time I checked, he was the one who fucked up your little group of friends and got me out of there, you lunatic," Kaela shouted the words from behind Landry's shoulder after he repositioned himself to stand between her and Theodore.

"And how do you think he knew where to find you?"

Kaela narrowed her eyes, trying to remember the answer Landry provided when she'd asked the same question.

"Maria told me." Landry said, one hand drifting to Kaela's hip as she moved closer to his side, the other closing and flexing.

"And who told Maria?"

A tremor registered below Kaela's feet, and her scalp tingled. The threat of violence merged from Landry's body into hers, and energy auras swam at the edges of her vision. A tick in her jaw caused her teeth to chatter.

"Okay, seriously, that's enough out of the two of you." Hailey threw her hands up in frustration. "He is telling the truth, Landry. We've stayed in touch all this time. I can vouch for him. Nisha tried to keep Kaela a secret, but somehow Jackson found out, and from the latest gossip I've collected, the Seville group knows too. Jackson reached out to Teddy, and we saw an opportunity to infiltrate. If he hadn't been a double agent, we never would have been able to ensure Kaela's safe return."

"You were working with him?"

"You knew about this and didn't tell me?"

Kaela and Landry shouted over each other in their anger.

"I couldn't tell you anything because you didn't know who we really were." Hailey started with Kaela, then turned her eyes on Landry. "And you hate Teddy. I couldn't explain the situation without you reacting in some unhinged, violent way. We had to let Jackson play his hand so we could flush out the whole team. Unfortunately, we still don't know who told him about Kaela, but at least we know he'll stay away for the time being."

"You knew him this entire time. All the conversations at the gym, you could have warned me, could have done something to protect me."

"He was never a real threat to you," Hailey responded warily. "And for the record, I did tell you he sounded like an idiot and you could do better. What do you want from me, Kaela? I am your friend. I kept an eye on you. When it came down to it, I put my body between you and those jackasses who kidnapped you. I did the best I could to be there when it mattered."

The two women stared at one another. Kaela couldn't bring herself to refute Hailey's statements but also couldn't bring herself to let go of her indignant anger. Each little lie, all the secrets that Hailey kept from her over the years, added up into one giant feeling of betrayal. First Todd, then Landry, and now Hailey.

Kaela felt like an idiot.

"Are you still Nisha's lap dog?" Landry's accusation broke the silence.

"I was never her lap dog." Theo moved into the room and dropped onto the couch with arrogant nonchalance. "An errand boy, maybe, but helping Jackson and then turning on them will hardly gain me any favor. At this point, I think I'm back to being a free agent."

"And I think we're getting the old gang back together."

Landry gave Hailey a look that vehemently denied the possibility of any such thing happening.

"Who are you?"

The slender male turned to Kaela with a look of surprise.

"*Uh*, my name is Chiro. I brought the new phone and your luggage from the hotel." As if to prove his innocence, he extended a hand, and a phone identical to the one she lost was clasped between his fingers. "Your contacts, files, and messages have all been restored."

Landry shrugged off her high-eyebrowed expression and took the offered device, forcing it into her hand. No security code was set, and when she thumbed on the screen, she found several text messages and three new voicemails waiting for her. Surprised, she scrolled through the callers' information.

"You can go now if you want, Kinichiro." The words had barely cleared Landry's mouth before the young man was down the driveway.

There were a few text messages from Caleb, asking when she would be back in the lab the following week and apologizing for 'losing track' of her at the gala. There was another message from her lab manager asking about time off, and one from her neighbor confirming the cat had been fed every day. Confusion set in when she saw that the three missed calls were from her ex-husband.

"What?" Landry leaned closer. "Is something wrong?"

Kaela looked up to find all three of them staring at her with concern. Her eyes flicked down to her phone and then over to Hailey before settling on Landry.

“Jason called me,” she replied dumbly.

“Your ex?” Hailey cried out in disbelief. “What does that turd want?”

“I don’t know,” Kaela said, tapping the voicemail icon and holding the phone to her ear.

She let the messages play through, one after another. She could feel the intensity of her frown deepen as she went back to the first one again. Landry’s stance grew stiffer with each minute that passed. Theo leaned forward with his elbows on his knees, eyes sharply focused on her expression. Hailey made a big show of settling on the couch next to Theodore with carefully crafted ease.

“Well?” she finally asked. “What did he want?”

“Just to check in,” Kaela replied slowly. “He says that he was interviewed by a government representative about me. He wanted me to know that he provided a good, clean reference for whatever high-priority funding I’d applied for. He said he hoped the higher clearance didn’t mean I was working on something unsavory for the state department.”

“Weird that he would need to tell you that, but he probably wanted you to thank him for being a decent human being. Typical.” Hailey grunted.

“I didn’t apply for a high-security grant. And he spoke to someone named Cassius Carver. I mean, am I crazy, or is that an unlikely coincidence?” The air was heavy with unspoken words. No one moved for several long heartbeats. Theo stared at Hailey, Hailey stared at Landry, and Landry stared at Kaela. “It would be really nice if one of you told me that I am crazy now. It is a coincidence, right?”

“It’s him.” Landry turned to Hailey and slowly moved away, letting Kaela’s hand slide free from where she was resting it against his arm.

Kaela immediately noticed the space he put between them. His eyes were frantic but calculating, some dark emotion buried there. The three feet between them became a yawning chasm as his expression settled into something colder. A thought whispered through her head. He was separating them in more ways than just the physical proximity of their bodies. He was afraid of being attached to her when his old boss inevitably arrived on the scene.

“It can’t be,” Hailey replied softly. “He is dead.”

“We never knew that for certain,” Landry responded, shaking his head and avoiding Kaela’s eyes. “That name, Hailey. That is bait. He knows we would recognize it. It must be him.”

"He knew about her before he disappeared." Kaela's eyes snapped to Theo as he made this announcement, annoyed that he would know this detail about her past. "He could have used Jackson as a test for her. That's exactly the type of thing he would do. You've probably already met him and didn't even know it. He fucks with your head. It's a hobby of his."

"Well, shit." The shocked realization raced over Hailey's face.

"Why would he care about me?" Kaela's pulse thumped in her ears. "I am clearly nowhere as powerful or controlled as him. I am nothing."

"You are everything," Landry choked out. "Just your existence is enough to upset the balance of power he controlled for the last thousand years. Don't you understand? He had to figure out if your powers were the same. Now that he knows what you can do, he must find a way to bind you to him forever or kill you."

"Nisha keeps a picture of him. It must be the only remaining evidence of his existence, but for some sentimental reason, she has a framed photograph." Theo scrolled through his phone before holding it out for her to see. "There it is. I took a picture of it on my phone in case it came in handy. Do you recognize him, Kaela?"

Every aging, mortal heart in the room skipped a beat when hysterical laughter erupted from Kaela. She responded with just two words.

"Fuck me."

Staring back at her from the phone screen was her neighbor, George.

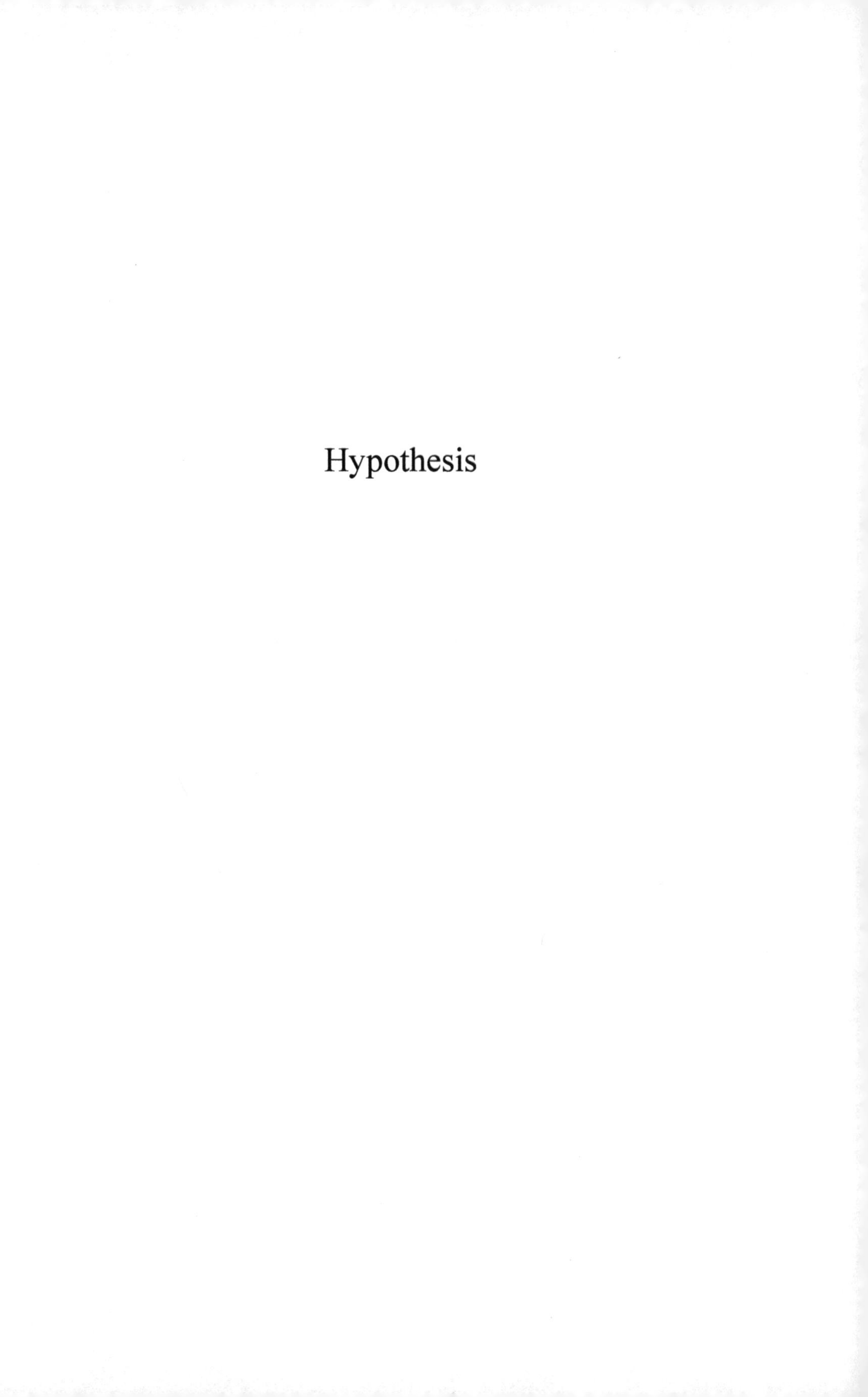

Hypothesis

Chapter 1

Dr. Mikaela Brookes, one of the most promising faculty members at her prestigious university, a mentor and role model for many brilliant young minds, and an outspoken advocate for the active recruitment of women to STEM careers, was drunk. And she was not just slightly inebriated, she was freshman year of college, sloppy lipstick, abrasively loud, drunk.

"You should have seen her dumb face. Staring at that pastry in my mouth like she was judging a pig at the fair. Like she'd ever be near a pig. Or a fair. *Stupid Uncultured Swine*."

Kaela turned her nose up into the air and delivered these last words with an elaborately slurred imitation of a transatlantic accent. She slouched back into the armchair, waiting for a reaction from the fluffy orange tabby on her coffee table and feeling the slightest spinning of the room around her. The feline offered a long-pointed look then raised one white-mittened paw and washed its face.

"You're right, I've had enough." Kaela braced herself and stood, letting the room come to the correct, static orientation before shuffling to the kitchen, where she poured the rest of her drink down the drain.

The last six months had been interesting, to say the least.

The trouble started when an annoyingly attractive man appeared in her life. Wasn't that always the case? Good-looking men could be such distractions, and Dr. Landry Griffiths was certainly a handsome diversion if she'd ever seen one. She gave a drunken, half-hearted grumble as she thought about their interactions. If she were being honest with herself, she knew the trouble started well before he entered her life on a delightful-smelling cloud of male pheromones.

It would seem the trouble began when she was a child, first showing the signs of her magical abilities, but no one around her recognized them for what they were. 'A budding naturalist,' her mother said when she exhibited an unusually green thumb with anything she tried to grow. 'A future entomologist,' her father intoned when she scooped up the butterflies dying among the leaf litter and sent them back into flight. 'An enormous scientific talent,' her graduate mentor bragged when Kaela's experiments with living cells or tissues in the lab displayed surprising results.

In just six months, Kaela's life went from world-renowned scientist (at least within select circles) to magical refugee on the lam. She went about her daily life, constantly looking over her shoulder, terrified of the next person who saw her as a means to an end. She needed to learn how to control her powers, and the sooner the better.

Yet, these world-altering, reality-shifting revelations were not the reason for Kaela's current state of intoxication. Oh, no. There was only one person in the world that could drive her to the edge of rage and lead her down this self-destructive drink-a-thon after only a few hours of interaction earlier in the day. That person was her former mother-in-law.

By the time Kaela had made her way from the overcrowded parking deck, through the glittering white marble and glass cavern that was the building lobby, and into the law offices of 'Harrison, Carson, and Scott,' she was two minutes late. The reception area was a smaller, but no less ostentatious, version of the building entrance. Pristine floors stretched beneath an impossibly high ceiling, a yawning expanse that ended in a full wall of windows overlooking the city. A thin brunette in a black pencil skirt, low-cut blouse, and ludicrously expensive heels was standing beside the reception desk, straightening a stack of papers on an otherwise pristine countertop. She plastered a bright, red-lipped smile across her cosmetically augmented face, and waited for Kaela to approach before directing her up the stairs to the left.

Each footfall on the treads added another layer of nauseous dread to Kaela's stomach until it felt as if she had swallowed an anvil. She shuddered, repressing the memories of the accusations and insults she endured during the divorce proceedings, which took place all too recently in these high-level offices. By the end of those weeks in which she was held captive by the legal hurdle of separating herself from her ex-husband's horrible family, she was emotionally numb, her pride lying dead in the corner, and her self-esteem just as defeated. It was the single most hateful treatment she had ever experienced, and it was all largely at the hands of one woman. A woman who was now waiting inside the third room to the right, her perfectly coiffed and colored hair shining like metallic gold under the fluorescent lighting as she cast her imperious gaze at the doorway.

"Mikaela!" The word was carefully crafted to deliver both a feeling of suffering and a tone of relief that this long-awaited arrival would *finally* allow things to get back on schedule. The sharply condescending glance at Kaela's clothing was a bonus. "So lovely to see you, my dear. Did you have trouble finding the place? It hasn't been that long since you last met us here."

"Wonderful to see you as always, Evelyn." Kaela offered Jason's mother a forced smile as genuine as the one she received from the receptionist upon arrival.

"Kay."

Her body tensed at the breathy word, and she turned toward her ex-husband, Jason, as he stepped forward to greet her. The remaining family members were settled in chairs around the large, varnished oak table and didn't bother to acknowledge Kaela with more than a nod or a glance before returning to their very important lives, which existed in a plane of reality that did not contain poor, white-collar workers no longer associated with their family. Jason's arms were elevated just enough to make it clear that he was going to embrace her, but Kaela quickly deflected by sticking her hand between them, forcing him into an awkward handshake instead. He was outfitted in his usual pressed suit with a variety of expensive accessories on display, an aged richling resisting the inevitable transition to family patriarch. Kaela noticed, with petty satisfaction, that he'd put on a bit of weight.

"You look good," he managed, stepping away and ignoring the angry stare this statement drew from the thin, sour-faced twenty-something sitting close by.

"Thanks," Kaela replied dismissively and eyed the empty chairs.

Evelyn was sitting next to her latest husband on the opposite side of the table, her slitted eyes still fixed on Kaela—judging her hair, judging her expression, judging the distance between Kaela and Jason, judging the length of the handshake. Kaela would rather jump out of the window behind them than occupy the empty seat next to Evelyn. To the right, Jason's two cousins were busy pretending to be the most important people in the room. One of them was wearing a costly, bespoke ensemble, likely having arrived directly from his symbolic position at the family firm. The other was outfitted for a day on the yacht despite the cool weather. Both were casting supercilious, bored stares in her direction. Their mother dying was probably low on their list of concerns, and they thought this meeting was just a formality to check off the list before gigantic sums of money could be officially bequeathed to them. On the near side of the table were Jason, his young girlfriend, and a man that could only be the lawyer for today's shit show.

The girlfriend tapped her long, manicured nails on the polished wood and kept her reptilian stare tightly fixed on Kaela from where she sat to the other side of the attorney. Those lacquered talons were clearly itching to sink into whatever amount of money would be allocated to Jason but would probably be just as satisfied with clawing Kaela's eyes out of her head right now.

"Well, since Mikaela has finally arrived, perhaps we can begin." Evelyn gestured impatiently to the lawyer.

Kaela maintained a carefully neutral expression while she witnessed Evelyn ruling over the room. She was a dictator accustomed to instantaneous obedience from everyone around her. Once, Kaela would also follow Evelyn's instructions like a blind sheep.

There was a tray of pastries sitting in the middle of the table between them, a towering assortment of baked goods coated with processed sugars and preservatives. Evelyn despised refined carbs and typically refused to let any near her, banning them from every menu she could control. Someone must have missed that memo when preparing the room, and they would surely pay for it later. The lawyer cleared his throat and began the traditional introduction to the processing of Aunt Gloria's will.

Kaela drummed her fingers against her thigh, the table hiding this signal of agitation from the room. The crown jewel of the piled confections was a fluffy croissant. The chocolate filling oozed from the swirled layers, and sparkling chunks of sugar were scattered across the top. No time like the present to reinvent herself as the bellwether instead of the trailing lamb. The lawyer paused in his spiel when Kaela stood, her chair rolling back a few inches as she leaned across the table to retrieve the delicious-looking treat, placing it directly on a napkin like a troglodyte. Evelyn's eyes widened, and her nostrils flared delicately, but Kaela just offered her a smile broad enough to be unhinged. Then she settled back into the chair, prize in hand.

"I will read directly from the will, and we can pause after each section to address any questions or concerns to the immediate material." The poor lawyer tried to continue as if the snack retrieval did not throw him off his pace. "To my dear nephew, Jason, I bequeath—"

“*Mmm*.” Kaela took a large, unseemly bite of the croissant and gave a satisfied moan in appreciation, licking the chocolate off her finger for good measure before speaking around her half-full mouth. “Evelyn, you must try one of these. They are to die for.”

Jason’s mother turned her hawk-eyed stare to the lawyer and made an impatient gesture, studiously ignoring Kaela’s outburst but unable to keep the faint snarl of disgust from her lips. Kaela couldn’t help a little chuckle at her childish victory but quickly sobered after accidentally making eye contact with one of the womanizing cousins. She avoided his revolting leer and continued eating the pastry in a more reserved manner as the lawyer droned through the current conditions of the estate.

Kaela still didn’t understand why the aunt would have left anything to her. Gloria was a silent presence at the larger family events (soirees, as Evelyn would call them), and they only spoke at length a few times. Kaela remembered her being distant and faded, as if all the joy was being siphoned from her petite, unimposing body. Jason and Kaela were newlyweds then, and although Kaela was never a rose-colored glasses type of girl, she hadn’t yet realized the toll that a bad marriage could take on a person.

Aunt Gloria avoided direct commentary about her husband, Evelyn’s brother, but in retrospect, the absence of words and the blank parts of her stories formed the picture of a man who demanded everything yet gave nothing. Kaela wondered if Gloria lost the better parts of herself to the marriage and recognized the same future looming over her newly minted niece. When Evelyn’s brother died last year, Kaela felt relief for the other woman. What a tragedy she didn’t survive him long enough to really enjoy her freedom.

“I do give, devise, and bequeath to Mikaela (Kaela) Brookes, my silver locket as shown in figure seventeen, and my estate in New Orleans, Louisiana, as described under the real property assets listing. In lieu of a monetary lump sum, the assets as described in section 10a shall be used to create a component fund with investments to be determined based on the provisions outlined in section 15a. The returns from these investments shall be redistributed to fund the estate taxes and necessary costs for upkeep according to the following schedules.”

Louisiana?

Kaela scrambled to remember any mention of Aunt Gloria’s home there. Evelyn was sitting even straighter than usual, her eyes glued on Kaela as she interrupted the practitioner.

"There is a mistake. According to the family prenuptial agreements, all estate assets and properties must stay with the blood relatives of my brother." She sneered as she continued. "I don't know how Mikaela managed to have herself named in this document, but distribution of these items will have to be disputed."

Evelyn calmly folded her hands on the table before her, waiting for the man to accept her proclamation and move to the next part of the will.

"I apologize, Mrs. Arnolt." The lawyer did look quite abashed as he held up his palms in supplication. "These assets, including the funds that are to be consolidated in support of the Louisiana property, are part of Ms. Gloria's pre-marital possessions and thus fall outside of the prenuptial restrictions."

"Well." Evelyn rapped a single finger against the table, one of the few times Kaela had seen her show such a display of agitation. "What is the value of these assets?"

The lawyer scanned through the documents stacked beside him. The back of his neck was red, although his demeanor remained calm. It gave Kaela a certain satisfaction to notice she was not the only person in the room who couldn't quite prevent Evelyn from getting under their skin. Jason was offering an apologetic smile over the lawyer's head, but Kaela refused to acknowledge it. The cousins were muttering about the lack of importance 'some hovel in New Orleans' had on the entire proceeding while Jason's girlfriend and Evelyn's husband sat in bored silence, waiting for the part where they learned what new financing they would be able to leech from their partners.

"*Ah,* the property is a large manor within the garden district. It is valued at eight point seven million dollars. The assets to be transferred to the component fund are currently valued at approximately twenty-four million. The locket is an old heirloom that has yet to be appraised."

The anger pounding through Evelyn's veins was practically palpable in the stunned silence that followed the announcement of the sums. Kaela was so amused by Evelyn being caught completely off-guard, it took another minute for this information to settle into her brain. She took a delayed, sharp inhale of air when she finally understood that in the last few minutes, she jumped in status from a middle-class academic with a minimally positive net worth to a multi-millionaire.

The room shifted. She was floating an inch above the chair as a dreamlike ethereal haze settled over her senses. After all the years of this family treating her like a lower-class citizen, like their own personal humanitarian project, she had begun to even the playing field. Granted, Evelyn's wealth started with a 'B' instead of an 'M', but Kaela was no longer a pauper in their eyes. She somehow took the one thing they held dear right out from under their noses, money.

"We will certainly discuss this again in private," Evelyn finally broke the silence.

By all accounts, Aunt Gloria was a shrewd, thorough woman. Kaela doubted that even Jason's snake-of-a-mother could find a way to contest the legality of this will, but just knowing she would have to try gave Kaela insurmountable joy.

The rest of the meeting was a repetitive drone of legalese. Most of the wealth went to the cousins, and smaller amounts were carved out for Evelyn and Jason. Kaela would be contacted with the final documents, house keys, and the locket within the month. At the earliest opportunity, she thanked the lawyer and slipped out. She had only reached the second stair tread when Jason caught up to her.

"Kay, wait!" He looked nervous when she paused, half-turned as if she might change her mind and bolt down the stairs instead. "Sorry about my mother. You know how she is."

"Yes, I do." Kaela gripped the railing tightly, hating every moment of the exchange.

"Listen, I meant it when I said you look like you're doing well. Did you get my messages about the good reference I gave for that funding?"

"Sure did." Kaela refused to applaud him for providing truthful information, particularly when it had been a fake background check in the first place.

The person calling to ask questions about her was Cassius, but Jason thought the call was from a real public servant, and she didn't see the point in correcting him.

"Well, I'll let you go." Despite this statement, he continued to linger. "Maybe when the lawyers finish crossing their T's, I can bring you everything. We could have coffee and catch up."

"I doubt Taylor would appreciate that." Kaela glanced up into the conference room where said girlfriend was continuing to shoot daggers through the glass wall with her icy stare.

"I don't intend to ask Taylor for permission." He grumbled stiffly.

"Goodbye, Jason."

Kaela continued down the stairs without looking back. Being around those people dredged up hurtful memories no matter what she did, and her head was swimming with unwanted emotions. She was tired of their particular brand of elitism. She spent the first few years of marriage struggling to do anything and everything she could to fit in. She smothered the parts of herself that were too loud or too aggressive to mesh with their superficial, polished images. She was constantly drowning under the pressure to be someone she didn't know or even like, and all along the way, they just kept dumping more water on her.

By the time Kaela reached the exit from the lobby to the main street, a wide grin found its way to her face. When she reached her car in the parking deck, she was chuckling under her breath. Once she buckled her seatbelt and started the car, she was laughing and crying in equal parts. She was a millionaire with magical powers.

Stand aside, Dr. Strange.

The euphoria was short-lived. Every condescending glance from Evelyn began to replay in the back of her mind. The perfect, high-fashion style of Jason's cold-blooded ingénue, the press of luxury brands and costly family jewels from every direction, the piles and piles of money casually divvied up between the beneficiaries around the room; all of it stuck in the back of her throat like dry toast.

She felt clumsy and dowdy next to their elegance. Her hair was a dull, limp, brown pile, pulled hastily into a bun at the nape of her neck before the meeting. While she drove, she ripped the hair band out, running her fingers through the released locks to straighten them. This only served to make her look like a bedraggled mess. At the next stoplight, she pulled it back into a ponytail. She was still staring at her dry cuticles and unpainted nails on the steering wheel when the light turned green and the car behind her honked impatiently.

Now, standing in the kitchen of her own home, surrounded by the details of her wonderfully ordinary life and seeing herself through the flattering haze of inebriation, Kaela's feelings of inadequacy morphed into disdain for Jason's family. Not one person in that room ever felt loved or understood. They were all born into a world where appearance was everything, reputation was the key to winning, and money made you better than everyone else.

"We are all living on a miniscule blue marble, spinning our tiny little webs in the broadest expanse imaginable, and I stopped to get my nails manicured on the way home." Hellcat perked its ears at Kaela's voice this time, offering a singular focus for her philosophical revelation. "Grandmother Anicette would remind me that painting your nails should always be about you, not about others. Your hair and your clothing and your jewelry should all be an extension of your feelings, not a mask behind which to hide to please people who don't deserve your energy. I think she would have been disappointed with me today."

Kaela inspected her iridescently shellacked nails and sighed.

There is perhaps no better demonstration of the folly of human conceits.

"But honestly, she would have been just as disappointed that I looked wildly unkempt at the meeting. Your physical expression of self is a personal choice, but you still must be put together in front of others. Man, when the Silent Generation offers advice, it's always full of conflicting ideals. Very confusing."

Kaela released an unladylike burp that would have scandalized her grandmother and walked across the living room with a large glass of water in hand. The cat gave an exaggerated yawn in return, the pink, ridged roof of its mouth flashing between small, sharp teeth. It voiced a halfhearted chirrup of agreement, circled once, then settled into a tight coil of fluff with its tail wrapped over its nose. Kaela stopped in front of a set of books on her mantle. She picked one up, a dog-eared autobiography with a yellowed fifty-cent sticker from a thrift store on the cover. She flipped through the pages, stopping at the occasional streak of neon highlighter to read a selected passage before moving on.

Stop, Look, Listen—then strike hard and fast with all the power you need.

Elites can become so inbred that they produce hemophiliacs who bleed to death as soon as they are nicked by the real world.

If you get the dirty end of the stick, sharpen it and turn it into a useful tool.

She grunted in annoyance. Fighting words. Each of the selected bits and pieces from the book spoke of a reader that was digging in, mentally fortifying themselves for a battle against the inequity of an unfair socio-economic system. Too bad they were just the random longings of a coward.

She flopped the book back on top of a well-loved Louis L'Amour novel. The leather bookmark jutting from the frontier paperback had not moved from its chosen pages in nearly a decade. It was the last thing her father read before he died. For all the anger she felt, Kaela still could not bring herself to donate the two books. Instead, they sat on her shelf in perpetuity, the bookmark waiting for the return of its reader like a frozen cross-section in time.

"Hello?"

The amount of background noise coming through the phone indicated that Hailey was enjoying her Thursday evening in a much more social setting than Kaela.

"If you had cancer, you wouldn't just fucking give up, right?" Kaela's blood alcohol level sponsored this unplanned outburst upon hearing Hailey's voice.

"*Woah,* hold on a minute." The noise dropped away, indicating that Hailey was retreating to a quieter space to converse with her emotionally unsteady friend. "What's going on? Who has cancer?"

"No one, sorry. Forget I asked that. Are you busy? It's ten o'clock on a Thurd—*hiccup*—on a Thursday."

"Wow, are you drunk?" Hailey's question was thick with amusement. "Yes, it's a Thursday, and I'm always out at ten o'clock, but you seem like you've been drinking more than I have. Was today that appointment with the Deadbeat Dick ex-husband?"

"Howdya guess?" Kaela slumped down on her couch.

"Bruh, I would ask how it went, but clearly not well."

"It was fine. I'm getting bunches of money from his dead Auntie."

There was a long pause while Hailey processed Kaela's matter-of-fact announcement.

"So, is this a celebratory drinking session? I totally would have picked you up and taken you out for drinks!"

"I'm not celebrating. I just really hate my mother-in-law."

"EX mother-in-law," Hailey quickly corrected. "Don't let that dry old bitch get to you, Kaela. We've talked about this. She's an absolute cunt."

"I hate that word."

"I know."

It was Kaela's turn to sit in silence while she decided how to respond.

"You're right, I shouldn't let her get to me like this." She drank half the glass of water she still clutched in her hand. "Okay, time to sober up. Thanks. Evelyn is a cunt. Hopefully, she dies soon."

"That's my savage bestie!" Hailey exclaimed. "Wait, is she the one who has cancer?"

"What? No. Why would she have cancer?"

Kaela bent her neck back and then forward, fascinated by the way her brain thought her head was still moving after it stopped.

"Because you said," Hailey drifted off with another laugh. "Never mind. I can send someone over to keep an eye on your house. Drunk people sleep entirely too soundly, and you need to be careful with everything going on right now. Are you going to be okay?"

After the events of the last few months, it was clear that several of the former immortal contingents were going to continue trying to control Kaela, by coercion or by force. The exhibition of her talents in the desert, along with Landry's very public claim as her protector, was enough to deter immediate kidnappings, but there were sure to be more attempts. When someone could stop, reverse, or redirect aging, no one in their right mind would walk away from the promise of immortality.

"No, I'm fine, I don't want anyone here."

Kaela's hiccup at the end of her run-on sentence was all Hailey needed to make the decision.

"I'm sending someone, and he will stay outside in his vehicle all night. You won't even know he's there."

"Not Todd. Shit, I mean, Theo or Theodore or whatever the hell I'm supposed to call him now."

"Teddy. And yes, he is the best person for the job. Like I said, you won't see him, hear him, or smell him. And Kaela, forget about Jackass Jason and his stupid mother. You cut them out of your life for a reason. Don't let them back in, even for a minute."

"Yeah, okay. Thanks, Hailey."

A subtle snoring drifted from the cat as it slept, oblivious to the world. Kaela finished the rest of her water, leaving the glass on the coffee table as she moved to her plant wall, her fingers trailing along the delicate fuzz of her Zebrina plant. She recently stumbled upon a reference to the plant by its common name, *Wandering Jew*. Her great-great-grandmother married into a Jewish family before the second world war. Although the practice was diluted out through the generations, Kaela felt a sharp filial allegiance, a compulsion to defend that came from a shared lineage in addition to simply behaving as a decent human being should. What were the odds that this plant, a spontaneous acquisition from a display at the local home improvement store, boasted that moniker? A man who taunted Jesus on his way to crucifixion, a Jew, who was cursed to wander the Earth until the Second Coming, never dying, as punishment for his unsanctimonious display: The Wandering Jew.

Kaela felt a wave of disgust. She cupped a section of trailing vines in one hand and reached across to her *Monstera deliciosa* plant, her delicious little monster. Previously, when she accessed her powers, it was a struggle to find the right headspace, to direct her mind into a realm where magic was real and the world around her could be manipulated with just a focused suggestion. Tonight, she barely finished her thought before the offending plant wilted in its pot, all the active energy from the cool, waxy leaves and long-reaching arms funneling through Kaela's body and fueling her suggestion that the *Monstera* grow. The other plant doubled in size, new leaves unfurling like a time-lapse.

Kaela laughed, a full-throated release of amusement at the power she finally wielded with ease. Her eyes turned to the cat, napping peacefully across the room. Why couldn't she manipulate animals the way she did plants? In her state of limited inhibition, she pretended that her feet set roots down through the floor and into the earth below the house. Her body was just a conduit for all life teeming across the planet. The cat was an adult today, but it couldn't be more than a few years old. Surely all those little cells and tissues remembered where they originated. Time was just a social construct after all. What if the energy that took things forward with such ease could also take things backwards?

For once in her life, Kaela didn't worry about the details. She didn't dwell on the science behind an organism moving backwards to a previous state. She just pushed the energy out and *thought* it into being. A dizziness even more potent than the alcohol swam through her system and made Kaela hunch forward, clutching her abdomen, eyes shut tightly against the feeling.

A screeching yowl tore through the air.

When Kaela recovered, she looked at the coffee table.

"Holy shit."

A tiny orange ball of fluff sat in the middle of the table instead of a full-grown cat.

France – 1522

Theodore let his head fall into his hands as he listened to the cheerful noise of tiny feet scampering barefoot across the floor. Faint echoes of bubbling laughter and little voices calling out for their Papa drifted past his ears, stirring a cold shudder along his spine. A burning, aching heaviness filled the space behind his eyes. It was just a memory.

He was alone in the cathedral. Before him, a stone lion stood half again the height of a grown man. The face and haunches had little detail, and the broad wings were only a rough outline along its back. Theodore shook off the residue of his memories and walked in a slow circle around the carving, listening to the stillness of the church before tracing his fingers against the surface. Beneath his careful touch, the stone crumbled like sand to reveal perfect, intricate cascades of feathers. He sat back to admire the results, absently holding out an arm. A giant rock rolled from the corner to rest below his downturned palm.

"That is a useful trick."

Theodore leapt to his feet as a man's voice echoed through the silence of the chamber. When he turned around, he found not one but two men standing at the edge of his makeshift wall, the fabric pushed back to allow them entry. The first man was large and muscular. The hair at his temples was frosted with age, and his eyes were the color of storm clouds. The second man was also tall but with the lean physique of youth and bright green eyes that were currently crinkled at the corners in amusement.

"A trick, indeed," Theodore blurted. "I practice such illusions when I am alone."

"You need not fear us revealing your secrets, monsieur," the young man was quick to remark, his lips pressed in silent laughter. "It is not a dark art that you practice."

"I am sure I do not know what you mean," Theodore replied coldly.

The two strangers exchanged a glance, and the older gave a consenting nod. Theodore felt his spine tense as the young man stepped closer to a large block of stone. His body moved with a sure-footed and fluid grace that was unsettling, as if each step whispered with the threat of violence. The stranger winked one emerald eye at Theodore and flicked his wrist.

Theodore blinked as the stone inexplicably shattered.

"We also choose to perform these types of magic in secret to avoid giving proof to the lie. However, you are among friends, and we are no consorts of the devil."

Theo scrutinized the older man who had just spoken. "Who are you?"

"I am Cassius. This is my son, Landry." The younger man gave a brief look of confusion at this statement, but it was quickly replaced with one of indifference. "We come from a large family of people with abilities like yours. We each have a particular talent, but we choose to live in secrecy. Given your response to our intrusion a few moments ago, I think you will agree that this is necessary for our kind to prevent unsavory reactions to any public displays of power."

"And what 'kind' are we?" Theo asked carefully.

"The kind that govern themselves," Landry responded seriously.

"The prejudices of the average man can be quite extreme." Cassius moved deeper into the room and found a perch on a small stool near the hunched, half-carved form of a stone gargoyle. "People like us are threats to their way of thinking, therefore, we are eliminated. The tendrils of hatred spread deep."

"How do you know I will not reveal you after this conversation?" Theodore looked between the two men.

Cassius' voice was hard when he responded. "You won't because it would also implicate yourself. And if you did rush out to betray us, you would not make it to the door."

"Are you threatening me?" Theodore snarled back.

"I am telling you that I always keep myself well protected. I have another family member you should meet. Ramla, please come in here where he can see you."

A dark-skinned woman stepped into the makeshift room, her movements graceful and silent. She nodded once to Cassius, and Theodore suppressed a shudder of distaste as her sharp, ebony eyes took in every detail of his appearance. A light pressure gripped his head and then vanished just as quickly.

"He won't betray you," she responded dismissively. "He is just frightened."

"I have always been keen to know everything about a person before I enter into any arrangements with them." Cassius dragged the stool closer to Theodore as he spoke. "Forgive my knowledge of the personal details of your life, but I am here to make you an offer."

"You wish me to join your group because you have need of a stone

mason?" Theodore kept a wary eye on Landry and Ramla as they stood guard in the background.

"I am not offering you a job," Cassius began. "I am offering new lives, for you and for your wife. I have lived for many years, and during that time, there were many wars. When I say that I have felt the pain of loss and seen more death than you can imagine, I am telling you the truth. I've witnessed people becoming consumed by their grief, unable to recover from what they have lost. I know what it is that your wife struggles to survive every day."

Theodore stared at this stranger who laid bare his greatest secret and deepest guilt.

"Have you lost a child?" he finally asked, voice choked with emotion.

"Landry, Ramla, please wait outside." The two being ordered away nodded and obeyed without question. After they retreated beyond range of hearing, Cassius continued.

"I have lost a child," he confirmed. "There is a sadness in the deepest part of my soul that will never leave. Every day, you must make the choice to live through it. I know that you can make this choice, but your wife cannot. Ramla can alter a person's memories. She can make your wife forget the loss, and she will be able to feel whole again. She could build a new life instead of digging a grave within the ashes of her old one."

"If what you say is true, you are offering to take something from her that she may not be willing to give." Theodore shook his head slowly.

"Here is my proposal. You may decide if you would like her mind altered, your mind altered, or both."

"I would not give up the memory of my children, no matter the pain," he replied.

"That is because you are surviving it." Cassius leaned forward, his voice soft.

Theodore remembered the unfiltered delight his wife effused after she became pregnant, and the purpose she displayed every day while nurturing the twins. Then he remembered the shell of a person that she became after their deaths.

"What is your asking price for such a thing?"

"There is not a price but an invitation to join our team. Let me tell you a story about a young man who found the world around him to be a cruel and terrible place until he discovered that he had abilities which set him apart."

Chapter 2

"Again."

In her dreams, Kaela was back in the desert. Hailey struggled to stay conscious through the pain of her broken arm. Theo was an emotionless block of muscle, restraining Kaela as she lunged for her friend. Jackson, the egotistical ringleader of the group, was watching with a condescending, sadistic leer. Landry was nowhere to be seen.

Kaela watched as they broke Hailey's arm, wordless screams ripping through the desert air from both their mouths, the sounds mingling into a reverberating cacophony of horror.

She could stop them. All she had to do was reach inside their bodies and make them suffer.

Kaela tried to raise her hands, as if the motion would help channel her abilities from some dark crevice of her brain into the space around her.

Her hands wouldn't move.

Kaela looked down and found her legs and lower torso encased in layers of rock, pinning her arms to her sides. Her breath came faster as panic set in. She looked into Todd's eyes, her stare sharp with accusation.

"I told you not to trust anyone, Kaela." His voice was cold and impassive. He looked over her shoulder as soon as the words left his mouth.

"This is the famous Dr. Brookes. I've been waiting for you."

The second voice washed over her, carrying a dark shadow of fear that crawled up her spine and sank into the primal drive at the base of her brain. The panic was all-consuming. She was screaming again, yanking her arms to the point of pain as she tried to break out of the granite restraints. The unknown presence pulled closer, making the hair on her neck stand on end. Tears of frustration slid across her cheeks as she spiraled out of control. He stepped in front of her, and she woke up from the dream.

The nightmare always ended without her seeing his face, leaving a dark blur in her mind where a face should be as she gripped her sheets and caught her breath. She knew what Cassius looked like. He paraded around, pretending to be her neighbor for years. Why did her subconscious think the identity of the ringleader behind her kidnapping was still a mystery?

Her clothing clung to her sweat-slicked skin, and her heart was pounding in her ears. She forced herself to get up and move to the kitchen, running her hands under the cold water and then patting them against the back of her neck. She cupped the water to her mouth, gulping it down in long pulls to soothe her throat. She was parched from the dry air of the desert.

No.

She reminded herself that she was only dreaming and the cottony sensation in her throat was from sleeping with her mouth open. Or from screaming in her dream. Or from her excessive consumption of whiskey the night before. Her eyes were heavy, a stinging exhaustion which caused a thin veneer of fluid to blur her vision. Even the air in her lungs felt thick when she took a breath. She stumbled to the coffee machine. Her head was saturated with a dull fog. Maybe the coffee would help.

On her way out of her house, the kitten greeted her at the front door, expecting to be let into the yard. The events of the evening came into focus, and she stared at the tiny animal as she considered her options.

She turned an adult cat into a kitten. She remembered the shock that was quickly followed by fear of this event being observed the previous night. She'd torn through the house, checking the blinds, and then circled back to pull the curtains closed over the windows for good measure. At the front of her house, she glared at a familiar truck parked at the top of her driveway and offered her middle finger before securing the coverings. When she was sure no one could have witnessed the event, she returned to the tiny feline and began a thorough inspection, sobriety making a swift appearance. Her attempts to revert the animal to its correct age failed, leaving her with nothing more than a pounding headache and bloodshot eyes. She eventually settled on collecting a few hair samples and collapsed on her bed for a fitful night of sleep.

After she pulled out of her driveway that morning, a truck followed her vehicle halfway to the university before it split off on another route. She offered Theo a crude gesture when she looked through the rearview and caught him waving goodbye to her as he abandoned the pursuit. By the time she walked into her office, having consumed two cups of coffee and an extra gooey cinnamon roll from the cafe near the campus bookstore, her body felt quasi-functional.

Kaela closed her office door behind her. She dropped her tote on the desk, envious of its slow collapse, filled with the desire to do the same—melt into the floor like a boneless heap of human flesh. Just standing in place was exhausting. She retrieved the vial of cat hair and held it up in the shaft of watery morning light oozing through the window. She contemplated taking the sample to the lab, but she couldn't decide what type of test to run first. Instead, she placed the vial next to her bag and returned to the window.

"Forward aging is a process of rapid energy consumption which forces the temporal degradation to increase."

The mumbled hypothesis was too simple, but it was a start. A dry-erase marker sat on the window ledge. The familiar chemical smell wafted to her nose when she wrenched off the cap, and her brain clicked into place at the sensation. Pavlov would approve. She hastily scribbled a series of equations at the top of the giant glass pane of the window, the squeaking strokes stimulating the residual neurons her olfactory trigger missed.

This was her kingdom: math, physics, hypotheses, and equations grounded in laws. These were the tools she could use to process the chaotic world that surrounded her. She crossed her arms, staring at the basic functions connecting time and energy to the continual process of aging. She reworked it, making the equations more complex. Life was a series of stages, each with a unique temporal component. Children aged rapidly; young adults hit plateaus interspersed with leaps that could be unpredictable but averaged to a slightly elevated pace over a lifetime. Building on the axioms by ignoring the obvious impact of diet or environmental exposures, and using the assumption of an average lifespan driven by telomere reduction…

Kaela had worked the math before as part of the ongoing research in her lab, but this time the proof felt different. Previously, she was structuring her deductive argument around the idea of repairing existing damage to treat diseases, not speeding the process up, and certainly not taking the phenomenon in reverse. She reached the end of the glass and stepped away, eyes retracing each number and symbol. She chewed her lip, knowing she was on the cusp of understanding but that she needed to approach it from a new angle. She started back at the basics.

"As tau approaches zero, the relative perception of time slows. If something were to accelerate quickly enough, it would age more slowly.

But we were both stationary. Therefore, the time dilation could be driven by a gravitational field."

Kaela glanced around her room but was out of available space to restart her work without erasing something else. She rushed down the hall to a storage closet, knowing that even one minute could be enough to lose the end of a theoretical thread she had plucked from the jumble in her mind. She managed to haul two large whiteboards into her office and closed herself back in, alone with her madness once more. The actual passage of time was meaningless to her body while her mind was engaged in understanding its theoretical passage instead.

Knock knock knock.

That part there described the scenario in which a person could age faster in a bubble.

Knock knock.

"I saw her carry some things from storage, but she shut her door before I could even say good morning. That was over an hour ago, but she's definitely still in there."

The muffled voice was like a mosquito buzzing in her ear.

The sheer power of the necessary gravitational component was mind-boggling, not to mention the overall effect of that increase in time on the body. No, this couldn't be the solution.

"Kaela!"

Knock knock knock.

"What?" Kaela finally snapped at the interruption.

"Hey, what are you…" The door swung open enough for Anjana to stick her head through, eyes wide as she took in the room. "*Um*, this is a very Beautiful Mind situation you have going here. Are you okay?"

From her cross-legged position on the desk, Kaela surveyed the three surfaces covered in small, tightly spaced markings. Her shoes and an empty coffee cup were abandoned in the middle of the floor next to several open textbooks. She had a habit of running her fingers through her hair when she was ruminating over a particularly complex problem, so her head was wreathed in a disheveled halo. She could see how this scene might be unexpectedly off-putting to her coworker.

"Yes, I'm good."

"*Mm.*" The noncommittal grunt was accompanied by a narrow-eyed assessment before Anjana pushed the door open the rest of the way to reveal someone next to her. "Look who I found wandering the halls."

“Good morning, Mikaela.”

Landry’s eyes twinkled, or was that her imagination? She last saw him weeks ago, just before they left California, and only two days after he rescued her from the kidnapping situation. A fuzzy twisting sensation rose inside her head. It was a peculiar feeling that only occurred when Landry was in close proximity. Along with it came hunger, thirst, and a dull headache. Those were unique to her hangover, though, not the man. She had been too focused on her work to register the various physical sensations before this disruption.

“Hi.” The breathy greeting tumbled from Kaela’s lips, and she was certain that she looked like a love-struck schoolgirl. She shifted her expression to what she hoped was polite interest, clearing her throat.

“I’ll let you two catch up.” Anjana’s sly smirk revealed that she missed none of the awkwardness as she backed away. “Let’s do lunch next week, Kaela. Good to see you again, Dr. Griffiths.”

Landry stepped further into the room after Anjana’s quick retreat.

“I thought you were still traveling.” The pressure of the air against Kaela’s skin and the feel of the table beneath her hands amplified as he approached.

He smiled and extended one of the drinks she hadn’t noticed him holding. “I was. I just returned from Spain yesterday. Soy latte?”

Kaila blinked at the question but then reached out to receive the offering. “How did you know I like soy lattes?”

“I asked Hailey.” His sheepishness was deeply charming as he made this admission. “She called me this morning to let me know you might need a little extra caffeine. She didn’t mention why you had a rough night but is it safe to assume that whatever happened provoked this intense fixation on,” his eyes roved across her equations, digesting sections of them with a quick intelligence, “Shapiro delays and gravitational fields?”

“I didn’t get anywhere with relativity.” Kaela stood next to him, gazing at the troublesome section of work she discovered just before his arrival. “I’m beginning to think that time evolution equations with closed timelike curves are a better avenue. You could explain the rapid aging at a microscopic scale, therefore staying in agreement with Hawking’s chronology protection conjecture.”

“An interesting approach.” Landry nodded in agreement.

“I have to understand what I did to Brady in the desert.” Her voice was small in her own ears, and she kept her eyes fixed on the board as Landry turned her direction, his face close enough that she could easily reach up to touch his cheek. "If I can just get a grasp on the forward process, I can work backwards, reverse engineer a solution for youth instead of old age. It's right there in front of me. This entire situation is unbelievably frustrating – starting with a solution and working back to a hypothesis instead of the other way around. You would think this would be easier."

"Mikaela, you have the ability. You don't need the theory and the deductive argument to explain it in terms of physical laws because you are the proof by yourself."

Landry lifted a hand to her shoulder, squeezing gently in support.

"No, this is much bigger than me." Kaela shrugged his touch away. "You don't understand. You've lived for a thousand years in your little enclave of immortals. You haven't spent the last decade watching people you love slowly lose their minds and their lives to something you could have cured. This ability I have, it shouldn't just be mine."

Landry crossed his arms and leaned back against the edge of Kaela's desk, waiting for her to face him. She stayed focused on the board until her heart stopped thundering and the moisture in her eyes receded.

"I have endured the deaths of nearly everyone I have loved." His words weren't angry or intended to cut, they were sad, resigned.

"I'm sorry." Kaela moved into his arms on instinct, folding herself into him in an embrace of mutual comfort. "That wasn't fair of me."

"I thought your grandmother was the only one who battled with Alzheimer's before her death." Landry was warm and wonderfully solid beneath Kaela's cheek as his words rumbled through her.

"My father also showed early signs." She closed her eyes; his arms around her were an anchor holding her back from her usual emotional spiral regarding her father. "When he was diagnosed with pancreatic cancer, he refused treatment. It was his way of dying on his own terms. It only took four months."

Landry didn't respond right away, holding her snuggly against him instead. Kaela finally broke the contact, stepping away and sniffing

"Looks like that dossier didn't contain all the details of my life after all." A half-hearted, smug attempt at levity.

"Grab your shoes and your coat, I want to show you something." He stood and moved to the office door.

Kaela followed him out of the building and across the courtyard, burying her hands in her pockets and lowering her head against a wintry gust that cut painfully across her face. It was the last day of classes before exams, and the campus foot traffic was sparse. Her surreptitious glances at Landry were clearly not as covert as she intended, because his mouth turned up and he met her eyes after the first few instances.

"What's on your mind?"

"I haven't heard from you in weeks." She scrambled to frame this statement in a way that didn't invoke an overly clingy first-date-gone-wrong persona. "I mean, I know you've been visiting these other groups of magical people and doing some type of as yet undefined, covert work to locate Cassius, but I was hoping to get updates or something."

Her ears burned despite the frigid weather.

"*Ah,* I apologize. I don't mean this to be as condescending as it may come across, but three weeks to you pass a lot more slowly than three weeks to me. Time paradox aside." Kaela snorted at his sly wink. "I was concerned that you needed a chance to process what you went through without my complicating anything. Although Hailey assured me this morning that you are perfectly capable of telling me to leave if my presence is unwanted. I wasn't avoiding you, Mikaela, but while we are on the topic, you should consider that being close to me might put you in more danger. Cassius and Nisha spent centuries manipulating me through the people I form attachments with. They want something from you, and they'll use both of us in any way they can to obtain it. As will anyone else."

"You once told me not to trust anyone, now that my abilities are common knowledge. Does that include you?"

Landry came to a stop in front of the entrance to the physics building, placing his hands on her shoulders, the physical connection approximating an intimacy in their exchange that lent weight to his words.

"A century ago, I would have given you a different answer, and perhaps when another hundred years pass, my answer will change again. But here, in this lifetime, I would do anything to keep you safe. You have my promise."

His response was honest but complex. Kaela didn't have the time or emotional energy to digest it in its entirety, so she took it at face value, cataloging the words for a later date. The underlying tone of the exchange was moving in a direction that Kaela wasn't ready to travel, and she steered them into a new topic.

"Did you learn anything useful in Spain?"

"Yes, I learned quite a few things, but nothing about Cassius or his location that we didn't already know." Landry dropped his hands from her shoulders and held open the door to the building, gesturing to an elevator across the lobby once they were inside. "They are aware that a new talent was unveiled in North America and that there is hope for their unnaturally long lives to be restored. Beyond that, they haven't decided how to approach you and are still collecting what information they can through their networks while they debate sending an envoy to make your acquaintance. They have a very rigid social structure to keep order, and they can never be expected to make quick decisions. Before they act, the entire board must propose a plan, and the members vote on its execution."

"Interesting, when you said there were groups of immortals, I thought you meant something less organized, more like a neighborhood watch and less like a corporation."

The glass-fronted conference room across from the main entrance was occupied, and when Kaela glanced up, she was immediately ensnared in a shared look with a tall, striking man. He wore an expensive suit, and his skin was the smooth, warm hue of terracotta. His hair, dark enough to be called black rather than brown, fell past his shoulders. His sharp gaze followed her across the tiled floor with a bright intensity. She chose to be a coward and turned to face the elevator, her shoulders slightly hunched against the continued feeling of his appraisal.

"Should I know that man in the meeting room?" Her eyes darted to Landry and then back.

"I assume you mean Ahtah?" Kaela was too focused on avoiding eye contact to notice the quick glance and head shake Landry gave to the man on the other side of the glass. "The man looking at us? No, I don't believe you've met. He is one of my long-time companions and is here to discuss a potential project that an economics professor would like to pursue about the intersection of poverty and history, within the view of indigenous economic systems. I suggested they use that room because it's typically unoccupied."

"When you say 'long-time companion'," Kaela began.

"Over two hundred years."

Kaela's mouth snapped closed, and she didn't ask any additional questions as they entered the elevator and traveled up to the fifth floor.

"Hi, Dr. Griffiths!"

A perky, young student politely waited to the side of the doors when they opened. His bright-eyed smile faltered only briefly when Landry's arm drifted behind Kaela, a gentle but noticeable touch to escort her off the lift.

"Hello, Joshua. Are you finished for the day?"

"Yep, and I'll need to study for finals most of next week. I'll just telecommute through the end of the semester if that's okay." The adoring, fixated look he maintained while speaking to Landry explained the less than flattering side-eye he offered Kaela. "Or course, if you prefer that I come in person—"

"No, that's quite all right. Good luck on your exams, and I will see you in January."

Joshua gave one last lovelorn glance to his mentor and then studiously avoided acknowledging Kaela while waiting for the elevator doors to close between them.

"Undergraduate researcher?" she asked benignly.

"Undergraduate researcher," Landry confirmed.

"I do enjoy the tour of another department's home base." Kaela nodded a polite greeting to yet another person in the hallway. There had already been four more people since the elevator debacle who appeared amorously happy to see Dr. Landry Griffiths. "But is there a reason you would like me to see your office other than to meet your fan club?"

"My fan club?"

It was endearing to note that he said this with full sincerity while smiling and saying hello to the latest person greeting him in the same breath. Kaela waved off the confusion over his popularity.

"What did you want to show me?"

"This." Landry stepped into an open office, and Kaela read his name on the wooden placard next to the frame as she followed. "I wanted you to see what obsessing over the fundamental explanations amounts to."

The office was spacious, much more accommodating to a party of two than Kaela's had been. The wall to the left was decorated with a large painting, a scenic western American view with mountains soaring high above a lake, drenched in the warm light of the sun, while the foreground was wreathed in shadows. Kaela thought she could see tiny dark figures standing in the shallows of the water. Flanking the painting were several oversized bookshelves. A desk and two large chairs took up most of the floor space. To the right were another bookcase, a floor-to-ceiling chalkboard, and an oddly shaped cabinet. Behind the desk was an impressively sized window.

"I hate being in an older building." Kaela crossed the room and turned back after inspecting the view through the sunlit panes, her body wreathed in a bright halo. "The original buildings have these tiny, wood-enshrined peepholes, but this!" She spread her arms wide, feeling the heat of the late morning sun against her back. "This is a real window."

Landry's chuckle was his only response as he approached a stack of boxes tucked into a corner near the painting. He removed the topmost container and placed it on the desktop, gesturing Kaela forward before he reached inside to retrieve a volume. She inspected the handbound leather spine and plain, unmarked cover before opening it to the first few pages.

The orange-red edges split like overripe fruit, revealing a tan interior with the yellow tinge of age. The handwriting was neat, falling within the precise confines of the lightly gridded parchment, but also paradoxically slanted and relaxed. At first, she found only rudimentary equations describing the ordinary state of things. The further she flipped through the ink-stained pages, however, the more complicated the mathematical propositions became. By the final page, she was beginning to identify an uncanny resemblance to the work in her office.

Landry handed her another volume.

And then another.

The notebooks eventually became more modern until she was holding a familiar, college-ruled composition pad with a black marbled pattern on the cover. These were obviously Landry's attempts at discovering the science beneath the magic. If she assumed correctly, these notebooks spanned at least a hundred years of continuous work. She didn't want to ask, but the question issued from her lips anyway, a tiny probe, evaluating the depth of her impending emotional destruction.

"Did you ever find the proof?"

"Those are only a sample of my life's work." Landry gestured to the stack of boxes behind him. "But no. I haven't solved any of it yet."

Kaela's chest could explode. It was as if every emotion she ever felt, or even contemplated feeling, was amplified and funneled into this singular moment. The grief, the anger, the resignation, and the despair, all squeezed together into an impossibly small space, her heart occupying the center of an emotional black hole. It was too much. The feelings compressed and compressed, doubling in on themselves until her body ached for release. And where was there to go at that point except for another dimension entirely?

"Good. Your work will give me a head start on the solution." She let the negativity siphon through a space behind her ribs, her stubborn nature rising to the surface. "Looks like we're going to be partners after all."

England – 1535

Theo drained the cup of wine in his hand and observed the revelry in the smoke-hazed room. He hated these parties. There was always an excess of wine, women, and candles. He offered a vapid sneer to a passing courtier. The choice was to appear entertained, or risk being marked by the king's disfavor. His sour examination of the room fell upon a young couple, spinning their way through the laughing circle of dancers. Sarah and Charles were perfectly suited for this type of event. Charles had been raised at court, his flippant chivalry and aristocratic bearing bred into him as much as taught. Sarah, though, was a wolf who was trained to prance beneath the spotted hide of a fawn.

After Cassius brought him to London from France, Theo was assigned three tutors. The first instructed him on languages, including both English and Latin. The second tutor provided training with various weapons and with his magical abilities. The third acted as a type of valet, selecting appropriate clothing and instructing him on courtly etiquette. This last training was by far the most challenging. Theo was not to slurp his soup like a common farmhand, nor was he to set upon the meat like a starved mongrel. How was he to know a gnawed bone was under no circumstances placed back on the trencher, and the square of linen was to be draped across his left shoulder?

Every day, he spent morning, noon, and night alone with his instructors, learning how to be someone else and not himself. One day, Landry brought Sarah into the room where Theo was receiving his language lessons. When the tutor asked him to translate a phrase from French to English, she spoke in passable French, inquiring whether she could be exempt from the instruction. The tutor then asked in German how she knew French. She responded in Spanish that she learned the languages of all the men who frequented the Inn where she previously worked. After that, her language lessons were separate from Theo's.

In combat, she quickly became decent with a bow, but when it came to magic, her ability to close the minor cuts and disperse the frequent bruises from training were nothing compared to Theo's ability to sling a boulder thirty feet with only a thought. Eventually, the tutor abandoned any hopes of having them spar one another and relegated her to the corner of the room to throw small knives at a target.

It was during one of their dancing lessons that Theodore first spoke directly to her. She only needed to watch the steps of a dance once, so the tutor demonstrated the selection of the day, and after Sarah successfully repeated the steps three times without error, she and Theo were paired together to practice. Theodore's inability to move his feet in time to the tempo finally caused the tutor to throw up his hands in frustration and leave the room, stating that Theo's wooden feet were now Sarah's homework.

"I suppose we will be here all day then." Sarah lifted a delicate eyebrow. "I don't know how to make you a better dancer."

"I do not know how to be a better dancer, milady."

"We both know I am not a lady." She offered a complex smile, a mix of merriment and chagrin, the smile of someone who was not one bit ashamed of who they were but felt it was required to observe social norms. "There is no need to pretend when it is just us two in this room."

"Well, lady or not, you should be trained to fight, not left to throw little knives at a stationary target. You accept your purgatory too easily."

"I accept nothing, and I am not a child," Sarah replied sharply.

"No, you are a young woman who needs to defend herself against malicious men."

"Are you concerned that men would try to force themselves on me?" She stopped dancing and dropped his hands in a show of annoyance.

"You are attractive. Am I wrong to assume they would?" he retorted.

"Attractive." She simpered. "Would you make advances on me also?"

Now it was Theodore's turn to appear offended. "I am married."

"Are you? And where is your wife, Theodore?"

There was a long silence while Theo struggled against a flood of unexpected emotions, and Sarah pretended to be unvexed by the pained expression on his face.

"I was married. She died."

"And you use her memory to win an argument?" Sarah tutted. "How chivalrous."

"I was mistaken." Theodore stepped back with a sharp nod of his head before beginning his retreat. "Perhaps you are a child after all."

Sarah eyed him for a moment and then shook her head with remorse.

"Don't leave. I am sorry. I am not used to men behaving as you do."

"You mean men who do not want to take you to bed?" Theo paused, looking at her over his shoulder as he reconsidered. "Yes, I suppose it's harder to have a conversation with someone who speaks to you as a person, not just a nice set of tits and a warm cunt."

Sarah threw her head back and roared with laughter.

"Our language tutor must be commended if he has already taught you such tasteless English words. In fact, you said them with such conviction I couldn't even tell you are French."

"Perhaps we can help one another. You teach me to dance well enough to be finished with these horrid lessons. I will teach you to fight so you won't have to rely on men's good graces."

Sarah nodded at Theo, the gesture as final as a handshake in cementing their alliance. Now, watching Sarah as she twirled on Charles' arm, her radiant laughter drawing the admiring gaze of many men in the room, Theo wondered if his lessons were helping Sarah protect herself or if he was just honing another deadly tool for Cassius' arsenal.

Chapter 3

Hailey's skin was glistening with the faintest shimmer of sweat, the sun refracting against the miniscule crystals. Kaela could taste the saltiness puckering her cheeks as if she had stretched out and licked it from her. They were lying on the ground, two radii coming together with their heads at the center of rotation and their feet spread, points along an endless circle. They gasped, sucking in the air to work past their exertion. The pounding of newly oxygenated blood through Kaela's body brought everything into sharp, vivid focus, and she nearly ran her tongue against that tan, glistening skin, but the moment passed, and Hailey rose from the ground to retrieve her bag.

They were enjoying a shockingly warm afternoon. It was one of those strange days that disoriented you with thoughts of spring flowers and vacations at the beach, while there was snow looming a few days away in the forecast. When Hailey suggested a trip to the nearby cabin for a trail run followed by a round of calisthenics, Kaela wholeheartedly agreed. It would be a dramatic improvement over their usual gym-bound routine. She closed her eyes as the sun soaked into her skin, and she listened to Hailey rummaging through her bag for a snack.

"That was a great run," Hailey stated around a mouthful of food before slapping Kaela's elbow. "What's up with you?"

"Nothing, just preoccupied," she responded noncommittally, peeking up from behind her hand.

"*Mmhmm.*" Hailey narrowed her eyes and took another slow, slightly aggressive bite of her energy bar. "Just tell me you don't want to talk about it. Don't bullshit me."

Kaela rolled over to her stomach. "Fine, I'm pissed off that I'm supposed to have all these 'powers', and I can't consistently do much of anything other than make flowers bloom unless I'm drunk. I feel incredibly useless. I am *also* pissed that the last three weeks have been filled with zero new information about Cassius. What is he waiting for?"

"And?" Hailey prompted.

"What do you mean, 'and'?"

"And you have very carefully avoided saying anything about Landry in the last two hours we've been together." She raised her eyebrows knowingly. "He said he went to see you yesterday, but he is also avoiding talking about it. Quite suspicious. Did you two knock boots yet or…?"

"No, we didn't do anything." Kaela stood and dusted off her clothing, not meeting her friend's stare. "I hate that I am even saying this out loud. I told myself after Jason and I were divorced that I wasn't going to get involved with anyone again. Landry obviously thinks that being with me is some sort of complication. We're just colleagues."

"First of all, don't let your trauma define you." Hailey pasted on the hard expression she inevitably used when scolding Kaela for her life choices. "Don't be that person that clings to the bad experiences in her past as if it sets her apart and makes her special because she is damaged in a dark and mysterious way. You are better than that. Do not let the very memory of Jason control you."

"This conversation is a moot point. When Landry realized Cassius was still alive, I *felt* a wall go up around him."

"How can the two of you be this frustratingly similar?" Hailey tipped her head to the side. "Have you tried to initiate anything with him?"

"I don't see why it always has to be me," Kaela retorted. "I mean, I know he was traveling around the globe, choosing to do God-knows-what and visit God-knows-who to get a handle on this whole Cassius situation, but he didn't think to text me even once? And now that I am saying this out loud, I feel incredibly ridiculous. Obviously, he was busy, and I'm being dramatic. THIS is why I shouldn't be dating anyone."

"Landry is focused on protecting you." Hailey finally stopped grinning and adopted a serious expression. "That is what he does, he takes the safety of people he *cares about* very seriously. It is a ridiculous, narcissistic pattern of behavior he's had for centuries. You have to remember, a few weeks doesn't seem like a long time to him. I'm sure he doesn't have a clue that you feel neglected. When he has a self-assigned mission to fulfill, he can be a stubborn man with a martyr complex. But he is also an extremely loyal friend and family member. If he were a worthless idiot like your ex-husband, I would steer you away."

Kaela gave Hailey a look that very clearly expressed her skepticism at this statement. Hailey polished off her snack bar, and an apple materialized in its place. She sat down, tucking her legs beneath her and leaning back to let the sun fall across her face.

"Don't look at me like that, 'Todd' was a different situation. I didn't know it was Teddy at first, and then when you showed me a picture, I didn't want to expose everyone right away by admitting I knew him. I thought it was harmless. I knew you weren't attached, and he was a good lay, which was all you needed at the time."

"And what do I need now?" Kaela gave her a hard stare.

"You need to figure out how to control your abilities," Hailey shrugged. "I got you a tutor. You also need to learn how to fight so you aren't such an easy target next time there's an attempt to snatch you. I'm sorry, but you seriously have the self-defense skills of a small child."

"Nice." Kaela kicked a rock at her. "And for the love of God, don't say Theo is going to be my tutor."

"Well, he used to help Cass with the newly discovered talent." Hailey suspiciously avoided eye contact. "I'm not suggesting that you start sleeping with Teddy again. However, he is a neutral party and can be trusted. He even trained with me a few hundred years ago when I first joined the team. It's a safe play."

"Safe!" Kaela exclaimed, incredulous at the very concept. "He kidnapped me. Twice."

"Okay, but hear me out," Hailey began. "He first kidnapped you in a moment of anger after he saw you were with Landry. He had already agreed to bring you to Nisha and knew Landry would never let you leave with him. If he hadn't gotten you to Nisha, she would have sent someone far worse to fetch you. And you know that we were working together in California. Both times, he made sure you weren't hurt in any way, right?"

"Other than shattering my sense of security in my own home and violating any trust I had in him, sure. Maybe, *maybe*, given enough time, I can get used to being around him, but you are asking for a lot."

"About that. He should be here any minute. We are starting combat training next, and I brought wraps for your hands, but prepare yourself for a lot of bruising."

"Are you ignoring me?" Kaela leaned down, bringing their faces closer together. "KID. NAPPED. Forced me into a car. Dragged me out of a hotel. Zip-tied my appendages. No matter what the explanation, he cannot be trusted, and he is definitely not safe. Did you discuss this with Landry?"

"Yes." Hailey's expression bordered on annoyance at the question. "Landry doesn't exactly see straight when it comes to Teddy, and he wasn't happy about it, but he said it was your decision."

"Will Theo even be an effective teacher if I don't trust him? Because I don't, and there isn't much of a chance I will anytime soon."

"I guess we just have to find out," she replied, her mouth twisting into one of her mischievous looks. "I can make him stand in as your practice dummy for combat drills."

Silence filled the clearing during the prolonged glare Kaela leveled at her.

"Fine." Kaela grumbled at Hailey, throwing a hand up in resignation. "Here is the deal. You show me how to get Bruce Lee on his ass, and I will continue to *consider* training with him on the magic part. But I don't trust him. I don't like him. And I currently resent you putting me in this position in the first place."

"Done." Hailey's hand gripped Kaela's arm, locking eyes with her to impress her sincerity. "If you are truly uncomfortable or need a break at any time, you just tell me. I am not dismissing your feelings. You went through two very distressing events, and that shapes how you respond, whether you want it to or not. You're strong and capable, but only you are allowed to decide if you are ready to do these things. I'm sorry if my bringing him today seems pushy."

The genuine concern with which she delivered these statements caused the anger in Kaela to wither. She could never stay mad at Hailey for long.

"Thank you. I know you generally have good intentions, even if it was a little 'pushy'. I'm okay for now."

Right on time, the shuffling crackle of dead leaves preceded the appearance of Theo at the head of the trail. The clearing with the cabin was at least an acre of smooth flat ground, and the two women stood in the middle, but even at that distance, Theo's presence gave Kaela an unsettled feeling. Hailey grinned and called out to him.

"Welcome back, Teddy. It's been a few years since you trained here with me. Glad you could still find it!"

"Kaela." Theo nodded.

She hadn't spoken to him since they left the desert, and for a moment, the direction of the conversation hinged on the path she selected. She could be stiff, hesitant with fear. She could be relaxed and flippant, ignoring the recent transgressions. Instead, she decided on something in between.

"I imagine I will have to hit you a LOT before I perfect my combat skills."

"You're the dummy today." Hailey shrugged in response to his confused glance in her direction.

"Well, you could have told me that I was going to be a punching bag, but okay." Theo grumbled under his breath and approached them.

"Where would the fun be in that, tough guy?" Hailey laughed.

Large targets of various designs lined the forest edge to the left, each pitted and gouged. One had a distinctly human outline and looked to have been recently decapitated. To the right was an empty wooden rack along with a strange contraption that stood seven feet tall, boasting a multitude of poles jutting in every direction like porcupine quills. When they first arrived, Kaela's inquiry about the archaic equipment was met with a dismissive statement that they wouldn't be using it any time soon.

"I thought you were about to make me swing a sword." Kaela had gestured at the wooden combat training devices.

"You have a lot of basics to learn before I slap steel in your hand, but it's going to happen eventually."

Hailey's response had been dismissive, leading Kaela to accept the fixtures as if they were just part of the background. Theo, however, approached the headless target with an air of familiarity and raised a questioning eyebrow at Hailey. She shrugged and started digging around in her backpack again. She found what she was looking for and walked back to Kaela, throwing a careless response over her shoulder to him.

"I got a little carried away when I was working out my aggressions with the battle axes a few days ago."

"First of all, it is the year of our Lord 2025, not the fifteenth century." Kaela eyed the strips of fabric in Hailey's hands. "When would you ever need a battle axe? And second, do you all own this property? The only green spaces close to the city are parkland. Are we even allowed to be here?"

"Ever the rule follower." Theo quipped as he returned to the middle of the clearing. "This is privately owned, and we have used this area to train for a very long time."

"I wasn't asking you, Douche." Kaela directed her next question at Hailey again. "If it's private, this land must be worth a small fortune."

"It is," Hailey took one of Kaela's hands and began wrapping it with a cloth band. "You will find that we are connected to just about anyone with money. 'We' being this group of former immortals you've fallen in with. Some of us are very good at predicting the rise and fall of powerful people in human society. Others are just really good at making friends and accumulating favors."

"Is that an actual gift, weaponized charisma?" Kaela joked, only realizing that she had said something wrong when Hailey's hands paused in their movements.

"Yes," Theo broke the silence, his voice uncharacteristically careful as he glanced at Hailey. "One of us was gifted with exactly that. He was loved by everyone he met."

Hailey resumed her task, studiously avoiding Theo's eyes as she finished the wrap on Kaela's second hand and pulled a roll of athletic tape from her pocket. She freed two long pieces, biting to rip each of them loose, and then finished the protective coverings before stepping back to fix Kaela with a quiet, sad regard.

"He died a long time ago, but there have been others with similar skills. Time to warm up. Have you ever thrown a serious punch in your life?"

Kaela shook her head, wanting to ask more but knowing from Hailey's dismissive tone she would refuse that line of discourse.

"We have a lot to work on, then." Hailey pulled her to the center of the clearing and made her face Theodore. "Pretend that you're about to fight him, hand to hand."

Kaela hesitated, then moved her right foot back, angling away from his body. She channeled everything she once learned from Billy Blanks as she brought her hands up to face level, fists clenched. She shuffled her weight back and forth on the balls of her feet.

"What is that?" Hailey laughed, distracting Kaela from the death stare she was giving Theo behind her fists of fury.

Hailey stepped forward and raised a hand, slapping the back of Kaela's right wrist, sending the associated fist straight into the middle of the cheek it was supposed to be protecting.

"*Ow!*" Kaela dropped her posturing and gaped at her trainer with an incredulous expression. "Why?"

"Sorry." Hailey cringed just enough that there was a slight chance the apology was genuine. "That is the worst guard I have ever seen. Let me guess, you took a cardio kick-boxing class once."

"Body Combat is a pretty demanding program." Kaela sniffed indignantly. "Also, I have seen every Jet Lee film from the 1990s, so I should be a quick study."

Hailey's head fell back as she released a full-bellied laugh. Theo managed to keep his own response to a reserved smirk, and Kaela felt that she had simultaneously passed and failed a test. She stepped forward again and positioned her guard hand.

"This hand has to be ready for an attack. That's why it's up here. The next time I reach out and slap you, it better be prepared for the impact. Also, you're a righty, so you should be ready to rain the pain with a haymaker right hook if there is an opening."

Hailey raised Kaela's left hand to eye level and pushed on her chin until it tucked back. She then reached down to Kaela's yoga pant-clad legs and pulled up on her left thigh until her weight shifted back to her right foot.

"Stay loose but keep your weight back there. The left foot should be ready to block, just like your right hand. If a kick comes in, you deflect and take it on the shin. You get a break in your opponent's guard, this leg is now a weapon, and you kick the shit out of him. Stay relaxed, don't keep those legs too close together or too far away. You have to be nimble but rooted."

"Like a bamboo shoot dancing with the wind. Got it."

Hailey braced herself on her knees as her shoulders shook with repressed mirth.

"Yes, Crouching Tiger. Like Bamboo."

"I prefer Shang-Chi." Kaela threw a wink to her friend. "I am training to be a superhero, after all."

"Let's see that left jab."

After Hailey gestured at Theodore, Kaela seized the opportunity and shuffled forward. Theo's eyebrows peaked in sudden alarm at the intensity with which she approached. Kaela closed the distance and started circling to the right. He raised his own hands and matched her steps despite the slightly baffled expression on his face. After half a turn, Kaela saw an opportunity and jabbed with every ounce of energy she had.

He sidestepped.

Kaela's punch went wide, and she short-stepped to bring herself back into a guard position. Theo placed a hand against her rib cage and pushed, gently, almost apologetically, but still firmly enough that she lost the little balance she had regained and tumbled to all fours.

"Yikes." Hailey grimaced. "That was pathetic."

"Shut up." Kaela seethed, taking three solid inhales to calm the rage inside her. "Let's go again."

Kaela focused on the way Theo moved as she returned to circling. After two slow revolutions, Kaela gave a quick, half jab with her left hand that wouldn't connect, and then moved toward him with her right hip, feeling the weight ripple up her side and down her arm as she threw a right hook. This time, she made contact and allowed herself a little spark of satisfaction as he blocked the punch and stepped away. His mouth twitched up at the corners in approval.

"Not as bad, but still not great." Kaela scowled at Hailey's statement but stayed in her stance when she approached. "Your jab has zero power behind it because you're popping up from your knees and dropping your shoulder when you do it. Here, move through it slowly, and I'll show you how to fix that."

The next thirty minutes are spent working on the mechanics of Kaela's left and right jabs. Hailey made her punch the air over and over while moving her feet, pushing her stomach in, lifting her arms, or lowering her chin. By the time Hailey considered Kaela's jab, the most basic of punches, acceptable, she could barely keep her arms up, and sweat was pouring down her spine.

"Teddy, my sweet." Hailey tilted her head and grinned roguishly. "Time to hold up your end of this. She gets one punch, and you don't get to dodge it or counter."

Kaela approached a resigned Theo and focused on keeping her feet moving while she assessed his defensive stance. When she saw an opening, she struck, and this time she felt the difference in the way her body moved with the rapid thrust of her leading hand. It was slow, her muscles having already expended most of their energy stores, but the movement was still tighter, more controlled than before Hailey's tutelage. Theodore brought his elbow forward and caught her fist on his right arm.

"Good!" Hailey exclaimed, coming forward to thump Kaela on the back and hand her a water bottle. "You are still so slow, you look like you're fighting in water, but we can work on that. Teddy, you didn't follow my instructions. The point was to give her a free shot."

"You said I couldn't duck or return fire." He gave an innocent shrug. "You said nothing about blocking."

Kaela squinted her eyes at Hailey as she shook out her left fist. Fighting in water, indeed. Todd took a drink from a sports bottle, looking infuriatingly fresh and energetic.

“Sparring with someone who has no idea how to fight is strange.” His quizzical expression shifted when Kaela’s scowl deepened. “No, I’m serious! You weren’t told how to circle or feint, and you just did it. You don’t blink when you throw a punch either. Stone cold killer.”

Kaela couldn’t help the curling of her lips and accompanying snort that escaped as he clapped her on the back. His relentless cockiness was fracturing the icy barricade of righteous anger she so carefully built. She ran the scenarios through her head, begging herself to remember why that boundary was between them. He kidnapped her. He dragged her from her home. He was standing right in front of her now, cracking jokes like they were friends. The disgust shifted inward. On two separate occasions, she proved to be helpless, unable to defend herself from a single, solitary man that decided to snatch her. Pathetic.

A fresh wave of indignation set her body on fire, and her arm moved without thought as she smashed her fist into his cheek. He didn’t see the sucker punch coming. The impact of it had him shuffling backwards on his feet before he lost his balance and fell to the dirt, water bottle flying.

“Oh, my god!” Hailey’s face was a mix of shock and pride as she stared down at Theo’s sprawled body.

He sat for a long moment, one hand reaching up to touch the spot of impact as he worked his jaw to assess the damage. He gave a long sigh and leaned back on his hands to look up at Kaela.

“I’m sorry.” All sarcasm and amusement were gone from his tone. “I know that does nothing to fix what I have done to you over the last few months. I would do it again if I had a choice, and I don’t expect you to understand, but I am still truly sorry for how my actions made you feel. I never wanted you to feel unsafe around me. Never. The situation forced my actions.”

“That’s not enough.” Kaela’s body sent a shudder through her arms, a byproduct of adrenaline or exhaustion, she wasn’t sure which. “You pretended to be someone else for a year, ‘Todd’. You are a stranger to me. You violated my trust in so many ways. ‘Sorry’ doesn’t cut it. Especially not when it comes with qualifiers.”

“I know.” He continued to watch her from his seat on the ground.

“Why?” Kaela finally asked.

“I thought I was doing the best I could for you.”

“For me? Or for you?”

He took a deep breath and stared into the woods as if searching for the best answer before responding.

"Both, I guess." He faced her as he said this, his eyes focused and serious, reminding her of the way he acted when they were in the desert.

It was Kaela's turn to gaze into the trees. There were two people in one body when she looked at him. There was the funny, charismatic guy she dated for a year with the intellectual depth of a fish but an ocean of charm. Then there was this new person that she barely knew with a darker, contemplative nature beneath that playfulness.

"They could have killed me out there. You knowingly put me in that situation."

"You would have been put in that situation whether I was there or not. I managed to insert myself into that group so I could make sure that you were protected. I wouldn't have let it go that far."

Kaela shook her head in disbelief. He really thought there was a level of control to the events in the desert. She was surrounded by nearly a dozen gifted people able to wield their powers. In no scenario would she have walked away unscathed if they all decided she needed to die.

"You could have just warned me and prevented my kidnapping in the first place."

"If I'd done that, they would have known I was on your side." He shook his head, frustration evident on his face. "They would have picked another time to go after you, and I wouldn't have known anything about it. We had to let them show their cards so we could understand their intentions."

Kaela was silent, her brain running through all the questions swirling around since those events.

"We all know that Cass is back now. You aren't ready to take him face to face, Kaela. Please let me help you prepare."

"You think he was the one who sent the team?"

"Not directly, no, but Cassius is a cunning bastard who spent thousands of years learning how to spin a web. I absolutely think he was involved at some level in everything that happened to you."

Kaela pulled the inside of her cheek between her teeth, rethinking her conversations with Landry and Hailey on the subject. Both of them spoke of Cass with hushed reverence and fear, as if he were the chess grandmaster and they were scrambling to anticipate his every move. Once again, she wondered if he was truly such an insurmountable opponent or if he just left a taste of fear in their mouths that tainted their opinions. According to Hailey, there were only three options: Cassius knew the attack was going to happen but did nothing to stop it, he planted the seed that turned into the plan to kidnap her, or he directly coordinated the entire thing.

"He is a master at manipulating people," Theo continued to beseech her. "He says and does things differently depending on who he is using. The Cassius I know is completely different than the Cassius who Hailey or Landry knows. He can mold himself into the exact person he needs to be to best control the other person. On top of that, he has the strongest powers of anyone. You aren't ready for him. You should be hiding, learning what your powers are, and preparing for an eventual confrontation while we can still protect you. If you really can do everything that he can, you are not just *a* threat, you are *the* threat."

"I won't be sent running." Kaela rested her fists on her hips in defiance, meaning every word. "I have clawed and scraped my way to where I am today. I am not giving that up just because some man with a god complex thinks I'm competition. It's not like I can even control it. What happened in the desert was a fluke."

"Accident or not, you altered the age of a person." Theo gestured as if she just proved his point. "He will come for you eventually."

"I'm not running," she reiterated.

"If you won't go completely dark, all I ask is that you consider a temporary sabbatical." He seemed momentarily resigned to her stubborn refusals. "Just long enough to figure your magical shit out."

Kaela shook her head slowly but then shifted to a noncommittal shrug, as if she would entertain the idea.

"Get up." She waved an exasperated hand at him. "It's weird to talk down at you like this."

"Well, that was fun," Hailey finally joined the conversation. "Are we all good?"

"We are nowhere close to 'good,' but I think Theo and I are ready to continue training now." Kaela gave him a sidelong stare.

"You can have a couple of free shots at me if that will help." He offered, sheepishly. "You haven't broken my nose yet. They say the third time's the charm."

A bark of laughter slipped out, and Kaela felt that wall fracture just a bit more. She turned to Hailey and found her standing with her arms crossed, monitoring the exchange and shifting her assessment between them. She gave a curt nod.

"Time to grapple."

Kaela looked at Theo. He towered over her by at least eight, maybe ten inches. He was broad with a wingspan one and a half times the size of hers. She spent many hours in appreciation of his muscular body and knew exactly how outmatched she was before they even began.

"I think I should grapple with you instead," Kaela responded to Hailey. "He's huge. Why are all the men Cassius selected for this group so big? I guess he didn't value the small-statured but highly intelligent type."

"Kaela," Hailey's voice was gentle and somewhat condescending. "You were born in the age where a person's ability to think is often directly correlated with their success. When Cassius started selecting people a thousand years ago, muscle and size were everything. No man fought with their wits except the solitary one in charge. Everyone else needed to physically provide protection. You can't practice against me because you need to be able to hold your own against these giant bastards that think the way to win a fight is with brute strength."

"I see." Kaela sized up Theo as if there were an ice cube's chance in hell that she could hold her own against him in hand-to-hand combat. "If I were in charge, I might want a few thinkers around to help validate my strategies, but I guess my ego isn't big enough to assume I could shoulder the mental load solo."

Hailey released a very undignified guffaw, and Theo cocked an eyebrow in her direction, though he kept the bulk of his focus on Kaela, no doubt monitoring for any unexpected attacks.

"You and I weren't born with that level of male audacity." Hailey winked. "Which is why we will one day live under a matriarchy where women don't waste their energy propping up overvalued males but instead will support other women in our global conquests."

"Hey." Theo held up his hands at the hostile looks he was receiving in stereo. "I am an exceptional acolyte. I would prefer my orders be directed from a strong, competent source, so you won't see me complaining when your prophecy is realized."

"Sure." Kaela scoffed. "The kidnapper is now the woke foot soldier."

"He actually is serious," Hailey admitted, somewhat begrudgingly. "He has always treated me as a person first, not just as a woman. That's saying a lot since we met in the sixteenth century."

The laughter that was bubbling up in Kaela's throat died out with a fizz. They met five hundred years ago. As with every other occasion where their ages were mentioned, her brain froze at the yawning chasm of time that their lives spanned.

"Well, let's grapple then."

The words left her mouth automatically, but her thoughts were still traveling through the years of unknown experiences these two seemingly normal individuals shared. They existed over centuries of life which Kaela could theoretically impart to someone on a whim, like a Greek god of old. What would her devoutly religious grandmother say to that?

We can accept God becoming Man to save Man, but not Man becoming God to save himself.

Did she have to become God to save herself and these strangers she was beginning to think of as family?

England – 1817

It was midday, but the noise of the tavern next door was just loud enough to camouflage the faint reverberations of metal striking against metal. Landry waited outside the building, straining his ears to deconvolute the sounds within. Two people were fighting with blades, the exchanges punctuated with grunts, taunts, and laughter. He tried the door handle and found it locked, but a quick mental nudge sent the interior bolt sliding free. He stepped into the broad front room just in time to see Theodore slice a blade across Anne's upper arm and shove an elbow into her face.

The crack of Anne's nose and the sight of blood welling up along her freshly carved flesh filled Landry with a sudden, swift rage. He flung out a hand, the concussive crack of energy pulsing through the room as his power launched Theodore several feet into the air, slamming him backwards into a wall. Landry's quick reflexes let him duck under the dagger Theo released in that same instant. A low rumble shook the floors.

"Enough!" Anne stepped between the two men and spat a glob of red-tinged mucus on the wooden planks near her feet. "Landry, it was well struck. Look, I've already healed."

"He injured you on purpose," Landry's voice was low and cold.

"It's called training, you overprotective ape."

"She can't learn if you keep treating her like she'll break," Theodore retorted. His stare was unwavering, but the vibrating of the earth faded. "She gives as good as she gets."

Landry glanced dismissively at the shallow cuts crossing Theo's biceps, then he scowled at the woman sitting in the corner. "And you just watch them do this?"

"I watch Anne learn how to protect herself," Cleda's voice was gentle and soothing as she stood, her skirts rustling like a breeze through soft wheat when she moved to Theo's side. "A woman with no fighting ability is just waiting for the wrong situation to make her a victim."

"Does he also cut you open to teach you self-defense?"

Cleda ran a hand slowly over the wounds on Theodore's arm, the skin smooth and healthy in the wake of her touch. When she finished mending the injuries, she gave Landry a reproachful look and focused her scrutiny on Anne, searching for any remaining lacerations.

"Of course not. He shows me basic skills. We do not use blades."

Although the edges of his mouth softened at Cleda's words, he did not relent his glowering.

"You wouldn't be offended if it was Charles or one of your other soldiers," Theo stated.

"No, I would not, because they are trained warriors who are matched to your skill set." Landry turned his fiery stare back to Theodore at this statement. "Anne is a spy, not a soldier. If you'd like to fight someone, I'd be happy to oblige. I won't even use my abilities."

Theo's face creased in a slight frown, and he returned his blade to the scabbard. Anne gave a wicked chuckle at his reluctance.

"Whatever is the matter, dear sir? Not interested in a sword fight with our master assassin?" It was Landry's turn to flinch as she said this. "Now, now, don't pretend that word offends you. Every time Cassius sends you on a secret mission, a former problem shows up in a ditch, the victim of an unidentified highwayman. We all know your mercenary skills are unsurpassed."

Landry adopted a deeply vexed expression as he continued to address Anne. "Please take more care in what you say among mixed company. I came here today because of your statements this morning in front of the servants and your continual, public declarations regarding global politics. It is decidedly unusual for a woman in high society to speak so. I must ask you to give the appearance of social compliance, even if it is just a façade."

"Fine."

Landry stiffened at the unexpectedly docile response and looked around at the other witnesses to the conversation. Theodore studiously avoided involvement, finding the cup in his hand infinitely more interesting. Cleda's eyebrows threatened to disappear into her hairline.

"Fine?" Landry repeated.

"Yes, fine." Anne said with exasperation. "Cleda started her courses today, which means I am only a few days away. I'm always exceptionally cranky at this time."

"Annabelle!" Cleda's face was a brilliant hue, and she tried to disappear into the wall.

Theodore's already intense dissociative focus on his hands redoubled.

Landry grimaced in shocked amusement.

"What?" Anne stared them down defiantly. "It's something my body does every moon cycle. I don't see why that should be a source of shame. No one ridicules men as animals for continually growing hair on their face. Our bodies have their own natural behaviors."

"Indeed." Landry gave a curt nod then promptly changed the topic. "I will be busy for the rest of the evening." He turned to Theodore instead. "I have an errand to run, but then I will go to the club, shall I see you there?"

"I can accompany you on your errand as I have no previous engagements this afternoon." Theo set down his cup and executed a quick bow to the ladies, following Landry out.

When they reached the carriage, Landry halted Theodore with a light tug at his elbow.

"This errand may be unsavory to you," he warned, observing the inquisitive tilt of Theo's head and the tightening of his brow as the other man processed the meaning of this statement.

"This is another missive sent from our Commander, then?"

Landry nodded in confirmation.

"Are you always such an obedient errand boy for him?" Theodore glanced at the driver and kept his voice low. "For all of your superior attitude, you condescend to the role of assassin quite willingly, it seems."

"You wouldn't understand." Landry stiffened, his icy tone a warning.

"What exactly would I fail to comprehend?"

The two men stared at one another.

"I am a gentleman driven by loyalty. I follow Cassius because I chose, a long time ago, to do this in exchange for the lives we live. I wouldn't expect someone devoid of moral principles to understand."

"I am going to disregard the very obvious stab you just made at my dignity." Theo settled onto the bench across from Landry, pulling the door closed behind him and slapping the roof through the open window to signal the driver. "My loyalty has never been questioned. I just don't claim a moral high ground while hiding the true nature of my deeds in shadow."

"I trust Cassius to know what is necessary for the greater good."

Theo shrugged noncommittally, and Landry maintained an indignant expression for the remainder of the very quiet ride.

Chapter 4

"Focus, Kaela."

Her mind snapped back at the sharp reprimand.

She and Theo were sitting on the floor of her living room, and she was holding his hand, staring at a thin, raised line along the back of it, the remnant of an injury from the epic sword fight he and Hailey waged the day they were training together. Kaela was supposed to be removing a faint sunspot that colored the skin near the knuckle of his index finger, but her attention continually drifted to the wound, tracing the pink puckering of the skin beneath the darker red of the scab.

"I said, FOCUS."

"You have awfully delicate hands for a stone mason," she grumbled in return.

Hailey sniggered in the background, and Theo's nostrils flared.

"I haven't exactly been carving stone for a living recently," he retorted, lowering his eyelids in a pointed glare. "And you never complained about my *fingers* before. In fact, I have gotten quite a few blasphemous statements out of your mouth by using just two of them."

Kaela grunted in annoyance and tried to drop his hand, but he gripped her fingers tightly, preventing the break in contact. Her jaw clenched in silent warning, but he persisted.

"I watched you in the desert. You need to focus, go into that weird stupor where you close your eyes and hum. Right now, you aren't even trying."

She rolled her eyes like an adult before she looked at the spot again. She tried thinking through the process like she did in the desert. Melanin was a normal response to sun exposure. This skin was aged, made of old cells that accumulated darker bodies in them from years of UV damage. They had embraced the response to physical assault over time, and become bruised, decaying things. So much melanistic drama at a cellular level.

The scab, though, was recently formed. It was the result of a stray swing of a weapon that cleaved the flesh along a tiny seam, damage that had nothing to do with aging. Honestly, Kaela was shocked Theo and Hailey weren't covered in injuries from head to toe after what she had witnessed.

First had been the hand-to-hand grappling. Hailey instructed Kaela on a few points before setting her against Theo. They started with the basics, self-defense maneuvers for breaking out of a hold. Theo grabbed Kaela from behind, his body pressed tightly against her as she dropped her weight to throw him off balance and alternated between jerking her head back into his face or stomping on his foot. After one particularly well-aimed head strike, Theo begged off any further demonstrations. They then moved to more advanced tactics, and Kaela was soon coated not only in her own sweat, but his as well.

At some point, Theo removed his shirt, and Kaela fought against a tugging feeling low in her belly when his hard body pressed into her, sweaty flesh to sweaty flesh. Her brain betrayed her, providing snippets of other times when their limbs connected in a heated tangle. His mouth near her ear made the skin tighten along her neck, and the strong, tangy smell of him coated her tongue. He was pulsing with the musky scent of testosterone, not unpleasant, but persistent. She tried to expel it from her nose, but each inhale just drew more of the oily pheromone into her, twisting her thoughts.

Theo reached around her shoulders again, and she threw him to the ground by pulling him forward over her planted hip. His weight drove the momentum, and he fell to the ground. Kaela attempted to capitalize on the opportunity by dropping over him, intent on pinning his arms. She belatedly realized she was now straddling his hips with her thighs, their faces only inches apart.

Kaela jumped back to her feet.

"Okay!" She gave Hailey a stilted half-salute. "I think we're all finished here. My arms are Jello, and I can use another gallon of water before I pass out."

She didn't wait around for a response. As she walked briskly to the cabin's porch to extract another bottle of water from Hailey's pack, she exhaled sharply through her nose, still seeking to rid her nostrils of Theo's scent. Hailey was a step behind, and Kaela turned, preparing to confront her about the abrupt halt to her training. Instead of stopping, Hailey continued up the steps and through the cabin door. Kaela leaned back, straining her eyes to see inside. There was no furniture, just shelves filled with vague, dark shapes. Her curiosity got the best of her, and she followed Hailey in.

Weapons.

There are shelves of weapons covering all four walls. Spears, bows, quivers of arrows, knives, swords, maces, something that resembled a long pickaxe, and several types of battle axes. Kaela forgot all about the large, sweaty man behind her as she ran her hands along the displays.

"So many." Kaela couldn't think of a reason anyone would own a cache of combat weapons this size.

"You did your exercises, but I think it's only fair if Teddy and I get some time to spar as well." Kaela was concerned about the wild glow in Hailey's eyes as she addressed Theo. "Choose your weapon carefully."

Theo made a great show of inspecting the choices before him, hemming and hawing until he finally selected a long sword. Hailey gave a condescending frown, as if judging his choice and finding it lacking. She reached over to retrieve a pair of short swords and held them out to the sides, taunting. Theo's free hand took up a thick, metal shield.

"Shall we?" Hailey asked with a dramatic bow.

"After you, milady," he simpered, straightening from his own elegant bow after she exited in front of him.

The two of them paced out into the clearing, swinging their new weaponry in slow, controlled movements as they loosened their muscles. Kaela perched on the steps, feeling like a tourist taking in a performance at a medieval dinner theater. Hailey bounced a few times on the balls of her feet and then settled low, her entire body coiling in on itself like an asp. Theo turned, his shield taking the lead as he brought his sword to the ready. An eerie stillness filled the space as they faced one another.

The clash was sudden and furious when it came. There was no indication that either of them would move, but as one, they broke their tableau and charged. Hailey's first strike was delivered with her right sword. It broke across the shield with a metallic clang, but her second blade was already swinging in tandem. She ducked behind Theo's guard and made a slash at his torso. He deflected the second strike with his sword, using the momentum to rotate his weapon around his head, bringing it back down at Hailey's shoulder on the cross-strike. Kaela stifled a gasp, but the worry that gripped her was unfounded. Hailey continued her two-handed attack by spinning in a tight circle, flipping her left blade to a reverse grip and bringing it up to catch Theo's attack in a single, elegant movement.

They stepped away from one another and circled.

Kaela was motionless except for the sharp rise and fall of her chest as she recovered from the shock of watching the exchange. They both moved with the control and balance of world-renowned dancers but wielded their weapons with terrifyingly lethal precision. Kaela could barely keep up with the speed of their movements. She reconsidered her preconceived notions surrounding the use of archaic weapons in modern times.

The two fighters continued to fall back and then surge together again. Each time they met, Kaela's heart was thundering at some near miss or faked stumble. The swords they were slinging through the air were very real and very dangerous. Any little mistake could be deadly for either of them, but they continued to attack and parry at full tilt.

A deep, anxious feeling formed in the pit of Kaela's stomach. In theory, the two individuals before her had survived hundreds of years filled with conflicts and war. In her head, there was only the Hollywood version of history consisting of staged special effects and slow-moving actors. Watching Hailey and Theo fight in person, each maneuver designed to impale or gut the opponent, brought a new level of understanding.

The clash of swords echoed in her ears even now, as she stared at the partially healed wound on the back of Theo's hand. What if her powers weren't tied to aging processes? Removing an age spot was just a matter of taking the cells back to a previous state. Repairing an injury, though, was that about taking something back to its un-injured form, or was it about fast-forwarding the healing process? Kaela thought about Hailey's ability to fix her own body. If she could direct her gift to repairing an injury, why couldn't Kaela do the same? She had already aged someone forward; why not age a wound forward until it was resolved?

Kaela's eyes were half closed as she considered the offending cut. She slipped into the dreamlike state that she was beginning to find familiar and *pushed* her mind into the mechanics of the skin layer. If the cells were damaged and the connections severed between them, new cells were needed and new unions had to be established. She thought about Hailey's lengthy experience with healing and imagined how her memories could help. Kaela's eyes drifted completely shut, and she envisioned a silly scenario in which she and Hailey were holding hands, laughing at the simplicity of this process as they intertwined their fingers and healed the wounds of the man in front of them with hardly a thought.

Hailey gave a sharp inhale, breaking the trance. Kaela opened her eyes and looked back over her shoulder. Hailey's hand was fisted into her abdomen, her eyes wide and fixed on Kaela.

"What did you do?" she demanded.

Kaela glanced down at Theo's fingers.

"Nothing, the spot is still there," Theo answered before she could say anything, dropping her hand in frustration. "This isn't working. I need some time to think about a better way to train you."

Kaela opened her mouth to correct him but closed it again. Half the cut was gone. She confirmed that before he broke contact. At the same moment Hailey cried out, Kaela felt a familiar dizziness and a pulling sensation deep in her gut. She was willing to bet Hailey felt the same thing. Her previous conversation with Landry repeated in her head.

I'm worried about what others would do if they knew.

No one would look kindly on a person who could control their magic.

"Fine." Kaela stood and dusted invisible dirt from her pants. "You go figure that out, and we can regroup another day. I need to get cleaned up anyway."

She tried not to wince at the tight pull of her shoulders and the ache in her thighs as she stretched. Their training in the woods took place two days prior. Yesterday, she woke up stiff and sore. Today was even worse. As a person who consistently visited the gym, she was ashamed to admit just how much pain she was in.

"We are going out tonight," Hailey beamed, incredibly pleased with herself for getting Kaela to agree to this plan. "I also need to get ready. You want to meet me there? Eight thirty still works?"

Kaela couldn't stifle her groan of regret.

"She is meeting you somewhere at eight thirty. Eight thirty *PM.*" Theo laughed in disbelief. "What terrible blackmail did you use to get Dr. Mikaela Brookes to agree to that?"

"Shut up, Theodore." Kaela snarled, despite knowing that he had every right to be incredulous. "It is a Saturday after all."

"Yes, and you certainly won't be in bed by nine if you are meeting Hailey at eight thirty." He dodged a decorative pillow and moved quickly to the front door, still chuckling. "Make sure you have a large coffee with your dinner."

"To be fair, eight thirty was a compromise." Hailey pulled a face at

Kaela over her shoulder as she followed Theo from the house. "She wanted to go at seven."

"Starting the night at ten o'clock is just absurd!" Kaela's shout of protest was lost in the slamming of the front door. "I mean really, humans aren't supposed to be nocturnal."

Kaela checked her watch. She had three hours to eat, dress, and catch a ride to the bar. After she finally agreed to this evening's activity, Hailey informed her that she was not allowed to wear work clothes, nor was she allowed to wear gym clothes. Kaela was fairly certain she had no other options beyond these and certainly nothing that would fit Hailey's instructions to wear 'something sexy and fun.' She probably should have thought about this earlier in the day. At least there was still time to research a solution.

Kaela grabbed her tablet and plopped onto the couch. She opened a browser tab, accepted her aging, hopelessly dowdy sense of fashion, and searched for 'trendy outfits to wear to the bar.' After a moment's hesitation, she added 'thirties.'

The Tin Cauldron was loud.

When Kaela first arrived, there were plenty of empty seats and the music was at a reasonable level. She and Hailey settled at the bar for a few drinks, their conversation relaxed. After an hour or so, the patrons started to arrive in groups. By half past ten, the music was blaring over the noise of the crowd, and there were no free seats to be found.

Hailey struck up a conversation with a stunning lavender-haired bombshell who squeezed between the occupied barstools to order a drink. Her lacy black corset flaunted her curves, ending just above her navel and revealing the flat, caramel planes of her stomach. Her ripped jeans hugged her generous hips and thighs. Kaela fidgeted with the hem of her fitted cotton tank as Hailey leaned over to speak directly into the other woman's ear. The woman turned her head to respond, her hand drifting to Hailey's hip as her lips shaped the words and brushed against Hailey's cheek. By the time the bartender brought over a glass of wine, the woman had her fingers looped into the waistband of Hailey's pants, and Hailey was playing with a long silvery-amethyst lock of hair.

"Her friends are sitting at the booth over there," Hailey yelled at Kaela, gesturing to a table where two other women were laughing together. "Want to join?"

Kaela considered the offer very briefly, but small talk with two complete strangers while Hailey hit on her lavender love interest was in no way appealing.

"I think I'll just call a ride and head out, but you go ahead!" She tried to look excited for her friend.

"Are you sure?" Hailey's forehead creased as she struggled to understand Kaela's extreme aversion to socializing with new people. "I can stay here with you instead. This is our night out together, I don't want you to think I'm abandoning you!"

"Tonight was super fun, but I really do want to go home. I'm tired and cranky. You go! I want you to. And she is really hot."

Kaela yelled this into Hailey's ear, knowing the woman in question couldn't hear anything they were saying over the noise. In all honesty, Kaela was thrilled with the excuse to slip away. Any stray thoughts about missing out on life-changing experiences by maintaining a sensible bedtime were soundly erased after this evening's activities. She offered a few more rounds of reassurance before Hailey accepted her decision. Hailey gave an exaggerated, lewd wink as she looped her arm through Purple's and sauntered to the corner table.

Kaela snorted, then flagged down a bartender so she could close her tab. A random man immediately occupied Hailey's empty stool while she waited. He looked over and said something incoherent in an attempt to start a conversation, and Kaela shook her head, hoping to politely decline the engagement. He didn't take the hint, and when she reached over to take her card back from the bartender, he leaned in to repeat himself, his mouth practically touching her earlobe.

"I'm sure you're usually very charming, but I'm not interested."

She yelled the words over the noise as she stood and stepped away from the bar. She walked away quickly, leaving him mid-sentence before he could respond with an aggressive insult or accusation. Turning down a drunk man at a bar was like getting a hungry octopus to stop going after a fish. No matter how many grasping tentacles you rejected, there are always more coming. And if you did, eventually, after much effort, successfully reject said cephalopod, he would just accuse you of being a rude bitch. Because clearly stating your lack of interest could only ever mean that you were a raging B-word.

As she walked down the street, Kaela realized her head was buzzing more than expected. After she reached a reasonable distance from the bar's front door without being followed, she allowed herself to release the breath she was holding and finished pulling on her jacket. There was always a chance a random man at a bar would choose to follow her out. The tension slowly eased from her shoulders with each unmolested step.

The well-lit downtown streets were crawling with loud, inebriated people. Kaela walked until the sidewalk widened and she could lean against a building without being trampled by foot traffic. After she requested a car through her ride-share app, she tucked her hands into her pockets and passed the time by watching the people around her.

Most of those walking past had the expected loose-limbed, exaggerated mannerisms of bar-hoppers. A few couples and groups were standing around in boisterous little clumps, waiting for their own rides to show up. The wall where Kaela had found shelter was the front of another bar, and the door of the main entrance released short blasts of pop music each time a patron entered. She checked her phone, shivering against a particularly cold breeze, and saw that her ride was still ten minutes away.

The skin on the back of her neck tingled, and her lungs tightened with a quick flash of anxiety. It was stupid for her to walk around by herself. She should have waited in the bar for her ride, but instead, she was out in the open, alone. A man was standing in the unlit doorway of a closed shop across the street. With his dark complexion, she couldn't make out his features very well, and when she looked his way, he dropped his eyes to the phone in his hand. Just someone waiting for a ride.

She was being paranoid. She shifted her gaze to a woman standing further down the street, her face bathed in the light of her phone as she leaned against a railing.

Everyone stands around with their phones. It's perfectly normal.

Kaela's eyes jumped back to the man across the street. She still couldn't see him very well, just the vague features of his face. With his phone held up in front of him, he should have been illuminated by the light of the screen. Unless he was just pretending to look at the phone.

Kaela's heart thundered in her ears. She glanced back to the woman and made eye contact. The other woman quickly turned away as if she'd been caught doing something suspicious. Kaela's concern became panic, and she bolted through the nearby door into the loud bar.

The blaring music, together with the overlapping voices, had a deadening effect on her hearing, the noise merging into a monotonous drone as if she were wading through a swarm of insects. She wove in and out of the crowd, doing her best to avoid the occasional slide of damp skin against her as she moved further away from the front door. Finally, she spotted the bathrooms. When she entered, there were a few occupied stalls, and a pair of women were having a loud conversation as they washed their hands. She canceled the car request and called Landry.

There was only one ring.

"Mikaela?"

"I need you to come get me."

"Are you still at the bar with Hailey?"

"Yes." She was too concerned with her own safety to ask if Hailey always informed Landry of her whereabouts.

"I'll be there in five minutes. Don't leave."

"Thank you." Kaela closed her eyes and breathed to slow the racing of her heart. "Wait, I'm at a different bar. It's further down from the one where I met Hailey. I don't know the name of it."

"Just stay on the phone and you can direct me when I get there."

Her eyes were still shut, but the sharp burn of tears started to form behind her lids. She took another long, slow breath, forcing her body to calm down. The panic began to ebb, and she blinked away the dampness in her eyes. The women at the sink left without even noticing.

"Are you okay? Where is Hailey?"

"She is still at the other bar. I was going to head home, but I ended up walking down the street while I requested a car. I think…" A toilet flushed, and Kaela lowered her voice, turning into the wall as she continued, "I think there are people out on the street, Landry. They were watching me."

There was a moment of silence on his end before he responded. The occupant of the toilet stall walked to the sink, glancing at Kaela in the mirror but then looking away. The stranger avoided eye contact until she slipped back through the door. No one wanted to get involved in someone else's business, particularly if it meant they might have to help in some way. Kaela scowled but couldn't claim that she would behave differently herself.

She remembered why she didn't rely on the kindness of strangers.

"Where are you now?" Landry asked.

"In the women's bathroom. As soon as I noticed them, I went into the bar and straight back here."

“Smart choice,” Kaela blushed at the approval in his voice. “I am three minutes away now.”

“Okay. Do you want me to come out?”

“No, stay put. I’ll come to you after I am sure the area outside is safe.”

She leaned back against the wall and noticed an employee checklist for bathroom cleaning. Given the state of the place, no one had followed the list in a very long time.

“Wait, there’s a sign in here. The bar’s name is ‘The Dirty Martini’. Wow, that’s a choice. Why would you have a filthy, disgusting bar and name it The Dirty Martini? I can’t decide if that was an ironic name selection or just a happy accident.”

Landry laughed. “There are a lot of other words they could put with ‘Dirty’ that would be worse.”

“If you say so.”

Kaela’s heart leapt into her throat when the door to the bathroom flew open. A highly inebriated set of women stumbled in, laughing hysterically and leaning against one another. Kaela averted her eyes and focused on slowing her pulse again.

“Mikaela?” Landry’s concerned voice pulled her back to center. “You are doing fine. I am about to pull up to the front of the building now. Wait inside the bathroom, and I’ll be right there.”

“Thank you.” Her words came out in a normal voice, but inside, Kaela felt like she might shatter.

“You don’t ever have to thank me for something like this. See you in a minute.”

Kaela hung up, restlessly tapping her phone against her leg, eyes fixed on the door. The drunk ladies managed to stumble from the toilets to the sink, still talking over each other and intermittently breaking out in wild peals of laughter. An eternity passed by the time she could *feel* Landry standing outside the door. When it swung open, his eyes instantly locked onto her. His relieved expression became the entire center of her existence for a long heartbeat. One of the women turned from the sink to leave and stopped at the door, shifting her hips in a slightly unsteady motion as she surveyed Landry from top to bottom.

“Hello, Daddy.”

Her friend giggled behind her, and a white-hot wave of annoyance traveled through Kaela as the first woman tossed her hair, leering invitingly at Landry. Kaela brushed past her with a condescending scowl, her voice a staged whisper as she addressed the younger woman.

"He's off the market, kiddo."

Landry's eyes didn't leave Kaela's face, but his smile shifted from relief to amusement. She took his hand and tucked her body against his side as they turned back into the bar. He used his size to carve a path through the crowd, keeping her pressed close until they reached the front door. When they stepped into the crisp night air, his black SUV was parked at the curb with the hazards on. The doorway across the street was empty. Landry walked her directly to the passenger side but pulled her into a hug, his lips brushing her temple, before opening the vehicle door. The gesture was quick and perfunctory, as if reassuring himself that she was physically safe.

"Let's get you home." He closed the door behind her.

"There wasn't anyone suspicious when you got here, was there?" Kaela's eyes continued to roam the street, checking behind the SUV through the side mirror as the vehicle pulled away from the curb.

"I couldn't find anything unusual, just a lot of drunk kids." He glanced at her as he said this, noticing the nervous picking of her fingers at the seam of her jacket. "That doesn't mean you were wrong about being followed, but you were smart. You stayed aware of your surroundings."

"I wouldn't call wandering off by myself 'smart'," Kaela muttered.

Landry's hand settled over the back of hers, fingers sliding together to stop her restless fidgeting.

"You shouldn't live in fear of walking down a crowded street." His thumb traced up and down her index finger, shooting little sparks through her arm. "Don't be too hard on yourself."

Snippets of her earlier abductions raced through her mind. Both times, there should have been other people around to notice what was happening, but no one intervened. Kaela pulled Landry's hand into her lap and clutched it against her stomach, feeling the weight of it like a reassuring anchor against the ebbing and flowing of her intrusive thoughts.

"Where are you taking me?" She looked out the window, watching the buildings pass, and focusing on the slow, careful strokes of his thumb against her skin.

"To your house." He looked surprised by the question as he responded.

"Can we go to yours instead?" Her voice was barely above a whisper. She was afraid to overstep but dreaded the thought of being alone.

"Of course."

The reply was easy, without hesitation, as he gave her hand a squeeze. After a few minutes of navigating city blocks, the SUV was moving along a highway, and the tension in Kaela's neck eased a little more. Months of inactivity, looking over her shoulder less each time she stepped out of the house because nothing was ever amiss. Why tonight? What changed? Maybe they were watching her all along, and tonight was the first time someone was sloppy enough to draw attention. Kaela balked at the thought.

"You look beautiful." Landry's words drew her back. "Did you have a good time before you left Hailey?"

"I guess." Kaela shrugged, turning pink at the compliment. "I'm not really the late-night-at-the-bar type. It was actually witch themed. As in, the bartender was wearing a cute little felt hat, and their drink special was a grape-flavored sex on the beach called 'purple ocean potion'. I can't believe Hailey wanted to go there when she is the closest thing to a real, live witch I've ever met."

"She does have a strange sense of humor," he agreed with a chuckle, taking an exit into an upscale district of the city.

"This is more than five minutes away from the bar. What were you doing out this late?"

"Running errands?" he proposed with fake innocence.

"Were you in that part of town just because I went out tonight?" The accusation was flat when it left her mouth, a metered average of the conflicting thoughts running through her mind.

"Would you be offended if I was?" His grin faded as he glanced over, waiting for her response.

"I am surprisingly not offended at all."

His thumb took another lazy circle before he placed his hand back on the wheel. They turned into the entrance of a new luxury condo development. Kaela's mouth dropped open as Landry stopped in front of the valet kiosk.

"You live in The Towers." He didn't reply as he stepped out, handing the keys to the night attendant before walking around to her. "Of course, you live in The Towers." She muttered as she took his hand, craning her neck to look up at the glass skyscraper.

"It was a conveniently timed investment," he offered by way of excuse.

"Your condo?" She followed him into the marble and glass spectacle of a lobby.

“The building.” He ignored her incredulous look at the correction. “It isn’t exactly homey, but it is very close to the university and was quite a portfolio booster. At least that is what I am told.”

“You basically live in a giant country club, which you own.” Kaela nodded at the concierge and kept her voice low as she followed Landry to the elevators. “Unbelievable.”

“It’s just a condo, Mikaela.” He grimaced.

She grunted.

When they entered the flat, she found herself surrounded by white, glass, and metallic surfaces in every direction. A sparsely decorated living area flowed into a dining room and kitchen with continuous snowy marble floors and floor-to-ceiling windows down the entire left wall. Even the enormous watercolor canvas gracing the space above the entryway console was mostly unpigmented with a few sections of black, abstract shapes. No plants. No pets. Other than a laptop with a stack of dusty old library books on the dining table and a few accoutrements on the kitchen counter, this could be a staged showroom.

Like many modern dwellings, it felt cold, vacant. A prime example of modern design declaring war on livable spaces. The impersonal decor could belong to anyone. There was no personality, no feeling in the choices that were made. Kaela’s home was filled with items that evoked memories, but this space reminded her of the way she lived when married, surrounded by an absence of individualism, with each expensive piece of furnishing meant to embody wealth.

“Your home is—nice.” She managed to keep her expression neutral as she offered the comment.

“It’s not.” Landry dropped his keys on the coffee table and silently offered to take her coat. “As I said, it is a lodging of convenience. Some of my assets are tied to the financial ownership of this building. Staying here is a perk. And I don’t think of it as my home. Can I get you anything?”

He gestured in the direction of the kitchen as he hung the coats. Kaela asked for a glass of water and started removing her heels while he retrieved one for her. The floors were entirely too clean for her to drag street filth across them. She placed the shoes next to the coat rack and followed Landry. Now that they were securely in his condo, the long night of activity was catching up. Her eyelids were heavy, and the tipsy euphoria from the bar had become a dull ache at her temples. She polished off the water as Landry waited.

"You must be exhausted." He took the empty glass and directed her to a doorway at the far end of the space. "The bedroom and bathroom are through here if you want to clean up. You are welcome to anything in the dresser for sleepwear."

The clock above the oven showed midnight. She nodded affably and followed his instructions. The bedroom was as empty as the rest of the dwelling. A grayscale abstract hung on a white wall above a pristine, linen-covered king-size bed. White furniture and a metal table occupied the small sitting area in one corner, and a low white dresser filled the space next to a second open doorway. She extracted a soft T-shirt and a set of cotton boxers from the dresser before wandering into the white marble bathroom. While she freshened up, she concluded that a cleaning service must use at least a gallon of bleach on the condo each week. When she returned to the main living area, Landry was sitting at his laptop. He immediately closed it and leaned back.

"I hope you don't mind. They were the first comfortable things I found. I used your mouthwash, too."

She refrained from fidgeting as Landry's eyes scanned the dark blue shirt, lingering on the Oxford logo across her chest before dipping to the cotton boxers. He absently scratched his chin with one hand, smiling in that cryptic way of his.

"Do you have a bag I can use for my clothes? I'm afraid if I set them down, I'll irrevocably stain these beautiful floors."

Landry grunted at her pointed joke and retrieved a fabric tote from the pantry.

"Had I known you loathed luxury real estate this much, I might have declined to invite you over." His light scolding was still enough to make her feel guilty.

"I'm sorry." She slid her folded clothes into the bag and avoided looking directly at him. "It is a very nice place. It just," she paused and then released the rest of her statement in a single rush. "It just reminds me of something that Jason's family would own. I don't mean to be rude."

"Jason, your ex-husband." Landry nodded once, acknowledging this explanation of her behavior. "If it makes you feel better, I don't blame you for the snide remarks. I meant it when I said this is not a place that I call 'home'. The monochromatic palette is a little pretentious for me. The on-site gym, pool, private lounges, restaurants, and bars are not too terrible, though."

“Wow, you really are suffering here.” Her eyeroll was negated by the upward twitch of her mouth. “I wasn’t raised in a household that was wealthy. When Jason and I married, his family treated me like a humanitarian project. No matter how outrageously wasteful or garish something was, I had to take it in stride to avoid the ever-ready chorus of ‘excuse her, she used to be poor’.”

“Do you know what wattle and daub is?”

“No?” Kaela responded, her eyebrows pinching together in confusion.

“Mud and manure that have been mixed with straw and layered on top of wooden sticks. I was raised in a household with a single room made from wattle and daub with a thatched straw roof. When it rained outside, it also drizzled inside because we couldn’t afford to fix the rotted thatch. You should never value the opinion of people who try to fill a hole inside of them with luxury and riches. They don’t know how to appreciate anything of actual worth.”

Something clicked into place inside her at this proclamation. They regarded one another as a new level of understanding unlocked. That stupid heat behind her ribs returned. A faded flare of alarm went up in her brain, warning her to keep her distance, but she chose not to heed the feeling.

“Did you walk to school uphill both ways?” She broke the silence with a characteristic, smart-ass retort.

“We didn’t even have school.” Landry’s mouth twisted into a lopsided smile.

“Touché.” Kaela couldn’t help her amused snort. She peered doubtfully at the stiff, stylish settee. “I am beyond tired. Did you want me to sleep on the couch?”

“You can sleep in the bed. I will take the couch.” Landry replicated her dubious expression as he assessed his furniture.

“Or we could both sleep in the bed.”

The pause that followed Kaela’s words was only a few seconds in length, but it felt like an eternity as she searched his face for a reaction.

“Mikaela,” he began, taking her bag of clothes and setting it on the table. “I am worried. I spent the last few weeks connecting with people who I haven’t spoken to in decades, if not longer. Cassius is up to something, and I still don’t know what. All I know is that it involves you. If we get too close, he will see what you mean to me. He will try to leverage that, use me to get to you somehow. I don’t want to be selfish if us being together will endanger you further.”

"Then I wasn't imagining this weird distance you were putting between us." Kaela watched him shake his head in a motion that could be confirmation or denial.

"You don't understand what he did in the name of his goals, what he is capable of doing." Landry took one of her hands in his, running a thumb along the center of her palm. "I know you have questions, but it's late. We can talk more about it tomorrow."

"Okay." Kaela's compliance was directly related to her exhaustion. "We can talk about it later, but all I want is sleep, and I would feel better if you were in there with me. I promise I will keep my hands to myself."

This time, he was the one to roll his eyes as she gave him an impertinent wink. He dropped her hand and nodded in the direction of the bedroom. Kaela walked straight to the bed and crawled under the covers, pretending to avert her eyes while he changed out of his clothes into a pair of sleep pants. He joined her, turning on his side so that they were facing one another across the expansive mattress.

"I know you said I don't need to thank you for this," Kaela began softly. "But thank you. You make me feel safe. I don't like to rely on anyone because when I do, I am constantly disappointed."

"You deserve more than that." As he said this, Landry ran his fingers up her jaw until he was lightly gripping the back of her neck. "You are used to being the strongest, most self-sufficient person in the room, but that doesn't mean that you shouldn't have other people you can rely on. Everyone needs support. Thank you for trusting me to be yours tonight."

He shifted over to kiss her forehead before releasing her. She shut her eyes and turned away, sliding back until his long body was spooned against hers. His arm wrapped around her midsection, drawing her even closer, and he tucked her head under his chin. His breathing was a stabilizing rhythm against her back, but the warm, hard press of his body against hers did not encourage sleepiness. She reminded herself that she promised to keep certain parts away from him.

"Landry?"

"Yes?" His response stirred the hair on the top of her head.

"The light is still on."

"Is it?"

The hand that was tucked against her stomach moved, and the room fell into darkness with a click of the switch by the door.

"Was that a frivolous display of power?" Kaela teased, impressed despite her mocking tone.

"Worth it," he mumbled, squeezing her closer again.

She closed her eyes, and his presence wrapped her with a feeling of security, lulling her into the comfort of a deep sleep.

Greece – 1821

"Is Charles still in Tripolita?" Landry's voice drifted under the closed door and into the hallway.

"Yes, he and Theodoros are going to redirect the actions of the forces there. I expect them to arrive here soon. After the recent victory, I think it's best for us to reunite and focus on a central commitment."

"I agree, we are more effective together. I could use Theo's particular skills if we become more actively engaged in combat."

"I know you do not like him," Cass's statement should have driven an emotional response from the eavesdropper in the hallway, but Theo felt nothing beyond an exhausted emptiness.

"I do not trust him," Landry's reply came quickly on the tail of this accusation.

"He has always followed orders and is adaptable to the greater need."

"Yes, because he has no conscience to hold him back. In all fairness, he does not like me either."

There was a shuffling from within the room, the creak of someone shifting in a chair, and the dull clink of a glass on wood.

"Theodoros has a thick vein of self-preservation running through him. He would never sacrifice himself for the cause, but he does emphatically support it, if only to ensure his continued immortality. He is not an idealist or a dreamer, which makes him an excellent foot soldier. Ultimately, it comes down to needing someone who can be trusted to follow orders precisely as prescribed. Not everyone can lead; most must follow."

This, at last, triggered a reaction from Theo, and an anemic feeling of annoyance trickled through him. He was certainly not a leader, but he only followed when it suited his needs, or when he saw no gain in going a different direction. The ghostly emotion gave just enough energy to his listless limbs that he reached for the handle of the door. Yet he still hesitated.

Charles was dead. He died on Theo's watch. He had to tell the two men on the other side of the door, but he feared how they would respond. He reminded himself not to think about the feelings and just communicate the facts.

Theo fought it, but the memory of his hands holding his companion's flesh together flashed through his mind.

"You're going to be just fine, Little Lord." Theodore forced the skin on either side of the sword wound closed with one hand, his fingers gradually losing traction beneath the deluge of blood that pulsed out with each beat of Charles' heart. "It looks worse than it is. We'll find a surgeon and get you sewn up."

The lies fell easily from Theodore's lips even as the color leached from the other man's face, replaced with the waxy yellow of death. Charles tried to talk, but all that came out were frothy gulps and exhales like a fish dying on the bottom of a fishing boat. When he finally fell limp against Theo's legs, days could have passed, but it was probably only seconds.

Theo let the lifeless body slide to the ground, turning to the dead body of the giant Turk. How had Nisha missed this one? Theo and Charles were following orders, moving through the city and bringing each of the military clusters to heel. Invading and sacking a city inevitably devolved into pockets of prolonged torture and rape for the inhabitants. Theo's job was to clean up the mess and minimize the damage without risking the feeling of victory that circulated among the troops. Why Cass wanted to include Charles, the softest and most sensitive of their contingent, in this mission, Theo would never understand.

The first corpse they came upon was the decapitated and mutilated body of a pregnant woman. Charles vomited profusely and nearly passed out. Theo left him to recover, talked the men down from their drunken fury, and then silently eliminated the two ring leaders that were the source of the depravity, replacing them with men of reasonable morals. The entire process required only a few hours of manipulation, a multitude of shared drinks to celebrate the victory, and a strong stomach. Charles' gift could have been extremely effective for the task if he only possessed the latter.

Each time they moved to a different region of the city, it was the same. Charles stopped eating breakfast on the days they relocated. He could never manage to keep it down. By the third week, it was clear he never would. Then the giant appeared.

Theo and Charles were traveling between camps with a handful of officers when the resistance fighters attacked. It wasn't unusual for the

Turks to hide themselves among the civilians and then jump into the fray when least expected. It was a desperate, suicidal justification for their survival. They didn't die in the main conflict. They wouldn't live through the war. But when they died, it would be on their own terms.

The moment that giant of a man stepped into the fight, Theodore knew there was something off. He hurled a wall of rubble at the enemy, but with just a flick of the Turk's hands, the stones fell to the ground. Theo charged, throwing stone after stone and wielding his broadsword with enviable precision, but each of his attacks was easily rebuffed. Charles only faltered for the briefest of moments as he considered the Turk towering above them. Were it not for his valiant charge, his rapier cutting a network of wounds into the opponent's exposed side, Theo wouldn't have found an opening. By the time Theodore managed to slip behind the enormous man, Charles had been skewered through the chest. Even as Theo's dagger dragged through the skin of the giant's neck, he knew that there was no saving his companion.

"Take care of him." Anne's concerned request the day they left England.

"Do not let him die." Landry's warning as they traveled to Greece.

"No one should trust me," Theo murmured to himself as he finally turned the handle to the door where he would face Cassius and Landry. "Someone always dies in the end. And it is never me."

Chapter 5

When Kaela opened her eyes after what felt like a single, long blink, the room was blindingly white in the morning sunlight. She squinted until the bright glow resolved into distinct shapes. Her hand drifted to the empty mattress next to her, finding the sheets cold to the touch. She sat up and brought a pillow to her nose, inhaling the woody citrus scent that made her stomach clench. She tossed the pillow back down with a huff, annoyed at her own sentimentality. The floor was icy against the soles of her feet as she slid from the edge of the mattress.

Her brain was reluctant to release itself from the deep, dreamless sleep. For the first time in weeks, she didn't have nightmares. What time was it, and where was Landry? Kaela closed her eyes and searched for the feeling that she always experienced when he was nearby. There was an initial off-balance disorientation that resolved into a low hum, a steady underlying pulse at the base of her skull that alerted her to his presence. She ran through a quick mental exercise, clearing her mind and focusing on that one familiar feeling.

There. She thought she had found it, just a faint feeling like a buzz of vibrations along strands of gossamer. She walked softly through the open doorway to the common area, the sensation growing stronger.

Landry was standing in the living room facing the windows, dressed in a pair of jeans and a green pullover sweater. The thrumming sensation was centered on him. As he stared across the city skyline, she noticed the steam rising from the mug in his hands, and the rich smell of coffee pervaded her senses. He looked deep in thought, and while she was loath to interrupt, the delicious aroma negated all patience. She cleared her throat with a loud cough.

"I left a mug by the carafe for you." The dimple next to his scar deepened, the skin pulling tight along his cheekbone. "I wasn't sure how long you were going to hibernate."

Kaela half-smiled, half-snarled and moved directly to the elixir of life without forming words. The clock in the kitchen displayed the time. It was eight-thirty. She blinked in disbelief. She couldn't remember the last time she slept past six, much less eight. She decided right then to never spend another night at a bar with Hailey. The first few sips of coffee burned on their way down, but she persisted, waiting for the liquid to clear her thoughts.

"Would you like me to make breakfast?" Kaela jumped, Landry's voice startling her by its sudden proximity.

"Sorry!" She raised her hand dramatically to her heart. "I didn't hear you come over."

"But, yes to breakfast?" He chuckled, running his fingers through his hair and letting his eyes drift over her clothing, the corner of his mouth tugging upward in a bemused expression. "Although I would love for you to continue wearing my clothes, I did send yours out to be laundered this morning. They should be returned soon. Your phone was in your pocket. I put it on the counter."

"Laundry service on demand is another burdensome perk of this condo?" She held the warm mug tightly between her hands and resisted the urge to step closer to him.

"It is a very difficult life here." He winked. "Eggs and fruit?"

Kaela watched him retrieve an egg carton and a container of strawberries from the refrigerator. Not counting a hired chef, she didn't think a man had ever cooked breakfast for her. He placed a pan on the stovetop, and her chest gave a heavy thump. She reminded herself that she was not allowed to form an attachment, but her body was completely disregarding the instructions from her brain. In a state of panic, she set down the coffee and took the eggs from Landry's hands.

"Let me. You can wash the strawberries. Scrambled okay with you?"

Before he could respond, she cracked four eggs directly into the pan and cranked the burner to high. She grabbed the spatula and started vigorously mixing, the shells abandoned on the countertop. When she glanced up at his motionless form, his face was oscillating between confusion and concern.

"Mikaela?" he finally asked. "What are you doing?"

"Making scrambled eggs," she replied, as if her behavior was the most normal thing in the world. "What does it look like?"

"I'm not sure what it looks like, but that is not how you make scrambled eggs."

"Of course it is." Kaela faced him and gestured to the pan with the yolk-coated utensil. "Eggs, pan, scramble."

"Can you please sit at the counter and drink your coffee?" He pried the spatula from her hand and replaced it with the abandoned mug. When he looked back at the stovetop, his expression settled into a pained half frown. "I would consider it a favor if you would let me cook breakfast."

Kaela contemplated arguing for a long moment.

"Fine," she responded instead, taking a seat on the other side of the kitchen island.

Landry immediately discarded the eggshells, then added the partially cooked eggs to the bin. When she made a grunt of protest, he silenced her with a single, cutting look. She settled back with narrowed eyes.

"I'm not much of a cook," she admitted.

"You don't say."

Kaela stuck her tongue out at his back and continued drinking her coffee. Landry retrieved a bowl and cracked four new eggs into it, whisking in milk and a selection of seasonings that she couldn't distinguish from her vantage point. Next, he coated a fresh pan with a dollop of oil and placed it on the burner set to low. The egg mixture was poured in, and he let this cook while he finished cleaning Kaela's mess. He then moved back and forth between the stove and the sink, cleaning and slicing the strawberries while intermittently stirring the eggs.

"Are you going to tell me more about these terrible things Cassius did to you in the past?" Although mesmerized by the live cooking show taking place in front of her, she couldn't keep her now caffeine-powered brain from churning over every part of last night's conversation.

Landry set a plate of food and a fork on the countertop in front of her, then gripped the edge of the sink, leaning onto his hands as he watched her.

"Maybe we should work up to that conversation," he deflected as she shoveled a heap of food into her mouth. "Taste better than your method of choice?"

Kaela wanted to make a snide comment, but all she could do was groan in happiness and eat the delicious, fluffy eggs. Landry made a sound of satisfaction and ate from his own plate. She didn't even consider resuming the conversation until her plate was clean and her belly finally stopped grumbling. She eyed the fruit bowl sitting on the counter in front of her and reached for an avocado.

"It's not ripe yet, I checked this morning," Landry warned.

Kaela poked at the green skin, and an idea began to form.

"Maybe you aren't the only one capable of frivolous displays of power."

He raised an eyebrow and waited. She held the fruit between both hands and focused, reaching for the mental place where she lost herself in the microscopic world beneath her fingers. The weightlessness and the dream-like blurring of her surroundings seemed to come to her with increasing ease. She was even beginning to recognize her gift moving inside her, tiny liquid threads of energy flowing through her skin and into the object she was holding. She opened her eyes and triumphantly handed Landry a brown, ripe avocado. As he took it, he squeezed the skin, and it yielded far too easily, squelching the dark interior out from between his fingers.

"Oops," Kaela looked at it sadly. "Guess I gave it too much juice."

Landry deposited the spoiled fruit on his plate and wiped his hands on a napkin. Kaela swallowed back a brief flash of lightheadedness. When she looked up at him again, she was greeted with a wide grin. His emerald eyes danced in the light from the windows, and he clapped his hands together.

"Spectacular!" he exclaimed. "I can tell you've been practicing. Is this what you have been doing in your training sessions?"

"Not exactly."

He tilted his head in question, and Kaela decided to relate the recent events from training. When she described her inadvertent manipulation of Hailey's abilities, Landry's amusement evaporated, and he grew pensive. He asked about the feeling when she drew Hailey's power to Theo's paper cut and if either of them felt weak or dizzy afterward. He quizzed her on the length of time she spent connected with Hailey. He wanted her to repeat the entire story in case she had forgotten any small detail. When he ran out of questions, he gathered the plates and started cleaning the kitchen. Kaela wanted to break the silence, but she was at a loss for how to start. After the dishes were put away and the counters wiped, he faced her.

"I don't have an explanation." He turned up his palms in resignation. "This is uncharted territory. If you can pull on any gift around you, this will put an even bigger target on your back than the one you already wear."

"I know." Her voice was barely above a whisper. "Hailey felt something happen, but I don't think she understood what it was."

A knock at the door startled them both. While Landry answered, Kaela retrieved her phone. She glanced at her messages and let out a soft expletive after reading a text from Jason. There was also a message from Hailey and there were a few dozen work emails she would need to prioritize that afternoon. Landry returned, holding out a stack of clean clothes and a new toothbrush, taking in her sour expression.

"I forgot my ex is supposed to stop by my house this morning to finalize a few legal details," Kaela sighed. "Also, I should call Hailey and let her know I'm alive."

"I already spoke with Hailey." Landry's tone made her glad she was not part of that particular conversation. "When do you need to meet Jason? I can take you home any time."

"Let me change, and then we can head out. He was supposed to show up by ten."

She retrieved a small bag from her jacket pocket and retreated to the bathroom, already dreading the meeting with Jason. The toothbrush was a luxury, and she felt like a new person after using it. She changed out of Landry's clothes, folding and placing them on the counter. The bag contained a few trial-size cosmetics and hair products. She made the most of what she had, determined to look reasonably put together when facing Jason. There was a certain level of unavoidable grandstanding in situations involving her ex-husband. After donning her earrings and lipstick, Kaela gave her reflection one last look.

Go get 'em, tiger.

Landry was waiting by the door when she emerged. She slipped on her heels and took her coat from him.

"Ready?" she asked.

"After you." He held open the door and gave her a slight bow. "I don't want to make you late for your appointment, but would you mind if we take a detour along the way?"

"*Hm*, that's mysterious." Her interest was piqued, but despite her inquisitive tone, he didn't volunteer additional information. "Sure, take as long as you want. Jason can wait."

The car was idling outside the lobby entrance with the valet, and in a matter of minutes, they were speeding off into the city. This time, they didn't take the interstate but drove along the urban roads into an older and less pretentious section. The buildings became lower, and the landscaping sparser. Landry turned the SUV onto a street packed with dilapidated buildings. Many of them looked abandoned, but a few of the houses further down had been renovated, and another handful were in various stages of repair. Landry parked along the curb in front of a house being re-sided. The familiar echo of hammers and the shouting of the workers felt like home to Kaela, and her face brightened reflexively.

"Half of the profits I receive from my real estate ventures are reinvested. The other half are funneled into foundations like the one that purchased these six city blocks. All these houses will be repaired and upfitted into affordable housing. The rent will be heavily subsidized. Therefore, parents can provide their children with comfortable homes without struggling to find the money to also feed and clothe them. The foundation directs resources into improving the available academic and artistic resources for the community.

"I am a firm believer in the working theory that each generation can improve through education and a deeper connection to humanity through the arts. We have a weekly farmers' market which accepts WIC EBT, and one of the booths provides free cooking and nutrition resources. Immigrants are often unfamiliar with regional produce and introducing them to the appropriate cooking methods boosts their confidence for purchasing local foods. Although, you could probably stand to attend one of the demonstrations." He winked at her. "We prioritize having a community garden and safe public spaces in the layout. There are free options for financial counseling and mental health resources as well."

Kaela was utterly speechless as Landry continued.

"I am not telling you all of this to impress you. I need you to know that my speech about a better future through sustainable changes was not said flippantly. I do believe that even one person can have a substantial, positive impact on the world if they are given enough time and resources."

"I feel like an absolute jerk." Kaela belatedly realized that she spoke this thought out loud.

"Don't." Landry gestured to the neighborhood around them. "This is an experiment. I decided a very long time ago that the way for us to become better human beings is by building communities and relationships. A stranger is a convenient target. A friend is not. People tend to shelter their own and protect things that they've invested their energy in. It is important to me that I explain my beliefs. I am sharing this because once you can fully use your abilities, you are going to be saturated with everyone else's ideas of how the world should work. I selfishly wanted the chance to tell you my vision of the future."

"A future in which you live forever, rolling vast sums of money into global campaigns against poverty?" The words started as a taunt, but halfway through, the teasing turned serious. "Do you really think that's possible?"

"Whether I live forever or just another fifty years, I will continue this work." He turned back to the steering wheel, shifting the SUV into gear. "I don't use my wealth this way on a whim."

"And reinvesting your capital in philanthropic ventures is benefit free?"

"Of course not," he admitted, eyes on the road as he navigated. "There are significant tax incentives. But the foundation is nonprofit, and I don't draw any salary or direct benefits. If I gave all my money away today, there would be nothing left to help others tomorrow. Instead, I accumulate the appropriate financial backing with a long-term plan. This is something you could do with your research as well. Think about the impact of continuous funding."

Kaela was silent as the last of the houses passed by the window. The community he described seemed like a dream. Only an obscene amount of money and political pull could have managed to navigate the sheer mountain of red tape something like this would involve. The extent of Landry's network and wealth were largely unknown to her, mostly patched together from the occasional, passing comment. From those conversations, she inferred that his money was amassed over centuries of shrewd investments. He was basically his own legacy, like the Vanderbilts or the Hearsts, without the generational loss of wealth over time from extravagant spending or gambling habits as the money was divided amongst the heirs.

"Did Cassius hold to these same ideals?" Kaela asked, noticing the way Landry's hand tightened then relaxed on the leather steering wheel as she posed the question.

"No, Cass and I did not see eye to eye on a number of topics."

She should have let the question slide as his jaw feathered beneath his clenched teeth, but she decided to push instead. She had waited long enough to hear about this enigmatic person who waited in the shadows. The mystery surrounding that man was infuriating.

“Tell me, Landry. How did Cassius view his responsibilities to the greater good?”

“Cassius had a more authoritarian perspective when it came to solving the world’s problems.” Landry stoically focused on the road in front of them as he began this explanation. “He took a ‘lose a battle but win a war’ approach to world peace. In truth, he was consumed by the questions surrounding divine purpose and spiritual guidance. He forgot the basic needs that drive societal hierarchy. The inner morality of men matters little when their pockets are empty and their children are hungry.”

Something in what he said struck a chord, a sudden and immediate connection between the person she knew as George and the unknown person that was Cassius. Divine purpose. Inner morality. How often had she listened to George pontificate on these subjects? Hearing Landry say them now carried a familiarity that made her wonder if George wasn’t much of a fabrication after all. Could she already know the real Cassius?

“If you disagreed on such a fundamental level, why did you stay with him for so long?” Kaela forced herself past the hitch in her brain. “You told me that you separated with him in the mid-1900s. That is a long time to let him dictate your life.”

So asked the divorced woman who took years to leave her controlling, cheating husband.

This time, Kaela managed not to orate her inner monologue.

“I fought his battles for two hundred years longer than I should have.” Landry glanced at her and shifted in his seat. “Cassius is very good at inspiring people. He knows how to change his arguments and shift his persuasions to match the person he chooses to manipulate. He knew I wanted to leave, but he wrapped Hailey, Cleda, and Charles too tightly into his schemes, and I didn’t have a choice. I couldn’t leave them behind. Not to mention the rest of my team.”

“Who are Cleda and Charles?” Kaela reached over and forced his arm from the wheel, holding his hand in support, wanting to keep him anchored like he did for her on many occasions.

“Cleda was Elizabeth’s, I’m sorry, Hailey’s companion that she mentioned at the restaurant in the desert.” He squeezed her fingers but didn’t look at her. “Charles died in the early 1800s. He seems so young in memory, but he was alive for over three hundred years. He and Cleda were twin ballasts for Hailey. The person you know today is much calmer, more even-keeled, than who she used to be. Back then, I worried she would never find her true course without the two of them righting her from time to time."

In the silence that followed this explanation, a swath of emotions flickered across Landry's face. There was loss and pain, but also a slow-growing contentment as he appeared to process events long past. She made a mental note to play poker against him in the future. Not only was he loaded, but his thoughts were completely transparent.

"There are certainly a lot of names to keep track of."

Landry snorted at the comment. "You have no idea."

"Let me see if I have them all," Kaela kept her tone light. "Cleda. Hailey or Elizabeth. Charles. Landry."

"Not even half of them." He chuckled. "Cleda and Charles. Hailey, Heather, Asmo, Elizabeth, Anne, and her birth name, Sarah. The original name stuck a little longer before she began using her disposable designations."

"Sarah." Kaela rolled the name around on her tongue, deciding how it fit with the woman she knew. "But always Landry?"

"Yes." He squeezed her hand. "Always Landry."

"Before we get to my house, I need to tell you something that happened the other night when I was, well, I was a little drunk. It's about Hellcat."

Kaela related the full details, at least what details there were, about the drunken cat incident to him on their way to her house. When Landry turned down her street, Kaela spotted Jason's pewter Range Rover. There was a fancy, exclusive-sounding name for the specific hue, but she never bothered to dedicate any brain cells to memorizing it. When Landry pulled into the drive, she spotted her ex-husband standing close to the front stairs, leaning down to pet Hellkitten. To Kaela's great amusement, the cat chose that moment to launch herself at him, a tiny but menacing ball of teeth and claws. When he realized a vehicle was approaching, Jason attempted nonchalance, straightening his posture and ignoring the seething demon of fur still swatting at his ankles.

"Well, there he is," Kaela offered from inside the SUV. "My glorious ex. Maybe I should just hop out?"

"No." Landry's grin was unsettlingly aggressive. "I will walk you to the door. That tiny thing is Hellcat?"

"I've taken to calling her Hellkitten."

Before Kaela could object to the escort, Landry parked the vehicle and walked around to her door. Through the windshield, she could see the way Jason appraised the other man, eyes widening at the size of his potential opposition. Kaela's smile when Landry offered his hand was in no way forced. While she was always acutely aware of his tall, muscular body, she was suddenly struck by the confidence with which he carried himself as they approached the front of her house. The gentle persona of ten minutes ago was replaced with a swaggering, assertive display of male dominance. Jason straightened his spine and sucked in the slight gut around his midsection.

"Hey, Jason. Sorry, we're a little late. We got sidetracked."

Landry slid his left arm around Kaela's waist, tucking his fingers against her hip with an easy affection. Jason looked in her direction, his eyes dropping to the arm around her, then quickly swinging up, as if acknowledging the contact wasn't allowed in whatever silent contest was being waged between the two men.

"No problem, I haven't been here long." He simpered.

"Jason, this is Landry," Kaela gave a simple introduction.

"Hello." Landry reached forward to take Jason's hand in a firm grip. "I see you have met the kitten."

"Yeah, it's completely feral. When did you get a cat, Kay? You never liked them."

As he said this, Hellkitten skipped down the stairs, her short little legs struggling with the unfamiliar height, and began to wind around Landry's ankles, purrs reverberating through her tiny body loudly enough for everyone to hear. Kaela hid her amusement behind a cough as Landry reached down to tickle the top of the kitten's head.

"She isn't that bad." His offhand comment and continued caresses along the kitten's back threatened to make Kaela burst out in laughter.

"She comes and goes," Kaela explained, swallowing her mirth. "She was a stray that thought I made for a good meal plan."

"Awfully young to be a stray."

"Maybe her mom died." Kaela shrugged.

After providing a reasonable show, Hellkitten voiced one ferociously adorable hiss at Jason, then meandered to a sunbeam on the drive and began to bathe herself.

"So are you two," Jason trailed off, unsure of the question he had started to voice.

"Are we… ?" Landry responded, looking confused.

"I mean, do you know each other from work?" Jason managed to correct himself.

"We do," Kaela replied.

"And you have the same kind of research lab as Kay?"

"Mikaela's lab is much larger and more successful than mine." Landry beamed down at her, where she was once again pulled into the half circle of his arm. "She makes it look easy, but very few people can secure the level of funding she is continually awarded. I guess we can't all do groundbreaking work."

"You're too hard on yourself." She nudged him with her shoulder and returned his look with a saucy wink. "I think your lab is more than big enough."

Jason cleared his throat uncomfortably.

"There is a package, I mean a piece of mail, for you." He stepped up to the door and retrieved the item in question. "I noticed it when I walked up, but the cat was there."

Kaela took the padded shipper from his hand, deeply entertained by his choice to remain standing on the lower stair tread. From this new position, he was approximately the same height as Landry.

"Well, I should let the two of you take care of your pending legal business." Kaela completely forgot that her ex-husband was standing nearby when Landry fixed his deep green eyes on her, the intensity of his focus making her breath catch. "Do you need anything before I go, *Cariad*?"

"Uh, no." She focused on appearing nonchalant despite her racing heart. "I think I'm all set. I'll give you a call later."

He caught her chin gently between his thumb and forefinger, brushing her mouth with a soft, intimate press of his lips against hers. Her body melted into his touch, but she managed to hold herself together under his lingering gaze.

"Good to meet you, Jason." Landry called over his shoulder as he headed back to his car, and the statement seemed vaguely threatening.

Kaela waved goodbye and turned back to Jason. He was still standing on the stairs, watching Landry's vehicle drive down the road.

"That was a Bentley Bentayga," he stated in disbelief.

"So?"

"So, no one spends three hundred thousand on a car if they are just an academic." He crossed his arms and shifted closer to her.

"He's also a physician." Kaela's smug response did nothing to change Jason's expression. "Okay, fine. He's ridiculously wealthy. Happy now?"

"Why don't I know him?"

She stared at him in annoyance for a full breath, then sent her eyes skyward. She stepped around him to unlock the front door and stood aside while the kitten sauntered through first—if a stumbling fluffball of a kitten could be said to saunter.

"I doubt you could possibly know everyone in this city, and you probably haven't crossed paths with Landry. He doesn't like to claim credit for his philanthropy, unlike some media-obsessed assholes."

Kaela heard indignant denial in the huff Jason exhaled behind her. She continued to the kitchen, dropping the package on the counter before bothering to turn around.

"I thought you hated my lifestyle." Jason's voice whined slightly as he made this insinuation. "You repeatedly told me that being wealthy made me 'less human'. Don't you find it demeaning to date that guy and rub it in my face?"

Kaela pinched the bridge of her nose, hoping for a sudden burst of patience but coming up short.

"Jason, this isn't about you, and my life is none of your business. Do you have the locket and the keys? I assume that DocuSign envelope I completed is sufficient for the legal part of this?"

He removed a small manila envelope from his back pocket and placed it in her outstretched hand. She peeked inside and found the items in question.

"Everything is done now." He said this like a question, waiting for her to contradict him.

"Yeah, I think it is," she replied.

They stared at one another, playing a familiar and yet novel game of chicken, waiting to see which of them caved first.

"Bye, Kay." He leaned in to kiss her cheek, but she stepped back.

"Goodbye, Jason."

When the front door closed behind him, she expected a flash of sadness or doubt, but the only emotion she experienced was the relief of completing a task. She turned the necklace and keys out into her hand, flipping the locket over to eye the delicate metal workings that wrapped around the beautifully crafted piece. When she cracked it open, she found a miniature of a woman she didn't recognize. On the back was an engraving:

There is the heat of Love.

Kaela wasn't sure what to make of it. She set the locket back on the counter along with the key and envelope. She needed a bath. A long, hot bath to cleanse the events of the weekend from her body. The locket and the final death of all emotional ties to her marriage could be processed later.

Russian Empire – 1858

"He is anything but safe."

Theodore lingered near the entrance of the salon, trying not to overhear the conversation inside and wondering why he always seemed to arrive at the wrong time. He nodded to the guard when they accidentally made eye contact, but the other man straightened and looked away.

"Landry is undeniably powerful, but you and I both know what he turns into if left unchecked. That's why I am sending you back to Cassius. I am too busy taking care of matters here. Nicholas needs my guidance, and this treaty has proven a nuisance. You know the importance of my involvement. I cannot be there to protect my beloved, so you must do it for me. I trust you to keep our little family secret secure. Don't make me regret that decision."

"Yes, my Lady." Theo recoiled in recognition of this second voice.

"Leave at once, and if that Frenchman becomes a problem, control him or snuff him out. I will not tolerate your failure should Cassius's pet decide to become a liability." In the pause that followed, Theo considered retreating down the hallway. "Theodore, you may enter now."

Theo smoothed the front of his semi-caftan with a sharp tug. Of course, Nisha knew he was hovering in the hall. He patted his hair in place with one hand then stepped through the doorway. He offered a deep, respectful bow to the commander's wife but did not acknowledge the other woman in the room.

"You arrived this morning." A statement, not a question. "Bring me the missives, then wait over there. I would be concerned that you overheard our conversation, but you know what Landry is capable of firsthand. And you are aware of the weakness my husband holds in his heart when it comes to that boy."

Theo was quick to place the sealed letters in Nisha's outstretched hand. Her eyes flashed with excitement as she withdrew to the upholstered bench near the windows, dismissing the two people attending her with a sharp wave. As soon as she sank into the cushions, her voluminous skirts settling into stiff, beaded peaks around her, the other occupant in the room approached Theo.

"Theodoros, my darling." To anyone else, the words would sound affectionate, but to Theo, they were the hissing of a snake.

"Ramla." His voice was devoid of any warmth as he greeted her.

She chuckled, moving as close as her dress would allow. She ran her fingers over the breast buttons of his new coat, letting her hand continue southwards until it reached his waist. When he pushed her away, she laughed again.

"This Russian court dress is quite dashing on you. Surely you can't blame me for appreciating it."

"Thank you for leaving your claws retracted, but I prefer if you keep your hands entirely to yourself from now on." Theo stepped back as he replied, prompting a momentary twisting of the woman's amused expression.

"You may leave now, Ramla."

The order from the other side of the room was met with immediate action. Ramla bowed to her leader, then blew a discreet kiss at Theo. Unlike the guard at the door, Theodore found it easy to ignore the tantalizing swing of her hips and seductive purse of her mouth as she glided out into the hall.

"Honestly, I am surprised at you," Nisha began once Ramla was gone. "I don't think I've heard of you taking any lovers since we turned you, and she is a very attractive woman. Do you at least find a few whores to keep yourself satisfied?"

"I am uninterested in reptiles for bedfellows, and women rarely become whores on a lark. I'd rather not contribute to the oppression such women already face." Then, as an afterthought, "Milady."

"Hm." Nisha beckoned him closer, then folded her hands atop the letter, her stare hard as she appraised him. "I won't waste time debating the choices of those who have a victim's mindset and do nothing to get themselves out of a distasteful situation. But I also won't have you compromised, and a man who craves intimacy is a man easily manipulated. Find a pretty Russian girl and see to your needs. The court ladies here are anything but maids, and you will find many of them are more than eager to bed a handsome man like you.

"Now, you have done well as a messenger, but I have more important tasks in mind. Your continued displays of loyalty are noticed, and I do love your lack of principles when it comes to following orders. Sit. It is time for your next assignment."

Theodore bit back a response and assumed a neutral expression as he followed her gesture to a chair nearby. He owed Cassius a great debt, and that debt might extend to Nisha, but he did not follow her orders out of loyalty. He did so out of necessity.

Deep down, Theodore balked at the mission Nisha began to detail when he was settled across from her. He was once a God-fearing Christian, a father and a husband, a person that knew right from wrong. Above all, though, he had always been a survivor. Three hundred years stood between that good man and the obedient mercenary he was today. He buried his conscience and prepared to execute her orders as instructed.

But beneath his docile compliance, Theodore was waiting. One day, there would be another who was more powerful than Cassius and this woman combined. When that person finally stepped forward to challenge Nisha, Theo vowed to do whatever was necessary to see them succeed.

Chapter 6

The dark blue sedan started following Kaela's car a few miles outside the University. It wasn't a very stealthy tail, which was concerning in and of itself. She spotted it almost immediately as it mirrored her movements, keeping one or two cars between them. When she turned into her neighborhood, it continued straight along the main road. She didn't see any other suspicious vehicles, and after she pulled into the driveway, she sprinted into the house, locking the door behind her. She stood in the entry, listening.

Why was this her life? She hated the anticipation, the slow dread that followed her like a persistent shadow. This was the third or fourth time a car had followed her around town, but the occupants never engaged in anything more than a brief game of follow the leader. Kaela went through what had become her usual routine upon returning to her home. She retrieved a folding blade from her purse and flicked it open before checking in every room and behind every door. Weeks ago, she told Hailey about her propensity to carry a kitchen knife around the house, and her friend had pressed the new weapon into Kaela's hand with a grim smile. From that day on, her combat training was carried out with a weapon, sometimes the knife, and other times a different blade from the cabin arsenal. There was something comforting about having more than her bare fists to wield against an intruder, even if she was nowhere close to achieving the level of skill Hailey and Theo demonstrated each time they sparred.

Kaela finished checking the second floor and returned to the kitchen. What was Cassius planning? Where were Jackson and his team? How was Nisha involved? The moving pieces still didn't have a pattern. Each group made contact in one way or another and then withdrew. Maybe they were waiting for her to make a move of her own. Jackson might be using a 'fall back and punt' tactic after the kidnapping in the desert did not go as planned, but that still left the other two players on the board. Nisha did not reach out again after she orchestrated their initial introduction. The stories Landry and Hailey shared about her made Kaela suspect that Nisha knew exactly what happened with the second kidnapping, but Theo claimed to have heard nothing from her in the months that followed.

While Kaela agonized over the missing information, she remembered the junk mail collecting in the corner of the kitchen. The daily additions were piled on top until a towering stack of envelopes and flyers engulfed the counter. Over the weekend, she would clear out the mess, but each week the cycle repeated. It was habitual, an anchor of normalcy amidst her carefully organized living space.

The package she received the day Jason brought her inheritance documents was just visible at the base of the clutter, a manilla corner poking out from under the cardstock flier for new windows. Curiosity renewed, she slid it free and inspected the return address. It was from a 'Professor C. Carver' with a return address at a university she previously attended. She dropped the package as if it were a living thing snapping at her hands. She remembered that name. Cassius Carver was the person who called Jason for a reference.

Cassius.

George.

She couldn't think of the mysterious man behind the immortals without comparing him to the neighbor he had pretended to be for years. The doting, paternal presence was a lie her brain still struggled to accept. Her hands shook as she ripped into the package. Inside was a book: *Dialogues Concerning Natural Religion* by David Hume. She opened the front cover, and written on the inside in a scrawling but legible script was a message:

Dearest Katherine, I hated to leave you with such haste. You deserve an explanation, and I will strive to provide a satisfactory one soon. For now, I hope you will enjoy this companion to An Enquiry. I look forward to renewing our philosophical discussions when we are reunited. Ever yours, George.

She flipped through the first few pages, pausing when she noticed the author listed for the foreword of this special edition.

"Professor Cassius Carver," she murmured in disbelief.

According to the short credentials after the name, Dr. Carver was on faculty at the University where she completed her doctorate. It would seem that in addition to recently inserting himself into her life, he had been watching her from the shadows at the very beginning of his mysterious disappearance more than twenty years ago.

Her surprise coiled inside her, transforming into something darker. She stormed through the entryway, gripping the Hume book in one hand, and threw open the door, stopping halfway into the front yard. The cold seeped through her socks as she stood on the nearly frozen grass. She held up the gift, shaking it as if to bludgeon a response from the air, and scanned the road for unfamiliar vehicles.

"I'm sick of your mind games you fucking coward!" she screamed, her words punctuated by the misty clouds of her breath condensing in the winter cold.

She made eye contact with a shocked neighbor who was standing near the door to their car. Kaela gave her a casual wave as if she was not behaving like a raging lunatic, tucking the book back against her side. A gentle chirrup came from behind her. Hellkitten was sitting at the bottom of the stairs, and if a cat could laugh with amusement, she would have been. Kaela grunted her annoyance and tucked the tiny ball of fluff under her chin as she stomped back up the stairs.

"The one time I don't want my neighbors to notice something," she grumbled.

When the front door was once again secured, she located her phone and texted Landry about the car that tailed her home and sent a quick summary of the mysterious package.

Cassius sent me a present, and I just realized I met him two decades ago. What a day.

While she waited for a reply, she retrieved the older Hume volume from a shelf and scanned the two works side by side, searching for any highlights or notations that would indicate why Cassius gifted her these specific works. The only thing unusual at first glance was a gift receipt for a coffee shop in Edinburgh. She tucked it back between the pages before her phone buzzed.

Are you safe?

Yes, just mad about Cassius.

There was a short pause before he responded.

We should talk about this. I am in a meeting. Meet around six?

She reacted with a thumbs-up emoji.

My place. I will be here stress-painting. Come over any time.

Kaela left the books on the coffee table and changed into more appropriate clothes for painting. As she worked, she considered her options for confronting Cassius directly. She was making significant progress in her training, both physical and magical. Although she was careful not to repeat the incident with Hailey's abilities, she was more than adept at forward aging. Thus far, she had mastered plants, but the kitten that was currently curled up on the sofa was her only mammalian success to date. One desperate night nearly a week prior, she had taken four shots of bourbon and attempted to de-age a sad, old opossum she found in her trash can by the garage. Clearly, being inebriated wasn't the key, but it could have also been an issue with the distance she kept between herself and the hissing marsupial. The day before, she came close to success with a moth during her training with Theodore.

"What are you doing with that?" She had peered into the clear plastic cage Theo brought to their meeting at Hailey's disheveled apartment near the gym.

Inside was a small insect with mottled gray and brown markings. It was perched at the bottom of the otherwise empty container, slowly opening and closing its wings. Theo grinned at her confused expression.

"I am tired of watching you try to un-rot fruit," was his response.

After her failed attempt with higher organisms, Kaela had hoped that a brown banana would be the key to unlocking her ability. That was also about as accurate as her alcohol-consumption hypothesis.

"Where did you find a butterfly?"

"It's a moth." He handed her the container. "A Winter Moth, actually, and there are a lot of them around this time of year."

Kaela waited for more of an explanation as she observed the movements of the one-inch insect, but Theo just walked to the corner and slid a chainmail shirt off an armchair before sitting. Hailey's apartment had zero wall decorations but enough random medieval weaponry to outfit the full cast of an eleventh-century-themed dinner theater show.

"Are you going to spit out your master plan?" She lowered the insect cage and glared at him. "Honestly, this is like pulling teeth."

"You are afraid of hurting people and animals." He leaned forward, bracing his elbows on his knees as he explained. "You only changed Brady in the desert because you had no choice. With me, you are full of hesitation. You don't feel confident in what you are doing, therefore you won't commit. You don't want to hurt me by accident. It's touching, and while I appreciate your concern for my well-being, you need to find a way to train on something other than dying plants."

"You might be overstating your importance to me." Kaela scoffed, even while accepting the truth in what he said. "So, you want me to make the bug younger?"

"This *moth* is about to die of old age. Worst case scenario, you royally mess it up and it dies now instead of tomorrow or the day after. Either way, you get to work with an organism from a higher taxonomic rank. I think it should turn into a little green caterpillar if you do this correctly."

She gave the moth another dubious look.

"Why not?" She grumbled and sat cross-legged on the floor, placing the container on its side in her lap to better see her latest victim. "How do you want me to start?"

"Do whatever you did in the desert, but the opposite," Theo said dismissively as he pulled a set of metal tiger claws from under the magazine stack on the side table. "She really should organize this place better."

Kaela bit back a snarky reply to his less than helpful instructions. Leaning forward, she fixed the moth with a serious stare and tried to summon her disconnected headspace. Falling into the trance, she lost focus on everything around her, and a familiar buzzing filled her head. While the part of her mind that was set on the insect became sharper, the rest of her vision faded into white snow.

She tried to follow the biology behind metamorphosis. She understood human aging at a deep level, but now she needed to understand the creation of youth for invertebrates. She went through the bigger concepts, like when she was setting up experiments in the lab, her brain repeatedly slogging through these processes.

When she was working with her plants at home, she didn't have specific ideas of what needed to happen, just a rough concept of how the energy flowed through the leaves and into the buds. She assumed this should be the same. Thirty minutes later, she had watery, irritated eyes and the beginnings of a headache. She set the cage down on the floor with a grunt of frustration and looked at Theo. After a dramatically large stretch, he wandered over and peered into the container.

"That is anticlimactic."

She punched the back of his calf.

"*Ow!*" He hopped away and shook out his leg. "That was uncalled for."

"I tried, okay?" Kaela snapped at him, getting off the floor and carefully unbending her back, feeling the pieces of her spine line back up with a series of pops. "I don't think it is even possible to turn this thing into a caterpillar again. I am not a developmental biologist. I'm not even a regular biologist. I barely remember how human development happens, much less that of an insect, and if I try to do it in reverse—"

"Kaela!" Theo gripped her upper arms and lowered his head until they were eye to eye. "Stop rambling. You are overthinking it. People were doing magic long before it could be explained by science. I don't need you to understand what is happening at the cellular level. I just need you to push yourself in the right direction and channel your energy."

She stared at him, dumbfounded.

"That is not how my brain works."

"Using your gift is about feeling your way to the result. It is not an intellectual exercise. When I move a stone, I don't think about how the energy conversions take place. I just know that if I *will* the stone to move, it moves. I know that using my power will drain me a little at a time. I have to pace myself and monitor the way my body feels."

"Again, not how I function." She planted her fists on her hips, and he took a small step back. "I am not a 'feel your way through it' kind of person. You should know that about me by now."

"Well, honestly, I don't know that much about you." He shrugged. "You aren't an 'open up and make yourself emotionally available' kind of person either."

She wanted to disagree, but he was right. They dated for a year, give or take. An entire year of her life, and she never told him anything too personal. She provided vague references to her work and a few minimal statements about her status as a divorcee. Otherwise, they stuck to the vapid small talk of a superficial, physical relationship.

Maybe he understood some things about the way she reacted to situations or how she really, *really* liked to dance after a few drinks, but he couldn't have gotten to know her in the ways that really mattered.

"I would apologize for keeping you at a distance," Kaela gave him a lopsided glower. "But you were a fake from the start, and I don't think my opening up to a lying psychopath would have been a good look."

"Brutal as always." He laughed and leaned down to retrieve the cage from the floor. "Come on, I'll walk with you to the cars. We can try again another time."

When she had left the university at lunchtime, the day was already frigid, but by the late afternoon it had become downright heinous. Somehow, the crisp chill of fall had turned into a polar vortex over the last week. She pulled a knitted cap low over her ears and turned the collar on her peacoat up. The branches above them had realized they were behind on their annual duties and dropped all their leaves, seemingly overnight, so she was slogging through a thick layer of dead foliage carpeting the sidewalk. Theo made surprisingly little noise as he followed behind.

"Should we plan to train again on Sunday?"

"That can work," Kaela replied amicably. "I have some house chores and a few errands to take care of tomorrow, but I don't have plans yet for Sunday."

"Why are you so agreeable today?"

Her feet gave a series of crunches as she turned in the leaf litter and faced Theo.

"What is that supposed to mean?"

"It isn't a bad thing." He held up his free hand in mock innocence. "You are just typically more confrontational. I didn't expect you to say yes that quickly about training. Or about the moth situation for that matter. Come to think of it, you are being downright friendly. What is happening?"

"Oh, come on." Kaela started back down the walkway. "I only give you a hard time because you're shady and you deserve it. It's the end of the semester. We are a few days away from a long winter break, when I can finally stop juggling an impossible professional workload with an equally ridiculous psychological burden from this new nonsense. Also, I had a few looming personal issues that were resolved, and I feel quite unencumbered at the moment."

"*Hm,*" he responded noncommittally. "Okay. Well, like I said, you are being oddly pleasant. I'm glad to hear you're in a good mental space. You have been on edge lately. Understandably so but even if I am a shady jerk, I know you accumulate stress and hide all signs of it. You could be ten minutes from death and only act off when you get down to sixty seconds."

"Thanks?" Kaela glanced back at him as they approached the visitor parking spaces. "I don't love the description, but I think I appreciate the sentiment."

"I just mean that you are strong." He came to a halt near her driver's side door. "You don't show weakness. That is how you are made. I understand that part of you, at least. I would never expect you to be any different, but it's nice when you're relaxed too."

"I see."

She didn't know what else to say. When they were together, he would sometimes surprise her with his sensitivity, and she would always brush it off as a fluke. She didn't want to admit they formed any amount of emotional connection. Instead, she dismissed the little details when they were staring her in the face. He acted like he cared for her. Maybe she even cared for him in some strange way. Kaela ran her eyes over his face, remembering the times when he would shift from an expression of mischievous flirtation to something softer, more genuine. Those moments were flickers in their shared timeline, but they still existed.

Kaela didn't know if one of them moved, but she was abruptly aware of how close their bodies were to one another. Theo breathed in a steady, unhurried rhythm, and his eyes were calm.

"See something you like, Kaela?"

Kaela took a quick, graceless step back and his cocky smirk returned.

"Did you want to take the moth home with you for practice?" He held the cage up in front of her face, and the insect flapped its wings. "Otherwise, I can just let it go."

"Why do I feel responsible for it now?" She pressed her lips into a thin line, still squinting at the winged creature. "Let me try again. Maybe if I'm touching it, I'll be more successful."

Theo shrugged, then held the little cage out for her. She crunched a few steps closer and unclicked the door in the plastic top. The moth stayed put as she reached in with one hand and carefully trapped it within her loosely cupped fingers. The wings whispered against her skin as it offered one last flutter then fell still.

She once saved a moth. The memory passed by, as insubstantial as the tattered wings she'd clutched sadly to her body. Somehow, as a child, she was able to do something without understanding all the little processes that drove her actions. Surely, she could do it again.

Kaela held the moth in front of her eyes. This time she kept it simple. She imagined the creature shrinking and shifting, becoming a little green worm. Some faint memory inside her emerged of a drawing with the life stages of a butterfly. She might have been in elementary school at the time. She lamented the lack of detail in the memory but focused instead on the idea of it *changing* into something different. A faint tug in her stomach announced the flow of her power, and she spread her thoughts to the trees surrounding her, taking some of the energy from them. In her hand, the moth's wings started beating a frantic rhythm against her skin. Then it disintegrated.

Kaela gasped in shock as the powdery wings broke apart into fragments, only to be blown away by the relentlessly gusting wind. She and Theo both bent their heads over her palm, and she slowly straightened her fingers to reveal what was left. The last of the debris blew away under a cold burst of air, and on her palm was a small, green caterpillar.

"Holy shit, you did it."

Kaela glanced at Theo's incredulous expression and then back to the insect body between them. Only then did she realize something.

"It's not moving." She poked it with the forefinger of her opposite hand. "I think it's dead."

He frowned in return. "Well, it was a start."

An unexpected wave of guilt doused any joy from the success. Kaela reminded herself that old age and death were natural parts of the life cycle. It was just a moth, and it would have died in a few days regardless of her actions. Besides, even if she could reverse the effects of age, she couldn't walk around making all flora and fauna immortal. She blinked and dropped the dead caterpillar on the ground.

"Right. A start." Something warm and wet trickled across her lip, and she reached up; her fingers came away with a smear of red. "That shouldn't have happened."

"Easy." Theo caught her as she swayed. "You might be dizzy for a minute, but you should be okay since it was small. That's just how it works."

She remembered that not all the people who used these kinds of powers knew to draw from the living beings around them. Did Theodore know this? Was she supposed to keep it a secret from him? She found it doubtful that he wouldn't have made this connection already, but out of an abundance of caution, she decided not to discuss it further.

Newly pledged to the immortal society and already keeping secrets.

"Maybe not the best start," she muttered as she pulled away from him.

"Any start is a good start," Theo had said before she got in her car to drive away.

Kaela wished she could agree.

She was half a gallon of paint in, and the kitten was meowing for her from the bottom of the stairs, pulling her from her thoughts of failure. She gave it a scoop of kitten chow in the kitchen and was watching it eat, contemplating the wisdom of attempting to age it forward again, when her doorbell rang. Her bare feet made faint pattering sounds against the tiles as she trotted to the door, brushing loose strands of hair back from her face before she pressed her eye close to the peephole. Landry stood on the stoop in his characteristically well-fitted jeans and a zipped fleece. In one hand was an easily recognizable pastry box.

"Is that Cannoli?" Kaela cried out as she whipped open the door. "Please tell me you got the chocolate cookie dough variety."

"Yes, and yes." He handed off the box of treats. "I wasn't sure if you were able to enjoy them the first time I brought them over, and I thought a second attempt would be appropriate."

"Yes, let's hope this evening doesn't have the same disastrous ending." She wasted no time getting the box to the kitchen and extracting a delicious-smelling confection.

"I was too busy painting. I haven't had dinner yet. I know, I know." She waved away the response he hadn't been forming, expecting a comment about healthy lifestyle choices.

"Who am I to judge?" He shrugged easily. "I would never tell you what to eat. I was going to ask if I could see what you are painting."

"Really?" She paused between mouthfuls. "Sure, I mean it's nothing exciting, but I'm happy to show you."

Kaela took another gigantic bite, her hunger driving away any good manners she might have harbored under ordinary circumstances, and she gestured for him to follow her up the stairs. Once they reached the top, she indicated the half-painted hallway with a sweep of her arm.

"My Mona Lisa," she joked. "It's therapeutic for me to do home renovations when I'm stressed or angry."

Landry's expression was one of surprise as he looked down at the paint rollers, then back over to her splattered sweats. He started to laugh.

"What?" she asked.

"When you told me you were painting, I thought you meant artistically, with canvas and acrylics or watercolors."

Kaela didn't immediately know what to say in response to this revelation but then joined him in laughter. "I did think it odd that you wanted to see a hallway."

"Yes, that would be strange," he agreed. "Do you also paint artistic renderings?"

"God, no." Her response was quick and firm. "I'm not a Mary Sue. I am an excellent scientist, a mediocre runner, and a decent dancer when I'm drinking, but while I appreciate others' talents in the area, I am no artist."

"You should probably finish this before the rollers dry out." He glanced around at the painting tools. "I can help, and you can tell me about this mysterious present you received. That was a very cryptic text."

"You don't need to," she trailed off as he started removing clothing. "What are you doing?"

"Well, I can't paint in these." He gestured to his very nice and probably expensive jeans before he unbuttoned and stepped out of them. "And I assume you don't have appropriately sized clothes for me to borrow, so my boxers will just have to take the brunt of the attack."

Kaela was certain a drop of drool gathered at the corner of her mouth where it hung, slightly agape. Her eyes ran across his bare, muscular body and his indecently fitted underwear. Dragging her gaze back to his face was a struggle, and the smug expression that greeted her when she finally managed to do it indicated that he was aware of his effect on her. She furrowed her eyebrows and gave a slow shake of her head.

"Not exactly fair when you specifically stated you would like this interaction to stay platonic."

"I certainly do not want this to stay platonic." He frowned at her. "I would very much like to revisit our night in the desert, but I cannot in good conscience pull you deeper into the position I have already put you in."

"No pun intended?" She bit her lip and dropped her eyes to his body again.

"Mikaela." His voice was a warning.

"Hey, you started it." She tilted her head saucily.

"I can't help it if the sight of me shirtless is enough to make you lose your self-control."

"Should I get topless and see how well you fare?" She toyed with the edge of her shirt. "I'm sure my nipples would in no way distract a seasoned warrior like yourself."

"No." His sharp tone made her laugh. "No, I would rather not test that theory."

Kaela pouted at him petulantly.

"Fine, then at least make yourself useful with the roller while I finish trimming in this edge under the window."

"Yes, madam," was his amused and somewhat relieved response as he followed her instructions. "But tell me about the present from Cassius while we paint."

They worked in tandem to finish the hallway while she described the situation. She repeated as many of her exchanges with George as she could, mainly the stories revolving around philosophy. Landry already knew that Cassius had posed as her neighbor, but until now, the theological discussions hadn't seemed pertinent. Although she tried to be thorough, these conversations spanned years, and she had likely forgotten a few key facts.

"He was testing you." Landry was standing in the middle of the hall, having completed the last section and discarded the roller. "Odds were that Cassius would eventually find someone who had similar powers to himself. That person would be a threat, a certain upset to the balance of power among our kind. I knew his response would be to eliminate the threat swiftly if it ever arose. I can only assume he started following you the day he discovered your skills and was deciding whether to kill you.

"He would have met with you when you were first starting school, found some way to stage a spontaneous interaction, and asked you questions to judge who you were and who you might become. Whatever you said kept him interested, made him think that you were worth investing more time in. If he didn't like your responses, you wouldn't be standing here now."

"Well, I guess it's a good thing I passed his test, even if I don't remember it happening." Despite the bravado of the words, Kaela's stomach twisted, and she worried the cannoli might not stay put. "It would have been terrible to die at the age of twenty-one when I thought that 'Drops of Jupiter' was the greatest love ballad ever made, 'Harry Potter' was a classic work of literature, and Von Dutch hats would never go out of fashion."

"The question remains, why is he still vetting you after twenty years?" Landry gauged her reaction as she began to clean up the painting tools. "Mikaela, I need to be honest about a few things. I knew there was someone Cassius was interested in around the time he disappeared. He and Nisha were always very secretive about details, and since I was not in their circle anymore, I didn't have direct knowledge. When Cass disappeared, everything changed. Nisha found you and asked for my help. I kept tabs on you from a distance, but I never knew Cassius was there too."

"I see." Kaela tried to pick apart this new information, but her brain was struggling to keep the details straight. "You told me that Nisha had certain ideas about how to approach me and that you disagreed. What were those? She must have known what Cass originally intended. Was she carrying out his wishes, or was it just her own plan to regain immortality after her husband supposedly died?"

"I don't think Cass told her about you," Landry's expression was perplexed as he replied. "She found out about you later, when we were all starting to get desperate. She asked that I worm my way into your life and make you fall in love with me. Then you would be convinced to continue the legacy of immortality that Cass once bestowed on us all. You were married at the time, but in her mind, that was entirely negotiable. Once you loved me, you would do anything to make certain I wouldn't die. Then, I could convince you to extend that to my 'friends', which of course included her."

"Of course." Kaela grimaced with disgust. "Honestly, did she think it would be that easy?"

"As someone who has done unnamable things for love, I am sure she did."

Kaela took a moment to fully digest his statement before responding.

"But that kind of love can't be forced or faked. Trust me, I've been on the losing end of this equation." She had finished cleaning up the painting accouterments, and they were standing at the kitchen sink while she washed the last of the paint from her hands. "And here we are. I didn't fall in love with her new decoy, 'Todd', and I am a wild card, free to do whatever I like while avoiding kidnappings and abductions."

"Mikaela, I am going to say this one last time." Although they were standing a reasonable distance apart, she could feel the pull between them, the nearly imperceptible way his body reached for hers, as he responded. "Eventually, we will have to face Cassius, and he will use every psychological weapon at his disposal to bend you to his agenda. Cassius turns me into a different person. There were times long in my past where he had me twisted beyond anything you would believe. There are periods with complete blackouts, where people died, and I have no explanation. You don't begin to understand the ways in which that man can corrupt the soul. I am here to protect you from that. Believe me, I would never hurt you if I could help it, but Cassius will try to use it against me if he realizes what you mean to me."

Kaela took a sharp, deep breath and let the air slide back out between her lips as she considered these statements. Landry's expression was open, vulnerable. While she should be concerned with the flags he raised, she couldn't help but blame all the negative fallout on Cassius, the absentee father that took advantage of his progeny.

"I know that I don't completely understand this situation," she began, reaching for one of his hands. "But when I would visit my parents as a functional, grown adult, I found that the instant they questioned my activities or choices, I became an angsty teenager all over again. We respond the way that we do because family gets to you in a way that no one else can. Cassius is family. He knows your triggers. I'm not saying you should forgive him for anything. Family can be destructive and poisonous too. But I think I understand how he can find and exploit weaknesses no one else would pick up on."

"I don't want you or our relationship to be the fallout when that conflict finally comes." He squeezed the hand she clasped and took a step closer. "That is why I keep telling you we need to maintain some distance between us."

"Such sappy bullshit." Kaela stepped further into his space, her body occupying the curve of his as she whispered against his lips. "Sex is sex. The only fallout will come from the vulnerabilities we allow ourselves in the process and those are entirely divorced from what we do with our bodies. If you promise not to fall in love with me after a little naked time, I can sign off on a tumble in the sheets."

"It wouldn't just be sex," his voice was strained, and his muscles visibly tensed as he replied.

"Maybe you haven't been with modern women enough to appreciate that a good lay might just be a good lay." Kaela raised an eyebrow and faked nonchalance, refusing to back down. "I am willing to pretend I have never seen you naked if Cassius decides to question me on the subject. Besides, I think it's obvious that we both want to be together physically. Even if we put it off, he'll still pick up on the tension."

“Are you sure that’s what you want?” Landry ran a hand softly down her neck, past her waist, and then pulled her into him by her hip. “As much as I wish I could walk away right now, you seem to be in the habit of getting me to ignore my better judgment.”

“I’m not asking you to make love to me. I’m asking for a release.”

“Just sex,” he spoke the words like a question.

“Just sex,” she confirmed.

The noise in his throat was a low rumble when he backed her up against the kitchen wall. His mouth met hers, swallowing her answering groan as he pinned her there. He savored her mouth, his tongue gliding in and around, tasting her. His hand slid beneath the edge of her shirt, and he hooked one finger into the waistband of her sweats, dragging it sideways along that sensitive skin just above her hipbones.

The unhurried pace of his explorations as his other hand slid up and over her breast was excruciating to Kaela. She gasped, trembling with sharp streaks of pleasure as he rolled and pinched her through the material of her bra. He gave a dark chuckle at the sound and his hard length pressed along her stomach, straining the fabric between them. She wiggled, smiling at the hiss of his breath at the contact.

“You make such delicious little sounds for me,” she whispered in his ear, dragging her teeth along the outer shell.

She was already tugging at the buttons of his jeans, pulling his shirt over his head, and generally trying to get their clothing off as quickly as possible. He didn’t resist but he also didn’t help as much as she thought he should. Clearly, she was the only one on a mission. At last, she managed to kick the last of her clothing away and nothing was left between them but skin.

“So impatient.” He teased her, his fingers burning as he ran them down her spine and around her thigh, then dipped them softly between her legs.

She grabbed him in one hand, the ache in her body now an unbearable throb. “Don’t make me beg.”

His eyes were blazing as he nibbled across her jaw. He spun her body around, so her back was to him, her hands now braced against the edge of the counter. She peered at him over her shoulder as he slid another part down the same path his fingers had taken.

Kaela’s breathy moan and his long grunt blended, and she arched her hips back, encouraging him. Through half-lidded eyes, she watched when he slowly pushed into her those first delicious inches. Kaela let out a sinful, lusty noise at the way he stretched her, forcing her body to make space for him. He placed a hand on her back, holding her flat against the counter so that her tiptoes were barely on the floor.

Her body had been aching for this, and it was worth the wait.

She lost all sense of time and self as they moved together. His mouth was on her neck and her hands were reaching back to grip him behind his head. The sounds from their bodies meeting and those coming from their mouths filled the room. She couldn't get enough of him.

After they finally cascaded over the edge together, Kaela pressed her cheek to the cool surface of the counter, catching her breath even as the last pulses of Landry's release sent waves of aftershock through her. He ran his nose up her spine, placing a soft kiss between her shoulder blades that made her shiver before lowering her to her feet. She turned on unsteady legs to face him.

"I was mistaken if I ever thought this was a bad idea." He donned his boxers and faced her with a lazy smile.

Kaela snorted and gave him a halfhearted shove as he stepped in close. Where he had been rough before, his caress as he tangled his fingers in her hair and traced the outline of her cheekbones was now sweet and somehow full of longing. A voice in the back of her mind whispered that she should pull away, but she leaned into his touch, closing her eyes and savoring the contact. His lips brushed the corner of her mouth, then trailed along her neck. He paused, resting his forehead against hers. She was looking at the dark flecks of gold in his emerald eyes when the words slipped out.

"Maybe you should go now."

Silence filled the kitchen for the span of a heartbeat.

"Just sex?" His words were spoken softly, part question and part resignation.

"Yeah."

He nodded and pulled away.

Each second spent watching him get dressed, Kaela was biting her cheek to keep herself silent. As she pulled her shirt over her head, an invitation for him to stay was on the tip of her tongue. She followed him to the front door, forcing the idea away. Those feelings were dangerous. Those feelings would wreck her again. She couldn't go down that path.

Just sex.

“I’ll stop by to see you this week at the office.” He gave her a chaste kiss, his lips the soft allure of a siren. “If anyone follows you or you feel at all unsafe—”

“I will call or text you immediately.” Kaela gave a reassuring smile to hide her warring emotions. “Goodnight, Landry.”

“Goodnight, Mikaela.”

She watched him through the peephole for a moment as he walked to his SUV, but pulled herself away, starting another scathing mental lecture.

Just sex.

Germany – 1924

Theo shifted his toes in his boots but otherwise remained still as he sat in the shadowy recesses of the loft. His dark green uniform matched those of the other officers, and with the smoke further obscuring the area around the gambling tables, he was reasonably disguised. On the main floor of the establishment, fresh air drifted in from the open doorways, and the lights were brighter, making it quite easy for Theodore to watch the people below.

Elizabeth was currently drinking three large, uniformed men under the table. Her arm flashed through a slit in the velvety blue material of her sleeve as she slammed her empty glass down on the center of the table and released a triumphant belch. The men's mugs joined hers a few seconds later, spurring a chorus of laughter. Cleda placed a flimsy diadem of twisted tin over Elizabeth's bobbed hair, and the crowd roared with delight as she gave a bow.

At the bar in the corner, a busty woman in a snug sequined dress was draping herself against Landry. The long fringe of her skirt left little to the imagination. She shifted her hips, and it parted to reveal a generous amount of skin near the apex of her thighs. Landry's fingers traced the bare surface of her back as she whispered in his ear, her heart-painted lips grazing his jaw. Theo noticed the sharpness in her eyes as she glanced around the room over his shoulder. Landry finished his drink in one long swig. He exchanged a look with Elizabeth over the heads of the men between them and then followed the woman through one of the back doors.

Theodore turned his attention back to the cards in his hand. "Well, I believe that does me in, gentlemen. I will withdraw and let you bloodthirsty sharks take someone else's money while I nurse my ego at the bar."

After a few good-humored claps on the back, Theodore extricated himself from the table and found his way down the stairs. No sooner had his feet touched the lower rung than an arm slipped through his, leading him to a table at the edge of the room.

"Teddy." Elizabeth grinned, her words measured and distinct as if she were completely sober despite the large amount of booze Theo knew she

had consumed that night. "You could just let me know when you'd like to visit instead of spying on me from a distance. I'm always happy to see you, you know!"

"Your overprotective commanding officer might say otherwise," he replied.

"This uniform is dashing," she teased, pulling him into the empty booth and leaning across the table to fiddle with his leather holster strap. "You did not join the army, but I'll assume this is part of your reason for being here tonight. A cover? What has Nisha decided to make you do now?"

"You know I cannot tell you." He grimaced and checked for anyone close enough to overhear. "What I can say is I am to verify that your dear leader is continuing to obey Cassius. I assume that this is an evening of revelry because you will all be shipping out to another location entirely in the next few days?"

Elizabeth frowned.

"You should stop working for that bitch."

"You know I don't have a choice any more than you have a choice about whether or not to work for Cassius," he responded with frustration in his tone.

"Well, you may tell your distrusting, evil dictator of a boss that Landry is following Cass's directives and, therefore, so am I. We are leaving in two days. I don't think anything would make him disobey that man, no matter how the rest of us may feel."

Theo gave her hand a quick squeeze across the table.

"We all knew what we were agreeing to when we decided to live forever."

Her face became sullen at this reminder, but she nodded.

"Yes, I suppose we did." Her eyes drifted to the back door and then across the crowd, checking on Cleda's location before returning to Theo. "I should get back to celebrating our return to action. Will you join me for a drink before you leave? I know that Cleda would like to see you, and since Landry found his mark for the evening, he shouldn't be back anytime soon. You know how he is, always eager to dip his wick. Sex is like a lovely bowl of pudding to him, enjoyed and savored in the moment but easily forgotten."

"I wish that I could." Theodore stood, wrapping his arms around Elizabeth as she pulled him into a hug. "Please be careful during this assignment. These games Cass and Nisha are playing could go sideways at any moment. I don't want to see you hurt."

"The same to you, Teddy. We've survived too many lifetimes to die in this one."

"Well, make it through this and I'll be sure we see more of each other in the next."

Elizabeth kissed him on the cheek and moved off into the crowd. As he left the building, Theo thought about everything they'd been through and wondered when their luck would finally run out.

Chapter 7

Kaela missed a deadline.

Fortunately, it was just her responses to the reviewers of a submitted publication, and she was able to get an extension from the editor, but it still filled her with rage and embarrassment. As all type A overachievers would admit, there were two imaginary prizes that they spent their lives trying to win. The first was awarded to the most organized, expedient, and low-maintenance person to travel through airport security. The second was for never missing even the most arbitrary deadline.

Kaela should have spent the weekend finalizing the draft manuscript Caleb had written and given it to her lab manager to submit before Monday morning. Instead, she did other things which put her behind schedule. She took the opportunity to daydream about those 'other things'. The fabricated image of Landry licking cannoli cream off her skin made her clamp her thighs together in frustration.

That was exactly the type of distraction that caused her to slip. It was past suppertime, the last day of work before winter break, and here she was, still in her office. She received the submission confirmation for her past due document in her email, relieved to mark that item off her mental checklist despite the lingering annoyance.

"Dr. B?"

"Hi Ashley." Kaela turned to the senior technician hovering in the open doorway. "Did you shut down the lab?"

"Yep, you aren't going to be here too much longer, are you?" Ashley glanced at the half-cleared desk.

"I was just packing up," Kaela assured her. "Did you get those culture samples sent off to the proteomics and genomics cores?"

"I did. I sent your cells that reverted and my cells that utterly failed to change, once again. I also sent the lotion sample to the mass spec lab, like you asked. I cleaned out the incubator stacks, took care of the final glassware from autoclaving, and emptied the fridges of anything that will expire in the next three weeks. All the grad students are gone. Caleb is going to be in and out of the building over break to work on some manuscripts, but he won't be in the lab. Everyone else has already taken off for the holiday."

"Thank you." Kaela stopped packing and gave her employee a genuinely grateful look. "Go home, enjoy the break, and I will see you in January."

"Okay, happy holidays!"

As Ashley left, Kaela felt the pressure of leadership lessening. She stuck to the career advice once offered by her father – hire good people, pay them well, and give them enough autonomy to impress you. She would fall apart without her senior staff.

I will be leaving the office soon.

Texting Landry before she transferred locations was a new part of her life. He never asked for updates, but with a car tailing her every day, she made the decision to keep him informed. She convinced herself it had nothing to do with what happened over the weekend, and it was just a way to mitigate the risk of an unanticipated attack. If she went missing, she wanted an energy-slinging, vengeance-seeking powerhouse to immediately search for her.

Kaela took a break from packing her bag and stared down at the empty parking square below the window. Something small scurried through the yellow pool of light spilling across the asphalt in the twitching, sporadic path indicative of a sentient creature. The campus had been mostly empty since lunchtime, and now the few stragglers hanging around the lab buildings had left as well. The absence of noise in the hallways became a persistent hum unto itself while she peered into the deepening shadows outside. Someone could be down there, watching her move around her brightly lit office, and she would never know. She glanced at the windows in the next building over. Most of them were dark, but a few overhead lights were on, illuminating unoccupied interiors like yellow eyes in a giant black face. Kaela jumped when her phone buzzed against the surface of the desk.

I was next door. I'll be at your office in a minute. Wait for me?

Her stomach gave a little flutter, and she instantly rationalized her decision to wait. It made sense to catch him up on the day's events, and an escort to her car wasn't a terrible idea either.

Okay.

She sat down in her desk chair to wait, fingers idly fidgeting with the locket around her neck, tracing the whorls of the engraving. When she was getting dressed that morning, it had caught her eye and she'd been struck by the impulse to wear it. The metal was warm against her skin, and she imagined a faint vibration emanating from it, like the purring of a cat. She turned it over to consider the inscription, but a triangle of white caught her eye. Peeking from beneath the residual clutter on her desk was a crisp linen envelope.

On her way to work that morning, she checked her mail, expecting junk but finding the letter instead. She was in a rush, and she tossed it into her leather tote with hardly any thought. Now, she retrieved it from her bag, inspecting the neat, compact lettering of the return address. It had been sent from Louisiana.

"What song is that?"

Kaela started in surprise as Landry's tingling presence washed over her. She was so engrossed in evaluating the letter that she missed his approach entirely. She really needed to work on her situational awareness. He stood in the doorway, his large body filling the frame. One of his hands held a white paper bag, the other was tucked into his front pocket, and his mouth curved in amusement.

"Hey!" Kaela dropped the envelope onto the desk and stood. "What song?"

"The one you were humming."

When she stopped in front of him, he lifted her chin with his fingers and brushed a kiss against her lips. She hadn't expected the gesture, and she fought the blush that rose to her cheeks. They had agreed not to become romantically involved, and this type of intimacy did not feel casual. At least none of her coworkers were around to witness it.

"I didn't realize I was humming." She shrugged and looked sharply down at his hand when the smell of food hit her nose. "What is in the bag?"

"Dinner." His dimple deepened when her stomach gave a very loud, aggressive grumble. "I didn't want to interrupt your workday, so I called Hailey and asked her what you like to eat when you are stuck at work late."

"How did you know I would be here late?"

"You have worked late every day this week. I made an assumption." Landry noticed the necklace at her throat, and he reached out, turning the locket over. "Is this a family heirloom? I've never noticed it before."

"This is one of the two items my ex-husband's Aunt Gloria left to me when she passed." Kaela waited patiently while he inspected the jewelry despite the continued gurgling of hunger.

"*The Iliad*," he commented. "Interesting choice."

"You recognize the words?" She looked at the inscription again. "It sounded like a message from a lover, but I didn't know it was a quote."

"I don't remember the full passage, but I can find it while you eat." Landry stepped past her to the desk and began to set out the food. "I can't continue to speak over the noises from your stomach for much longer. Were you close to her?"

"Not very." Kaela's mouth started salivating as she inspected the Mediterranean feast. "She died a few months ago. It was bizarre because she also left me a pricey property in New Orleans. I don't know much about it, but I received a letter today with a Louisiana postmark that might shed some light on the mystery."

It took her a moment to notice the stillness that fell over Landry. He looked faintly concerned when he turned to face her.

"What was Aunt Gloria's maiden name?"

"I don't know, actually." The sharpness in his expression was unnerving. "Please tell me that she isn't part of all—*this*."

"I will try not to be insulted by the way you just gestured at me." Landry laughed a little stiffly. "No, I'm sure it is a coincidence, but the name and location are familiar. I will look into it. New Orleans is a popular place for our kind."

"Why is it that when supernatural shit hits the fan, New Orleans is always involved?" Kaela sighed dramatically. "Drunk tourists in voodoo shops don't notice boring, everyday magic, I suppose."

She plopped back into her chair and pulled her sleeves to her elbows before she set to work on a gyro. She peered at Landry out of the corner of her eyes as he took his phone from a pocket. She couldn't believe he picked up dinner from her favorite restaurant. It was thoughtful to feed her. It was beyond thoughtful to do the legwork of identifying her go-to meal and hand-delivering it.

"There is the heat of Love, the pulsing rush of Longing, the lover's whisper, irresistible—magic to make the sanest man go mad."

"Wow." The words danced smoothly across her senses, his low voice giving them a metered rumbling like a pulse. "That is quite lovely. Not something her husband would have selected to go on a gift. He was a dick.

The locket isn't expensive or pretentious enough for him to have bought it in the first place. More layers to the mystery instead of answers."

Landry perched on the far corner of the desk. When she offered him the hummus, he gently took her wrist and turned it to inspect a long, scabbed-over cut across the back of her forearm. The explanation that it was inflicted during knife training with Hailey and Theo earned a disapproving scowl, even after she assured him it was her own knife that managed to do the damage. Despite the claim that he had already eaten dinner, he consumed a fair portion of the hummus, continuing to frown at the injury.

"I had some interesting successes today in the lab." Kaela tapped her fingers against her leg and watched Landry bite into a dolma, her eyes lingering on his mouth. "I had my technician start a few cell culture plates the other day, and I attempted some very nonscientific mumbo jumbo with them this morning."

"Mumbo jumbo?" He raised an eyebrow.

"Hocus pocus?" she teased, smiling at his slow, unamused blink.

She had arrived at the lab earlier that day, completely preoccupied with the latest iteration of hypothetical equations she'd been investigating. They matched some of the work from a journal Landry used in the late 1970s, but her approach contained subtle differences, fewer constants, and variations on the relative assumptions. As she related the day's events, she tossed him the notebook in question as well as her tablet running an open-source software for her calculations. She jokingly apologized for using digital equations instead of creating her own hundred-year-old paper trail. He studiously ignored the jab at his anachronistic use of handwritten notebooks.

"There is definitely a distinction here," he pointed to a section displayed on her screen and flipped to the corresponding part of his own work. "I think that is worth pursuing further. But the theoretical discussion can wait." He carefully stacked the materials on the desk and waited for her to continue. "Tell me about the lab work."

"I don't know why I haven't tried to manipulate the cells on purpose before," she admitted. "It was a logical place to start and probably a better representation than mushy bananas and over-ripe avocados."

It was early enough in the morning that her lab technicians and graduate students were still struggling out of bed as she walked into the brightly lit laboratory space, the windows dark and the air carrying only the automatic whirrs of the equipment. She carefully removed one of the plates from the incubator, sliding it onto the microscope stage and flicking on the light source. She clicked the optic into place and turned the knob, finding a relative focus that placed most of the cells in view.

They were mature neural cells, long and stretched thin like pulled pieces of chewing gum. She moved the plate, scanning the well to confirm that they all looked healthy and happy. Then she closed her eyes and held the plate between her hands, thumbs and forefingers at each of the four corners, while she framed her thoughts around her desires, running through the pathways she knew would drive the processes that needed to occur. This time, she relied on her own energy to feed it, and she aired a monotone hum from deep inside her, like a dirge.

When she opened her eyes, she could barely feel the difference in her body from the exertion, and she peered through the eyepiece, anticipation coiling in her stomach. The cells were now crumpled little spheres, the wadded paper appearance of stem cells. She leaned away from the scope, looking around in shock at how easy her success was to achieve.

Surely it couldn't be that simple.

"But it was. It was so simple that it hurts me to admit." She threw her hands in the air with exacerbation, aware of Landry's cautious appraisal. "I did it to two of the cell plates. Then I took one of those plates and drove it forward, making those cells into functional neurons again. All the years of work, and it was never science that made any of my successes happen. It was me. Me and my mysterious control over living things like Hebe reincarnated, feeding magical ambrosia to the cells of my choosing."

Landry remained silent, watching her frustration ebb and flow in a chaotic dance before speaking. "Your lab has produced plenty of ironclad scientific findings. The only thing that caused you problems was this one specific set of experiments that never repeated and were therefore never published. You are being too critical of yourself. Your calculations and your legwork are fine. You need to discard any data from recent experiments performed by you and leave the lab work to your employees from here on. Honestly, you shouldn't be in there, regardless of this situation. You don't want to be *that* professor who can't let go and focus on their managerial role."

Kaela tried to dismiss the accuracy of his last statement. "You're right. I may contaminate anything I touch and should just stay out of there. For now. I had my technician send the cultures for a full evaluation of the gene expression and protein production of the cells. If anything comes from those analyses, I'll tell you, but the core labs are closed for the holiday. I won't know anything until at least mid-January."

She decided not to mention the other sample that she sent for analysis. She wasn't sure how Landry would feel about her decision to reverse engineer the herbalist ointment she obtained from Marlene in the desert. Landry started cleaning up the empty food containers and nodded at the envelope at the edge of the desk.

"Are you going to open that?"

She picked up the piece of mail and carefully ripped open the top. Inside was a letter written in the same concise, flowing script as the address on the outside. Both the envelope and letter were heavy, high-quality stationery. Who sent physical letters these days? She scanned the contents before tucking it back into her bag.

"Also mysterious." She shrugged away Landry's quizzical look. "The caretaker of the estate has written to let me know they will continue to maintain the grounds and home as Gloria previously desired. However, they look forward to making my acquaintance and assured me that they will immediately institute any new or additional instructions regarding the estate if or when received."

Landry snagged a few olives from the last food container, and Kaela pinched her eyebrows together in mock annoyance. Something about the way he popped them into his mouth felt sensual. The back of her neck turned clammy, and she refocused on straightening the items on her desk, choosing not to acknowledge this distraction. The effect he had on her libido was disconcerting.

"Why were you on campus today?" she asked him, desperate to bring her body back to equilibrium.

"You do remember that I am on faculty at this university, don't you?" he teased. "I needed to check in with my staff before the break. Since most of our work is theoretical, they are remote all but two days during the week, and we have a standing in-person meeting on Friday mornings."

"I thought this job was a cover."

"This job was a convenient cover, but I still made a commitment to the people I hired, which I intend to keep." He wiped the desk with a napkin and threw it in the garbage before turning to face her again. "Besides, physics was always my favorite doctorate."

Kaela snorted at Landry's reference to his multiple degrees and collected the standard-issue black plastic bin, placing it outside the door for the night janitor to collect. It only took another minute to finish clearing the desk before she ushered him into the hallway.

"May I walk you to your car?"

His smell wrapped around her, and she imagined the heat of him against her back as she locked her office door. She nodded and moved down the hall beside him, trying not to stiffen when their shoulders touched or when the back of his hand brushed against hers.

She was being reckless. She knew she was slipping into a comfortable dependency months ago, even before they had sex. Being with him made her feel different, like she could relax and just breathe instead of keeping her spine straight and tackling every challenge in her path like she was waging a battle. She was losing her edge, smothering some of her drive with this warm blanket of normalcy. This wasn't who she decided to be after she finally freed herself from the last major relationship mistake. She feared shrinking again.

Landry seemed to notice the shift in her thoughts. He cleared his throat and moved farther away as they approached the elevator. "So, you are planning to compare the cells you manipulated to the ones that you didn't handle to see what pathways light up?"

"Yes." Kaela was relieved by the change of conversation as she stepped into the lift. "But like I said, it will be a while before I have that data."

"Still, it should prove interesting." Although he maintained a relaxed position on the opposite side of the small space, his proximity was making her skin heat again. "Once you've compared the data sets, you will try to work backwards from there?"

"Exactly," she said with determination. "I can deconstruct the processes that I am manipulating through my abilities and then find a scientific approach that mimics them."

"Science-derived magic." He looked impressed as he followed her out of the now-open elevator doors. "If you can make this work, there is an entire realm of scientific advances waiting to be discovered."

"I would start with that impressive salve your healer gave me in the desert." She glanced at him, hoping this was her opportunity to get his permission, to ease the slight strain on her conscience. "And if the aging reversal could be turned into a wrinkle cream that also treats bruises or blemishes, can you imagine the money we'd make off something like that? I bet we could finance construction of accessible clean water to an entire third-world nation."

"I cannot express how much it means that your first thought is solving a global crisis." Landry held her winter coat while she placed her arms through the sleeves, leaning in so the words he spoke next caressed her skin. "You are truly amazing, Dr. Brookes. You bury yourself in your work, but for all that society frustrates you, there is a deep-rooted need to fix what is broken. You would die happy if you never spent another night on the town, but you would spend your riches solving the socio-economic problems of a nation of people you have never met. Maybe there is an optimist buried deep down inside you after all."

Her fingers froze on the final button of her coat. The way he described her was different from how she saw herself. Her brain constantly sought solutions, but she never considered herself a humanitarian, just someone who wanted to solve problems in a world full of them. Helping people was a good idea, but his statements painted her as a compassionate person driven by hope. His view of her was kinder than she deserved.

"You can't possibly know that much about me in such a short time."

"It doesn't take centuries to know those parts of you," he answered earnestly. "We are the same in many ways. I saw that the first night we had dinner. You don't typically vocalize those feelings, but I could always see the goodness in your spirit, lurking below your carefully crafted cynicism."

The emotions that these words provoked were anything but simple to Kaela. She saw herself as he did for a brief second, and there was a brightness from the perspective. When she tucked the locket behind the collar of her coat, her thumb traveled across the engraved letters. She couldn't stop the words from tumbling through her head again.

There is the heat of Love, the pulsing rush of Longing, the lover's whisper.

She turned and set a brisk pace in the direction of the parking lot. Landry's long legs allowed him to catch up in a few steps, and when she glanced at him, he looked relaxed, unfazed by her mercurial reactions. She would not allow herself to think about the ember in her chest. She wouldn't make the comparisons or use the words. She would remember that strong, independent core that propelled her through her life, framing it in the context that she chose.

He could be a friend, and maybe something a little more, but she would not tether herself to anyone the way she did with Jason. She refused to be shaped by the relentless wear of a serious relationship: the repetitive smoothing of a corner or sanding of an edge that didn't quite mesh with the other person.

"I'm going to visit the house in New Orleans." The statement surprised Kaela as it left her mouth, but as soon as she voiced the words, she knew the time away was exactly what she needed. "I can ask Hailey to come with me."

There was a brief pause before Landry responded.

"I understand. May I suggest someone with more firepower at their disposal to accompany you in addition to Hailey? I know your training is advancing, and Hailey can easily handle ordinary threats, but I won't be there if an attacker with more interesting abilities comes after you."

Kaela considered the offer while they approached her car. It did make sense to have someone close by. She nodded in agreement.

"Who were you thinking?"

"Do you remember Ahtah?" Landry asked. "He is a trusted companion that already knows Hailey, and he is what we call a dream walker. He's still in town and can meet you as soon as tomorrow morning. How long will you be gone?"

Kaela turned back to Landry, her eyes lingering over the details of his face from the mark on his cheek to the curve of his lower lip. Maybe she was overreacting. It was a stressful week, and her emotions were heightened. She pulled herself together and made eye contact. The green of his eyes seemed to glow under the streetlamps. Ordinarily, the edges of his irises appeared brown, but here in the semi-darkness, the veins of deep gold reflected the light, and Kaela couldn't breathe around the ache inside her. An edge of panic crept in. His expression softened as he read something in hers. He took one of her hands.

"I am only asking so that I can tell Ahtah what to expect, if you're comfortable with taking him along as a bodyguard, that is." The tenderness in his eyes made her heart constrict even more.

"Two or three weeks, I think."

Kaela looked at their joined hands and remembered their first date at the cute little restaurant a few blocks away from where they were now standing. She had no idea who he really was at the time. Her powers were still a secret, and he was just the new, unbearably attractive colleague at the university. She considered their first meaningful conversation during their dinner, and she realized that although he talked around the parts of his world she couldn't yet understand, he had been honest about everything else. He shared his mortal, human life with her that night. The stories and jokes were from the twenty years of his existence when he aged like everyone around him and thought he would live a normal lifespan.

When they said goodnight later in the evening, he kissed the inside of her wrist like a perfect gentleman. As if remembering the same thing, Landry brushed his thumb across that sensitive section of her skin, leaving goosebumps in the wake.

"Hailey and Ahtah can both come with me."

"Thank you, I will be far less worried while you're gone." He brought her wrist to his lips. "Just tell me if you need anything at all. I'll be here."

The feel of his mouth against her skin was almost enough to make her change her mind. She placed a hand on his cheek and kissed him softly along his scar.

"I'll text you my flight information and you can coordinate with Ahtah. See you in a few weeks, Landry."

She could see him again when she leveled out and got a grip on her raging emotions.

Proof

Chapter 1

Dr. Mikaela Brookes was a coward. She stood on the sidewalk in front of an impressive manor home in New Orleans, having just fled over a thousand miles to avoid her feelings, and she still struggled to keep Dr. Landry Griffiths off her mind. Her first thought upon seeing the nineteenth-century mansion she'd inherited was that she was at the wrong address. Her second thought was that Landry would empathize with her impostor syndrome as she took in the massive, uptown property that now belonged to her, the daughter of blue-collar workers, descendants of poor European immigrants. She would never be ashamed of her family or upbringing, but the image of her mother, smiling as she handed over a stack of carefully organized coupons to a grocery store cashier, flickered in Kaela's mind, desperately asynchronous with the physical manifestation of her *nouveau riche* inheritance.

"Don't let this nice weather trick you." Theodore's words interrupted Kaela's brooding. "When it's hotter than Satan's ball sack in the summer, that house will be much less attractive."

"Nice." Kaela faced her companions, giving Theo a reproachful glare. "Can someone please remind me why he was invited on this trip?"

Hailey and Ahtah stood a few feet away. The various roller bags and carry-on luggage had been pulled from the departing ride-share cars and were spread along the pavement. A carrier was grasped in one of Kaela's hands, Hellkitten peering silently through the mesh front. The flight to New Orleans was direct and uneventful. Kaela's seat was a single at the front of the plane, and her companions were several rows behind. Other than the occasional question from the flight attendant, she was able to spend the trip in silence, watching the clouds through the window or working on her laptop.

"Are we going to knock or just stand out here on the sidewalk all day?"

Kaela started to provide a witty retort to Theo's question when movement within the shadowy depths of the front porch caught her eye. The house sat a fair distance from the front of the property, and the space between the porch and the road was filled with oak trees. Their thick, straight trunks were topped with sturdy upper limbs that bent and twisted into a broad, overlapping canopy. Being winter, the missing leaves left a bare grid of lines against the bright sky, but she could imagine the deep blanket of shadows they would create during the heat of the summer when they were heavy with foliage again. A wrought iron fence delineated the edge of the sidewalk from the property, and square stone pillars topped with gas lamps bracketed the walkway. Wide front steps politely introduced a low-lying veranda that wrapped around both sides of the structure. Waiting at the top of the landing was a woman.

"I think our hostess is ready for an introduction," Hailey responded with a nod. "We shouldn't be rude and make her wait. And Teddy, maybe just let Kaela talk so you don't offend anyone."

Kaela huffed a laugh at the comment and was the first to wheel her bags up the path, assuming the others would follow. The woman was tall, and though she did not have an unusually large build, she possessed a sturdy quality in her posture, as if she was carved from stone rather than grown from the ground. Her eyes were dark but warm, the smudged makeup around them giving her a gypsy-like quality. A colorful silk scarf tied a thick mass of locks away from the ebony skin of her high forehead, and metallic braid cuffs glinted under stray tendrils of light that slipped beneath the gallery roof. When Kaela was close enough to be heard at a normal speaking volume, she called out a greeting.

"I'm Mikaela Brookes. Are you Angelique?"

"Everyone calls me Angel." The woman moved to the bottom of the stairs, shaking Kaela's hand and then reaching for one of the suitcases, her words slow and thick with the local dialect.

"Thank you. Everyone calls me Kaela." Angel nodded in understanding and then looked over Kaela's shoulder to the remaining members of the party while Kaela hastily turned to make introductions. "These are my friends: Hailey, Theodore, Ahtah. They will be staying for the duration of my visit, but if there isn't room, we can find lodgings nearby. I'm sorry I didn't warn you there would be this many of us."

"This is your house, Sha. No need to apologize. There's plenty of room for y'all." Kaela waited, but Angel didn't lead the way into the home. Instead, the taller woman kept her eyes on Ahtah. "I see you're still involved in business you ain't got no right being involved in, Ahtahkakoop."

Kaela's spine involuntarily straightened, and Hailey's eyebrows crawled past her hairline as Angel produced this name, the full given appellation like a scolding intended for a naughty child. Theo, unflappable as ever, gave Ahtah a brief, disinterested glance.

"*Tân'si*, Angelique." This was only the eighth or ninth time Kaela heard Ahtah speak during the entire trip, and she was once again surprised by the deep, calming quality of his voice. "I see you are as ready as always to judge the actions of others despite your lack of knowledge around the context."

Kaela's immediate instinct was to diffuse the situation, and she scrambled to think of an appropriate tactic to do so, even as she puzzled over the relationship between the two of them. Before she could find a solution, Angel waved her hand dismissively and turned to Theo, saving Kaela from her discomfort.

"Your face is familiar." Angel's words shot into the air, heavy with accusation. "I don't see how I would've forgotten a good-looking man of your caliber."

"I once visited your mother. It was nearly twenty years ago, and you would have only been a child," Theodore offered with a cocky shrug. "Even my beautiful face is forgettable after that much time."

"*Ah,* yes. *That* woman must have brought you with her to threaten Manman. Didn't quite know what she was getting into, did she?"

"You know Nisha?" Kaela asked with a tone of resignation, accepting the fact that nothing in her life would be left untouched if she kept digging at these tangled connections. "Of course you know Nisha."

"I know her name, and she knows to stay out of our way. That's enough for me. You may as well come in and tell me who you're involved with. I didn't realize Gloria read you in before she died. I assumed I'd have to orient you to everything myself. Ought to help if we just air it out before we get any further along. Maybe you can explain why you showed up with a kitten if you're only fixin' to stay a short while." Angel nodded meaningfully to the carrier in Kaela's hand, then lifted the large suitcase as if it were a paper box containing nothing but feathers and carried it into the house. "Come see."

Kaela exchanged a quick look with Hailey before the two of them followed close behind. The initial step into the home filled Kaela with an intense, bracing sense of rightness, the fleeting impression of a memory that she tried to latch onto before it dissipated. The air was a warm billow that carried an earthy mix of sage, lemon, and vanilla. The entry opened into a large foyer, white walls segmented by wide doorways and life-sized portraits. She paused in front of one painting depicting a laughing young woman, her hair wrapped in white fabric, shocking in its contrast to the rich, dark skin of her face. The painting was oddly informal, the woman slouching over the back of a chair, a book propped open in her lap, and one hand reaching over as if to call someone forward from just beyond where Kaela stood.

"She was lovely, a real looker." Angel set down the bag and stood beside Kaela, looking at the painting with warmth and a bit of sadness. "Manman knew it, and she could charm the pants off just about anyone."

"She died." The words were gentle when they spilled from Kaela's lips, said with a softness that conveyed understanding.

"As we all must."

The statement would have been an insignificant truism, a casual observation of the common fate shared with all humans, if it was spoken by anyone else. Kaela looked at Angel, noticing as the other woman cast a pointed stare in Ahtah's direction. Hailey cleared her throat.

"Should we take our luggage up to our rooms?"

"Top of the stairs. There are four bedrooms to either side. The last one on the left and right are currently occupied, but any of the others are available. The master is on this floor for you, Kaela. I can show you where."

Kaela nodded in response to Hailey's questioning glance. Then Ahtah, Theo, and Hailey carried their luggage up the staircase that rose from the ground in a straight shot to the second level before it split in either direction at the top.

"Who stays here with you?" Kaela asked as she followed Angel past the stair landing and through a long corridor to the entrance of an expansive bedroom suite.

"I have my son with me and a woman I keep track of. She's like family. Since my job as the caretaker required constant attention, your aunt thought it was easiest if we all stayed under this roof. If it's an issue for you, though…"

"No, not at all!" Kaela was quick to interject. "I don't plan on moving here, and I'm glad that you're taking care of the place. I just haven't quite wrapped my head around what it means to be the new owner. Honestly, I came here because—well, I don't know why, but it wasn't to make any big changes. And she wasn't really my aunt. Gloria was my ex-husband's aunt, and for whatever reason, she decided to leave this place to me." Kaela stopped rambling and looked around the spacious room, the four-poster bed and oversized fireplace catching her eye as she placed the pet carrier on the ground. "Do you mind if I let the cat out? We probably need a litter box. I didn't think that far ahead."

"I'll say it again. I won't tell you what you should or shouldn't do. I'm your employee now, and you set the rules. Besides that, I love animals. The more the merrier. But you should just know that Estè is constantly taking random critters in, and she may have something hanging around that your kitten won't like."

"Estè is the woman you care for?" Kaela opened the door to release Hellkitten, and Angel nodded.

"We can go to the sitting room to share our stories if you think it'll be fine." Angel looked at the tiny cat, and it returned her appraisal with a cold, aloof stare before slinking across the carpet, sniffing each object it passed.

Back in the foyer at the front of the house, Kaela and Angel were joined by Hailey. The other woman was just stepping down from the last stair, and together, with the kitten in tow, the small group filed into one of the front rooms. The space was brightly lit by the oversized windows spaced evenly along the two outer walls. Kaela craned her neck to inspect the ornate plaster over her head from the cornice molding to the large medallion embellishing the base of a chandelier.

The archaic designs above were juxtaposed against a mystical aesthetic below. Clusters of crystals and dried herbs cluttered the antique furniture, a tray of mismatched pillar candles sat atop the low-lying coffee table, and a broken animal skull crowned a stack of old leather-bound books on the mantel above the fireplace. Dark pigmented paintings of the bayou graced the walls, the images dripping across the canvas as the vertical lines of hanging moss gave way to long streaks of tree trunks reflected in swampy water.

"This is giving voodoo. The spiritual vibe is very on brand." Hailey plopped onto one of the large, leather couches and irreverently grabbed a handful of small bones, buttons, and shells from a bowl on the table before her, letting them trickle back into the container through her fingers.

"Only tourists practice the kind of voodoo you're thinking of in Nola."

Angel frowned as Hailey moved on to carelessly leafing through a set of hand-painted tarot cards. "This is more like a hobby to explore the trendy occultism this town offers as part of its business model. Please be careful with those. I like the artwork."

Hailey set the cards back down, the top card of the deck facing up. Kaela's eyes snagged on the image as she joined Hailey on the couch. A dark-faced Queen in black regalia with a crown of bones atop her head stared back. Kaela started to ask about it, but movement near the entrance to the room distracted her. A willowy, delicate woman hovered in the doorway, her eyes riveted to Hellkitten, who had jumped onto the coffee table and was cautiously investigating the bone bowl.

"Estè." The concerned, sisterly tone with which Angel addressed this woman spoke volumes to their relationship dynamics. "Come in and meet the new owner of the manor home, Mikaela Brookes."

"Hello." Kaela greeted her warmly. "It's just Kaela. This is my friend, Hailey, and this is my cat. We call her," she paused, embarrassed. "We call her Hellkitten. It's nice to meet you."

The silence didn't stretch for long before Hailey burst into laughter.

"You call her, what?"

"Shut up, Hailey," Kaela muttered.

Estè didn't acknowledge the newcomers with more than a nod before she went straight to the kitten, dropping to her knees next to the coffee table and engaging in a prolonged stare with the animal once she was at the same level. Hellkitten angled her head, and a loud, slow purr began to echo through the air. Estè held out her hand, and the feline offered a solid head boop against it. The woman laughed, a toneless exhalation of air, and scooped the fuzzy little creature up, settling back into a cross-legged seat and letting Hellkitten move freely around her lap.

"Is Isaiah still out with his friends?" Estè nodded a respose, then Angel turned to address Kaela and Hailey again. "Estè is mute. She hears and understands just fine, but please don't expect a verbal answer to anything. Isaiah is my son. You should know that just about everyone y'all will meet in this house can do some magic except for him. I call him my little squib. I borrowed that term, I didn't make it up myself."

"Yeah, I know where it's from." Hailey leaned forward with sharp interest. "I forgot there were any of you down here. I'm surprised you're after Kaela already. I thought your lot didn't want to be part of the world the rest of us live in."

"I don't know what you're talking about." Angel looked at Kaela. "I didn't go after you. I first heard your name when Gloria decided to make you the beneficiary of this place. Didn't hear it again until she passed. I thought you were just a normal member of her family. I didn't realize you might be something more until you showed up with your very *interesting* entourage. Maybe you could tell me what Gloria got herself into for perspective?"

"I feel like there are too many pieces missing for me to understand what's going on right now." Kaela leaned back. "Until a few months ago, I didn't think I was anything other than one of her normal relations either. I'm new to the world of magic, and I certainly didn't expect Aunt Gloria to have any ties to it. My attendance was requested at the reading of her will, and I suddenly owned this place and this necklace."

"*Mais*!" Angel's eyes widened when Kaela produced the locket from beneath her shirt collar. "She gave you that, too."

"You recognize it?"

Angel reached beneath her own shirt, producing a matching necklace.

"My grann was Creole. She lived a small life, but Manman, she set her sights on bigger things even as a child. When she was old enough, Manman hid her roots under layers of false pretenses and made connections with 'better' folks in the city. She managed to meet your aunt at some fancy club, and they fell in love. Now, that was back when you were only allowed to love someone if they fit a particular category that society deemed appropriate for you. Opposite races and same genders were not part of the approved list.

"But you can't stop feeling those feelings once they start. They both married men and had babies, following the expected steps of the dance. They met in secret but never for long and not with any steady frequency. My papa died when I was little, but your aunt couldn't get free of her tether as long as her own husband was alive. Or maybe she never wanted to. Either way, I reckon she would have eventually come around, but Manman died ten years ago and that was that."

"Your mother, Manman, had powers?" Kaela caressed the necklace, distracted by the brief but intimate story.

"She did. All the women in my family do. Hers was called the 'gift' of foresight. She could catch glimpses of things, impressions of the future. It was a curse, really." Angel's eyes followed the movement of Estè's hands as she tickled the edge of her shirt, inciting a flurry of paw strikes and a fluffy sideways dance from Hellkitten. "I gave you plenty of information to hold up my half of this *tête-à-tête*. Now, I would like to know more about you. Start with how you ended up with these people, and then what you're fixin' to have us involved in."

Kaela remained silent at first, considering the implications of Angel's involvement in the current power struggle. Estè stroked her long, elegant fingers across Hellkitten's spine. The silent woman sat in a rich beam of sunlight that spilled into the room, swirling with movement as illuminated motes of dust drifted through it. Estè's arms were a patchwork of creamy caramel intermingling with splashes of delicate pinkish skin. The bright pattern of light across her created a riotous dance as she moved, a blurring of the distinctive melanin borders.

"I spent my entire adult life thinking that the world was filled with rigid laws and clear divisions between one thing and another. Then, about six months ago, I found out that all those black and white scientific principles upon which I built my career were not always so organized. In fact, I think most of them are just flimsy explanations for things we really don't understand at all."

The silence was filled with the weight of Kaela's revelations, the feeling that something significant had taken place, and she was suddenly able to process it within the context of this exact moment, here in this strange house, watching a woman she didn't know weave illusions in the sunlight.

"She's an incredibly smart and well-known scientist who found out she has magical powers, then went into a deep existential crisis over the meaning of her life." Hailey provided this synopsis with an exaggerated shrug.

"Did I miss the part where she claims she can't actually do anything, and that we are mistaken about the importance of her abilities?"

Kaela frowned at this new addition to the discussion. Theo crossed the room and flopped onto the couch next to Angel with a suspiciously disarming smile. Ahtah remained hovering in the doorway, his eyes touching Angel's for only a second before he looked back at Hailey.

"So, you discovered your powers, and this crew showed up at your doorstep?" The caretaker looked between Hailey and Theo, ignoring Ahtah entirely. "You must have quite the power if the Old World Crew wants to recruit you. I've kept up with enough of the politics to know that Cassius is gone, and your side has divided loyalties. What can you do, and who owns you?"

"No one owns me, and I can't do much of anything yet." Kaela avoided the pointed look from Theo. "From what you've said, you know Cassius and Nisha. Do you know Landry?"

A long, cryptic stare in response.

"We've met," she stated.

"What about someone named Jackson?"

"That one doesn't ring a bell."

Kaela lost the thread of the conversation as she once again weighed her options. She could be vague about the backstory and hope that Angel was content with minimal details. She could also just take the plunge and decide to trust someone she barely knew.

"Why did Nisha visit your mother?" she asked.

"This is a safe place for people with abilities who want to live a normal life. When that husband of hers went missing, she was desperate to find someone who could do the same thing that he could. She was also in a precarious position when it came to controlling everyone around her. She came here to force Manman to join her little gang and to rifle through our collection of talents to see who we were hiding. It was a short visit."

Kaela glanced at Hailey and saw that her friend's delighted but feral expression reflected her own feelings about this statement. Someone standing up to Nisha was a welcome thought.

"She was the first person to try to recruit me." A plunge of trust felt appropriate. "I don't know all the details, but she might be using other groups to scare me into joining with her. I think some of them have been following me. Right now, the only people I know and trust are Hailey and Landry."

"*Ouch.*" Theo pulled a face at the omission of his name and shifted to address Angel. "I am also on Kaela's side, even if she won't admit it. Ahtah's cool, too."

"Why are you willing to share this information?" Hailey interrupted. "Why do you trust us?"

"I'm not willing to share it because I trust y'all, I am willing to share it because I trust Kaela. Gloria created this property as a gift to Manman. It was her way of protecting the woman she loved, even if she couldn't be with her. She never would have made a succession plan without consulting her first. Did you forget the part where I told you Manman could see the future? She would have known a thing or two about you, long before you even arrived in Gloria's life."

"But by being here, I'm bringing awareness to your existence again." Kaela rubbed the bridge of her nose in tired exacerbation. "I'm sorry. I shouldn't have come down like this. I wish I'd known more before barging into your lives."

"Sha, a safehouse is meant for anyone that needs it. You stay a bit. We ain't scared of Nisha or those loyal dogs that work for her. You're one of us now, and we take care of our own." Angel leaned over and patted Kaela gently on the knee. When she straightened, it was with an air of finality. "Now, y'all must be hungry. I got enough food in the kitchen to make a round of sandwiches, but tomorrow we'll have to go make some groceries to stock up for this many mouths. Come tell me how you want 'em dressed. Maybe after you get something in your belly, we can talk about these mysterious powers you seem hesitant to discuss."

The warm feeling in Kaela's stomach started to cool with this last statement, but Angel waved her hands in the air when she caught the nervous glance from Kaela to Hailey.

"*Mais*, child. I was teasing. Keep your secret as long as you need. It's up to you to share it when you're ready." Angel breezed across the room, speaking to Ahtah without looking at him. "You better come see about these sandwiches with me, Ahtahkakoop, unless you're too busy lazing about in this doorway."

America – 1996

Celine Dion belted her latest ballad through the car speakers as Kaela's mother drove along the twisting, rural street. This was the only compromise that Grandmother Anicette would agree to when it came to Kaela's musical preferences. God forbid, they listen to that 'banshee' known as Alanis Morissette or that 'talentless screecher' called Mariah Carey. Even Celine was received with little excitement.

"Son chant français est supérieur." She sniffed.

Kaela's sigh was filled with youthful melodrama. "I don't have her French CD, Grand-Mère."

Despite the disagreeable statement, her grandmother's hand maintained a rhythmic tapping against the leg of her polyester pantsuit as she gazed out of the passenger window. When they finally reached the end of the road, the trees dropped away, and a sprawling field opened before them.

Kaela's neck whipped forward, and she nearly smashed her face into the upholstered headrest of the driver's seat as her mother stomped down on the brake pedal. A deafening, discordant burst of squawks assaulted her ears, and a group of birds ran from the center of the road. Their pinpoint heads sat atop long necks, and their legs scurried frantically from beneath oversized, football-shaped bodies.

"Ugh, fucking guineas!" her mother shouted the uncharacteristic vulgarity.

"Mom!" from Kaela.

"Susan!" from Grandmother Anicette.

"Sorry, sorry." Kaela's mother held up her hands in apology, then gripped the wheel again, easing the car down the driveway. "I remember those birds from the last time we visited Great Aunt Violet. They are such a nuisance. Unfortunately, someone must be feeding them."

After a moment of silence, Kaela began to laugh, and her mother joined in. Grandmother Anicette even cracked a smile. They parked in front of an old two-story farm home. The broad mass of the stone chimney bisected the main gable near the drive, and the front porch wrapped asymmetrically in the opposite direction. It was charming, in a rustic, anachronistic way. When Great Aunt Violet died a few months prior, the white clapboards had been repainted and the roof replaced in preparation for sale. The garden was still reasonably well maintained, but it still held an essence of wildness in the haphazard sprays of forsythia and the mounds of creeping jenny that covered several large stones.

"Kaela, you can go explore while your grandmother and I meet with the realtor. Just don't go too far, it should only take about fifteen minutes."

"If you're looking for the chickens, they're hiding in that barn over there," Grandmother Anicette whispered in Kaela's ear as they exited the car and walked to the porch.

Kaela immediately headed toward the building her grandmother pointed out. There were a handful of low-lying structures off in the distance, and this one seemed indistinguishable from the next, but Grandmother Anicette was always right about these things. She called it her seventh sense, her sixth sense being her ability to determine the right amount of tarragon to add to her famous chicken and morel dish without needing to measure it.

The wooden door to the small shed was hanging ajar. Kaela brushed a spider web from her face as she stepped through into the dark, cool interior, the musty smell of dirt filling her nose with its richness. The rustle of wings and the soft, nervous clucking of hens greeted her. Once her eyes adjusted, Kaela could see at least a dozen full-sized chickens roosting among teetering stacks of old potting buckets. She stepped around the cluster of chicken-sized wallows that had been scratched into the dirt floor, moving deeper into the structure to get a better look at a solitary bundle in the far corner.

As Kaela passed, one of the hens jumped from its chosen tower, voicing a loud cackle of fear. Plastic pots cascaded across the floor when the other chickens joined the panicked retreat, wingbeats filling the air as they launched themselves toward the doorway. Kaela gripped her ears and hugged her elbows tightly against her body. When the last of the buckets rolled to a stop, she let her arms fall back to her sides. She continued in the direction of the dark shape, fixated by the strange heap. She was a step or two away when the image finally came together in her mind. It was the lifeless body of a dead rooster.

"Oh, you poor thing!" Her eyes filled with tears as she carefully

pinched one of the stiff, cold legs between her thumb and forefinger, dragging it around until she could see it more clearly. "Not a single injury. Were you just old? I wish we could all start over when we get to the end of our lives. Wouldn't that be wonderful? It's called reincarnation."

A strange urge took hold of Kaela, and she reached back to the rooster, placing a hand gently over its shiny black feathers. A jolt passed through her. It reminded her of the nauseating pulse of electricity she once experienced when she was plugging in the vacuum and accidentally touched the metal edge of the plug. Her hand jerked back as the rooster's body gave way under her palm, disintegrating into a pile of loose feathers. She gasped when the feathers shifted as if stirred by a breeze. From beneath the pile, a tiny head emerged.

Kaela ran back to the house, one hand clutching the miniscule black chick to her chest and the other holding her nostrils closed to stave off a sudden nosebleed. Her mother immediately fussed over her nose, brushing aside her story about the baby bird with an apologetic glance at the realtor.

"She has such an active imagination!"

She was right, of course. Kaela let Grandmother Anicette take the chick back into the field to join the other chickens. The little baby bird must have been there all along. It was the only explanation.

Chapter 2

The air burned in Kaela's lungs as she sucked it down in deep, greedy gulps. Her feet slapped the pavement in a sharp rhythm, and she rounded the last street corner at a dead sprint despite the stab of pain in her side. When she reached the front of the house, she slowed to a walk and turned, a triumphant expression across her face even as she tried to keep her jelly-kneed legs moving. Theo had just come into view behind her, his face red with effort and annoyance.

"Like I said, you're hot girl fit," she slung the insult at him between breaths, enjoying the twist of his features as he finally caught up to her.

"I'm not…" He braced his hands on his legs, bent forward, and panted like he might faint at a moment's notice. "…hot girl… fit… just don't… like… running."

Kaela gave a snide laugh and continued walking to the end of the block, listening to the painful struggle of the man trailing behind her. When she woke that morning, drowning in the fluffy bedding of her posh, king-sized bed, she decided an early run around the city would help clear the confusion still occupying her thoughts from the revelations of the previous day. When she crept through the front door, she found Hailey and Theo waiting for her on the porch.

"You weren't seriously planning to go running by yourself." Hailey's crossed arms and sharply peaked eyebrows instantly filled Kaela with guilt. "You're taking Teddy."

"I am not taking him with me."

"What is the point of having all of us here to protect you if you won't let us?" Her friend gestured vaguely through the air, her movements sharp with frustration. "Just because we're in another state doesn't mean you're free to dismiss the threats. Nisha's reach is long. Take Teddy."

"Can't you go?" Kaela's voice held an embarrassing hint of a whine.

"No, I'm going to the grocery store to 'make groceries' as they say."

Kaela scowled at Theo.

Theo scowled back at Kaela.

"Hey, don't act like you are the only one who is put out," he said. "This is not my ideal way to spend a morning. No one likes to run."

Once she acquiesced, it didn't take long for Kaela to realize that although he continued to vocalize his distaste for the activity, Theo wasn't in terrible shape. He managed to keep up with her through the first mile but quickly deteriorated as she continued to lead them along the city sidewalks. She checked the distance on her watch from time to time and carved a long three-mile loop through the grid of houses and shops. At first, he kept pace a dozen feet behind, which gave Kaela the unsettled feeling of being chased. She made him run next to her whenever the width of the path allowed.

"Only a mile left, big guy," she teased as they passed the front of a delicious-smelling French bakery. "Maybe you should spend some time on the cardio equipment in between those sets of deadlifts and curls. Then you would actually be in good physical shape instead of just looking that way."

"I do cardio… just not… this kind of cardio…"

"What other kind of cardio is there?" Kaela unwittingly played into his teasing.

"The kind… you used to enjoy… with me…" Despite his ragged intakes of air, Theo managed a loud, triumphant chortle at the look that crossed her face when she finally registered the innuendo. "Maybe… we could try that… tomorrow morning… instead."

"Shut up." She snarled and picked up the pace, doling out her choice of passive-aggressive retaliation. "Better keep up. You shouldn't waste any of the air in your lungs in case you need to defend me from an attack before we're finished."

Her sprinting the last stretch before they reached the house was a low blow, and she felt the smallest, most insignificant bit of remorse as he labored to pull himself together before following her up the front stairs.

"How was it?" Hailey held out two glasses of water when Kaela and Theo entered the kitchen. "Bruh, you look ready to fall over. She didn't take it easy on you, I see."

"Does she ever?" Theo groaned and gulped half the water down. "It was as painful as you would expect a 5K to be."

Kaela rolled her eyes.

"Kale or spinach in your breakfast smoothie?"

Groceries littered the island that took up the center of the room, and a blender already sat on the counter near the oversized copper sink. With

Hailey leading the expedition, the selection of food consisted mainly of fruits, vegetables, and lean meat.

Kaela rummaged through the freezer, locating a bag of frozen peas that she pressed against her right knee to stave off any swelling while her eyes trailed across the dozens of bundled herbs and plants strung up to dry above the countertop. She thought about the delightful aromas of the business section nearby as she'd been running past.

"There is a bakery close by. With all the kidnapping and random stalkers following me around, I find carbs bring me the greatest sense of security."

"And do you like changing your lifestyle just because a couple of misdirected milksops decided to assault you?"

Kaela considered the question, eyeing her friend who was channeling the personal trainer energy which once defined their relationship.

"No."

"Right. You and I, we stick with our goals, and we aren't changed by misogynistic agendas. You got me? Now, kale or spinach?"

They stared at each other, Hailey resolute and Kaela oscillating between wanting to hug her friend and wanting to strangle her.

"Spinach, please." Kaela grumbled, setting her empty glass by the sink. "And I was being dramatic. I just really love eating bread after I run."

"Well, in that case, you should try one of these." When Hailey turned back, she had produced a plate of beignets, seemingly out of thin air. Two of them were already clutched in Theo's hands. "Food is fuel, not a coping mechanism. Eat up."

"Thank god!" Kaela elbowed Theo to the side and grabbed her own sugar-dusted piece of happiness from the plate, abandoning the peas on the counter. "And while I am incredibly thankful for your support, who uses the word 'milksop'?"

"It isn't my fault you've never noticed my archaic vocabulary and wondered if I'm actually four hundred years old." Hailey winked and then switched on the blender before Kaela could reply, yelling over the noise. "Angel wants to see you in the solarium. I'll bring this out to you in a minute."

"I'm going to take a shower if you'd like to join me. Otherwise, the solarium is through the door back there," Theo shouted and gestured to the back of the kitchen. Kaela gave another eyeroll and followed his directions, punching him in the arm as she passed. "Tomorrow morning, then." He gave a lewd wink, ducking away from her second swing before he exited the kitchen in the opposite direction.

The solarium was astonishing. Thick, curved glass stretched up into the sky like a translucent gothic vault, held in place overhead by sturdy, metal ribs. Three of the walls were almost entirely constructed of windows, and a wide brick path marched a perfectly straight line into the center of the room before spreading into a semi-circular courtyard. While the brick patio held an ornate table and chair set, the remainder of the room was filled with a variety of plants. Thin leafy trees rose from the corners, their branches stretching gently into the air, dangling small fruits: lime, lemon, fig, and persimmon. On one side, purple and green foliage mingled with flowers of a dozen different colors and shades. In the opposite direction were clusters of vegetables and herbs. One potted vine spilled across the floor, nearly reaching the entrance, and Kaela spied tiny cucumbers beginning to form along the spiky arms.

"This is beautiful!" Kaela exclaimed when she found Angel kneeling among a cluster of potted tomato plants. "I've always dreamed of adding something like this to my house. Is there an irrigation system, or do you water everything by hand?"

"There's a drip for the bigger trees and such, but the pots I water by hand." Angel continued to inspect the vegetables as Kaela moved close enough to peer over her shoulder. "I think these are spent. I'll have to pull them out and start some seeds. It's too bad the new ones aren't producing yet. I hate having to buy tomatoes at the store. They never taste right."

Kaela glanced at the immature plants a few feet away and then back to the old ones, chewing on her lip as she considered.

"You asked about my powers." Angel looked up at her sharply, eyes narrowing with interest. "Let me show you."

The old tomato vines were prickly and dry under her fingers as Kaela grasped one of the thick bases. With her other hand, she reached in the direction of the newer pots, using the line of her arm as a focal point, directing her intention from plant to plant. She settled her mind down into her body, feeling for the thrumming pulse she'd grown used to. It was there, always waiting, always eager to rise. She smiled at the feeling of it moving from hand to hand, pulling what it needed from one plant and transferring it to another. She was a shuttle for the energy, a purposeful vessel that encouraged the old growth to collapse. Each cell in the mature tomato vine shriveled and released the last of its stores as she hummed a low note. The new plant shivered with potential, and tiny tendrils became substantial new growth as it stretched to the sky, unfurling and blooming in moments. Before the old plant crumbled into the dirt, the blossoms on the new vine became little green orbs, shiny and waxy in the morning light.

Kaela let her hands drop back to her sides, feeling the release of the magic and the empty sensation it left behind.

"*Mon Dieu*! I knew it would be impressive, but this exceeds my expectations, Sha." Angel stroked the little green tomatoes with wonder. "Is it always plants?"

"No." Kaela forced herself to meet the other woman's eyes, and in that exact moment, Hellkitten traipsed into the room. "There have been a few other incidents, where my powers have worked on animals or people, but plants are the only thing I've been able to master, the only consistent use of my power."

Angel nodded, her eyes settling on the cat with understanding.

"I see why she wants you."

"And you should know why she can't ever have me."

They exchanged a charged look.

"Voila! I bring your well-deserved breakfast, my lady. What did I miss?" Hailey pranced down the brick path. She set a small plate with additional beignets and a glass filled with a frothy green liquid on the table, planting her fists on her hips as she faced them. "You both look very serious right now."

"I showed Angel what I can do." Kaela walked over to the table, waiting for her friend's reaction to this leap of faith.

"If you trust her with your secrets, I guess we're all about to be part of the same, big, happy family. I can heal myself."

"Hailey!" Kaela lunged forward when Hailey drew a butter knife firmly across her inner arm, applying enough pressure to break the skin. The wound dripped blood for only a second before the edges sealed back together. "She was probably okay with just a verbal description!"

"A demonstration is worth a thousand words, or something like that." Hailey shrugged, then looked at Angel. "Your turn."

"I'm strong."

Hailey drew herself up to her full five-foot two-inch height and stared the larger woman down.

"Are you fucking kidding me?"

"No, I'm serious," Angel returned, hands poised in a gesture of peace. "I'll show you."

And that was how Theo and Estè walked in on Angel holding a chair out directly in front of her with one arm while Hailey clapped her hands in schoolgirl delight from her seat on top of it.

"Are we showing off?" The chair returned to the floor with a loud thud, and Hailey stepped free as all eyes turned on Theo. A quick nod from Kaela was enough to convince him. "Good. Here's my contribution to the Chosen One's retinue."

The pathway of bricks rippled in a dramatic cascade like an oscillating waveform. At the abrupt shifting of the floor, a pair of startled rabbits leapt from the shelter of the flowers, eyes wild. In an unfortunate turn of events, their movements placed them directly in line with Hellkitten.

"Shit." Kaela immediately set into motion, meaning to grab the tiny cat before it could try to attack the other animals, but she only took one step before Estè was there, lowering herself to the ground next to the creatures. Angel held Kaela back by the arm.

"Don't worry, she can handle it."

For a few seconds, there was a standoff with Estè, the feline, and the rabbits forming three points of an unusual triangle. Then the moment broke, and the animals gathered next to the kneeling woman, receiving their reassuring strokes like an anointing, before wandering off. After the rabbits hopped back under the cover of the flower patch and Hellkitten was silently bathing herself near the table, Estè rose from the floor.

"She communicates with them." Kaela didn't need to see Angel's confirmation to know she was correct. "There actually is one of you, one of us, that can speak to animals."

"Does that surprise you?" Angel placed her arm around Estè with sisterly affection as the other woman joined their circle.

"Not at all." Kaela shook her head, thinking about how much she would enjoy telling Landry that he was, in fact, wrong about that particular talent being in use. "How many more of you are there in New Orleans?"

Angel moved to the table and settled into one of the chairs, gesturing for them to join her. Estè gracefully took up a cross-legged position on the floor nearby, Hellkitten instantly occupying her lap, leaving three of the chairs available. Kaela retrieved her smoothie and complied, trying not to breathe in the freshly showered scent of Theo that filled the air in sharp contrast to the stink of her own sweat. He claimed the seat to her left, and Hailey took the one to her right.

"About forty of all ages and abilities. Some are still babies who don't understand why they can't let anyone know how special they are. Some are old enough that they simply tend their gardens and do little more than concoct the occasional coughing tonic or mix a poultice for a bruise. Others live normal lives, work normal jobs, and do their best to hide whatever strange proclivity their magic decides to take on when it rears its head. But a few have found a way to embrace what they can do, and they use their magic as best they can to either help themselves or help others. My favorite is Bernice who runs a tourist operation down on Canal Street. She happens to be an illusionist who gives the best ghost tours in the city!"

"All those people grew up here in New Orleans?" Kaela's voice rose in surprise. That number of magical people together in one place seemed absurd.

"No, lots of folks came here over the years to be among others with the same strange talents. This house has become a beacon for people like us." Kaela noticed how Angel managed to direct this statement at her, to the exclusion of Hailey and Theo. "Things are always easier with family, whether it's the ones you were born with or the ones you choose to love. Especially when those things you're afraid of are driven by hate."

Kaela's first thought was of her mother. The warm feel of her hugs and the annoying way she always knew if Kaela was having a bad day, despite what her daughter told her to the contrary, the odd tilt to her head when she was choosing to remain silent and let Kaela talk first, and all the other little eccentricities that were wrapped up inside Kaela's memories of an ordinary woman who had an extraordinary impact on her child's life. The hole of her passing had been filled with an expansion of her relationship with her father, a forced dependency that had swollen to fill the vacuum of her mother's absence. Then he, too, abandoned her. Now, there was no family. Hailey caught and held Kaela's gaze; something about the way her friend's face remained carefully neutral made the sensation of exposure even more pronounced.

"What sort of hate would make people leave their homes?" Kaela looked away from Hailey and followed Estè's fingers as she gently combed through the kitten's tail fur. "I mean, sure, seeing something that looks like magic would be a shock, but why would there be such a strong rejection to something like being able to mix up a killer hangover cure with a handful of random ingredients?"

"You are an open-minded person." Angel patted her hand. "Most people are not that way. Most people are immediately terrified by anything they can't explain. And fear is only a heartbeat away from hate."

"It wasn't that long ago when we were all being unfairly tried for witchcraft and burned at the stake." Hailey was also observing Estè's interaction with Hellkitten, a ghost trail of emotions flickering across her features. "Showing any hint of something bigger, be it a particular skill or even just an independent happiness, was enough to make a woman a target for execution. All it took was one little word from someone important."

"Witch," Angel confirmed.

"Not just women," Theo reminded them.

"No, but women were more likely to offend the men in charge, and more of us bore the brunt of that method of retaliation," Hailey retorted.

"True enough," he acquiesced.

Kaela looked between Theo and Hailey, imagining their experiences with witch-hunts over the centuries. Estè reached up to tap Angel on the knee, gesturing from the cat to Kaela and then producing a series of hand movements that appeared to be sign language. Kaela lamented the lack of ASL education in the public-school systems as she tracked the gestures without comprehension.

"Estè says that in the 1600s, this animal would have been considered your familiar," Angel translated.

"You knew about the cat, didn't you?" Hailey sat up, rigid in her seat as she blurted out this revelation. "You talk to the animals. You must have known something was off. Did you tell Angel about it?"

The woman on the floor shook her head emphatically and then signed a response for Angel to relay to the group.

"She says that she knew what happened to the cat and knew about Kaela's powers, but she didn't think it was up to her to reveal those details to anyone. She didn't tell me anything. Which, by the way, I'm a bit upset about now that we're discussing it. I would have liked a heads up given the importance of Kaela's skill set, but I understand you not wanting to tell someone else's business."

"Well, thank you for the discretion."

Estè nodded to Kaela.

"I think we've cleared up quite a lot." Theo leaned his chair back on two legs as he surveyed the group. "We now know each other's abilities, we have established that we're all trustworthy individuals, and we know if Nisha raises an army, our new friend here can summon all the gators in the Bayou to fight them off. I, for one, will sleep like a baby tonight."

"Thank you, as always, Teddy, for the lovely perspective." Theo caught the beignet that Hailey lobbed at his head, grinning as he took a big bite.

A grounded satisfaction flooded through Kaela at the exchange, and she found herself smiling. Perhaps she was finally surrounding herself with people that made her feel like a part of something. She wiped the thought away, not quite willing to accept the idea for what it was.

"Maybe we can spend some time coming up with a training schedule now." Theo switched gears, becoming much more serious as he dropped all four chair legs to the ground. "Angel, if you've trained others to use their powers, I would appreciate your help with Kaela. She flits in and out of control like a short-circuiting wire. Maybe you have fresh ideas."

The long, assessing stare Kaela endured from the caretaker was unnerving, but she steeled herself to withstand it.

"I may have a few ideas, but you'll have to trust me, Sha."

Kaela found herself returning Angel's steely look.

"I trust you."

The honesty of the words was surprising but hearing them out loud made Kaela realize she meant them. She had already lost one family. Building another was a frightening concept, but maybe, just maybe, she wanted to give it a try.

America – 2012

Kaela fished the olive from her gin martini, chewing it slowly and repressing the grimace of disgust that threatened to seize her features. She hated gin with its astringent smell and nauseating taste of pine. But at every family gathering, Evelyn prepared the drinks, and Jason pressed one into Kaela's hand with an air of finality. He knew she didn't like them but forbade her from giving any indication of that revulsion for risk of offending Mother Dearest. Eventually, the mushy fruit in her mouth lost the overtones of kitchen cleaner and coated her tongue in its own tangy, complex flavor instead.

She should be interviewing for an assistant professor position at Columbia right now. Instead, she was watching Jason's mother select the flowers for their wedding. From the start, Evelyn had made it perfectly clear that although she would occasionally ask Kaela for her opinion, she did not, in fact, want anything of the sort. All that was required of Kaela was for her to nod and completely agree with each decision imperiously handed down by the family matriarch.

Kaela shifted on the delicate settee so she could look at the street in front of Evelyn's brownstone. She tried not to think about the fight with Jason. She tried to focus on the joy she should be feeling at marrying the man she loved in a few short months instead of the interview she'd been forced to cancel due to Evelyn's change of schedule. The position at Columbia would likely be awarded to someone who appeared more engaged and eager, not someone who put off responding to an invite and then rescheduled at the last minute after plans were set. She told herself there would be other positions at other universities. There was only one Jason.

She should be happy.

"Everyone has calla lilies. I want something unique for the bouquet. What did you call these? Tricyrtis. Add these with orchid stems and eucalyptus. What do you think, Mikaela?"

Kaela plastered on her mask and nodded with faked enthusiasm. She set her glass on the side table and accepted a spray of the flower du jour. The florist was quite crafty when she decided to use the scientific instead of the common name. She wondered if Evelyn would reconsider her selection if she knew that the Tricyrtis blooms in question were typically referred to as toad lilies. Such an undignified name for a decoration in Evelyn's grand design. Kaela rolled the sprig between her fingers, appreciating the blotchy speckling of purple along the delicate little petals. Several of the buds on the stem were still closed, and Kaela ran her fingers across them as she returned to wistfully watching the sunlit avenue, humming softly to herself.

Her mother should be here. It shouldn't be lonely to plan a wedding. She felt a deep wave of sadness that tugged against her like a physical drain. She blinked away the tears that threatened to gather in her eyes and began to tuck her emotions back into their hiding place. She used a cocktail napkin to wipe away the moisture at her nostrils, surprised when the tissue showed a spot of blood.

"May I join you?" Aunt Gloria lowered herself to the cushions before Kaela could respond, her eyes fixed on the flowers. "Those are lovely."

"Yes, I suppose they are." Kaela looked back down, noticing with some curiosity that the buds seemed to have opened in the last few minutes.

"She does mean well, most of the time." Gloria continued to stare at the flowers.

"Does she?" Kaela didn't mean to reveal her annoyance, but the words slipped out easily.

"Not really," Gloria admitted, her voice distant as she finally looked up from Kaela's hands and considered her with a strange expression. She looked puzzled, surprised in some way, but Kaela didn't know what she had done to cause this.

"Mikaela," Evelyn's sharp voice broke Gloria's silent inspection just as it was becoming awkward. "Do come over here and help Jason pin the boutonniere to his jacket. Honestly, child, one would think you did not want to be involved in the planning of your own wedding."

Kaela stood and moved in the direction of the flower table on the opposite side of the room. As expected, Jason didn't offer a single word in her defense. She took another martini from the tray on her way over, waiting for the dull gloss of the alcohol to make the day's experience more tolerable.

She should be happy.

Chapter 3

"Hailey is pissed you won't let her be part of these new sessions."

Kaela shrugged, eyeing Theo as he circled opposite her on the little brick patio in the solarium. The furniture was pushed to the side to free up the space for use as a fighting pad. Angel and Ahtah stood on the path further away. Kaela adjusted the grip on her boot knife and let her thoughts slide over to the dream walker.

She had been training for ten days. In her first lesson with Angel, the caretaker did nothing but discuss magic theory with her new student. She pushed Kaela to describe how it 'felt' when she performed certain tasks, and how she thought her powers worked. Kaela walked her through the situation with Hellkitten and then provided full disclosure on the events in the desert. Somewhere along the way, Kaela even found herself rambling about the incident with Theo's paper cut and had to abruptly change topics. By the end of it, Angel was silent. They adjourned to let her 'think on it a spell' before deciding how to proceed. On the second day, Angel brought Ahtah into the session.

"You have more than one ability," she announced, settling on one of the three mats placed together on the bricks.

"Excuse me?" Kaela blinked in feigned confusion.

"You can manipulate age. You already know that. You can force something to become older or younger. You can rot a banana or grow a plant from a seedling, taking it backwards or forwards in age. But you can also borrow powers from people around you. That makes you dangerous. Ahtahkakoop can help you learn to control it."

"You can't let anyone else know." Panic crawled up Kaela's spine, and in that instant, she second-guessed every detail she'd provided to Angel during their sessions. "If someone like Nisha found out – "

"I thought we trusted one another." Angel took both of Kaela's hands and squeezed reassuringly. "Take a breath. Take two. We are family now whether you admit it or not. You can't hide your abilities by pretending they don't exist. You have to understand them, learn to harness them, and then decide where to go from there. I just want to help."

The following two sessions consisted of sitting cross-legged opposite of Ahtah. At first, he didn't talk. Then he began telling her stories about his life. The soft resonance of his deep voice and the quiet rustle of the plants around them became hypnotic, a repetitive soundtrack that made her thoughts loose. He was an exceptional storyteller. His ability to move in and out of other people's thoughts, to create visions that took over the mind whether waking or sleeping, was a surreal backdrop for his life. Kaela grasped at the stories as he told them, slippery things that left her uncertain of where the truth started and the dream ended.

On the fifth day, Kaela could close her eyes and feel Ahtah's presence. He was a pillar rooted in her awareness, and when she focused on him, her nose filled with a thick woodsy fragrance. Her mind felt lighter, like it was untethered from her body and gliding on a strong wind. She learned to reach further, to feel Hailey, a burning, chaotic energy moving around the front room that left her ears crackling but her skin feeling tender if she focused on it for too long. Theo was a cold, rigid shadow pacing across the front lawn, and the taste of salt, like the ocean, spilled across the sides of her tongue and made her jaw ache.

In their sixth session, Ahtah fabricated a scene, pulling it from Kaela's mind and draping it across her sight. It was a memory of her father's fiftieth birthday. It was a large family gathering with her grandparents smiling in the background, her father's now deceased siblings laughing and joking loudly in the foreground, and her cousins slipping through all the spaces between with the social ease available to children.

It was the family she knew for only a brief time in her youth. It was an interconnected warmth that was ripped away and replaced with the sad, lonely reality of adulthood. She knew the vision was fake, but no matter how she thrashed and fought, it remained, shockingly vivid and authentically detailed from the odd quiver of her grandfather's lips when he laughed to the quiet fidgeting of her youngest cousin's feet any time a serious question was posed to him.

By the eighth session, Kaela could easily remove Ahtah from her mind, shoving his suggestions away and even attempting to plant her own imagination into his perception, her ability allowing her to siphon and redirect his powers. She won the occasional snippet of memory leaked from behind the walls, but despite hours of focused effort, Ahtah's mind remained a secure vault, the contents inaccessible to her amateur attempts if he wasn't willing to share.

Now, ten days into her training, Kaela pulled at the unyielding pillar that was Ahtah, drawing some of his gift into her body. It filled her with a strangely solid sensation, the bloated feeling of eating too much food. She funneled it carefully outwards, forming a mental appendage that prodded directly into Theo's mind. She focused on disorientation, the dragging of a movement after muscle fatigue, and the slow motion of fighting against water.

Kaela laughed as Theo stumbled and blinked in confusion. She reached out to Angel, the caretaker's power wrapping around her muscles like a joist, merging together with her intentions in an easy coupling. The strength of that bond burned as she stepped forward, locking her unarmed hand around Theo's neck and sweeping a leg behind him. She pulled him several inches into the air before he began the downward trajectory and slammed him to the ground with a little more force than originally intended.

"Shit, Kaela!" Theo gasped against the hand that was pinning him to the ground. "You know I like it rough but damn, that one hurt."

Kaela felt the borrowed powers fade away, retreating back to their original sources, and she withdrew the knife she held pressed into Theo's side. She let the fingers of her other hand linger against his neck, feeling the steady throb of his pulse beneath her skin. She was panting, the movement contradicting his calm stillness while their bodies remained pressed together.

"Keep your dick in your pants, *Teddy*. It's not a come-on that I just kicked your ass."

"Isn't it?"

His words were a blatant invitation. He slid his eyes over her mouth, sensuous and slow. She responded with a hasty retreat, scrubbing her palm against the rough denim on her thighs as if it would rid the afterburn of his skin on hers.

"That was an impressive improvement over the last time I saw you train." Angel stepped forward, offering a soft clap of appreciation.

"Did Ahtah help you?"

Kaela's eyes jerked up to meet the dream walker's, and she shook her head slightly in denial.

"She did not need my intervention," the tall man responded.

"Definitely not a direct answer to my question. I think it odd that I lost focus due to an inexplicable mental fog while in your presence."

Ahtah and Theo remained in a silent deadlock after this, neither willing to give an inch to the other just to end the discomfort.

"If the two of you are finished growling at each other, we should start on Kaela's magical training now." Angel and Kaela exchanged a look, confirming their unspoken agreement to keep Theo in the dark about her ability to manipulate other powers. "I think it's time for that kitten to become an adult again. You don't need to be here for this part, Theodore."

Theo was still lying on the floor, knees bent up at right angles. Kaela offered her hand, willing to meet him halfway after the devastating physical slam she had administered to him. He accepted the olive branch and groaned as she leveraged him to his feet.

"I might just sit in one of these chairs for a bit to recover. Don't mind me, though. Continue with your part of the training, Angel."

Angel scooped up the kitten, who was always within a few yards of Kaela, and brought it to the middle of the patio. She gestured for the others to join her before sitting directly on the brick patio with the feline firmly held on her lap, ignoring Hellkitten's squirming protestation.

"I've watched you do this with plants, and I don't think it's any different for you with animals or even people. You have to commit to it, though. The only times my magic has failed for me is when I've doubted myself."

Kaela listened to the words but couldn't quite let them penetrate. "We've talked about this before." She thought through her sessions with Angel that occurred each day after she and Ahtah finished battling for mental supremacy. "I control a certain flow of energy, but I need to understand where the energy starts and ends. I can't just blindly shove the cat back into being a full adult. The energy required for that would be vast, and I don't understand how much that really equates to. I could kill every plant in here and still need more. Then what? I use myself as a battery? I don't like the odds here."

"You are overthinking it, Sha. You can simply make her what you want. You put her back into her proper time."

"This isn't about time, it's about energy. Trust me. I've done the math."

Kaela really had done the math—multiple times. She had files and files of equations on her tablet upstairs. The only thing that could describe what she did with plants was a shifting of energy that drove something into or away from a state of senescence. For this to be about time, all the equations she and Landry had agonized over would need to come together into a proof of the theorem, and the likeness of such a law had never been shown before. It would be groundbreaking.

Theo cleared his throat from his side of the room.

"I think we should talk about Aristotle's wheel paradox."

"What?" Kaela lowered her brows at the sudden shift in topics.

"Do you remember it?"

"Yes, of course I do." She struggled, once again, with the fact that Theo was not the shallow playboy he once pretended to be.

"Explain it to Angel and Ahtah."

Kaela narrowed her eyes in annoyance, recognizing a trick she often employed with her students. If you couldn't explain a concept to someone who had no prior knowledge of your specialty in a way that they would understand, you didn't really understand it yourself. She let the silence stretch before she addressed the others.

"Imagine you draw a two-dimensional wheel with one circle inside another, a co-centric pair like a hubcap inside a car tire. Then you draw parallel lines that run under each, like a road that each wheel needs to travel along. When the wheel moves forward, it appears that each circle is moving a single rotation. The tire itself moves one full revolution, and the hubcap remains in the same orientation relative to the tire. This means it has also moved one full revolution. However, the tire and the hubcap have different length circumferences. How did they each moved only one rotation and also moved the exact same distance?"

Understanding and confusion dawned on their faces in equal measure.

"And now give them the solution." Theodore's eyes gleamed.

"Why don't you give it to them, since you are eager to use this as a lesson?" Somehow, he always managed to raise Kaela's ire, no matter how innocuous his sarcasm or gentle his teasing, she found herself immediately on the defensive.

"If you stick to a strictly two-dimensional view and perform a theoretical evaluation of the problem, you create a paradox. However, if you literally placed a wheel on a road and rotationally locked it with a smaller wheel traveling its own path, the problem disappears. You can force the larger wheel to turn one rotation, but this makes the smaller wheel drag against its own surface as it rotates at a slower pace. Conversely, you could force the smaller wheel to turn, and then the larger wheel slips as it travels faster than the little one. But when a wheel is on a road, there is only one surface touching one wheel.

"The point of the problem is that a black and white, purely analytical evaluation of a situation creates a paradox that doesn't really exist. Your ability to control age and your ability to redirect energy are bound together, inseparable because they are parts to the same whole. Sometimes you use one at the sacrifice of the other, but that give and take is fluid. You are putting unnecessary restrictions on your magic because of your own cognitive distortion. Just do it. You don't have to understand the basic laws of physics to do anything else in your daily life. If you make the cat the correct age, the energy works itself out. Stop thinking so damn much!"

Kaela scowled at him, but for once, didn't respond with snarky sarcasm. He was right. She didn't agonize over gravity each time she jumped. She simply returned to the ground because gravity followed its set of preordained rules. If her magic already followed its own pattern, she just needed to focus on the end goal and let the details sort themselves out along the way. As long as she connected a broad enough net, there would be more than enough energy in the world to make the change. She had to let go of her reservations.

"Are you okay with this?" Kaela addressed the kitten as Angel released it from her lap. Hellkitten padded forward and then sat in front of her, wrapping its tail around its front paws and staring up at Kaela with an unnaturally serious expression. "All right then. I guess we're doing it."

She held out her hands, letting the kitten come to her. Then she cradled it to her chest and closed her eyes. At first, she felt nothing but the thrumming vibration of its purr echoing deep in her body. Then, bit by bit, she found the vein of quicksilver in her. It pulsed with her need and flowed in ephemeral threads into everything around them. Her magic was deeply interconnected to life, and she felt this on a visceral level as she focused on the warm bundle of fur calmly molding its little body against her, yielding itself to fit her shape.

Kaela remembered the first time she'd seen the cat, small but impressively self-assured as it strutted up to her front door and demanded entrance to her home. Kaela pulled on that image, needing it to materialize between her hands. She felt the first drag of energy and rooted outwards, using her lessons with Ahtah to identify and connect to every living thing in repeated radii, moving further out the longer the energy continued to siphon from her. Then, it stopped.

She opened her eyes and looked at the fully-grown cat in her arms.

"Holy shit!" Theo exclaimed, his tone incredulous.

Before Kaela could say anything, a loud voice called out from the kitchen.

"Knock knock! Where you at, Teedy Angelique?"

"Of course he shows up now." Angel stood and gave Kaela a lingering smile filled with pride. "That was amazing. Remember the way it felt to use your power like that so you can do it again when you need to. Theodore, you did good, too. You knew what to say to push her into that place. Good on you. Don't let it go to your head."

"Auntie?" A female voice now called out from the main part of the house.

"I guess our lessons are over for the day. I invited some of the family to meet y'all, and it looks like it's time for those introductions. Ready to meet more magical folks, Kaela?"

Kaela stood on steady feet, holding Hellcat close, astonished by the expansion of her size and weight. Her success wiped away her usual hesitation.

"Yeah, I think I am."

America – 2014

The dark lace along the edge of Grandmother Anicette's dress was startling against the white lining of the coffin. The funeral director had offered a standard gown during the review of the ceremony packages, and Kaela scoffed. The very thought of her grand-mère in anything less than her finest clothing was laughable. Later, as Kaela's hands ran over the silky, wine-red material in the closet, she remembered the extra stiffness in her grand-mère's spine when she'd worn the dress to a wedding or special event. At the time, Kaela thought it was a perfect burial gown. Now, seeing it draped across the interior of the coffin, accentuating the yellow of the body that wore it, Kaela thought only of blood.

As a child on a cross-country trip in her family's brown-paneled wagon, Kaela had the misfortune of visiting a presidential wax museum in a fly-over state. The signs proclaiming the attraction appeared on the edge of the highway just after the fatigue of monotony had begun to set in, and her mother, in a spontaneous attempt to infuse fun into their adventure, insisted on making the four-mile detour. There was a display showing the assassination of JFK. Kaela remembered her amusement at the tableau of a dead president surrounded by sallow figures that were supposed to be alive but looked equally alien and lifeless.

Part of her wanted to trace her finger across the cold, waxy skin of her grand-mère, just to see if dead skin felt less human than that of the living. She shuddered and turned away, hands clenched at her sides.

The guests were starting to arrive. They paused at the memory book by the doorway, adding their condolences, prayers, and other trivial, sentimental words. They trickled slowly down the aisle to the casket. Pictures of Grandmother Anicette littered the small table below the white floral wreath, varying from the faded black and white of her youth to the more vibrant colors of recent photographs.

Kaela greeted each of the guests with the expected sadness on her face. She hugged them and thanked them for coming. Some were only vaguely familiar, but she pretended they were all close associations. She stood alone, for what felt like hours, greeting them one after another.

Later, she would be glad Jason was too busy at the firm to attend. She would realize that his presence would have made the experience even more unbearable. For now, though, she felt adrift in her isolation.

Her father had been in the hospital this week. He had an episode on the job site, and the doctors were doing a full evaluation. So far, the test results were inconclusive, but Kaela suspected the truth. He was beginning to show signs of Alzheimer's. The countdown was starting, and she was hopelessly behind.

Almost two years ago, she finally secured a position at a university to pursue her interest in neural diseases. Her resume hadn't been the most competitive, thanks to a certain gap around the time of her wedding, but she found a senior professor willing to take a gamble on her. She had recently been awarded a grant with a significant dollar sign attached to it and could start to establish her own laboratory.

Her marriage continued to deteriorate around her, flaking away in little pieces, although she tried her best to glue it back together each time a crack appeared. She hid her academic efforts, sacrificing sleep on the nights Jason worked late or stayed out with friends to complete her long to-do list during his absences. She minimized her achievements, pretending her career was a hobby and not a soul-consuming obsession. When he was around, she put his needs above all else, desperate for him to think their marriage was her only priority.

But now, her grand-mère was dead. Her research hadn't even gotten off the ground before she lost someone that she loved due to a lack of therapeutic options. She had to work harder, achieve more, before she lost her father as well.

"Kaela, my dear." One of Grandmother Anicette's friends from church approached her. "I am sorry about your grandmother. How are you doing? Do you have someone helping you with all of this? A small group or a prayer partner?"

She tried not to stiffen at the question. She reminded herself that the words were well-intended, despite the insinuation that some mythical being could impart comfort. She once listened to her grand-mère talk about how God always managed to provide for her in hard times. Grandmother Anicette worked hard her entire life and made smart choices with her finances. When she needed something, her own forethought provided. But to her, it was divinely delivered. She chose to pin her successes on an abstract deity and justified her misfortunes the same way.

Kaela took full responsibility for her wins and losses. She couldn't fathom letting divine purpose control the course of her life when she made decisions every day that determined her trajectory, decisions like choosing to prioritize her husband's needs above her own. The man who couldn't be bothered to help her through the death of her grandmother had taken precedence over the deep sense of purpose she felt when she was working at the lab. She made that decision. She chose her fate. And she could still change it.

As she accepted the sympathetic grasp of the woman's hands around hers, Kaela made herself a promise. She would refocus on what was the most important to her: her research that wouldn't revolutionize medicine but could change the world for a select group of people like her. She would take the fallout of that as it came, but she would never, ever prioritize someone or something other than herself again.

Chapter 4

Estè sat on the floor, this time in a shaft of moonlight. Her legs were straight in front of her and her shoulders pressed against the cushioned edge of a sofa. A fox draped itself across her thighs, the white tip of its bushy red and black tail twitching as it slept. Hellcat perched on the cushion behind Estè, occasionally batting at a stray hair along her neck when it danced in a phantom draft. Plants trailing from pots on a nearby table seemed to reach their tendrils in her direction. She was as silent as a specter, flipping slowly through a stack of Tarot cards, Gaia embodied.

Kaela had just entered the house after an hour sitting on the porch, swinging and ruminating in solitude. Her phone battery was approaching an alarming nadir but she couldn't stop opening her emails and messages, repeatedly reassuring herself that she hadn't missed anything of importance and pretending not to notice the lack of communication from one particular person. She had suddenly felt the absence of Hellcat, who was her ever-present shadow those days, and went in search of her missing familiar. That was when she came across Hailey, hovering in a doorway just past the foyer stairs. When Kaela approached her, she found her friend gazing into the sitting room with a melancholy stillness.

"Hey," Kaela bumped Hailey's elbow and leaned against the door frame across from her, smiling at Estè when she glanced up. "You okay?"

"Yeah, I'm fine. She just reminds me of someone." Hailey abruptly straightened and smiled the large, bright kind of smile that people employ to make others forget there was an unfinished topic to discuss. "I'm feeling like some wine in the plant room, join me?"

Before Kaela could respond, Hailey's light, bouncing steps carried her halfway to the kitchen. It wasn't until they were settled in the solarium that Hailey finally looked her in the eyes.

"I don't want to talk about it." The skin between Hailey's eyebrows creased before she turned away to uncork one of the bottles she'd placed on the table.

"I wasn't going to ask." Kaela's false reassurance drew a cutting look from Hailey, and she grinned in amusement. "But if you *did* want to talk about it, I'd be happy to listen. And before you say it's none of my business, I would like to remind you that you are the one who keeps telling me to 'open up' and share my feelings more."

"Have you told Landry about the cat?"

Kaela frowned. "No."

"Have you even texted him since we got here?"

"Touché." Kaela's eyes were nearly slits, arms now defensively braced in front of her body.

Hailey offered her a glass of wine with a satisfied smirk. The usual patio set was pushed off to the side, and a collection of wooden lounge chairs had been pulled from storage to occupy the patio space. Kaela accepted the drink and settled on the closest chair, feet tucked beneath her.

The Hellkitten transformation had occurred four days prior, and the immediate result of Kaela's success was the manifestation of equilibrium in her mind and actions. The deep-rooted dread with which she faced each day had faded to a slight agitation. When she thought about the unresolved threat of Nisha or Cassius, she panicked a little less. She started each morning by running or doing combat drills with Theo. His sarcasm and innuendo became a normal part of her routine, like chicory coffee or crawfish. After showering and eating, she would spend the remainder of the pre-noon hours reviewing lesson plans, curating her grant application tracker, and creating experimental outlines for her lab staff to follow when they returned from the break. Lunch with Hailey was followed by an afternoon lesson with Ahtah and Angel. Then she would read or explore the city until dinner.

If Kaela left the house, an entourage consisting of Hailey and at least two others would follow. Sometimes she knew the additional people; other times, they were new faces that never repeated with enough regularity for her to learn anything about them. Earlier that day, on one of these brief forays, Hailey and Kaela wandered into a boutique near an art museum and discovered an impressive collection of stationery and paper gifts. Kaela lingered at a section of intricately embossed leather notebooks, selecting a soft tan volume that reminded her of the boxed journals sitting in her office at the university.

Now, lounging in the solarium, starting her second glass of wine after thirty minutes of conversation filled with nothing but trivialities and inconsequential chatter, Kaela's mind drifted back to the journal in her room. She'd purchased the notebook with the intent of gifting it to Landry when she returned home, but after weeks of pretending she didn't notice his absence, she worried about the awkwardness of the gesture.

"He checks in with me every day."

"How is he?" Kaela asked after a brief pause in which she determined that pretending she didn't know of whom Hailey spoke was a waste of energy.

"Worried about you but won't admit it. It's astounding how similar you two can be. Wait, have I said that before? Well, it's just as true today. Would you like me to tell him of your successes with the magical training? I've been reassuring but vague so far when he asks how *everyone* is faring."

Kaela felt the warmth of the wine spreading through her body and shifted to a reclining position. There was a giant knot in her stomach each time she reached for her phone. She knew there was nothing but heartache and disappointment waiting on the other end of the line if she followed through. Why did she so badly want to do it anyway?

"No, I will call him in a day or two." She abruptly sat up. "It's nearly Christmas! Wait, does your lot celebrate holidays?"

"Of course we do. I mean Landry, Teddy, and I do. I've never asked Ahtah. But it doesn't seem as if Angel is very festive this time of year."

"I noticed the lack of decorating in the house compared to the rest of the city. Maybe we can hold off on the present exchange until we get back home."

"Christmas is about being with family anyway." Hailey winked at Kaela and reached over to squeeze her knee.

That one, simple statement drowned Kaela in a flood of feelings. She wanted to pull her friend into a hug, to explain to her what it was like to finally have someone she could lean into without any physical complications. She felt the words swelling on her tongue, but before she could voice them, three more people entered the room.

"Who forgot to invite us to the drinking party? Don't worry, we brought additional provisions."

Angel's niece Zoe slunk over to them, her lean body flowing with a liquid grace. She slid onto the chaise with Hailey, dropping her head onto the other's lap with a contrived ease. The increasing displays of affection between the two of them suggested they were getting to know one another quite well in the four days since Zoe's arrival.

Adam, who was Zoe's brother, and his partner, Basille, deposited several bottles of wine and additional glasses on the table before melting together onto a third lounge chair. Kaela momentarily envied them for the youthfulness that made their movements carelessly lithe. Their dark, strong limbs were casually intertwined, and Basille toyed with the edge of Adam's sleeve where his arm draped across the other's body. The movement was unthinking and endearing to witness.

As the three of them started a rowdy conversation about their plans for getting high and attending the Christmas bonfires on the levee in two days, Kaela peered at Hailey. Her friend's face was lit with amusement, her laughter clear and easy as she joined the chatter. She was always quick to transform, shifting to fit any situation and rolling with the social scene like a wave of bright water. Kaela thought about the words that she could no longer speak, feeling the weight of them in her chest. But Hailey had moved on, and the moment was broken. After a reasonable amount of time passed, Kaela excused herself, consciously suppressing a grunt when she stood, and one of her knees popped. She hadn't iced it long enough after her morning run.

The house was quiet inside. Kaela tiptoed through the kitchen, stopping at the sink for a glass of water. She listened to the faint laughter that continued to drift from the solarium. The competing sound of hushed voices from the front of the house drew her forward, creeping along the old wooden boards with slow, flat steps to prevent creaks. Ahtah and Angel were standing in the foyer at the base of the stairs, her voice sharp despite the whisper and his a low murmur of comfort. His shoulders held a slight bow as he wrapped his arms around her waist, her body leaning into his as if they were two halves of a familiar shape.

"Still such a hopeless romantic," Angel whispered fiercely. Her mouth was inches from his, but her voice carried down the hallway.

"*Kisâkihitin*, Angelique. Not all people who love are romantic."

"You can stop talking now, Ahtahkakoop." Angel kissed him gently, then took his hand and led him up the stairs.

Kaela retreated, a nagging feeling of guilt leaving her stomach unsettled after the unintentional snooping. She placed one careful step behind another until she bumped into something hard and warm. Her foot elicited a loud creak from an unwieldy board, and she gasped, afraid of who she would find when she turned around.

“Spying on people isn’t nice.” Theo’s chest rumbled against her back. “Although they do make a handsome couple.”

“I wasn’t spying, I was just getting some water before bed and didn’t want to interrupt them.” Kaela hissed over her shoulder, noticing how close his mouth was to her neck and how hot his hand was where he had braced it against her hip.

“Sure.” He pressed into her more firmly, his fingers tight against the exposed skin between her shirt and pants, his lips now inches from her ear. His smell wrapped around her, clean and citrusy like the ocean but with a heavier undertone, similar to the feel of his magic when she reached out during her lessons with Ahtah. “Keep telling yourself that.”

She tried to appear calm when the sensation of him against her sent a vibration clawing across her body. She stepped away, the movement feeling more like a desperate lunge than an unaffected retreat. She avoided his knowing leer and retrieved her glass from the counter, putting the island between them in the process.

“What are you doing down here?”

“Well, I’m not sure if you know this, but I have been staying in one of the guest rooms of this very house.” Theo’s snarky reply elicited the usual eyeroll from Kaela. “I was finished with my turn on guard duty. I took a shower and thought I’d get a snack before I head up to the crow’s nest for a while.”

“Guard duty?” She frowned as he retrieved an apple from the bowl on the counter and carefully peeled off the sticker.

“Yes, guard duty.” He took a bite, the juice shining against his lips as he chewed. “We rotate, but there is always someone on watch.”

“Why didn’t I know that? And what is the crow’s nest?”

“You don’t need to know about guard duty because you’re the one we’re guarding. You aren’t part of the rotation. That would be rather pointless, don’t you think? And the crow’s nest is the weird room on top of the house. Come on, I’ll show you.”

Kaela looked at his outstretched hand. His hair was still wet from his shower, and a chunk of it fell forward into his eyes. His shirt was snug, hugging his biceps and torso before it met the edge of his black joggers, and a few splotches of water darkened the fabric. They hadn’t been alone in months, other than when they went running. Each time she tried to sneak out the front door, he was waiting to accompany her. Yesterday morning, he even managed to match her pace without looking quite as wrecked at the end.

Another chorus of laughter erupted in the solarium.

"Sure, why not?" She set down her glass and took his hand.

He pulled her along a small hallway that she thought led only to the pantry, but when they reached the end, there were two doors. She scolded herself for doing a subpar job of mapping the house. Theo opened the mystery door, revealing a narrow set of stairs. He dropped her hand, allowing her to enter ahead of him. She swallowed her claustrophobia and walked up the first flight, turned a corner, and traversed a second run of steps before entering a square, window-paneled room.

"A crow's nest." She breathed as she turned in a circle. "Like a ship's lookout."

"Took an advanced degree to figure that one out, did it?" Theo avoided her scathing glare and stopped at a low bar cart, opening the globe on one side to reveal several familiar amber bottles. "Drink?" Kaela gauged the swimminess of her brain and nodded, deciding she could handle one more for the evening. "It's a full moon. If I turn off the lights, we should be able to spy on the neighborhood but still see our own hands. I know how much you enjoy playing the role of peeping tom after all."

"It would be nice to see the stars," she admitted with a dismissive gesture to his taunting.

She followed him with her eyes as he prepared the drinks and walked to the switch near the door, relaxed and confident as always. Her thoughts drifted to Ahtah and Angel, wondering if they were together in a room just below her feet. She thought about Zoe, draping herself across Hailey's lap while Adam and Basille laughed quietly together, wrapped up in each other's bodies. She accepted the drink Theo held out to her before sliding down onto the floor pillows piled in the center of the open room. There were no other furnishings, and Theo remained standing, his side to her as he looked through a window to the street below.

"Do you ever think there's something wrong with you?" Kaela broke the silence, her words not quite forming as she intended.

"Should I be insulted by that question?" He laughed but didn't look at her.

"Sorry, that's not what I meant." She mumbled the contrite apology and tried again, watching the liquid sparkle in her hand under the moonlight. “It’s just, some people are really good at making friends, at connecting with other people, at loving other people. But I somehow always feel like an extra in the play, important to myself but replaceable to everyone else.”

“How much did you drink tonight?” Theo’s chuckle was softer this time. “Yeah, some people can attach themselves to every person they meet, like all connections will become a tether between souls. But that’s not you, Kaela. And it’s not me. And there’s nothing wrong with that.”

“Sorry, I’m being ridiculous.” She finally looked up, meeting his eyes in the dim light and finding a strange comfort in his nearness. “It’s hard not to compare myself to the blaze of passion that is Hailey.”

“Everyone likes Hailey and Hailey likes everyone.” Theo sat down on a cushion next to her, facing the same direction, their thighs side by side, close but not touching. “But Hailey has only ever loved two people, and both of them were ripped away from her. Don’t be fooled by the way she draws other people’s affections. Her heart was sealed off a long time ago, and I don’t think anyone is getting back in.”

A gnawing sadness worked its way into Kaela’s chest at the realization that they were all equally alone, some were just better at hiding it. Tears threatened at the corners of her eyes, and she wondered if she should have turned down the drink after all. She felt lost and needed something to keep her there, engaged and present, something that reminded her that her existence was connected to someone. Maybe life meant more than just the little sliver of perception a person is allowed when it was part of someone else’s reality, too.

“What was it your mother used to tell you? Sometimes friends are here for a short part of the journey, but there will be others to take their place. Friendship is a sum of all those you’ve touched and those who have touched you.”

“How do you know that?” Kaela’s head whipped around, and she stared at Theo in surprise that bordered on anger.

“You told me.” He shrugged and leaned back on his hands, watching her reaction. “Remember when we went to that terrible concert on the waterfront and you ran into a friend from undergrad that kept insisting you exchange numbers and reconnect? You hated the idea of forcing a friendship and told me you stuck to the advice your mother gave you when you were a teenager.”

“That was over a year ago.”

“I have a good memory.”

Kaela turned back to the window. She wondered what other personal details she’d let slip during their time together and how well he really knew her. She was surprised by the way that made her feel. She scooted her cushion closer and slid an arm around him, leaning her head against his shoulder. His body tightened in surprise but relaxed again as he brought a hand up to stroke her hair.

“I may not be a deep, soul-searing connection, but I’m here for you if you need me, kid.”

This time, one of the tears escaped and traced a silent path across her cheek.

“I mean, I have *touched* you.” His suggestive use of the word brought an unexpected chuckle to Kaela’s throat. “I’d be happy to *touch* you again, if you want.”

“Oh, my god, stop ruining the moment.”

She closed her eyes and let his smell and physical presence wrap around her like armor against the cold fingers of loneliness that tried to grip her heart.

America – 2018

"I already miss you inside me..."

It was the day before their six-year anniversary, and Kaela was staring at the face of Jason's watch, where it rested on top of the nightstand. She reread the words. They were the first part of a text from someone named Taylor. Her brain halfheartedly searched for a word that began with 'me,' which could explain the text in any way other than the obvious. The screen darkened again, but her eyes couldn't move away. The shower handles squeaked when Jason turned off the water.

Kaela was propped against a pile of pillows, working on her tablet. The university recently implemented a progress report system for providing contemporaneous feedback to her students, and the dean was aggressively interested in which of the faculty adopted the initiative. Her career was just beginning, and it would receive a positive boost if she demonstrated her commitment to the program, which meant that she spent several hours a week checking the communications. On top of her very heavy teaching workload, she was struggling to expand her funding and therefore increase the footprint of her research lab. She needed more brains working on more projects to get more publications. The tenure struggle was new to her, and she couldn't quite parse together enough hours or resources in the day to make headway.

The text should make her angry or, at the very least, hurt. A yawning emptiness occupied the place where her heart should be breaking. She didn't have time to deal with her husband's philandering bullshit. Acknowledging it would only mean facing a family drama that would inevitably end with a faceoff against Evelyn. Jason would never fight his own battles.

"Always working." Jason stood in the doorway to the bathroom, watching her.

"Well, I've got a lot to do." Her voice was calm, almost deadpan.

"It would be nice if you spent as much of your time on me as you do on your work. I'm starting to feel like you don't want to be around me."

Jason strutted across the room and pried the tablet from her fingers, discarding it on her side table. He hadn't bothered to dry himself off, and beads of moisture dripped from his naked skin as he leaned over her. He kissed along her neck, one hand sneaking under the blankets and between her legs.

Was he with her today?

The thought bubbled up, and Kaela's stomach turned when Jason slid one of his fingers into her, bending his neck so he could capture her nipple in his mouth through her sleepshirt. She wondered if those fingers had already participated in their fair share of intimacy for the day. He noticed her stiffness and pulled back to look at her.

"What's wrong with you? You're like a corpse."

Like a corpse.

Like the dead bodies she cried over at the funeral for her grandmother and then for her father. But since he didn't attend either of those, what would he even know about corpses?

"Nothing, I think I'm coming down with a cold." Kaela heard the words from a distance, as if it weren't her own mouth forming them. "I should probably sleep in the guest room to keep you from getting sick too."

"Seriously?" He moved back and pouted, his erection at face level. "Can you at least give me head? I mean, he's ready to go."

For half a second, Kaela wondered if sucking him off to shut him up was the easiest solution. Her stomach twisted again. "Not tonight, Jace."

He continued to grumble as she gathered her charge cables and carried her devices out of the room with her, biting back the automatic apology that rose to meet his disappointment. She walked across the hall and down the stairs with a disconnected calmness.

Somehow, she already knew he was cheating on her. The idea wasn't fully formed and had never presented itself with enough surety for her to acknowledge. There were plenty of signs. Thus far, their marriage was the loneliest six years of her life. The confirmation of his adultery was almost satisfying, as if she were glad he was with someone. That couldn't be right, though, could it?

Kaela deposited her items in the guest room but then stepped through the balcony doors. The cool evening air wrapped around her bare legs, and she hugged her arms across her shirt, staring out at the gibbous moon, hanging low in the sky and coating everything in a silvery wash. Rustling at her feet drew her eyes to the luminescent green of a luna moth's wings tangled in an abandoned cobweb. The breeze made the moth's body stir again. She reached down and carefully extricated it from the trap, cleaning off the dangling bits of silky fiber as best she could without damaging the diaphanous membranes.

Kaela held it close to her face, marveling over the long trailing tips of its wings. Such a lovely creature. She knew from childhood science books that they only lived for a week and didn't have a digestive tract. Like all lovely things, they weren't built to last. Moisture formed in Kaela's eyes, but she bit back the emotions threatening to emerge. She threw the moth up into the air. It spread its wings and flew away. She shook her head and blinked at the blurriness in her vision. Her eyes were tricking her. The wind had carried the dead insect away.

She wiped at her nose, noticing that one of her frequent and unpredictable nosebleeds had started. She paced softly back into the guest room and picked up her tablet, using a tissue from the nightstand to stem the tiny trickle of blood.

She had work to do.

Chapter 5

Another week.

Just one more week and Kaela would be back at the university, giving lectures and overseeing the advancement of science. The time spent in New Orleans was developing the surreal fuzziness of a strange dream as the return to normality drew closer.

Last night, she stood at the bathroom sink and combed her fingers through the hair at her temples, letting a tingling spark of magic flow into them. The feel of the power still surprised her. It was the opposite of a phantom limb. It was the solidification of an abstraction, the manifestation of something her brain still told her was make-believe. In the morning, no one appeared to notice the darker locks of homogenous brunette. If anything, that only made her feeling of delusion more acute. She went about her day, training and preparing for the two very different lives she was leading, pretending the dichotomy was manageable.

She found herself in awe of the slumbering powers in her body as she wandered around the city with Hailey that evening. People were too calm, moving past her without even registering her presence, because why would they? She was just another person in the crowd. No one around her could know that she wasn't an ordinary human on the prowl for a good time in one bar or another. No one could know how unusual she really was.

Yet her immediate concern was not one that required any amount of magical intervention. It was one that relied entirely upon the street smarts most women in their third or fourth decade of life had acquired through common social exchanges. A man in a bar was hitting on Hailey.

"Ya'll been hangin' out by yourself all night. We don't you come on over to our table? My friend over there keeps lookin' at you, boo." Kaela tried not to cringe at the pet name and avoided following the indicative jerk of the man's head. He turned back to Hailey, leaning against the counter near her stool with a practiced flippancy and slouching even further to bring his face close to hers.

Kaela should never have let Hailey drag her into this hole in the wall.

They shared nice, expensive cocktails and small plates at a chic wine bar to start the evening, but as usual, the devil in Hailey couldn't be satisfied until she found some dirty, dimly lit dive where she could down a few beers while they yelled at one another over the noise of a drunken crowd.

Even by Hailey's standards, this place was a mess. A Ouija board was nailed haphazardly above the entrance, and the walls were coated in stickers, graffiti, and dirt. Cheap multi-colored string lights crisscrossed overhead, a marginal addition to the glow cast from a single neon beer sign and a dilapidated claw machine in the corner. Kaela tried to about-face when her shoes crunched against the sticky floors on the way in, but Hailey refused to let her retreat to the sidewalk. Kaela allowed her friend to shove her into a seat at the dingy bar top and began grumbling about health inspections until the bartender was close enough to hear. Kaela politely held her tongue regarding the hygiene of the establishment while they ordered drinks, but was still concerned that the sagging, water-stained tiles of the drop ceiling would collapse on her at any moment.

The half-lit suitor currently attempting to sweet talk Hailey was the latest of three men who approached them while they sipped their beers. The first two were quickly and firmly dissuaded by Hailey, but this last one was turning out to be more persistent, likely due to the number of drinks he'd consumed.

"No thanks, you aren't my type," Hailey yelled, her words competing with Brian Johnson begging for a present from his Christmas mistress through the ceiling speakers.

"Come on, Sha, don't do me like that." Despite the loud rejection, he didn't change his stance. "What, you don't like men?"

Kaela sized him up as she waited for Hailey to deliver some scathing response. He was reasonably large, probably a football player in high school a few decades past, but the softness around his middle and the heavy way he relied on the bar to steady him was reassuring in the event that he decided to get physical. The bartender caught her eye and moved in their direction.

"I like men fine. You specifically aren't my type." He leaned back slightly as Hailey's stare became flinty. "I'm sure you can find someone else here that is interested in you, since I, clearly, am not. Have a good night. *Laissez les bon temps rouler* and all that shit."

"Y'all doin' fine?" The bartender interrupted, nodding to the spurned suitor. "How's it going, Big Man? I'll bring the table another round in a minute, right?"

The man took one last look at Hailey, then mumbled his agreement to the bartender before trudging back to his friends. For his part, the bartender just winked at Hailey and moved on.

"We can leave," Kaela offered.

"Why?" Hailey ran a thumb up and down her glass, collecting the condensation. "Because some idiot who considers himself a Gigachad doesn't understand how to take a hint the first time? Nah, girl. I'm not uncomfortable, even if he is."

The man was drinking a fresh beer with his friends, occasionally scowling in their direction. While she listened to Hailey, Kaela covertly peeked back, not quite comfortable with the unresolved tension.

"Have you always refused to be intimidated, or is this something that evolved over time when you were surrounded by the 'Old World Crew', as Angel calls them?"

Hailey let out a laugh. "I've always been this way. It's one of my many charms. Besides, if he picks a fight, you can just zap him like you did Brady."

"You're the worst." Kaela sent her eyes skyward but couldn't prevent the corners of her mouth turning up.

"Bet." She punched Kaela on the arm.

"What does that even mean?"

"You bet. Betcha. That can't be the first time you've heard it." An incredulous look crossed Hailey's face. "How can you stop adapting to the new slang? You are practically an infant in the grand scheme of my existence. Language is a living thing; if you stop adapting, you stagnate."

"I don't think speaking like I'm a teenager is going to add a depth of culture to my existence." Kaela scoffed in response. "Although you have a point. It would be quite odd if you were sitting here speaking Middle English."

"*In youthe is bothe cheef and heigh servys*e." Hailey's laugh rang out again, impish and bright but quickly fading as a serious expression took over. "Shifting between languages, absorbing slang, immediately fitting into new cultures. Those were the lessons Cassius stressed in my education. Anything to make me a better spy."

"Do you hate Cassius?" Kaela asked after Hailey fell silent.

She was thoughtful for a moment before responding. "He was the reason I lost things that I loved, but he isn't the monster I sometimes thought him to be. He used us for his own agenda. Landry most of all. But sometimes his intentions were true despite the inevitable fallout of his actions. You know he spent years in America as an abolitionist? The Lion of White Hall. He prioritized Women's Suffrage, too. He thought everyone should have equal freedoms, but he somehow held himself above the rules. I do hate him, but I also love him. I pity him and I envy him for his beliefs. I resent him, but there are happy memories, as well. It's too complicated for one feeling. You can't summarize hundreds of years in simple terms."

Kaela rolled the bottom of her glass on the bar surface, fidgeting as she considered this response. "And do you hate Nisha?"

"That bitch can die a slow death." Hailey chugged the last of her beer and slammed the glass down. "Let's get out of this seedy joint and find some place where I can dance! I've had enough of this classic rock Christmas garbage."

Hailey tossed enough money onto the counter to cover their drinks, with a healthy tip left over, and turned for the door. As they navigated across the sour, residue-coated floor, Kaela was relieved to see the unwanted admirer and his friends had already vacated the premises. The two women moved out into the street, wandering through the crowd of revelers singing drunken carols on the sidewalks. Hailey looped their arms together and pulled Kaela along as she stared up at the sky.

Stars were barely visible above the washout of light from the buildings and streetlamps. Kaela remembered how clear they had been when she visited the crow's nest above the house with Theo. She was leaning into his shoulder, digesting the words they'd shared when the clouds shifted in the obsidian sky, splitting apart like a rip along an overstretched seam, allowing a broad cascade of moonlight to shine through. Her hand reflected white where it rested on Theo's leg. She looked at the stars scattered within the patch of open sky.

"Olber's paradox," she had murmured.

"*Hm*, that's the one where the universe can't be infinite if there are visible dark spaces between stars?"

The rumble of his words distracted her, lessening her surprise at the comment. "I still can't believe your vapid, pretty boy routine fooled me for so long," she grumbled.

"Hopefully, the new me doesn't disappoint you too much." His tone was casual, but his words seemed more direct than usual, as if he were prodding her for a genuine answer.

"Actually, I prefer the real you. Even if you are an asshole most of the time."

Her words drew the desired grin from him, and he returned to his usual flippancy. "It's okay, I'm still a pretty boy *all* of the time."

"You're an idiot."

"Yes, but an idiot that knows Olber's paradox has been resolved."

An amused exhale left Kaela's mouth before she responded. "Yes, but it's such a wonderful example of perspective. The assumption is that what you see in a single, isolated moment is the reality you must accept and live with. The Universe is finite. But when you step back to consider your own little spot in the bigger picture and consider that time is never static, the reality changes. The Universe is infinite. It reminds me that whatever I'm feeling right now will change. Just give it time."

Theo gave her shoulder a comforting squeeze. "That is an oddly reassuring, if extremely nerdy, way of looking at things." He left his arm resting around her. "Personally, I thought the moral of that paradox was that most people, including Newton, don't grasp the physics of light traveling through interstellar space or the concept of expansion leading to red-shifted objects, but I like your version better."

"I take it back. I liked Todd the Playboy."

He pinched her ear in retaliation, and she laughed, closing her eyes and settling firmly against his side. She opened up her powers to feel around them, and the salty ocean breeze of his magical signature washed over her.

She must have fallen asleep because the next thing she knew, she was waking up with his arm under her head. They were snuggled into the pile of pillows on the floor with the first light of dawn streaking through the windows. He was breathing with the deep, steady rhythm of sleep. She'd swallowed her panic and carefully extracted herself from his embrace, fleeing down the stairs at a snail's pace to avoid any accidental noises.

Hailey, of course, had been in the kitchen when Kaela crept through the door on her way to her room. Her friend took a long look at the crumpled clothes she'd been wearing the night before, raised one highly expressive eyebrow, then turned back to her meal prep without a single comment. Kaela completed her walk of shame without further encounters and emerged later showered, changed, and pretending the entire evening had never occurred.

Now, walking down the street with a few drinks on board, caught up in the fresh air and companionable holiday revelry, she felt a certain level of shame remembering Hailey's minimal but significant acknowledgement of the situation.

"I wanted to talk to you about the other night," Kaela started, pulling Hailey closer by the arm but not looking at her. "Nothing happened with Theo, we just fell asleep talking."

"Bro, you could sleep with everyone in that house including Angel and it would be none of my damn business." Hailey led Kaela down a side street. "I think this is the way to a bar Zoe talks about. Much better than the last one. On God."

"Okay, but I didn't want you to think that I was doing wrong by Landry." Kaela trailed off when Hailey stopped walking and grabbed her by the shoulders.

"You're an adult. Landry is a very, very old adult. What's between you is seriously none of my business. You realize most of us stopped adhering to the societally fabricated concept of monogamy after a century or two of blindly following a system of beliefs forced on us when we were entirely human? I am your friend, not your judge and keeper. Besides, Teddy is part of our security detail tonight and might be close enough to hear you. Maybe not the best time to talk about it."

"What!" Kaela glanced around in panic. "What do you mean, security detail? I didn't notice anyone following us after dinner."

"They were following us before dinner." Hailey's pace never wavered as she replied. "Two more blocks, I think. It should be right up against those warehouses along the water if I remember correctly."

"Why don't you use your phone to navigate like a normal person? Honestly, I'm always surprised when people don't use a resource when it's right there." She trailed off as a parallel thought took shape, and she flared her magic, searching around her for any odd sensations.

The familiar salt and citrus immediately alerted her to Theo's presence, but there were others. One was rich and earthy, a strange coupling of the smell of the ground after a heavy rain and a boiling pot of bone broth. Another was both dark and bright, like seeing an afterimage on the back of your eyelids after glancing at the sun. The last was a heavy, pressing weight that dragged against her, a boulder in the middle of a river. She previously felt the first two from a distance while she was practicing with Ahtah but had yet to meet them. The last one was Angel.

She threw a slightly wider net, and four, no six, clustered sources of magic popped into her awareness up ahead. She strained to untangle their signatures, but they were too close to one another, and she could pick up only a jumbled mass of feelings, smells, and tastes. If she kept stretching herself farther, there were even more, wavering little pricks of sensation that would normally be too weak for her to notice. Were they just faint due to distance, or were these people with lesser abilities? She tried to compare the distance between one of the little points of energy and Theo's signature aura.

Kaela stumbled when she realized how close Theo was, her eyes flying to a spot near the dark window of an office building. She squinted into the shadows by the door and could imagine a darker shape there, but her eyes kept slipping away, as if something was turning them to the side.

"About time you figured it out." Theo stepped into the light of the street, his body materializing out of the shadows exactly where she had been staring.

"How?" she asked, peering back at the building.

"Remember the light bender? Kat is something similar." Theo exchanged a fist bump with Hailey as he responded. "You had me pegged the whole time. What gave me away?"

"You have loud feet," Hailey offered with a shrug.

"Well, don't let Kaela fool you, we spent an amazing night together on Tuesday. Very intimate. You should definitely report back to Commander Griffiths on the situation."

Judging by the burning sensation, Kaela's face had spontaneously burst into flames. She couldn't put together an intelligent response, just a wordless sputter before Hailey gestured for them to be silent. A group of people were approaching.

"It's giving stalker, Jackass," Hailey yelled at one of them.

Kaela gaped in disbelief as the man from the bar sauntered forward, accompanied by a half dozen others. A few faces seemed familiar enough to give her pause. Hailey was standing with her body just slightly in front of Kaela, endearingly protective but also somewhat obscuring the view of the whole group.

"I tried to make it easy on y'all, but now we gotta get dramatic out here in the open." The bulk of him seemed much less impressive now that Kaela was standing close to Theo. "I'm just supposed to bring you to her. It didn't have to be kickin' and screamin'."

At the same time, Kaela placed the familiarity of the faces and realized that these were some of the stronger magical signatures she'd registered earlier. Two of the men in the group were Jackson's flunkies, one of the polo brothers, and the young fire thrower.

"Shit, Theo—" she murmured under her breath as he stepped closer to her, forming a tight flank of protection with Hailey on the other side.

"Yeah, I know," he whispered back.

"I hate to ruin your optimism here, but I'm still not interested." Hailey exchanged a quick glance with Theo but otherwise remained focused on the cluster of men that now fanned out in front of them. "You should just move on. Trust me, I'm way more trouble than you're looking for."

"Not very tough the last time," Polo-guy spoke up, his voice grating against Kaela's ears, dredging up memories of the desert. "The fuck are you doing with them, dude?"

Theo shrugged in response to the question.

Kaela probed the group and discovered that half of them were likely the muscles of the operation, only three had significant magical signatures, including the man that had hit on Hailey and the two she knew from past exchanges. Fire-boy smelled of charred wood, and whispers of crackling heat filled her ears. Hailey's nemesis made Kaela's body feel too solid, as if gravity had somehow intensified. The other was a mixture of sensations that she didn't quite understand. She hoped his powers were less impressive than the flamethrower. How could she have been so stupid tonight? She should have known him for what he was the second they entered that bar.

"Glad to see you haven't gained any intelligence since then." Hailey snarled. "Maybe you could go back to being the thug of the party and let the adults talk. Teddy, take her where we discussed and keep her safe. Ahtah, Angel, and Lunk are more than enough backup to handle this. We can meet up with you after we're finished here."

As Hailey spoke, three figures stepped out from the shadows of nearby buildings to join them. Kaela wanted to kick herself for not realizing her own teacher was hidden nearby, but even now, she couldn't sense Ahtah as she could the others. She made eye contact with him and tried to communicate her concern about the fire manipulator. He nodded as if he understood.

Next to Angel was a gigantic mountain of a human who stood nearly seven feet tall. The dark skin of their neck and arms was completely covered in even darker tattoos, and their hair was cut into a crazy, jagged mane that accentuated their wildly intimidating presence. They were the source of the earthy sensation Kaela had picked up earlier. She was sure they would be able to handle all three of the nongifted attackers without breaking a sweat.

"Dibs on the Fuck Boy, he has a few appendages that require compound fractures." Kaela recognized the manic gleam in Hailey's eyes as she winked at them. "I'll see you after I've had my fun."

"What? No. Hard pass. I'm not leaving you to fight my battles. I'm more than capable of helping take them out."

Despite Kaela's protest, Theo started to pull her away by the arm, and the others closed ranks in front of her, shooing her along like a flock of overbearing mother hens.

"Come on, Kaela. Now isn't the time to stretch your new magic muscles. The whole point of us following you all night was to keep you safe. Let's not waste that effort." Theodore continued to guide her away from the conflict. "Hailey lives for this."

Kaela's struggles flagged when a pair of brass knuckles materialized from Hailey's pockets. She spun them around her index fingers before slipping them on with a wild-eyed cackle. She was already advancing on her intended target while she shouted back over her shoulder.

"Katarina, keep the street empty of onlookers and cover us."

The entrance to the side street underwent a disorienting shift, and then all four members of Kaela's volunteer army faded into the surroundings. The half dozen men facing them began to lose their nerve, glancing around in surprise as they took a series of backward, hesitant steps. They should have turned and run. Before they could realize their mistake, the dark shadow that was Hailey reached Jackson's lackey.

It was a bloodbath.

Kaela gasped as the man's head snapped back with what could only be a series of invisible collisions. Sections of his face blossomed into bloody, lacerated bruises. Before he could pull himself back together, one of his arms twisted at an odd angle and then bent violently away at the joint.

The pyro stood close by, staring into space with his arms limp at his sides. Ahtah must have received Kaela's panicked nonverbal communication loud and clear. She wasn't sure the kid could summon fire without his twin, but she didn't want her friends to risk it.

Lunk snatched a knife out of a man's hand as if it were a toy. A single punch to the face sent the assailant flying back and collapsing into a motionless heap. Angel tossed another attacker across the sidewalk like a straw dummy.

This time, when Theo guided her away, Kaela didn't fight him.

"I told you; Hailey barely needs the backup she already has." The alleyway dumped them onto a much busier thoroughfare, and Theo calmly walked Kaela down the street. "You've seen her playing around with me when we spar, but this is the first time you've really seen her in action."

"I had no idea. I mean, I knew she was a unit, but what she did to that man was something different." Kaela struggled with processing the rapid succession of violence she'd witnessed.

"Come on, we can go through the warehouses to keep off the street in case more of them are following us. I'll get us a ride when we're on the other end of River City."

Theo led her past a tall, metal-shrouded warehouse with a smiling purple and green jester leering down at her from its perch above the entrance. At the corner of the building, he tugged her into the narrow walkway between buildings, his fingers firm on hers. She was momentarily distracted by the ease with which she held onto him, letting him steer her by the hand without any resistance. He paused to look at a stray chunk of asphalt on the ground. The rock hurtled into the handle of an exterior door, slamming into the lock with enough force to shatter it. The door creaked open a few inches, the lock and latch mechanisms broken.

"*Um,* isn't this trespassing?" She finally thought to question Theo's plan as he escorted her into the building. "Obviously, this place is closed. Maybe we could just get a cab from here?"

"It's okay, Angel knows the owner. Well, her mother knew the current owner's father before he died. It's complicated, but just trust me, they're on the list of allies."

"I didn't realize there was a list."

Kaela's words echoed into the steel rafters. Their feet against the polished concrete floors seemed jarringly loud as they moved deeper into the warehouse. Dim lighting cast sinister shadows across and among the dozens of sculptures lining the sides of the walkway. She blenched when a five-foot-tall, disembodied head caught her eye, grinning up at her from between two giant birds. A collection of rainbow-colored peacocks flocked around another grotesque head, this one was at least fifteen feet tall with a long, curling tongue like a serpent.

“What is this place?” A particularly odd bust of an old hag came into view, and a crawling sensation spread across Kaela’s neck like whispers of spider legs against her skin.

“Old floats and decorations from the Mardi Gras parades.” Theo indicated an open doorway, the light from beyond the threshold spilling across the concrete floor. “That way.”

When she stepped through, Kaela was relieved to find a much less crowded space beyond, but the room was already occupied. The woman she’d met at Nisha’s residence was standing in the middle of the open area, fisted hands on her hips. She turned her narrow-eyed stare on Theo and raised an eyebrow in accusation.

“It took you long enough. I managed an entire kidnapping without falling off schedule. Though I suppose you never follow instructions to the letter these days.”

“Nice to see you too, Ramla. You could just say thank you for delivering her to you with minimal fuss.”

Kaela tried to process the rapid turn of events, but the ringing in her ears drowned out all reasonable thought. Theo had betrayed her again. He was working with Nisha. At least ten others were standing in the room behind Ramla, likely waiting for orders. And someone was tied to a chair.

It was happening again.

Except this time, the person on the chair was not Hailey.

America – 2020

The box of lo mein was hot against the skin of Kaela's legs. She watched a bird hopping along a branch through the living room window and felt a proprietary connection to the creature, as if its presence was enough to cement their alliance in her new beginning.

She was sitting in the middle of a completely empty room, enjoying her first dinner in her brand-new home, a ceremonial moment of celebration. Her signature was still freshly inked on her divorce papers, and tiny little sparks of happiness were finally taking root.

She was free.

She didn't have to be anything that she didn't want to be. She didn't have to swallow back the words she wanted to scream or fake meekness when she wanted to scratch and claw.

She had no family. She'd buried her father.

She had no friends. She'd lost them over time.

But it was better this way. She never really needed family or friends. She was always enough on her own. She just didn't know it until now.

Kaela dug another mouthful of noodles out of the container with her chopsticks.

This window could use some plants.

Chapter 6

Why were hospitals always intolerably warm? Kaela remembered the damp trickle of sweat dripping along the centerline of her lower back. She remembered the unnecessarily stiff cushions of the hospital recliner. Everything was designed for a specific function, not for comfort.

"Hello, Mr. Brookes. My name is Jessica, and I'm your Care Specialist. Somer is going to be your primary nurse, and she'll stop by to introduce herself soon. If you need anything at all, an extra blanket, some ice chips, whatever will help you feel more comfortable, you just let me know."

There was that word, comfortable… comfort.

"Thank you, Jessica. This is my daughter, Mikaela. She's a doctor. She knows more about this than me. She is here to ask all the questions and make sure I don't miss anything. She's an expert in these types of things."

"Just a research scientist with a Ph.D." Kaela found herself saying, a sense of embarrassment creeping over her as she rushed to minimize her expertise. "I'm sure I won't know anything more than his doctors. Just here for emotional support."

"Nice to meet you."

Kaela could feel the nurse's annoyance hiding beneath the friendly demeanor. She was sure the poor woman faced an untold number of know-it-alls with access to WebMD. Her undergraduate degree in biology and doctorate in neuroscience weren't medical degrees, but she was still certain she knew more about the science of her father's disease than most of the hospital staff. She gave the nurse a meek shrug and let the tension fade.

Grandmother Anicette, her father's mother, had died in this same hospital. The strongest, most opinionated woman Kaela had ever known passed away in the most unremarkable manner within that very building. And now, as her father proudly introduced her, she knew at any moment he would also forget who she was.

Alzheimer's was an asshole.

When Somer entered the room to check his vitals, he gave the same boastful introduction to his doctor-daughter. He beamed as he listed Kaela's credentials and declared that her brilliance came from her mother, "God rest her soul". Kaela blushed and deflected, eager to escape the stuffy confines of the room.

Her father was admitted for a series of targeted procedures to shrink the tumors peppering his lower abdominal cavity. The treatments were like anything else designed to attack cancer: slow-acting poisons that didn't discriminate between healthy and diseased tissues as they steadily ate through his body. He lasted two full weeks before he declined further treatment. Kaela begged and cried, but he refused to change his mind. In another few weeks, he would be discharged to hospice and wait for death.

His mental condition continued to deteriorate at a rapid pace. She swallowed her anger at his choices and tried to reason with him. She considered having him deemed unfit to make his own medical decisions, but when she looked him in the eyes and listened to him turn down every option she presented, she knew it was the man who raised her to respect others' autonomy and not the Alzheimer's talking.

She became increasingly thankful for Somer. Each time her father dipped into a forgetful state, the nurse was there to help him. She wasn't particularly kind or warm in Kaela's interactions with her, but she was tough and efficient. Somer managed to keep Kaela's father calm during his increasingly frequent episodes. Kaela remembered the nurse from when her grandmother was housed in the neuro wing of the hospital. It was a strange but wonderful coincidence that she also attended to Kaela's father. When he was discharged, Kaela's reliance on the nurse was difficult to break.

Nine and a half years had passed since then. Nearly a full decade in which many of the names and faces from that time at the hospital had faded into the back of Kaela's mind. But now, standing in the middle of a giant warehouse filled with parade floats, something clicked into place.

"Somer?"

The woman Theo had addressed as Ramla turned her haughty expression on Kaela. She ran her eyes slowly from head to toe, inspecting Kaela like she was an interesting new plaything.

"Now, that is a name I haven't heard in a long time." Ramla leaned on the back of the chair, and Kaela tried to focus on her words rather than on the occupant tied to it. "I should introduce myself. I worried you would recognize me when we last met, so I gave you a little forgetful nudge. Good thing, too, because it seems those memories were there after all. My name is Ramla, and I'm not really a nurse."

"I gathered." Kaela felt a slow rage beginning to build as this new revelation sank in. "Was Nisha using you to spy on me when my dad was in the hospital? And my grandmother? What did you do to them?"

"Your family has such a remarkable ability to resist me. In fact, your family is remarkable in general. It took me longer than it should have to understand why that might be. Every few generations, a very interesting ability pops up in your family tree, but by some stroke of luck, it happened three times in a row."

The sinister flash of teeth behind Ramla's sneer made this event seem anything but lucky.

"I don't know what you're talking about. My dad was just a contractor. He didn't have any special powers." Her brain hitched, remembering Grandmother Anicette's unusual intuitions, but she plowed on. "And my grandmother was no different."

"You can lie to yourself if it makes you feel better but we both know Nisha wouldn't have been determined to wipe their minds if they were just ordinary people." Ramla tutted and tilted her head in fascination as she watched Kaela's reaction. "You really didn't know.

"Cassius was unusually interested in your family. He should have eliminated your entire lineage centuries ago, but he never had the balls for that kind of wet work. How fortunate for him that Nisha cleaned up the messes when he wasn't looking. I've spent years stripping away your ancestors' thoughts but you're all too resilient for your own good, and I end up making you forget everything. It's quite tragic. At this point we should start calling it your family curse."

"You stupid bitch." Kaela snarled. She felt an edge of hysteria creeping in but focused on her anger.

Everything that she had lost was at the hands of this woman. It wasn't a disease that stole her family, piece by piece, until they no longer recognized her. It was *her*.

Ramla. Nisha. Cassius.

They were the ones that would pay.

Did her father and grandmother have the same powers as her? Did they know? How many members of her family tree had been cursed with these abilities? Why had Cassius tracked them across generations? She needed answers, but first she needed to deal with the creature in front of her.

Kaela's eyes shifted to the figure in the chair.

"Darling," Ramla cooed. "The concern is clearly written on your face when you look at him. But it seems that our little Landry has been keeping secrets again. I would ask him why he left you in the dark, but as you can see, I had to give him something to keep him—compliant. Isn't it funny that I'm the one that first told him about you. And here we are, all together for the first time since then."

Landry's eyes were closed, and his chin rested on his sternum He was breathing, but he didn't respond to any of the words being spoken. Three empty chairs sat to one side of him.

"What's the plan, then? Are you going to use him to get me to agree to something? That tactic ended with failure before, and I don't know why you think it will work now. In fact, I'm not the same helpless person I used to be."

Kaela stretched her mind into the room, feeling the spark of abilities in Ramla and Theo. The men standing in a row behind them were watery, vague impressions rather than the distinct auras she was used to sensing. As she pondered this, she felt more coming from the direction of the entrance, growing closer with each passing second. Ramla's presence was an oily, insubstantial thing that stuck to her thoughts, clinging deep in the crevices of her mind. She tried to shake it off, and the other woman chuckled.

"You aren't the main character this time, sweetheart. You're a pawn. Nisha sends her regards, but now that we know Cassius is back, you equate to a loose end. Thank you for that bit of information, Theodoros. It makes everything much cleaner this way."

Theo shrugged, his hands in his front pockets as he ambled over to Ramla's side of the room.

"I'll kill you." Kaela's eyes were knives as she made him this promise.

"I gave you all the help I could." His blue eyes were piercing, but his tone remained unaffected. "You'll be fine without me."

"She'll be dead." Ramla laughed at her own response. "Now, if you'll give me a moment, I have a few minds to grab before we complete this reunion of ours, Mikaela."

Hailey, Ahtah, and Lunk made it five feet into the room before they froze. Their expressions fell slack, and their arms hung limp at their sides. Hailey's brass knuckles slid off, clattering against the cement in a series of metallic clanks. Angel stepped around them and approached Ramla with a furtive glance in Kaela's direction.

“My people are not to be harmed; that was our deal.”

“The big one will be fine.” Ramla waved dismissively. “The other two are no longer your concern. Our deal is complete, and your brat will be dropped off at your house. You can leave whenever you’d like and take that giant with you.”

“Angel?” Kaela’s stomach plummeted through the floor. “You’re working with her?”

“I’m sorry, Kaela. They have Isaiah. I have to keep my family safe, and Nisha will leave us alone if I stop keeping you from her. This was the only way to get my child back. I don’t have a choice.”

Kaela gauged the desperate tremor in Angel’s normally steady voice. She bit the inside of her cheek, refusing to say the words that rattled in her head, knowing the other woman had been put in an impossible position.

But we were supposed to be family, too.

Angel took Lunk by the hand, leading them out through the door like a disoriented child. She didn’t look back.

“Let’s all have a chat, shall we?” Ramla gestured to the empty chairs. Hailey and Ahtah crossed the floor, movements as jerky as marionettes. They dropped bonelessly onto the seats but somehow remained vertical.

Ramla must have penetrated their minds, forcing them into a submissive, nearly catatonic state. That meant her powers were similar to Ahtah’s but why was he not fighting her? Kaela thought about their rapid entry from the front of the warehouse. They had been moving quickly but hadn’t looked like they were expecting trouble. Ramla must have surprised them. And maybe the thin sheen of sweat along Ramla’s forehead and lip indicated that keeping the dream walker under control was a struggle.

Kaela made eye contact with Theo, and he made a nearly imperceptible nod in Ramla’s direction while widening his eyes.

“Now, like I said before, Dr. Brookes, you are an extra in today’s events.” Ramla tapped her nails against the backs of the chairs. “Our handsome hunk here decided to betray Nisha, and she does not take kindly to betrayals. He is a master of secrets, but can you believe he didn’t tell her that her own husband was still alive? Her husband, that she has searched the globe to find over the last twenty years, never knowing where he might be or if he had met his end. What kind of person gets in the way of a love like that? There were other, worse things he hid from her, including some spicy details about you, but I won’t bore you with all of that. I just wanted to make it clear that everything you are about to experience is his fault. This is his punishment."

As she listened to this tirade, Kaela reached for Ahtah with her mind. She still couldn't feel his magic. He was shielding her, which meant he was in control of at least some of his powers. She couldn't steal his abilities if he was keeping her out, but maybe she didn't need to.

She considered the slick, clinging feel of Ramla's magic. If she could gain control over just a part of it, perhaps Ahtah could break free. She might not be able to use Ramla's abilities against her, but she had a feeling that Ahtah would be more than capable of taking Ramla in a fair fight. Kaela needed to distract the other woman long enough to test her theory.

"Cass hid from Nisha this entire time." Kaela offered a condescending look to her adversary. "Clearly, you've never experienced love, or you would recognize the issue there. You don't let someone you love think you're dead."

Ramla drummed her fingers against Landry's shoulder, scowling at these statements. Behind her, the ten men remained silent and still, statues guarding something Kaela didn't yet understand. Ramla leaned forward, wrapping her arms around Landry's neck in a loose embrace, her ample bosom pressed against his back.

"I suppose you would know better. I know your history but didn't care enough to remember all the details. You are a divorcee, aren't you? I guess your ex-husband isn't the one you love, then. Could it be our devastatingly good-looking commander?

"I admit, I have seen the appeal. It isn't often that an intelligent man is both a grower and a shower, but you must know that already. Cute little dragon ink, did he ever tell you about it?" She dragged her slender fingers up Landry's side, circling the area where Kaela knew the tattoo crossed his ribs, and nuzzled his ear. "It represents his little mortal human family that he left for dead when he chose immortality. I know the man he really is. I know all the secrets, too. Sweet, innocent doctor. He wouldn't look twice at you if you weren't gifted with these powers."

Ramla looked at her with mock sympathy, her hands still on Landry, possessively stroking him. "He was the only one who could really keep me out. The rest of them had pathetic defenses. Even Ahtah unless he was really concentrating. And now look at them, unable to throw an ounce of magic at me. Nisha taught me and helped me grow more powerful than I've ever been before."

Kaela tried not to follow the other woman's fingers with her eyes as she traced the edge of Landry's jaw. Theo was frowning with distaste and staring at one of the large floats stored against the far wall, uncomfortable but not willing to interfere. One of the men standing behind Ramla fell to the ground, his body seizing in rapid jerks. Ramla glanced at him in disgust.

"They don't last very long. That's why I bring so many. Oh well, I guess I'm starting to run low on time. I should wrap this up."

Kaela suddenly understood how Ramla had the energy to control all these people. She was draining the men behind her. Kaela desperately searched Ahtah with her thoughts, looking for any hint of the foreign magic that was keeping him captive in the chair. A cold, slippery feeling informed her of success. She tried tugging at it, but that only made the feeling spread until she imagined it greasing her tongue, and her mouth filled with a coppery aftertaste. She thought of oil spilling on a hard surface and realized that moving it around wouldn't help. She needed to absorb it. The thought was nauseating, but she pulled a tiny bit of it into her, waiting for some terrible result that never came.

"Time for your punishment, naughty boy." Ramla snapped her fingers in front of Landry's face, and his eyes opened. "You have never seen what he can really do, Mikaela. It's terrible and beautiful at the same time. I'm going to do you a favor and introduce you to the real Commander Landry Griffiths. Of course, the result will be your death, but at least you can truly understand the man you love before he kills you. Such a romantic end."

"Ramla." Theo finally reacted as she gestured, and two of the men moved forward to stand directly in front of Landry's chair, their steps labored as if they were half asleep.

"Stay out of this, Theodoros." She hissed. "It's too late to be a hero."

Landry stood, his movements stiff and robotic. His eyes stared blankly ahead. Kaela dragged more of the oily presence from Ahtah, desperately working to break him free. She thought his eyes flicked in her direction for the briefest of moments.

"What are you doing?" Ramla angled her head and looked at Kaela in surprise. "You aren't supposed to have *that* ability. Tricky little bitch. No wonder she wants you dead. Curious though. Can you actually control it?"

Instead of a gentle pull, Kaela yanked on the slimy tether of Ramla's magic, desperate to free Ahtah. Ramla's lips flattened into a wicked scowl, and Kaela felt an icy slick of magic coating her brain. Her entire body was disconnected. The cold feeling of a hand that's fallen asleep spread into every part of her.

"Kneel." Ramla snapped her fingers for dramatic effect, and Kaela dropped to the ground.

A humorless laugh left her crimson lips, and then she turned, tilting Landry's head down and pressing the curves of her body into him. She brought his lips to hers for a long, sensual kiss. "It's a shame we couldn't have a little time together. I imagine after being with that girl, you need a good lay. I guess I'll just have to live with the memories though." She stepped back, gesturing to the two men. "Kill them."

His cold, vacant eyes turned to the men, and a concussive wave of energy rocked through Kaela. Something insubstantial erupted from their bodies, coalescing into a glowing mist that spiraled into Landry.

They exploded.

One second, the two men were standing there, lifeless as statues, and then they vanished in a spray of blood and bone. The sound, like the bursting of a water balloon but magnified a hundred times over, rent the air, echoing in Kaela's ears. She released a muffled scream, her hands clamping over her mouth when Ramla's hold disappeared.

Theo watched it all with suspicious familiarity.

In the stillness that followed, Landry turned and fixed Kaela with eyes that were no longer human. His nose flared as he sniffed the air. The bright green centers had become the deepest black, so dark that they seemed to devour all light, consuming it like a rip in the fabric of the world. She balked under the appraisal, drawing into herself. Her feet involuntarily shuffled away, some instinctive part of her seeking to escape the cold predator she faced.

"Kill her first, slowly," Ramla's voice was strained, sweat now dripping along the sides of her face as she struggled to keep Landry captive. Two more men fell to the ground behind her. "Then kill the others, too. Don't leave anyone behind." She retrieved something from one of the men who remained standing and stepped to Landry's side, a knife in one hand. "I just need to make sure you don't walk away from this in the end, my love."

Ramla slid the blade into Landry's side, stopping only when it reached the hilt. He barely flinched, though blood began pouring down his side. He took a step in Kaela's direction.

Ahtah abruptly stood, his attention on Ramla. Kaela could have cried in relief, but whatever conflict ensued was no longer her concern as she faced the man-turned-demon before her.

"Landry," she pleaded, holding her hands out in front of her. "Please snap out of it. It's me. It's Mikaela."

He continued stalking her, one measured step after another. Kaela managed to maintain eye contact, though she shrank back from the pulses of power radiating from him. The usual swimming of her brain when he was nearby was now an all-consuming thrashing. Her vision narrowed until the only thing she could see was his face. She barely registered the press of plaster against her spine as she ran out of space to retreat. She frantically stretched her magic into him, seeking traction against the tidal wave of power consuming her. His hand closed around her neck, and he held her against the surface of the float, his breath a panting growl.

Then she found herself deeper in his mind, and an empty calm slipped over her as if she had broken into the eye of the storm. Landry froze; his eyes were still black, but his breathing shifted to a deeper rhythm. His hand was firm, pinning her in place, but she could still breathe. The smell of him embraced her, unchanged despite his current state.

She carefully raised her hands to his chest, not wanting to startle an already mad beast, and pulled the tiniest tendrils of energy out of him. She felt the tugging of her own powers as she manipulated that small part of his ability, convincing it to flow into her. She instinctively knew it was too much for her to hold, and she reached out, blindly attaching herself to the others in the room and directing the power outwards. The feeling was similar to when she drew on other living things, but instead of taking from many sources to feed a single change, she was pulling from one endless well and redistributing it in multiple directions.

"Landry," she whispered.

He lowered his head, drawing his nose along her neck with another deep inhale. His teeth grazed her skin. She dragged more from him, finally feeling a subtle shift in his body. His hand loosened around her neck, and the raging storm became a hard wind. Her vision seemed to sharpen, and she finally heard people shouting from the other end of the room.

Ramla crumpled to the ground in front of Ahtah, and the remaining men helped Theo grab her before making a full retreat. Hailey rushed to Ahtah as he collapsed too. Kaela lost focus in the chaos, and the body leaning against her became heavier.

"*Cariad*?" The word manifested from deep in her memories, one that he previously used as a pet name for her, and it felt right as it slipped from her mouth.

"Mikaela?" The word was a whisper as it left Landry's lips.

Kaela pulled one last line of energy from him and then cut her connection when he dropped his hand from her neck to her shoulder. His eyes had returned to their vibrant green with normal pupils, and he managed a small smile. Relief flooded through her. She started to place her hand on his forearm but froze, momentarily confused by the blood coating her fingers.

He looked down at her shirt with a disoriented panic. "You're hurt!"

"No." She glanced down, realizing that her shirt and hands were wet with blood while Landry realized the blood was coming from him.

His hand drifted to his side, eyes wide in disbelief as he touched the handle of the knife and stumbled half a step to the side.

"No!" Kaela reached for him, wanting to help but hesitating because she was afraid of hurting him further. "Oh, my god. Don't move, we'll fix this. You'll be okay."

"I don't think this is fixable, *Cariad*." He placed a hand against the side of her face when she finally moved forward to steady him. "*Je t'aimerai jusqu'à mon dernier souffle*."

Landry collapsed to the ground, slipping through Kaela's blood-coated arms.

Someone was screaming.

Kaela wasn't sure if it was her or Hailey.

"No, no, no." Hailey threw herself next to Landry, crying and shouting his name as she attempted to hold him together around the knife that protruded grotesquely from his body. The new blood coated her hands and arms, mingling with the darker flakes already there from her earlier activities. "You cannot die this way, you stupid ass! Wake up, Landry. Wake up. Wake the fuck up!"

Kaela sank to the ground and looked at her hands, lying limp in her lap, Landry's blood thick and sticky between each finger.

"Hailey," she whispered.

Ahtah was now kneeling on the other side of Landry's body, his face already heavy with grief.

"Hailey," Kaela said again, her voice low and even, a reflection of the empty stillness she felt in her body. "You have to heal him."

"I can't! Not again. This cannot happen again. I can't save him. He'll die and it will be my fucking fault!"

"Hailey," she intoned for the third time. "Give me your hand."

Hailey reached for her with a confused, desperate sob.

Kaela felt for Hailey's bright, open flame of power and found it right away. She used the line of their connected hands as a guide, drawing a stream of pure fire from Hailey's body and into her own. She reached down and pulled the knife from Landry's side, surprised by the amount of force required to yank it free. Hailey gasped and reached to intervene, but Kaela just gripped her hand tighter, shoving Hailey's other arm out of the way and placing her own hand on top of the wound.

She pushed the searing, hot line of energy down into Landry. Hailey cried out again, but this time it was shock at the feeling inside of her that drove the noise from her mouth. She took a breath, the whites of her eyes flashing when she looked back at Kaela.

"How are you doing this?"

Kaela closed her eyes in concentration, pulling energy from her own body as well to bolster the process. She wasn't sure how much would be required but when she started, the flow of energy was like water being sucked into a drain. After a few minutes, she felt the beginnings of exhaustion, and the energy slowed on its own. She released Landry and Hailey at the same time, hoping for the best. She tried to catch her breath. Her body wanted to melt onto the floor beneath her, but her spine was rigid. She felt like a used towel, wrung out and pinned up to dry on a line.

Ahtah let out a low chuckle.

"Looks like it was fixable after all." Landry's voice wrapped around her.

Hailey dropped onto Landry with a sob. Kaela closed her eyes, listening to his laughter and holding his hand. Inside of her, something broke open, pouring a river of emotion into her body that was equal parts bracing and terrifying.

America – 2022

All the people Kaela had loved fell into one of two categories: those she left and those that left her.

She should have asked more questions before she agreed to marry Jason. She should have contemplated the idea that love did not endure, that the very concept of soulmates was fiction.

"Which one are you?" she could have asked. "Will you be one that ends with the bitter aftertaste of soured love, the kind that aches along my tongue and fills my mind with cynicism? Or will you leave first, your abandonment eating holes in my heart because you chose to reject what could have been and decided I was never enough for you?"

She thought about the family and friends she had loved. Those relationships were filled with temporary happiness that stemmed from a fickle, overinflated affection. For two years now, she had managed to go about her life, finding her own fulfillment while keeping everyone around her at arm's length. She poked and prodded at her own boundaries, reinforcing them when she found a weakness. Her defenses were ironclad. She was at no risk of losing herself to another person again.

She slipped through the front door of the apartment, tiptoeing down the stairs to her car. It was late, and she didn't want to wake the other tenants. Even if she never planned to visit again, it was just good manners. The man from the bar tonight was unbelievably attractive, and her time with him had been well spent, but it was just a one-time event.

She cranked up the air conditioning and listened to the radio at an obnoxiously high volume on the way home, smiling at the book on her stoop when she pulled into her driveway. Reading materials from George, no doubt. Once inside, she stood in her pajamas, brushing her teeth and looking at her window of plants with a sense of satisfaction.

There was no place for love in her life anymore, and she couldn't be happier about that.

Chapter 7

The tension in the room made the air crackle inside Kaela's ears. She glanced at Landry with disapproval. The angry scowl on his face remained, but the popping of energy faded. It was probably the best she could hope for.

She turned her attention back to Angel. They were in the front room of the house, facing one another from their respective couches across the coffee table. Hellcat was crouched between the bone bowl and the tarot deck, motionless except for the occasional twitch of her tail. A low growl occasionally emanated from her furry body. The humans were packed into the room along the walls, lined up like chess pieces on opposing sides of the board, their two queens occupying the center.

Angel held Isaiah tightly against her. The boy was watching the cat with a wary expression, but he otherwise seemed at ease next to his mother. Angel claimed he had been sitting on the stoop when they returned, unharmed and unaware that he had been missing in the first place. Ramla had done them a favor by keeping the boy unconscious, but it was unlikely that the kindness was purposeful. It was more likely that she didn't want to listen to him crying.

After the events in the warehouse, Kaela had come to terms with Angel's actions. While she didn't fully understand the bond between a mother and her son, she suspected that Angel would have done anything to keep Isaiah safe. At least the betrayal came in the form of inaction. If Angel had brought the entire New Orleans group to support Ramla against them, Kaela wouldn't be sitting where she was now. Her willingness to accept the unfortunate series of events did not necessarily extend to the others in the group, though. Landry was still seething at Angel's willingness to turn against Kaela, and the caretaker avoided eye contact with him as he loomed over the couch.

"Where do we go from here, Sha?" Angel finally broke the silence.

"I want to forgive you." Hailey gave a loud snort of denial from the back wall at Kaela's words. "I know they had your son, but why didn't you talk to me instead of throwing me, throwing us, straight to the wolves?"

"I trained you. Theodore trained you. Ahtahkakoop trained you."

"Do not add me to your list, Angelique," Ahtah warned from his position near Hailey.

"All I'm trying to say is that we know you are more than capable of handling yourself against Nisha's people. If I'd told you about her demand to deliver you to that woman and she found out, well, I wasn't willing to gamble with my Isaiah's life. I tried to come up with another solution, I really did. There just wasn't enough time."

Kaela tried to put herself in the other woman's place. Would she have done anything differently? Nisha was cold and calculating, not someone that was likely to balk from hurting a child as punishment for a betrayal. She certainly hadn't hesitated to send an assassin to kill Landry. Kaela glanced back at him, reassuring herself that he was nearby. She was momentarily distracted by the image of him lying in a pool of his own blood as it spread across the concrete, a red veneer that shone under the warehouse lights.

He should be dead.

Landry's eyes shifted to hers, the skin around them softening when their gazes met as if he knew where her thoughts traveled. She let her attention linger on his face, tracing the unfamiliar smoothness of his skin and uniform, black of his hair. When she'd tapped the power within him, she had turned it back on people nearby, latching onto the auras that were familiar in addition to herself and Landry, to prevent overloading her own body. In the process, she'd managed to taint the energy with her own magic. It wasn't until after Landry's wounds healed and they could collectively breathe again that they noticed the changes.

Hailey, Ahtah, Landry, and Kaela were each at least ten years younger. She was obsessed with understanding every little detail of the magic, calculating her actions to within ten thousandths of a unit before using her powers, and once again, she got it right when she acted on blind impulse.

Hailey cleared her throat, and Kaela pulled herself back to the conversation at hand. "The fact remains that you and Theo conspired to get me to that building. Even though I disagree with your choice, I can forgive you for it, but I can't trust you, Angel. You must understand that. We need to decide what to do next, but those plans can't include you. We'll leave in the morning. Until then, you have to go somewhere else."

"Isaiah and I will stay at a friend's house tonight. I'll tell the others to clear out as well. Does this mean you'll be looking for someone new to watch over the place?"

The misery was obvious on her face as Angel looked around the room, taking in the surroundings as if she were already making her final goodbye.

"No." Landry gave Kaela a sharp look and Hailey produced a sound of exasperation at this statement. "Although I don't trust you with my secrets or my well-being, I trust you to do what's best for all the people who rely on you here. I can't take refuge from people who need it. You can come back tomorrow after we're gone and continue with your normal duties."

Angel stood, gripping her son's hand as if he would disappear at any moment. He suffered the affection stoically. Lunk, Basille, Adam, and Zoe peeled themselves from the back wall. Estè rose from her seat near the doorway to join the others and they all followed Angel out of the house. Zoe paused just before the threshold of the exit to cast a mournful gaze at Hailey. When Kaela looked back over her shoulder, Hailey's face offered nothing but icy rejection to the young woman. When they were alone, the three members of Kaela's group settled near her on the couches. As soon as Landry's lap became available, Hellcat occupied it, staking her claim now that he had proven his loyalty to her human.

"If nothing else, your traumatic experience has won the cat over." Kaela said with amusement.

"Ramla will inform Nisha of Kaela's ability to control others," Ahtah interrupted Landry before he could reply to Kaela's teasing. "If Nisha was not planning to kill all of us before, it will be a priority for her to do so now. We cannot remain here, but returning to your home may not be the safest route either. We need a secure location where we can determine the best way to resolve these threats."

Hailey leaned forward onto her knees, assuming an equally serious expression. "I would like to have a discussion about why all of you knew Kaela had a second ability and thought it wise to keep me in the dark." The aggrieved expression Hailey offered everyone suggested that conversation should happen sooner rather than later, but she continued. "Nisha will quickly learn that Landry didn't die. Ramla was trying to end every person in this room, but she failed. Nisha will send an entire team to do it correctly the next time. She does not suffer failed missions calmly."

Landry stretched his legs out in front of him, the cat matching his sprawl from atop his thighs. He released a long, slow breath. "Nisha does not suffer anything calmly. The last few years, I've been tracking her movements. Before she found out about Cass, she was driving some radical changes in the eastern hemisphere. I had to put out more than one fire in the private sector that she seemed happy to light then walk away from, regardless of the consequences. And then there are the political aspects of her meddling. There used to be a balance for these types of things, and she is violating every unspoken understanding between factions."

"If she eliminates the last of the competition, she can do whatever she wants." Hailey grumbled.

"But now that she knows Cassius is still alive, will she bring the crazy back down to a reasonable level?" Kaela looked at Landry and Hailey, knowing the two of them had the best grasp on Nisha's motivations.

"Maybe." Landry stared at the ceiling, his head resting on the back of the couch.

Kaela stared into the empty sockets of the skull on the mantel. She suppressed a shudder when she thought about Landry's inky orbs during the height of the conflict the night before. He remembered none of the events prior to staring down at the knife protruding from his side. Ramla had shown up at his apartment when he'd returned from a recent trip. Although he was ashamed to admit it, she'd wormed her way through the door and stabbed him with a needle. Hailey ridiculed him mercilessly over the cliche nature of his drugging. The next thing he knew, he was lying in his own blood while Kaela saved him.

"No," Hailey contradicted. "She won't go back to playing by the rules. Cassius won't come to her willingly. He's shown that he doesn't want to be found. What do you think that rejection will do when it ultimately sinks in? She'll be sad, but then she'll be furious, and she'll lash out even harder than before. Cassius was the saner of the two."

"But she needs him to come back to her. She needs him for her immortality," Kaela said.

Hailey and Ahtah shared a look.

"Tell them, *nimis*."

"Tell us what?" Landry sat up straighter, staring at Hailey expectantly.

Hailey looked uncomfortable. "I may have overheard a conversation about Nisha and Cassius several years ago that led me to believe something unfounded. That is, it was unfounded at the time, but now that we've been through everything that we've been through in the last few days, and decades, I don't think it's completely unfounded anymore. In fact, I'm mostly certain that it's accurate. And it might change what we're planning to do next."

"Well." Kaela blinked at her friend as she processed the vague, circular sentences. "That certainly clears things up. Maybe just spit it out and stop being obtuse."

Ahtah chuckled in amusement, surprising Kaela with the brief appearance of his sense of humor.

"Nisha can control the powers of others. I think she's been controlling Cassius for centuries, and he finally decided it was better to live a short life of freedom than an eternity as a slave."

That was certainly not what Kaela had expected. Judging by the deathly silence filling the room, Landry was just as surprised. Ahtah, however, looked pensive.

"How many years ago did you reach this conclusion?"

Hailey didn't respond to Landry's question. Instead, she squirmed in her seat and cast a pleading look at Ahtah, who shook his head in response.

"How many, Hailey?"

"Not that many, maybe fifty?"

"And you?" Landry turned on Ahtah. "Have you known all this time?"

Ahtah shook his head calmly. "I only knew she was hiding something from us after last night. I slipped into Hailey's mind to take away Ramla's control in the warehouse. She was thinking about this at the time, and I picked up on the general idea."

"Fucking dream walker." Hailey grumbled under her breath.

Kaela stood, a restless energy prompting her to move her feet. She paced near the windows, staring at the floor but registering nothing beyond her jumbled thoughts.

"Nisha can control powers, like I can. How are we able to do the same thing? I thought you expected everyone to have a different manifestation of their energy, except on the occasions when children took after their parents, like the herbalists in Maria's family. But somehow, my family keeps manifesting an ability that intrigues Cassius enough to follow us across multiple generations and threatens Nisha enough that she wants us all dead." She stopped pacing and fixed her stare on Landry. "Please tell me I'm not related to her. I don't think I could take that level of entanglement right now."

"No," he immediately replied. "You can't be related to her."

"But how do you know? She is thousands of years old, even older than you!" Now it was Landry who looked uncomfortable as Kaela spoke, shifting and clasping his hands together in agitation. "I thought we agreed to no more secrets. What aren't you saying?"

"Not secrets, exactly. There are just a few details that I still need to tell you about your family. I was planning to talk to you, but I hadn't found the right time."

Kaela threw her hands into the air with exasperation. "Well, no time like the present."

"There was a woman, a healer." Landry cleared his throat as he searched for the right words to convey the history he knew too well. "We were together for a very long time before she decided to give up her immortality. I made her a promise to watch over her children after she died. She was your ancestor over twenty generations ago."

Kaela's stomach turned, and she shook her head. By her rough math, Landry had known her family for over four hundred years. She wanted to laugh at the absurdity of it, but at the same time, was afraid that she might vomit right there on the floor.

"You stalked me as a child?" Her eyes prickled with tears even as her face heated in anger.

"No! Your grandmother lived in France until she married your grandfather. He was an American soldier in World War II. I met her once, just before she emigrated, but she showed no magical abilities. I had her tracked and monitored by people who worked for me. By the time you were an adult, you were the last of Marguerite's bloodline, descended from her eldest daughter. I told you the truth when I said that I first met you about twenty years ago."

She searched for honesty in his expression as he pleaded his case. Hailey and Ahtah were silent as ghosts in the background. Kaela pressed her fingers to her temples and breathed in slowly, holding the air in her lungs for the count of six before letting it escape back into the world. She shook her head again.

"I need time to process this. I can't right now."

Hellcat bristled and removed herself from Landry's lap, digging her claws into his leg in the process. She placed herself on the arm of the sofa closest to Kaela and twitched her tail in agitation.

“I think I’m with the cat,” Hailey stated, drawing an annoyed glance from Landry. “And before you ask, Kaela, I did not know about this. I mean, I knew about Marguerite, but I didn’t realize you were her relative.”

“We still need a plan,” Ahtah, the voice of reason, spoke up, effectively ending the exchange.

“I already spoke to the department chair and dean of the university this morning. Since I’ve been on faculty for seven years, I’m allowed a teaching sabbatical for the semester. I can manage my lab remotely. We did it during the pandemic, and we can make it work again.” Kaela’s voice wavered at the end of this announcement, but she plowed stubbornly ahead. “Besides, I can’t just show up with a face that magically matches the ten-year-old headshots on my social media profiles.”

Hailey moved from the couch to embrace her, seeing through the weak excuse for humor. “This is temporary. You are not giving anything up, just buying us a little time to wipe the floor with Nisha, and then you can go back to saving the world with science. I, for one, would appreciate staying this youthful, but you are welcome to give yourself those laugh lines and crow’s feet again before this is all finished.”

Hailey glared at Landry over Kaela’s shoulder as she made this attempt at levity.

“I have the best technical staff,” he chimed in, words chipper despite the glower he leveled at Hailey in return. “Wherever we go, you’ll have an encrypted connection and all the bandwidth you can possibly need. Any of my resources are at your disposal. It will be like you never left campus.”

“Okay.” Kaela straightened, sniffing away the momentary break in her composure and letting Hailey retreat to the couch before she continued, “What’s next, then? We need a way to stop Nisha.”

“First, we need to collect Cassius,” Ahtah offered.

“In the conversation I overheard, Alban was discussing something with Cassius. He kept referring to our commander’s ‘troublesome marriage’. He said several things about Nisha’s ‘control’ that didn’t make sense to me at the time. Then Alban said that he might have found a way to keep Nisha at bay.”

“Who is Alban?” Kaela looked at Hailey, who looked at Landry.

“He was the most loyal of Cassius’s personal guards and a firestarter.” Landry supplied the answer and exchanged a look with Ahtah. “He defied Cass’s orders on a few occasions. Therefore, he has shown he is capable of thinking for himself. He might be willing to help us, and he knows where all the bodies are buried."

"Both literally and figuratively," Hailey chimed in.

Kaela couldn't help the amused smile that crossed her face.

"No one has heard from him since Cassius disappeared," Ahtah reminded them.

"Which leaves us back at step one, find Cassius." Landry looked around at the group with a grim expression.

Several things popped into Kaela's mind at once and she wanted to kick herself for being so oblivious.

"I think I know where he is." Kaela returned to the couch, sitting a little further from Landry than she had before. "He and George each gave me a few clues that I didn't recognize until now. I'll get into that later but for now, let's make a plan.

"High level overview. Relocate to someplace more secure, find Cassius, get information from Cassius to find Alban, get information from Alban to beat Nisha, and then I get to strangle Ramla with my bare hands. If I have time, I'd also like to make sure *Todd* never breathes again. After that, I return to my position at the university and continue my work, hopefully culminating in a Nobel prize nomination. Did I miss anything?"

Hailey was the first to giggle, which quickly grew contagious, causing Ahtah to chuckle in a very undignified manner. Landry's bass contributed to the mirth, leaving Kaela no choice but to release the laughter bubbling up from her own chest. The shock of yesterday's violence and apprehension for the days to come reduced the four of them to hysteria for several glorious minutes. Finally, Hailey wiped the corners of her eyes and looked around with a more somber expression.

"Cassius and Nisha have lived for a millennium. When I met them, it was like coming face to face with Zeus and Hera. I never thought I would be sitting here deciding how best to destroy one of them."

"That is an apt comparison. The Greek and Roman gods were selfish. They cared nothing for those weaker than them." Ahtah turned to Hailey with a serious expression again. "Cassius and Nisha were two spoiled children who realized they were stronger than anyone else and could get away with whatever they desired. You and Landry made the right choice to leave them all those years ago. Mikaela considers the lives around her as much as her own when making choices. She is a capable leader, and I am proud to join her team."

His statement solidified Kaela's place at the head of the group. She looked at Landry, knowing that he was used to being the leader in the past. When their eyes met, he nodded easily.

"I wouldn't want it any other way," he admitted. "Ahtah's right, you are the best choice as leader of this group. We all need your sense of humanity, and I need you to keep me under control if Nisha or Ramla tries to use me as a weapon again."

"Thank you, I'm honored to have all three of you with me." The corner of her mouth pulled up into a lopsided smirk. "At least I know I have a demon on a leash, a healer with a nasty set of brass knuckles, and a man that can control minds. What's not to like about these odds? For my first order as your new Commander, I demand that you all get food and plenty of sleep. Tomorrow, we put together the details of our plan to defeat two immortal gods."

"And kill Todd," Hailey added.

"And kill Todd," Kaela agreed.